Surviving Amelia

Surviving Amelia

NAOMI RAND

Bink Books
Bedazzled Ink Publishing Company • Fairfield, California

978-1-960373-75-5 paperback

Second edition, 2025

Cover Design
by
Cody Fitzgerald

Bink Books
a division of
Bedazzled Ink Publishing
Fairfield, California
http://www.bedazzledink.com

For Susan L., Helen M. and Nancy L.

They really were the best of times.

This is a work of fiction.

Acknowledgements

I began writing *Surviving Amelia* just after my father died. Over the course of the next six years, I lost my mother. Anna Rand had been one of only three women in her medical school class. She'd carved out a career as an OB GYN for herself against all odds. She was an abortion rights activist, a radical whose political views informed my own, and a true force of nature. Anna was a voracious reader, she subscribed to all sorts of magazines including *The New Statesman* and *I.F. Stone's Weekly*; she read nonfiction, mainly history and political science, and loads of fiction. She had a soft spot for mysteries. It's one of life's cruel jokes that by the end of her life, she could barely string a sentence together.

When I began to write this book, a friend said, "I don't understand why you want to write a literary novel when you figured out how to write mysteries." She meant well, though I took umbrage at the time. She knew how hard it was to sell a literary novel. I could sell mysteries, so why change course? Looking back, I often wished I'd been able to take her advice. But the thing is, I couldn't. This novel was what I had to write. By the time I finished, my parents were dead, one of my closest friends was in the process of losing his own mind to Alzheimer's way too young, and my sons had grown up and had gone off to college and real life. Write what you know, they say. Apparently I took those words a little too much to heart.

Surviving Amelia is a work of fiction and that should be apparent from the first chapter. After all, a ghost comes to life and is a main character through the course of the novel. Still, I did read several books that grounded me in reality; *Letters From Amelia* by Jean L. Backus, *The Sound of Wings* by Mary S. Lovell, Amelia Earhart: *The Mystery Solved* by Elgen M. Long and Marie K. Long, *Lost in Flight* by Amelia Earhart, *The Fun of It* by Amelia Earhart and most crucial of all, *Courage is the Price* by Muriel Earhart Morrissey. Humans crave certainty which is why the where, why, and how of Earhart's disappearance has proved to be such an enduring mystery. I have no allegiance to any particular theory though the book does find her stranded on an island.

I wish I could thank all my readers. But, in truth, there were far too many, and I wrote so many drafts. I am afraid of leaving someone out and so I thank you collectively and hope you will forgive me for not naming names, thank you for reading whatever draft you read and offering such wise editorial advice, thank you for supporting me through what has definitely been a mind bending process. Most of all, I want to thank my husband David, and my sons, Travis and Cody. Having the three of you in my life gives me such pleasure. You make me feel like I truly am the luckiest woman on the face of the earth.

1

Amelia
October 1937

AMELIA DUG HER navigator's grave all day, using rocks and shells to shove back the earth. Her fingers were blistered, torn. But at least Fred was decently buried underground. On the forty-seventh day you rest, she told herself. Yet, it was more than that long. She knew from the notches carved into the bark of the palm tree. Fred had been dying for much of the time and she'd been nursing him through. It rained as she dug, making a mess of the grave. The hollowed out coconuts were filled to the brim. Not that it would do him any good now.

To think she'd imagined herself lucky, managing the landing without dying on impact. Fred had been able to pull the emergency radio out with him. That first day, they gathered wood to light a signal fire. Amelia's lighter was still in her pocket, but soaked so thoroughly the flint wouldn't catch. It took over an hour for the old scout method to work, sticks rubbed together, then finally a spark. There was a flame; a funnel of smoke that blasted up into the empty night sky. As it grew, they were both elated believing that the Itasca, the rescue boat that was tracking them just in case, would have no trouble spotting that tornado shaped cone.

Wrong.

Even as the battery weakened she sent out distress calls. "This is Amelia Earhart. I am stranded due west of Howland Island. Can you hear me?" No one responded.

It was hard not to lose hope, hard not to blame yourself. The jungle beyond the beach was impenetrable. And no one had emerged from it to find the castaways.

Amelia ran over it in her mind again and again. It always came out the same. The storm clouds had been too thick. She'd had no choice but to cruise at a higher altitude. Of course, doing that meant the fuel burned faster. And when the sun came up, there was no landing strip, nothing but choppy green water. The glare reflected off it, the sun all but swallowed up. She radioed to the Itasca again and again. She got no answer. Finally, Amelia used what was left of the gas to ease the descent. It worked and they were able to ditch instead of crashing into the water and dying on impact. It was truly a miracle.

A miracle of a sort. Every day, the sea birds wheeled above. They had no rifle, so they built a makeshift hunting implement using Fred's pocketknife, attaching it to a branch with a strip of cloth torn from her shirt. Fred's wound was infected. She kept cleaning it with salt water, but it still went septic. Thus Amelia was de facto hunter, gatherer, and cook. She waded into the surf, stabbing the fish to death, roasting them over the fire, sucking the flesh off the bones. She made him soup out of them when he could no longer chew, Amelia using a handmade spoon to ladle it into Fred's mouth. The wound in his chest was swollen by then, the odor foul. He was feverish, delirious.

She promised him many things as he lay dying.

She would tell his wife he loved her.

She would make it clear it wasn't his fault.

She would swear they'd been on course and Amelia had been the one to make the critical miscalculation.

She'd bring him home and bury him decently.

No, she would never mention the drinking. Amelia would say he'd been sober as a judge.

When it was over she couldn't bear to leave his body out to rot. She told herself that if they were ever found, she would point out the grave and they could unearth him. Then she dug as best she could, scooping out the earth with shells. Amelia recited the Lord's Prayer over him, although she hadn't been to church since Grandfather and Grandmother Otis took her in Atchison.

"Our father who art in heaven, hallowed be thy name."

She had termed religion claptrap, and had been known to spout Marx when pressed. Yet, after the prayer, Amelia raised an invisible glass. Would that there was a bartender up in heaven. Then Fred would be having his usual Scotch. A psalm sprang to mind. "Though I walk through the valley of death I will fear no evil." Fred had never been afraid, even when he realized he was dying. It's the breed, Amelia thought. We're all fatalists. It's how we explain what we do to ourselves. Exhausted, she shut her eyes. Above her the night sky glittered with stars.

2

Samantha Barry
August 1980

SAM WATCHED HER mother dig into an oversized purse and emerge victorious, emery board in hand. Brooke used it to file her blood red nails to a razor's edge. Her outfit was classic, the tight yellow Capri pants and black sleeveless v-neck leotard topped off with a signature Isadora Duncan length, caught in the wheel-spoke scarf. Mom and daughter were headed uptown by train, making for Barnard and freshman orientation. Although Brooke would have preferred to sit together, Sam was the one who separated, choosing the vacant corner seat across from her. Now they perched, like boxers, waiting in their opposing corners.

She'd tried, oh how she'd tried, to leave Brooke behind in their Brooklyn apartment. Sam had already suffered through four hours plus of tearful good-byes with "my little girl is leaving me" as the refrain.

"I'm not leaving you, I'm just going to college," Sam repeated.

"You don't understand at all," Brooke insisted. "Wait till you're a mother."

"I'm only moving to Manhattan. It's not even the suburbs. Mom, please."

Brooke refused, sobbing as if her heart had broken.

Imagine if I'd actually applied to one of those other schools, Sam thought. Every time the guidance counselor gave her a brochure, her mother made her feelings abundantly clear.

"Berkeley? You'd be lost there. It's far too big!"

"Michigan, you deserve better."

"I did *The Music Man* in Chicago, the wind whips right off the lake. You'd hate it there. You'd freeze to death."

"New Haven? Are you delirious? It's not a place one lives. And who cares if it's Yale, for god's sake!"

"Georgetown? What are you studying, government? You're pre-med!"

"Sweetheart, you're not going to even consider Swarthmore. It's stultifying."

There was only one place worthy of her, Barnard College. It was the same seventh sister her mother and grandmother had attended. Lineage was important. Brooke's plan for funding the four years was beyond optimistic. "Think of how happy we'll make your grandmother. I'm sure she'll offer to pay."

What was she smoking? That is, besides the pot Sam's brother, Win, had left behind. Grandmother Katherine never forked over a dime to help any of them out. The grandchildren were expected to prove themselves and pull themselves up by their bootstraps. This was odd advice, coming from a woman who had never had to work a day in her life and was living off of inherited wealth. Katherine owned houses in Bar Harbor and Palm Beach, plus a grand apartment on Park Avenue. Meanwhile, Sam could only afford college because of a financial aid package that included loans and a work-study assignment. When Sam graduated, she would have to pay the loans all back, something her grandmother had never been expected to do. Which was just as well.

Sam reminded herself that she could have gone to school to several other colleges and not had to pay a dime. The offers had been made. It was her choice to stay close to home. That was because being close meant she could hop on the subway. And doing that was a lot easier than hitching a ride to NYC on a plane. If Brooke needed her, she'd be there in a half an hour. Not that Brooke would. She'll be just fine on her own, Sam told herself, then forced herself to mentally change the subject, playing a game she'd made up long ago. The goal was to figure out what advertisements lurked underneath the spray-painted graffiti tags in the subway car. As they rolled uptown, Sam found the hotline poster hidden under a huge orange "R." The poster showed an anguished woman clutching a phone, begging the viewer to dial **1-800-I Confess**. Under "A," scales of justice touted **Bail Bonds Available**. And a "T" cut off the shoulders and face of a lanky model clutching her Virginia Slim. "R. A. T." What a boring tag. Sam missed good old "Taki 183."

The car made a perilous jerk as it pulled into the Wall Street station. Well-groomed men in perforated brown and black leather shoes lifted their briefcases, preparing to disembark. If only this subway would turn into a rocket. If only they were hurtling towards a distant galaxy. Once they docked, Sam could hug Brooke goodbye, Brooke sobbing and waving as the ship retreated. Ah well. Instead Sam was inside the train, clattering north, making for the thickets of the Upper West Side.

AT THE CITY Hall station, Sam spotted Keith Haring working away, his canvas a papered over advertisement panel on the station wall. He was wiry, balding under the ubiquitous cap. Haring wore soda bottle thick glasses. Sam had dubbed him "the chalk man." He used white chalk on a black background. She loved the drawings. Dancing dogs. Flying fish. Faceless figures sprouting angel wings. Dabs of white lines round the edges of each indicated they were in motion. Because if you stop, you die, Sam thought. She waved, trying to get Brooke's attention and point him out. But her mother was oblivious, foraging in her purse to emerge with a pack of Gitanes. "No Smoking. No Fumar." Signs were posted in every car, not that you could read the warning under the tags. Still, everyone knew the law. Sam let her hand drop, embarrassed, as her mother puffed away. Brooke leaned back, shutting her eyes, savoring her nicotine soaked moment of defiance. Sam felt torn. Part of her couldn't help but admire Brooke's infernal, self-satisfied, fuck the world smile. The other part wished she could be anywhere else.

Sam wondered if anyone in the car guessed they were related. She had inherited her Mediterranean coloring from her father's side of the family. Her eyes were brown, her hair jet black. Brooke's naturally red hair was highlighted to hide the grey. Her complexion was pale, sprinkled with freckles. Brooke's eyes were a brilliant jade green, courtesy of brand new color contacts. Sam's mother was all girlie girl and "look at me!" Sam was purposefully, diligently the opposite, dressed in frayed jean shorts with a t-shirt bearing a faded photo of Exene Cervenka, the lead singer of X. A pair of gold stud earrings was her only bow to vanity.

Sam Berry emerged at 116th street and accelerated. She was already through the Barnard gates and asking for directions when she realized her mother wasn't bringing up the rear. No Brooke in sight. Sam twisted round. The air was thick and slightly rancid. She was sweating bullets. Brooke knew the room number. Still, guilt licked at her. Instead of heading upstairs, Sam perched on the ledge outside Sulzberger, eyeing her soon to be classmates as they strolled past. Here, a Jewish American Princess; there, a preppie queen. Most undergraduates were accompanied by both well-dressed parents and toted more bags than the paltry duo Sam had packed. Trunks and valises and suitcases stamped with exotic ports of call rolled by. Who would she find here to talk to, Sam wondered? Who looked like they lived a life even remotely like hers? Panic gripped her. Just then Brooke appeared, accompanied by a clean-cut Columbia undergrad toting Sam's suitcase.

"This is Matt. Matt, my daughter Samantha."

"Hey," Sam tried.

"Matt's my knight in shining armor."

He blushed. "Come on, this isn't your daughter. You're sisters, right?"

"You didn't just say that," Sam said, lifting an eyebrow. Matt ignored her. Her mother's laugh tinkled. Matt's gaze veered to Brooke's ample cleavage. Sam's humiliation was complete. Not that he was going to get anything for his trouble; Brooke used and abused and discarded boys like him routinely. In your wet dreams you tool, Sam thought.

Upstairs, her last name was one of two on the card next to the door of room 316. Inside a family was seated on the far bed looking like three ducks all in a row, albeit incredibly large, blond-haired blue-eyed ducks.

"I'm Lucy," the youngest duck said, standing and extending a hand. Sam tilted her head back. Her roommate, Lucy, had to be close to six feet tall.

"And you must be Samantha," the mother duck said. "I'm Alma Westcott, Lucy's mom."

Alma wore a yellow print calico dress with frills at the bottom of the sleeves. It was demure, sweet, and completely without pretension. No one within fifty miles of New York City would own something like that. Alma might as well have gone and painted the word "Tourist" on her forehead.

"Tom," the father duck said. He gave Sam a firm and hearty handshake.

Alma was plump, a smiler. Tom was clean cut, serious, and wide as a house. Lucy was lanky, blond, and drop-dead gorgeous. Sam felt immediately outclassed. Lucy literally glowed. Sam decided that, being so attractive, Lucy must have drained the light from everything else and sucked it into her own body.

Brooke stood at the door saying goodbye to her new best friend. "You're a doll." She bestowed a high beam smile. The callow youth trotted off.

Taking a seat on the empty bed, Brooke homed in on the male in the room. "Brooke Barry," she said to Tom. He took her extended hand and shook it hard enough to cause a dislocation. She opened her purse and dug inside and extracted the ever-ready pack of Gitanes. "Smoke?" she offered.

"Sure," Lucy said.

"What?" Alma was clearly shocked.

"Just kidding," Lucy said, catching Sam's eye and exchanging a complicit smile.

Sam allowed herself to hope. Maybe it wouldn't be a complete disaster, this room, this roommate, this seventh sister and its exclusively female college.

The room was tiny, the air fetid, the window shut tight. Sam would have opened it but Alma barred the way. She was at work unloading a huge steamer trunk. Sam set her duffel bag on the desk chair and unzipped it. Her skin caught in the metal teeth. "Damn!" she exclaimed.

"Oh dear, did you hurt yourself?" Alma asked.

"It's okay," Sam said, sucking the wound.

"We have Band-aids."

"I'm fine. Really." Her protest fell on deaf ears. Alma flourished a box. Extracting one, she un-stripped the paper and held it out so Sam could set her wounded digit down. "Good as new," Alma said, wrapping it tight. Was she going to kiss it next, the way the school nurse used to?

Brooke hadn't even noticed. She was too busy conferring with Alma's husband, exhaling perfect smoke rings.

The room had two generic blond wood desks with matching dressers. Lucy's side was already pretty in pink. Her bed sported a rose flushed comforter with matching bolsters, and twin pillowcases.

Sam unpacked her own vision of independence, posters of Joe Strummer and Elvis Costello wielding guitars. A pile of her favorite art books sprouted on the small desk. Joseph Beuys was her current obsession. Sam had gone to the retrospective at the Modern five times. Her favorite piece was the Volkswagen bus with sleds trailing off the back. Each sled held a roll of tightly wrapped felt. Sam had been moved to tears.

Here she was. Here she was with Joseph Beuys, Elvis C., and her roommate Lucy Westcott. Sam had done her best to get a single. She'd even had her therapist write a letter about her social anxiety (it was a lie; still, she wielded a certain amount of power since the kitchen shrink episode when she'd walked in on him on top of Brooke spread-eagled across the kitchen table). When the college persisted in their perverse desire to sequester her with a stranger, sending her a questionnaire asking her what her likes and dislikes were, Sam answered the questions with her characteristic honesty. "Favorite hobbies? Listening to punk rock music several decibels too loud. Describe your perfect roommate? Invisible." They'd ignored her warnings and chosen this girl who looked every inch the prom queen.

But there was that comment about the cigarette, there was that. Hope does spring eternal, Sam thought ruefully.

Alma was at the window, trying to pry it open. "It must be stuck," she said.

"Let me," Sam offered.

"Oh no, dear. Tom will do it."

Tom showed no signs of doing anything. He was focused on Brooke.

"I can't believe you were really a football player," Brooke said. She used her best "aw gee whiz" tone. "A sporting man. Well, I'm not surprised. You have that firm look."

Tom didn't notice the artifice. Most men didn't. They were fools when it came to Brooke, at least initially. Sam cleared her throat. Her mother ignored her warning. Brooke's head was inches away from his. It was embarrassing and pathetic that she needed this kind of constant attention and approval. Sam took out her frustration on the window, slamming her hand hard into the frame. It came unglued. She lifted it.

"My, but you're strong!" Alma exclaimed, her voice several decibels too loud.

Sam flexed her nonexistent muscles. Inner strength, that's what does it.

"Sam's father doesn't believe in this sort of thing," Brooke said. Sam winced. Not that one!

"What sort of thing is that, Brooke?" Sam interjected, flushing.

"Why, you know," Brooke threw out vaguely. She used her hand to encompass the room with its stale air and standard issue furnishings. Sam knew where her mother was headed. By pretending she had a loving husband at home, Brooke could sanctify this as an innocent flirtation. Tom was not even close to her type. Brooke fell for aging rock stars, alcoholic painters, and euro trash.

"My father lives in Vermont," Sam said under her breath. She shot Brooke a warning look.

"Your father adores the country," Brooke continued, ignoring the implicit threat.

Yes he does, Sam thought. And when he got divorced, he left the city and his son and daughter far, far behind. She hadn't seen him in eight years, although she still kept a photograph of him in her wallet. Originally, it had showed dear old dad with his brand new family, a bouncing boy named Damian (who names a child after the devil?) and their former au pair, the bountiful Eliza. Sam cut them out and kept him. She looked at it from time to time, reminding herself of how disappointing fathers could be. Hey, she could share it now.

"Did you folks have to travel far?" Tom asked.

"Just from Brooklyn," Sam said.

"This is our first time in the city," Tom allowed.

"Really?" Brooke managed to sound authentically surprised.

"We're from Appleton. Appleton, Wisconsin."

"Wisconsin. I've been to Milwaukee," Brooke told him. "Beer. The Brewers. The Milwaukee Rep."

"Tom and I, we don't get down to the city all that much. We're just settling back in," Alma said brightly. "What with Tom's retiring."

"You're retired?" Brooke inquired.

"Tom was a lieutenant in the Navy," Alma explained. "They give you a real nice pension."

"A Navy man. Now isn't that interesting. I'll bet you went just about everywhere," Brooke said.

"I guess we did travel quite a bit," Tom agreed.

"A bit? My lord!" Alma exclaimed. "Japan. Germany. The Philippines, why you name it. Lucy here was born over in Germany. She's our youngest. We have six."

"Alma," Tom said quietly.

"What?" Alma asked. She made a clucking noise and bent over, then dug into the trunk to emerge with more pink towels.

"Six children? God, two almost killed me," Brooke exclaimed.

Sam thought about grabbing her and yanking her to her feet, then whisking her away. *Stop. Please just stop!* Sam couldn't do it. It would be too humiliating. She told herself this would be over in a few more minutes. Brooke would go, Lucy's parents too, then she and this girl Lucy would finally be alone. What would that be like? What could they possibly have in common? Then Sam realized Lucy was staring at her. Lucy's expression said, "When will our suffering end?"

She smiled and Lucy rolled her eyes.

"Is your other one a girl?" Alma inquired.

"A boy. Winston. We call him Win."

"Is he in college too?"

"He's finding himself," Brooke said, dully.

Alma had unwittingly stumbled into the thicket of true despair. Brooke stared down at her scarf, stunned into silence. Win wasn't finding himself. He was escaping her clutches for the umpteenth time. His avowed desire to flee from his mother had broken her heart. Sam had mixed feelings. Growing up, Win had been both protective of her and abusive. There were childhood games like Fifty-Two Card Pick Up and Hostage (guess who was the hostage?), and all those mornings when he woke her with a dousing from a squirt gun, then chased her through the apartment and right out onto the street in her pajamas. He was like that comic book villain he'd introduced her to back when, Two Face. It was also Win who made sure she didn't break her neck on the jungle gym when Brooke was rehearsing for her next big break. And without his guidance, Sam would have been listening to what was on the top forty on WABC. Win had patiently schooled her in music, from the Beatles to Otis. Sam sympathized with her brother. He wanted to just be a kid; instead, at twelve, he'd been stuck caring for her. He didn't exactly ask to be the man of the house. No wonder Win alternately loved and despised her. It was kind of his right.

Sam's possessions were stashed. She plopped down in her desk chair and spun round. Alma was still unpacking. On the surface, their families couldn't have been more different. Lucy's was honest to god, dyed in the wool, All American. These people probably said grace at every meal. And look at how well prepared they were. Alma had packed her daughter a first aid kit. Yes, all that pink was cringe inducing, but at least this mother had thought to provide her daughter with actual new bedding. Sam's own sheets were stripped off her bed at home then stuffed into the duffel bag.

These Westcotts were solid. They knew how to parent. Sam visualized Lucy's home. It featured modest décor. There was a dining room table with a seasonal centerpiece. For fall, a cast iron turkey surrounded by orange and red autumnal leaves; for winter, a snowman with sprigs of rubberized fir; for spring, lilacs and tulips; for summer, daisies, gladiolus, and dahlias. At dinner, after saying grace, they'd devour a hearty meal. And round that table, five other male children. All were undoubtedly youthful versions of Tom.

"You'd think for all the money it costs to go here they'd invest in air conditioning," Brooke said.

Alma retrieved another pink item from the trunk. As she unfolded it, Sam realized it was a curtain.

"Mom, stop, please just stop," Lucy begged.

"Stop what?" Alma asked innocently.

"Stop fussing over me."

"I'm not fussing," Alma said. She dug into the trunk again and emerged with a brand new curtain rod wrapped in plastic.

"Alma, sweetheart," Tom said. "Why don't you sit down for a while and rest?"

Alma ignored him, stubbornly working the rod out of its sheath.

"Mom, Samantha is living here, too. She might not want those curtains."

"I'm just going to try them out," Alma said.

"And we're just going to take them down when you leave," Lucy told her.

"Let's just see how they look."

"God, let's just not," Lucy said.

"What's gotten into you?" Alma asked, clearly hurt. "I'm only trying to help."

"It's her room, Alma," Tom said softly.

"Yes," Alma agreed, yet she headed for the window. Tom stood, going for the interception.

"You're upsetting Lucy," he told her, grabbing hold of the rod.

There was a brief struggle. Then Alma managed to wrest it away. He shook his head. Her face reddened. She spun round and found Sam. Sam saw she needed an ally and she would have been one, she did feel sorry for her, but Sam had to live with Lucy. The lines were already drawn. Poor Alma was starkly, completely alone.

"You said you liked the curtains," she tried. "They're your favorite color."

"I haven't had a favorite color since I was five," Lucy said bluntly.

This was evidently a private family matter. Sam tried to catch her mother's eye, but Brooke ignored her. They should go but Brooke was clearly enjoying this. When they were alone again, Brooke would have at the Westcotts, disemboweling Tom, the decommissioned naval officer and former jock who was stupid enough to imagine himself as hot as he was in high school and Alma, the housewife who had six, count them, six children. Oh, the plebeian misery of their boring, Midwestern, Middle American lives! Look at them, Brooke would crow. Look at her. Her dress was just ridiculous!

It was Sam's job to defend them. She'd have to beg her mother to stop, although she knew that Brooke would refuse to relent. If pushed, she would beat her breast and swear she'd done as much and more for her children. Sharper than a serpent's tooth, these children of hers. If that didn't work, she'd crank it up another notch, sobbing. In the end, everything was always about Brooke.

Alma held the screwdriver in one hand, the case of screws and rod holders in the other. She was also attempting to hold onto what was left of her dignity. Her mouth was a thin line. She'd tamped down the tears. Alma was brave, Sam thought. And stalwart. The woman was doing her best. Impulsively, Sam got up and went to her, then hugged her from behind. "Oh my," Alma said, turning. There was a glimmer of disappointment in her eyes. She'd hoped for Lucy. But then she gamely smiled, accepting this last minute replacement.

3

Muriel Earhart Morrissey
September 1980

IT WAS ONLY September and yet the house was already chilly. It wasn't even below thirty-two degrees outside; soon enough, winter weather would come. It would be unforgiving and bleak with snowbanks rising up the sides of the path dug along the street. On sunny days Muriel would be blinded, going from indoors to out.

Muriel went upstairs to her bedroom, took a cardigan out of the top drawer, and pulled it on. She checked in the mirror to make sure she'd buttoned it right and recoiled. It was still a surprise to see her reflection. How had she gotten this old? When had her hair turned whitest white? When had she become this snow queen?

Enough!

Downstairs, she went to get her purse where she'd left it on the kitchen table.

Only it wasn't there.

Where on earth?

She checked the living room, then the hall, then sighed and made her way back upstairs.

If your mind went, you went with it. She had had too many friends who had fallen prey to criminal mischief because of it. Fearing their nest eggs would no longer suffice, the poor fools had entered contests. When the phone call came to congratulate them, the supposed winners were ecstatic and eager to give out all their pertinent information. A million dollars was to be wired to their bank account. One week later, those same foolish souls discovered their accounts cleaned out. Then they had to choose between the spare room at their children's house and an old age home. Muriel had told herself she'd exit gracefully before her mind went south. Ah yes, the best laid plans.

Now where was that purse? It wasn't on the dresser or on the bed or hanging in the closet. Muriel stood in the hall, trying to think. She was getting senile along with everything else.

It came over her then. She missed both of them so much. She doubled over from the pain. You expected that you might outlive your husband. You saw the walking wounded, a society of widows all around you. But outliving your child? It didn't bear imagining.

Muriel had a sudden memory of her own mother standing in this same house, waiting. That time, it was Amelia. Mother, irredeemably broken, clutching at all the what ifs. The plane was lost over the Pacific. That time, the word "lost" called forth its optimistic opposite. Once lost, mightn't she be found? Their mother had kept her bag packed just in case right up until the day she died. She'd always believed that Amelia would come back.

In my case, Muriel thought, the word lost is truly a euphemism. They're dead. *Dead.* If only I could pretend otherwise.

She couldn't. All those trips she'd made to the hospital and the hours spent standing by the bed as the machines ticked both their lives away. Some of her clothing still retained that horrid antiseptic smell. She'd washed it and dry-cleaned it, but the stink was still there. After their son died, her husband, Albert had been her rock. He'd said they would stay right here and take whatever came to them. They would die with their boots on. What a bald faced lie. Muriel had held his hand in the ambulance as he gasped for breath.

"Don't let them take me there," he'd begged her but Muriel had ignored him. She'd been selfish. She'd needed him alive and with her and what if they could save him?

Here was the purse, right where she'd left it, hanging off the coat-hook in the mudroom. Muriel locked the door behind her and set off down the street.

HER HOME SAT on a side street in Medford. Albert had been house-proud, and his son helped out. The two of them toiled through long, hot summers on their projects. Wiring. Plumbing. Painting. They were handy men, handy men to have around. Now they were both gone and things were going awry. One toilet flushed itself as if a ghost was using it. There was a steady drip in the kitchen sink. The electric door opener for the garage was on the fritz. She would have to call someone eventually.

It was a relief to get out. To be heading somewhere else. Muriel was the only pedestrian. Everyone drove these days, no one bothered to walk even a block when they could drive, making you eat their dust.

Muriel walked with determination. Watching the speed walkers at the Olympics, Albert had said, "Why Muriel, that's you." It was true. She was hard to catch up with, even with Albert's big strides. She headed for town.

Virgil Washinawok stood at the counter inside the Book Nook on High Street. He was talking to three college age boys. Underneath the register, stands held the daily papers. There was the *Boston Globe*, *The Boston Herald*, *The Medford Transcript*, *The Boston Phoenix*, and those big city standards, *The Wall Street Journal* and *New York Times*.

Muriel headed to the back, past the stock shelved alphabetically in the handmade wooden bookcases. Virgil had set books aside in a reading area. He'd put in two big armchairs and a coffee table. New releases were cracked open so many times in the first week that they looked secondhand. Muriel had told him it seemed a little foolish, giving books away like that, for free.

"If they wanted them for free, they'd go to the library," he replied.

She couldn't quite see the logic there. Of course, reading a book at Virgil's was much more pleasant than sitting in the library, with its fluorescent lighting and hard wooden chairs. There it felt unwelcoming and sterile, like a hospital ward. Here, you could settle in.

Virgil believed that after a few hours of reading, they'd buy something. Muriel knew better. Why spend the money? Then, there was the thrill of doing something illicit to reckon with. Muriel had spotted more than one Tufts student slip something into his or her pocket or purse. She'd alerted Virgil. It was curious how he responded, doing the same thing each time. As the thief left, he'd ask if they had something they needed to tell him. Nine times out of ten they would pull out the book and pay for it. It was a dance, Muriel thought, and even when they brazened it out, Virgil didn't threaten them or call the police. He said that their conscience would get to them eventually. Muriel doubted it. Her own Albert would have done things differently. He'd been a strict man. He believed in teaching a lesson. He would have called the police and had every one of them arrested.

Every so often Muriel bought a paperback. That assuaged her guilt for taking up this space, for sitting down and starting to read then looking up and discovering it was already dark outside.

At first, Virgil only exchanged pleasantries with her.

But now he set books aside for her. Kept them by the cash register and gave them to her and even asked her opinion.

Muriel had always been a reader. When she was young, she and Amelia had had to sit for centuries in their grandmother's library. They'd read all of Dickens, all of Eliot, all of Thackeray. Once out of school and able to choose for herself, Muriel discovered she preferred humor. It was Huck Finn and everything else Mark Twain wrote. She adored Oscar Wilde. There was always an importance in being earnest.

Irony abounded.

Years ago she'd imagined herself having her own great adventure, back when she and Amelia were so young. Then, they'd both known how to shoot a rifle, how to cut down a squirrel in the prime of its life, and not bat an eye or feel a twinge of regret. But then boys came into the picture. For her, there'd been Daniel Roberts in high school, and Bertram in college who went to Harvard and pinned her, and then of course Albert. Thus her fate was sealed.

"I put away childish things," she said, said it aloud then looked around furtively to see if anyone had overheard. Virgil was up at the cash register. Virgil, whose own wife had died over ten years ago, had chosen to stay faithful to her memory or at least not remarry. They'd had no children. He'd stayed put right here in Medford. His looks were the cause of a lot of gossip. He was originally from Minnesota, but his wife had been Medford born and bred. They'd met out west; Muriel didn't really know the details. But she knew that he was Indian, or rather, Native American. Growing up, she'd spent some of the best summers of her life in Worthington, Minnesota. She guessed he was Chippewa. His black hair had finally turned salt-and-pepper gray and his face had gotten lined, but his coloring was still tawny, and his dark eyes gleamed.

"Here's one I think you'd like," a voice said. Muriel started. How long had Virgil been there, watching her? It was horrible what happened these days. She went into some kind of trance. Better here than on the street, she thought. Sometimes she'd start out from home and the next thing she knew she was clear past Tufts and heading for the highway.

Muriel took it from him. On the front she read *uncorrected proof.*

"It's a galley," Virgil said. "We get them for free before the book comes out."

The cover was dark blue. There was a map on it, but not the kind you hang on the wall in the back of a classroom and pull down with a snap. Instead, it was from one of those old-world globes, like the ones on display in libraries and museums that showed bodies of water stretching out and the countries mashed together.

Muriel read the title aloud, *The Transit of Venus.*

"I'll let you tell me what you think that means," he said. Then he was off, waving to someone up at the front.

Muriel opened the book and read the first line, "By nightfall the headlines would be reporting devastation." Turning back to the cover, she tried to guess what the book would be about. Of course, there was absolutely no way to tell. That was part of why she liked to read; when you got deep inside, the suspense could be killing. But Muriel never let herself read the ending in advance. She held out, no matter how nervous she got for the characters. It was a point of pride.

The book had been thumbed through. She guessed that Virgil's hands had done that.

Dust yourself off, get yourself up and start all over again. The lyrics came to her out of the blue. She'd loved that song when it was at the height of its popularity. It was a song meant for young people's ears. Only the young could forge ahead so easily. They knew that there was so much to look forward to and so little left behind. At eighty, what lay ahead looked grim. All that had mattered most could be spotted in your rearview mirror.

Two funerals. One had been more than enough. Muriel didn't want to think yet here it was, the truth. Her truth. Your body was a husk. It had held onto what made you, you. Once you were dead, the person fled. Where they went was anyone's guess. As for mourning, Muriel was intrigued by the

Hindu tradition. There was an appeal to the idea of piling a man's worldly possessions up with him and shoving it off into the Ganges or, in her case, the Charles. Muriel knew what she'd load onto Albert's funeral barge. The Zeiss binoculars he'd used for bird watching, the power mower, the tools in the basement, the electric carving knife, and, of course, his beloved Caddy. She'd crawl onto the hood and have them shove the damn thing off. When the barge was a safe distance away from shore, she'd strike a match. Muriel smiled at the image of herself, perching atop the flaming wreckage of that once gleaming, wing tipped car.

"How is it?" Virgil asked.

She shivered and turned. Muriel blinked and looked past him. It was dark outside. The store was deserted.

"Albert bought a gun for himself," Muriel said. "I don't know what to do with it."

Virgil took his time responding. Finally, he said, "Turn it in to the police."

She nodded. "It's the shock, I guess. I didn't even know he had it. I found it sitting in his desk drawer."

Virgil slipped into the other chair.

It had been quite the surprise, finding that gun. Albert had carried on as if nothing were wrong. He'd been the one to go out every day, into the day. He'd been the one to try to force her out of bed. "Get up, girl," he'd said, like she was a horse. Then she'd found the gun and known exactly what he'd bought it for.

"Maybe he wanted it for protection," Virgil tried.

"From me?" Muriel let out a choking laugh. It was odd, telling him what she'd not told anyone. Why Virgil, why him, of all people?

"I never did like how it felt killing things myself." Virgil crossed his right leg reflexively over his left. "That's one of the ways I diverged."

"Your family liked to hunt?"

"We had to eat," he said.

Muriel smiled. There was her comeuppance. "The thing that bothers me most is that I can't ask him about it."

She could see he knew what she meant. But she'd overstayed her welcome. Muriel stumbled to her feet. Her right leg had fallen asleep. She tottered. Virgil put his hand out, lightly, to steady her. She couldn't help pulling away as he extended it, even with the pins and needles coursing up her leg.

"Thanks for the book," she said, feeling ashamed. Confiding in him had been a moment of weakness. She paused, realizing, it had been six months since she'd lost Albert. There, another euphemism.

"You let me know what you think now," Virgil said as he walked her to the door. He let her out then locked it behind her. Relocked it, she realized. He'd closed up without disturbing her.

Outside, the air was so cold it almost robbed her of her breath. Muriel took her time. There was no reason to rush. What was the point? Dinner was leftovers from the night before, a roast she'd made that she would heat up, and some potatoes.

A mother and son had a special bond. Sometimes she thought Albert was jealous. He'd come upon the two of them at odd moments and she'd see the look he gave them. Albert had his rules. "Keep your elbows off the table," he'd say to their boy. "Stand up straight when I talk to you." His advice always started off with one proscription, "Now if I were you. . ." That was the moment every child stopped listening, but Albert never realized.

Letting herself in, Muriel smelled his scent. All this time and it lingered on, as if he still lived here with her. She set the book down on the side table, went into the living room, and attacked the mail. Inside the top envelope, Hallmark's best sported a bouquet of white lilies on a pink pastel background. The inscription read, "Condolences for Your Loss." It was from Charlotte, who had been on the board of Grace Church with Albert. She'd retired to Arizona and specialized in generic letters that began, "Dear Friend," detailing the exploits of everyone in her entire extended family. There were cruises to the Galapagos, safaris in Kenya. Charlotte always enclosed a photo, a jumble of old and young perched on some rocky outcropping. Why bother? No one wanted to be treated as an interchangeable cog in the wheel of friendship. The card was oddly familiar. Then Muriel realized why. Charlotte had sent the exact same one after their son died. She must have a packet of them squirreled away.

"Jesus," Muriel said, chucking it in the trash.

It was only the beginning of a floral avalanche. Roses. Mums. Lilies of the field. They were scattered between the bills. Inside, empathy in script, some with personal notes scrawled below.

"When I lost Sy, I thought I'd never be able to breathe again. Please call me anytime."

"I can't imagine what you're going through. I would do anything to help."

"You think life will be fair, but it isn't. Dear Muriel, you've been such a rock for me. Such a beacon of hope."

Was she a beacon? Muriel saw herself more as a lighthouse, stuck on a promontory, a staid, brick-faced entity. When daylight came, it showed its true self. Erosion had battered it, the paint was chipping, the edifice was crumbling and who on earth cared? She wanted to crumble. She would have liked to be swept away. What I am, Muriel thought, is exhausted. Exhausted from bearing up under the weight of all of this. What I want is to go back to bed, to hide under the covers, to play that game that Amelia and I used to play where we would pretend to be asleep until she would tickle me mercilessly.

But there was that poster Virgil had up on the wall in his store. "This is the first day of the rest of your life."

Goodie.

An official cream envelope came next. The sender was a Dr. Fabian Price, chairman of the Biology Department at Columbia University. Perhaps he was a friend of Albert's from his youth?

> Dear Mrs. Morrissey,
>
> We are most pleased to inform you that a generous benefactor has endowed a scholarship in your sister Amelia's name. The deserving recipient will receive a full stipend for their remaining three years. It will be awarded to an undergraduate female chosen by our committee and deemed Barnard's most promising pre-medical candidate. Obviously it is inspired by your sister's example. These benefactors are alumni themselves. They are also great admirers of your sister and have only lately become aware of her short tenure here.
>
> The initial award recipient will be selected this year. A ceremony to honor her is planned for this January. We would be gratified if you would agree to attend and give the keynote address. Of course, we will gladly pay all expenses. Our anonymous donors have made a special request and are offering a generous honorarium. If you have any further questions, feel free to call.
>
> Yours,
> Dr. Fabian Price

The man signed his name with a flourish. There was that joke about doctors not being able to write legibly. Here was an academic. You couldn't make out one letter in his name. Muriel set it aside. A note fluttered into her lap.

> Dear Mrs. Morrissey,
>
> It's Samantha Barry. I know you must get lots of invitations so I have no idea what you'll think about this one, but I at least wanted to take the opportunity to write and say hello. I hope you remember me. You were so generous about my paper. I'm a freshman at Barnard now and work for Dr. Price. He had me typing up a press release about this new scholarship. I mentioned how I'd gotten a letter from you and knew how to get in touch. He was so gung ho, wanted to know your address and if I thought you'd want to speak. I know you're probably too busy to come all

the way down here plus New York in January isn't exactly *fun in the sun*. Still, if you do decide to brave it, I promise to show you the sights and make sure they put you up wherever you want. I'd so love to actually meet you. Your words of encouragement meant so much.

Always the best,
Samantha Barry
P.S. Thanks again for taking my work so seriously. I hope you don't regret it now.

That Barry girl had written quite the paper. Was it really only last year? The topic had been *Amelia Earhart: The Icon*. According to its youthful author, her sister had been a master of public relations, maximizing her popularity by inventing an innocent alter ego, a "perfect" Amelia. This alternate self had benefited from luck and timing; fame happened to her and kept on happening. The charmed and charming version of Amelia was both decent and all American, plain spoken and modest, although she was also a woman who opted to wear men's clothing and fly planes. The public forgave her these eccentricities because her invented persona was so convincing and so disarming.

"You've done an excellent job here," she had written Miss Barry. "I was impressed with your research and your diligent analysis, though I will tell you that the thesis is, at the core, misguided." Misguided, now there was a plum word.

The girl had written a thank you note. That thesis was clever, and frankly a little too close to the truth for comfort. That young woman did know her subject. But Muriel wasn't about to give Amelia away at this late date. She knew things about her sister that no one else knew. And she would go to her grave, keeping them secret. It was how Amelia would have wanted it.

Muriel walked down the hall and into to her office. She opened the file drawer. Here was Miss Barry's opus, typed on onionskin paper.

Biographers have spent a great deal of time recounting the events of Earhart's life. Some focus on her accomplishments and her outsized celebrity. Others delve into the mystery surrounding her last flight and disappearance. Her public pronouncements are a matter of record. Her private life is a mystery. Amelia Earhart was politically progressive and an ardent feminist. She went where no woman and few men had gone before. All that was known, but what we don't know, we continue to guess at. Was she trapped in a loveless marriage with G.P. Putnam, or was it a mutually beneficial arrangement? Did she have lovers?

Was she a bisexual? Was her ambition always there, or was it just luck that made her into a household name? It's a very modern view, believing that our heroes and heroines owe us the truth and should expose themselves to us warts and all. Amelia still refuses. Who was Amelia Earhart? We know what she accomplished, but her story is incomplete mainly because even forty plus years after her death her image is still tightly controlled. That is the legacy of the real Amelia Earhart.

It was a dare, the sort of dare young people specialized in making when trying to get a rise out of their elders. Her own children had done it.

The yellow kitchen curtains rustled. A front was coming through. Out with the old weather and in with the new. There were changes one longed for, while others were too painful to contemplate. Muriel thought of those cables Amelia had sent to their parents once she was aloft and safely away, flying east, over the Atlantic.

"No matter what happens it will have been worth the trying."

Muriel's letter from Amelia arrived the same day. She didn't tell Mother she'd gotten it. By the time she got a chance to read it, it was after two a.m. Their mother had been frantic with worry, imagining every possible horrible scenario, but she'd finally gone to sleep.

"Dear Pidge," Amelia wrote. "You're thinking why didn't I confide in you? You think I don't trust you and of course that makes you angry. But if I did tell you about going, then I would have had to swear you to secrecy and that would have been cruel. You couldn't have told Mother, yet every minute you'd have to be with her would have felt like a lifetime to you. And who's to say you wouldn't have blurted it out just to stop that feeling from overwhelming you. If you had, Mother would have tried to prevent me from risking my life. It's what a mother is supposed to do, isn't it? Protect her child and prevent her from doing something foolish and dangerous?

"To be honest, there's more. I suppose it scared me, thinking of how I would have to explain this to you. You would have asked me, 'What if you die?' What does someone say to that? How do you say that you only have a certain number of chances to try things in life, and that this is the one I couldn't pass up? It was so much easier to pretend with you and go on as before. It wasn't sisterly of me to hide this from you, yet I had to. I couldn't let myself be dissuaded. I couldn't take the chance of that happening. If not now, when? There was only one right answer for me. I know it was selfish. I only hope you can find it in your heart to understand and forgive me.

Your loving sister, A."

Why not go back to Columbia? She hadn't been there since Amelia served as her amateur guide, giving her a tour of the campus. She'd been so low, but the more she thought about it, the more the idea intrigued her. Besides, it was months away. She'd work on the talk. She'd put something in for the girl, this Samantha Barry, a sly response to the paper. An inside joke, as it were.

Muriel opened the right hand desk drawer and pulled out some notepaper. Then got to work, composing her answer.

4

Amelia
September 1980

AMELIA OPENED HER eyes and discovered a cracked plaster ceiling. Scrambling to her feet, she knew where she was. She was in Muriel's living room. Grandfather Otis' secretary sat in the corner. The blue drapes were tied back. Sunlight streamed in. It was hot in the room. It would be, it was boiling hot on the beach, where she evidently lay dreaming. Things in the room had shifted from the way she remembered them. The sofa was no longer upholstered in a plush maroon. It wore a natty plaid. Standing in for the matching loveseat were bookended Windsor chairs. The floor-to-ceiling bookshelves were the same and cluttered with family photographs. Here was Mother, showing off the string of pearls Amelia had bought for her. Her brother-in-law Albert wore casual attire, snapped on the garden seat. And Amelia waved to admirers from the cockpit of the Electra. Perched to her photograph's right was one of a young man in uniform. Army? Navy? Marines? Amelia reached for the frame to lift it closer. Her fingers slid through. She gasped, pulling back as if stung, then tried again. And got the same result. It was going to be one of those dreams, rife with frustration.

Amelia had had them before. In truth, not being able to grab hold of a picture was child's play. On the nights before a potentially record-shattering flight, she'd fall asleep and discover she was taxiing down the runway alone, without a navigator, charts, or a working compass or Amelia would be driving to the airport when a wall of water appeared, lifting the car and tossing it down. Worse, a stream of burning lava, the source a seething volcano spewing dust and ash, barred her way. She'd put the car into reverse and find the gears stuck. Once, after all of this, she arrived at the airport to see her plane soaring off without her.

Luckily, she'd learned that dreams were malleable. You had to have the stomach for it. And the presence of mind. It was a funny way to put it, but all too true. The mind was a surprisingly supple tool. Amelia had learned that if she took hold of her own dream, she could reinvent it. She redirected the flight back to the landing strip and retrieved Fred. If that didn't work, she reminded herself to look under the jump seat. There she'd hidden a treasure trove of navigational charts. As the water from the tidal wave poured into the car, she rolled up the windows and hit the switch that turned it into a submersible. H.G. Wells had done it first. She was only following in his hallowed footsteps. Inside, she was safe in her underwater, motorized house. Boiling lava met an ice storm and froze in its tracks. As for that plane shooting off into the ether, it wasn't her Vega at all. That was being prepped in a nearby shed.

It was a useful skill, one she'd forced herself to learn early. The first time she and Muriel stayed at Grandmother Otis' house on their own, the nightmares began. Amelia was six when the witch arrived. She'd trap Amelia in the hayloft, her grandmother's bedroom, or that cave where she and Muriel went spelunking. Grabbing Amelia by her hair, she'd emit a cackle as she dragged her off to shove her into an oven. Smoke filled her lungs. Gasping and screaming, Amelia woke and discovered she'd woken the entire household. Muriel was at her side, hugging her tight. Grandmother Otis had run to see who was screaming bloody murder. Even Grandfather was there, stroking his moustache. It was so humiliating.

And went on for a full week.

Finally, Amelia decided she'd had enough. She told herself that as soon as the witch appeared, she would force herself awake. That night, the hideous creature showed up on schedule. She looked even worse than usual, with a horrid snaggletooth and breath that reeked of onions. Amelia pinched her arm until it felt sore. Even though she was dreaming, it turned out she'd done it. Waking, she saw the outline of the witch fade away on the bedroom wall. Relief buoyed her. She'd made good her own escape! Her victory was a turning point. After that, she tested the limits. She let the witch touch her before waking. Then let her stuff Amelia into a dungeon. Once she felt confident of her power, she even let the creature wrap her stringy hands around Amelia's neck. "You're not real, now go away." The witch was amused, but Amelia knew better. "Shoo." She made a triangle with her fingers and flicked her away like a mosquito. On cue, the witch dissolved.

Amelia blinked. She was here. Here in Muriel's house. And positive she could leave whenever she wished. Where was the harm in staying put?

The bookshelves had evidence of pivotal family events. Her niece and nephew grew older, wearing caps and gowns, claiming trophies, marrying, holding children of their own. So the soldier in the uniform was her nephew. Look at Muriel and Albert dressed to the nines! Muriel wore red satin, Albert sported a tux, his gut swathed in a cummerbund. Muriel's hair was white. That was a shock. And Albert was going bald.

Amelia struck a habitual pose. Her hands slid effortlessly into her trouser pockets. She felt the lighter and next to it, what felt like a pack of cigarettes. Luckies! Amelia lit one and inhaled, greedily.

There was a horrid squealing noise like old pipes releasing dead air. Curious, Amelia traced the source. Down the hall in the kitchen, a woman was heating a kettle. Her white hair was pinned atop her head. As the burner lit, flame coursed out. She turned round and Amelia saw it was Muriel writ old. This dream was Dickensian. Was it meant as a vision of things to come? Muriel opened the icebox and retrieved two large, perfectly formed white eggs. She cracked them into a bowl, mixed them to froth, then poured the liquid into a frying pan. After unwrapping a rectangular package of Wonder Bread, Muriel selected a slice. There had never seemed to be anything remarkable about the bread, but then again, there had never been much truth in advertising. Muriel dropped it into a sleek, silver toaster. Amelia's stomach rumbled. In her present, near starvation condition, it was torture watching the preparation of this modest meal.

Amelia had smoked her cigarette down to the nub. She dropped it on the floor, meaning to stamp it out. As the butt hit the black-and-white tile, it fizzed and vanished with a pop. Now that was different. Come to think of it, so was the kitchen. The avocado icebox she'd sent as a surprise Christmas present was white. The cast iron stove was gone, replaced by a smaller, four burner model. The color scheme was now off-white.

Muriel scrambled the eggs. As the scent coiled out, Amelia's knees wobbled. Dizzy from hunger, she leaned against the icebox for support. The metal gave underneath her, and she plummeted. Suddenly, she was admiring a chicken carcass and browning salad in a Mason jar. If she kept going, there was no telling where she'd stop.

That scared Amelia. She managed to right herself. On her way out, she spotted a lonely twig of wilted celery.

Muriel sat down at the breakfast table. In front of her, the window framed a busy birdfeeder. A blue jay perched, shoving sparrows and chickadees aside. "Pest!" Muriel tapped the glass. The bird gave her a hostile look. She banged again and it finally took wing. Satisfied, she turned the dial on a rectangular metal box. Music poured out. It was Brahms piano concerto number two. So this was a radio. Muriel adjusted a long telescoping metal rod and the fuzzy reception improved. That had to be an antenna. Muriel was admiring her garden. And what a garden it was, chock-full of dahlias, asters, red, pink, and yellow roses. Pidge had always had a green thumb, but she'd outdone herself with this stellar display. The hardy oak was gone, in its place a cast iron table with matching chairs.

Muriel ate her breakfast and then set the dirty plate in the sink. She refilled her teacup and headed down the hall to the spare bedroom. Like everything else in this topsy-turvy world, it wasn't a bedroom. It was an office, complete with desk, bookcases, and an oak filing cabinet. Muriel sat, opened the top drawer, and withdrew a piece of parchment paper. She reached for a fountain pen. After uncapping it, she held it aloft like Damocles sword. Time ticked on.

Amelia surveyed the room and found her image everywhere; a framed advertisement for that ill-conceived clothing line she had started, the Steichen portrait of her from Vanity Fair, a corkboard layered with fading snapshots, the photo Pidge had taken of her at the wheel of her old car the "Yellow Peril." She stood next to Neta Snook, her first flight instructor. She was in rolled-up shirtsleeves, poring over maps at her house in Toluca Lake. Framed front pages proclaimed her newsworthy achievements: *First Woman Flies Atlantic; Sails Blindly Through Fog Blanket to Coast of Wales, Ireland Greets Earhart After Solo Hop Across Sea from Harbor Grace, Amelia Makes Oakland Ending Hop From Hawaii.* There was even a wall dedicated to amateur renderings of her likeness. Some were in pen and ink; others, pencil. One had the title "Saint Amelia." Hardly a saint, she thought wryly. Funny that she would dub herself one in her own dream. Well, not funny as much as egotistical. What was more unlikely, that she was a saint, or that Muriel was the keeper of the flame? Both were a wry bit of wish fulfillment. She turned to the far wall and read the boldface headlines. *Amelia's Sister Not Worrying, She Says. Amelia Earhart's 7-Year-Old Nephew Worries in Medford at Letter's Fate. Planes Poised for Hunt. Last Gift From Amelia Arrives. Navy Gives Up Its Hunt For Amelia, Lost Pair Declared Officially Dead by Authorities.*

"Oh!" Shock gutted her. Here was the trick ending. Time to return to reality. Better to be alive, stranded on that beach. Better a chance at rescue than this. In this dream, she was gone.

Amelia pinched her right arm.

The pain was real, but nothing changed. She was still here, standing behind Muriel who had finally decided to set pen to paper. The nib made a scratching sound. Amelia tried pressing down hard on the tender spot where her hand met her wrist. That always worked.

Not this time. What to do? She slapped herself. Her cheek stung, her eyes watered. Yet she stayed put, planted firmly on the hardwood floor.

"Done!" Muriel announced. She set her writing utensil aside and read aloud to her captive audience. "Dear Professor Price, It was a great pleasure to speak with you. I look forward to visiting New York and trust that my talk will not disappoint. I am positive my sister would have been honored to have this scholarship given in her name. She looked back at her time spent attending Columbia with great fondness."

Muriel signed with a flourish, folded the notepaper into thirds, and then tucked it into an envelope. She affixed a stamp. Gripping her now empty teacup, she rose and spun to face Amelia. Only scant inches separated them. Muriel had shrunk. They'd been exactly the same height. They used to, literally, see eye to eye. Now her younger sibling's nose pressed against Amelia's clavicle. Amelia dodged and feinted but Muriel walked right through her, bisecting her body. Amelia shut her eyes, bracing for the pain.

And felt nothing.

She spun round to catch Muriel slip out the door. She was humming a song Amelia knew. It was from Freddie Astaire's movie. Why, she'd been at the premiere and shared a booth with him at the after-party. "I love the way you dance, it looks so effortless," she'd told him.

"I love the way you fly a plane," he retorted.

A joke. But he understood. Years of planning and practice went into making something look this easy. He clicked his heels in midair. She soared off toward the horizon.

That night she'd written a letter to Muriel, telling her about the premiere, about Astaire and their tête à tête. Reading it over, she'd decided not to send it. She'd torn it up. Amelia thought Muriel would see it as a boast, that the confidence would encourage jealousy. Why stir that pot? And to think, they'd once shared everything.

Muriel was singing that same song. And here was Amelia; trapped in this "Mudford" prison, trapped in the town she'd fled from a lifetime ago. The words taunted her.

Nothing's impossible I have found, for when my chin is on the ground, I pick myself up, dust myself off and start all over again.

5

Sam
September 1980

"LOOK WHAT CAME for me today," Lucy said. She took a baggie stuffed to the brim with marijuana buds from a cardboard box, gaily decorated with postage stamps.

"You had that sent to you at the dorm? We'll get busted. That's crazy."

"Don't be so paranoid."

Lucy's confidence was incredible. Sam was positive it had to do with her looks. Sam assumed that when you were as attractive as Lucy was, you believed the world was your oyster. Sam was good looking enough. She got her fair share of male attention. But she didn't consider herself a great beauty. And she certainly saw the world in a wholly practical light. For one thing, she knew that drug-sniffing dogs were immune to beauty, and that when it came to striking a deal, it would be too late for Lucy's looks to work their undeniable charm. She also knew better than Lucy what could happen if you were caught and ended up on the wrong side of the Rockefeller drug laws. Win was an excellent teacher. He had friends who were doing hard time, so he took every precaution, renting three different post office boxes under assumed names and wearing a different elaborate disguise using a wig and moustache as well as a hat when he picked up his mail. The drugs he received were packed inside teddy bears lined with impermeable plastic. They'd been made specially so even bloodhounds couldn't sniff through. The floor of his closet had a secret hatch for his metal lined stash box. Win sold the best cocaine, pot, and hash that money could buy. The drugs were the reason for his ongoing popularity with the sons and daughters of New York's Upper East Side upper crust.

Lucy constructed the perfect joint, dropping the crumbled remains of the bud onto EZ rolling paper. She made a straight line with the debris, then rolled, licked, and lit it. After drawing in, she handed it over.

"This is strong," Sam said, her throat already burning.

"Hawaiian," Lucy noted. "We were posted there for a while."

"You've lived everywhere. I'm so jealous."

"Don't be. Naval bases are full of pre-fab housing and military brats. My dad would throw a fit if we went off the base. We had to sneak around or toe the line."

"And you toed the line? Come on."

"I was the youngest," Lucy said. "I didn't have a lot of choice."

Lucy squatted cross-legged on her own pink bed. Sam leaned against it, her legs making a v on the floor. They shared the joint in companionable silence. The crack underneath the door was stuffed with a towel, just in case someone in authority wandered by. There. They were done. Lucy swallowed the roach. The evidence was carefully tucked away.

Lucy thumbed through the milk crate that held her records. She selected one and set it on Sam's KLH turntable. A woman's voice emerged, her quaver ripe with longing. Before meeting Lucy, Sam had had contempt for country music. Then Lucy played Patsy Cline for her. Sam was now officially addicted. In return, she had introduced Lucy to Elvis Costello and his angelic red shoes. Share and share alike was their motto. It was grand bunking together in this room that was fast becoming Sam's sanctuary.

Classes officially began today. Being pre-med meant Sam took two lab science classes, trigonometry, an English seminar, and advanced French. Sam's Bio professor had wasted no time. Their first lab was due in two weeks. They'd been given cages and fruit flies and were supposed to prove or disprove Mendel's laws of inheritance. Everyone knew what the results should be, but that didn't matter. You still had to test it out. Superior genes trumped inferior. It felt morally reprehensible to be proving this when Sam considered the bastardization of genetics and how a simple biological law had been used to justify the extermination of Jews, Gypsies, and various other non-Aryan members of German society. Sam and Lucy got thick milk shakes and French fries at a place everyone called the "survivor's coffee shop." The owners' tattoos were souvenirs of their other life. The wife had bleached blond hair and she joked with everyone. Her husband was quiet and dour. There were questions everyone who saw those tattoos wanted to ask, yet who could bear to hear the answers?

Grim.

Patsy was wooing Sam, singing about her sweetest dreams. Moral issues were important, but they would keep for another day. Sam sank down onto the floor. From there she admired the infinite variety of patterns made by the cracks in the ceiling. She was so incredibly high. That had to be why she was certain her fortune was up there waiting to be read.

Sam spent Monday and Friday afternoons perched at a desk in the windowless alcove outside of Professor Price's office. She filed papers, typed up his research, and answered the phone. Some would call it her work-study job, but Sam knew it was destiny that she'd been given this post. Literally her first day there, she'd typed up the announcement inviting applications for the Amelia Earhart Scholarship. Sam mentioned to Professor Price that Earhart's younger sister, Muriel, was still alive and well and living in Medford, Massachusetts. He lit up. Did she think that Miss Earhart's sister would come and speak at the ceremony? Sam said, "Why not write her? I've got her address."

Generally Sam believed that luck meant you ran down the steps to get the IRT into Manhattan, and the doors were just opening as you hurtled through the turnstiles. There. You would be on time after all. The idea that she had written an entire paper on Amelia Earhart for her Feminism class last year, that Muriel Earhart Morrissey had actually read it, then sent back her comments, and that now Sam was instrumental in getting Muriel invited down to Columbia to speak was a lot closer to destiny. Or so the pot said.

Of course, Sam was applying for the scholarship. That was a no-brainer. Or rather, she was hoping someone would nominate her. Muriel had been nice enough to critique her paper. Now Muriel had agreed to come speak. It had to be significant.

Winning the scholarship would be incredible. It would spare her ever having to hear another conversation like the one she'd listened in on when Sam received the acceptance letter to Barnard. Brooke starting off proud as punch. But, within minutes she was reduced to begging. Pleading. "Mother, don't you think she deserves a chance at a great education? No, I don't think going to City College should be enough. It wasn't for you or me, was it? Look, father always told me he would help out. Yes, I know I've been a disappointment to you. I'm not expecting it. I don't live my life hoping for charity from you. Sam is your granddaughter. What do you need all that money for anyhow? You have everything anyone could ever want. Yes, I understand it's your money, not mine. Yes, I certainly understand why I am not worthy. But Sam isn't me. God, why do you have to be such a cunt?"

With that, Brooke slammed down the phone. Sam could have told her it would end this way. Brooke knew it too, but she kept going back to the dried out teat. Sam hated her grandmother in principle, but principles were hard to hold onto when you actually had to interact with the person. Katherine was vain and cruel, but she had also made it clear that Sam was her favorite. She would take Sam aside and tell her how special she was and gift her to prove it. Sam owned a pair of ruby earrings, a Navajo necklace, and an antique sculpture of an ancient Chinese warrior astride an ivory horse. All were tucked away in Sam's safest place. The last thing she needed was for Win or Brooke to know that she'd been given special treatment. If Brooke had let Sam ask Katherine, things might have turned out differently, but instead it was Brooke on the phone demanding her due. Then the two of them went spinning off until it ended in the usual, painful free fall.

Sam was already busy ingratiating herself with the Professor. It couldn't hurt. After all, he was in charge of organizing the scholarship committee. Was it wrong to do it? Yes, and no. Sam wasn't naïve enough to believe that you got anywhere on talent alone. You also had to have luck. And know the right people. Amelia Earhart's career was a lesson in all of that. Professor Price's wardrobe gave him a slightly homeless air. Shirts were stained. Jackets missed buttons. While he worked, she cleaned the stains off his jacket. She found his lost pens. She kept faithful records of all his calls. He'd already told her she would have to do research. She said she looked forward to it. He was a dear sort of man and on Friday she'd had a horrible urge to clip the stray tendrils of white hair growing from the edges of his earlobes.

This pot was way too strong. There was a prickling in the back of her neck. It felt as if an alien were taking her over. "Did you ever see *Invaders from Mars*?" Sam asked Lucy.

"No. What is it?"

"This creepy movie from the fifties. A kid wakes up and he sees a flash of light. It turns out a spaceship is landing. The Martians get to his family, his friends, everyone in the town. When someone is taken over, there's this telltale zipper on the back of his or her neck. I've had nightmares about it ever since I saw it. Did you see *Village of the Damned*? In that one, all the children are in control and they have these strange eyes that turn yellow. They make the adults do whatever they want, but there's this one teacher, I think it's a teacher. He decides that he has to save all humanity and the only way to do it is to make sure the kids can't find out what he's up to, so when he's about to kill them he constructs this wall in his head, brick by brick. Oh, and the kids can read minds, did I mention that? All they can see is the brickwork."

"Aliens, really?" Lucy was laughing. "There aren't any aliens. There's just us poor humans. We're the only conscious life form out there."

"How can you be sure? We're just this tiny dot. Not even a dot. The universe is huge, I mean, there are galaxies on top of galaxies. We're a smidgen, no, make that a speck or an infinitesimally tiny point of nothingness. Plus, the movies aren't about the alien menace. They're about the communist threat. The big fear back then was having our minds controlled. Hollywood made sure that Americans felt scared of it. They were complicit in the whole approach. The movie makers were channeling the zeitgeist."

"Wow. That's quite an analysis. The zeitgeist? Do explain."

"The major ideas that were floating around at the time because of McCarthy and Truman. It was basically that the Russians were out to get us and the Communists were evil, ready to suck out our souls."

"You're pretty convincing."

"I didn't invent the concept," Sam admitted.

"Still, you explain it so well. So what's the big fear now?" Lucy asked. "It's not drug crazed youth. That was the sixties."

"Black people," Sam said. "There's one that never dies."

"No kidding," Lucy agreed. "I went out with this boy for a while. Whenever Lee came over, my father would leave the room. Dad couldn't out and out forbid me from dating Lee, but he made it clear that I was upsetting him. When I asked him what was wrong, he said he was protecting me from disappointment."

"You kept on seeing Lee?"

"For a while. But we fell out of love. That happens. But you know all about that."

It was as much a question as a comment. Lucy had been working on the lost loves angle for days. Sam was embarrassed to admit that she'd had exactly two romantic interludes and neither had lasted more than a few months. Or progressed past mutual groping. To admit that to Lucy was to admit her inferiority. She was a virgin. Lucy wasn't. Sam could act as if she was jaded and superior, but it was only that, an act. Lucy was the one who actually knew about sex, and love, and boys. It gave her an incalculable edge. Not that this was a competition exactly. Still.

"You're so different from who I thought you'd be," Sam said, changing the subject.

"How do you mean?" Lucy gave her a sly look. "Prom queen gets brain transplant?"

"You're the first prom queen I've ever met."

"And you're my first native New Yorker."

Lucy extended her hand. Sam shook it hard. They dissolved into laughter. Sam really liked her roommate, which was more than a little surprising.

Sam had a vision of those pink curtains suffering in the bottom of the closet. She was sorry they had hidden them away. Lucy's mom was decent and sweet, the polar opposite of, say, a certain Brooke Barry.

In that movie *Invaders From Mars,* the little boy woke from the nightmare and had a moment of pure relief, realizing it had just been a dream after all. Then he looked out his bedroom window to find a spaceship landing. That was what living with Brooke was like. You woke up every morning imagining the worst was over, but then you walked out of your bedroom and the day unfolded. By the time dinner rolled around, you were just like that boy, terrified and alone and wishing you could go to sleep and wake yourself up to discover you were actually living on a different planet where all the girl's rooms had pink curtains and comforters, and all the moms missed you solely because you were their baby daughter. Those moms didn't want to live without seeing your bright shiny face at breakfast. They were there to love and protect and honor and fold you into their arms. Plus, they got up early to cook you French toast with real maple syrup, calling to you as you left the house, "Have a great day."

"Your mother is intense," Lucy said, reading her mind. "It must be weird, living with her."

"Weird doesn't even begin to cover it," Sam said. "Your mom seems nice."

"She's nice, all right." The way Lucy said it made it sound like an insult. Lucy stared at their makeshift curtains hanging limply. There was no breeze, not even a gasp of air. "I'm starving."

"Me, too. It's the pot."

"This is nothing compared to Thai sticks. That stuff's lethal. My brother Jack had this friend who would ship it in to us when we lived in Texas. Then Jack went and found religion and became a crusader for Christ."

"How'd that happen?"

"No idea," Lucy said a little too quickly. "Apparently when you make a vow to give yourself to Jesus you give up drugs and start proselytizing like crazy. The first sign is a loss of any sense of humor whatsoever. It's like Jack got his soul snatched away. Maybe there are aliens, only they're masquerading as evangelists. He keeps trying to change my heart and mind. I tell him I don't want reeducation, thank you very much. He went from being fun and great, to being like dad, straight as an arrow."

"At least you have parents who act like actual parents. Brooke used to keep these tabs of acid in the freezer. I was six when I went looking for ice cream and found them. She told me they were postage stamps with Donald Duck on them, a special limited Disney edition. I wanted to mail a letter with them. So there my mom is, dropping acid, and a few years later she can't see that Win is dealing drugs out of our apartment. She just thinks he's got such great pot and coke because all his friends are rich and generous."

"Families are nuts," Lucy said.

"Tell me about it."

"I'm starving. Where do you want to eat?"

"The West End," Sam said. The West End Bar, fabled land of Kerouac. As a callow tenth grader, Sam had been infatuated with all things Beat. She'd read Burroughs and Ginsberg and Kerouac, then traveled north to pay homage. Inside that dingy bar, she'd nursed a burger and fries and imagined her ever so macho heroes sitting in the next booth. Jack, Bill, sad-eyed Lucien. A year later, she was a year wiser. By then, she knew those former heroes were sexist swine and that Burroughs had fully intended to miss the apple in his William Tell moment and kill his wife. *I have seen the greatest minds of my generation,* Sam thought. She still recognized their talent, but now it came with a disclaimer. Women were most definitely not allowed on pain of death.

Times had changed. It was all to the good. It was 1980. Sam was a woman, or soon to be one. She would make her own history. Or was it herstory? Sam found a crumpled five-dollar bill in her pocket and pulled it out for show and tell.

"I'm getting ready," Lucy said, tugging her sneakers on. "Your mom may be a little out there, but at least you know where she's coming from. My mom is sweet. It's painful. No one in my family except my dad even raises their voice. You should see us at dinner. All we do is tick off the events of the day as we pass the mashed potatoes and smile. One day we'll smile so hard our faces will peel off from the strain of it."

Creepy, Sam thought. She slipped her thongs on. Her toes gripped hold of the rubber, sending a shock of pleasure through her. Drugs were bad for you. They messed with your brain chemistry. On the other hand, they certainly made life interesting.

"After you," Lucy said, ushering her out the door.

They walked south past Salter's Bookstore on the corner of 115th and Broadway and down to the bar. Inside, they slid onto stools and ordered. Drinks came first, burgers second. Sam downed a rum and coke. Lucy chugged a shot of tequila. The rim of the glass was coated with salt. She bit down on the slice of lime with professional aplomb.

"I got to like tequila in Texas," Lucy said. "I was a barrel racer down there, but I had to sell my horse when we left."

Their all American food arrived at that juncture. Lucy hit the bottom of the Heinz catsup bottle with the palm of her hand. Red slop doused her fries.

"You can share mine," Sam offered, nudging her plate closer. "So when you say you were a barrel racer, what does that mean exactly?"

"They set up these barrels and you ride round them on your painted pony at top speed."

"Why would anyone choose to do that?"

"Because it's fun," Lucy said. "Better than getting high. Can you believe it?"

"It wouldn't be for me. Horses are way too big and inscrutable."

"You have to connect with them."

"I don't think I want to," Sam said.

"Don't knock something you haven't tried. We should go riding together."

"Not in this life."

"Don't be afraid," Lucy said.

"I'm not afraid. I'm clear about my limits," Sam said firmly. "I prefer to keep all my limbs intact."

"You're too much."

"Am I? How exactly?"

"Because you're funny and original and I don't know." Lucy's attention was drifting, "Where did you get those?"

She was touching Sam's legs. They were clad in the black jeans that were oh so skin tight with perfect, narrow bells. "Canal Jean."

"You have to take me there."

"Can do." Share and share alike. Lucy had offered the pot. She could offer shopping tips. Sam observed the rest of the room in the mirror above the bar.

She realized every male was eyeing Lucy. Sam felt a stab of jealousy. Why did it have to be a competition? Still, Sam was used to being noticed.

It began when she turned twelve. Overnight, she went from a child to jailbait. Sam never understood why, she was still flat as a board. Yet, suddenly indecent comments were flung at her from strangers, construction workers whistled, she got felt up on the subway. Brooke told her to ignore it. So it was up to Sam to learn how to protect herself and walk the New York City gauntlet. Men three times her age whispered, "Mamacita, te amo." Sam learned how to jeer at them and deal.

Before Sam started hanging out with Lucy, she was positive that she only felt contempt and hatred for these weaklings, these males without self-control. Now, she discovered to her shame, being ignored was equally discomfiting. When she was with Lucy, it was as if she were invisible. It was shallow and stupid, but she kind of missed being hit on. Who would ever have thought it?

"I can't believe I'm in New York," Lucy said. "My parents didn't want me to go to college here. They think this city is the birthplace of sin. Really, it's my dad who thinks that. My mom doesn't. She's just sad I'm so far away but she wants me to be happy."

"So she's on your side."

"I guess. But no one's really ever happy, are they? You can be pissed, or pissed off, or thrilled, or elated, or bitter, or mellow, but you're never just happy. It's such a bland word."

Sam saw her point. Happiness was what you were supposed to aim for. But did it even exist? Buddhist monks didn't call it happiness. They claimed *enlightenment.*

"I would have killed to go to college somewhere else," Sam said.

"How come you didn't?"

"It's a family tradition," Sam said. There was another, darker reason, but she wasn't going into that.

"As in your mom bullied you into it."

"It's complicated," Sam told her, then changed the subject. "You got to live everywhere. That's what I want."

"You've never been to an exotic clime?"

"I got to go to Paris," Sam admitted.

"That's pretty nice."

"Not really. Brooke decided to move there with her boyfriend. He rented her an apartment so he could cheat on his wife with her. Jean Claude used to give me money. *Mademoiselle Samantha weel be parfait. It eez good zee fresh air.* I spent every day of the month we lived there at the café down the block. I'd read and get free refills on my hot chocolate."

"While I was bored out of my mind, trapped inside a Quonset hut, learning how to insult people in a whole lot of other languages. Childhood, bushels of fun." Lucy chewed a piece of burger and swallowed before elaborating. "Aho Kono kuso-ttare. That's 'stupid asshole' in Japanese. So do you ever call her 'Mom' or is it always Brooke?"

Sam smiled. "I'd like to think it's always Brooke, but sometimes I forget and call her Mom."

"Does it drive her crazy when you call her Brooke?"

"It used to," Sam said.

"That's cold," Lucy said. "Why did you start?"

"I have my reasons."

"Tell me."

Sam didn't want to. Certain things were just too painful to expose. She prayed that Lucy wouldn't press her further.

Lucy reached into her pocket and pulled out a crumpled pack of cigarettes. She knocked one out and stuck it in her mouth. After lighting it, she took a long, pensive pull. Then she placed it in the ashtray. Nestled there, next to the advertisement for Cuervo Gold, the death stick smoked itself.

A jazz band set up on a small stage at the back of the room. The drummer skimmed a wire brush across the drumhead, making a hissing sound.

"You should have gone to the University of Wisconsin," Lucy told Sam. "Then I'd be here, and you'd be there. You could have dinner with my parents on the weekend. You could be their surrogate daughter. You know what? I'll trade my family for yours. On Thanksgiving you can have my spot at the table."

"I think they might notice."

"I doubt it. In the Land of Lakes, no one ever notices anything. It's a place of peace and prosperity where nothing ever goes wrong. You'd be just fine. Just say, 'It's me, Lucy.' No one will be so impolite as to doubt you. And you'll love it there. Us Westcotts are all about our Thanksgiving. We are so grateful that the Native Americans let us infect them with the influenza virus and sold us their land for a handful of trinkets. Thanksgiving is the only day of the year that the entire family gets together. Dear Uncle Jerry. He's our family lech. He feels you up when he's giving you that big hug. Then there's cousin Rory. He's got a little trouble telling the difference between drinking to relax and drinking till you're a brain-dead idiot. My dad joins right in. The two of them sit in the den and watch whatever football game is on. They grunt and pound the table when their team is ahead and eventually end up plowed under it. All the women, Aunt Sheila and Aunt Mary and my mom, huddle in the kitchen and bitch about their husbands. Well, my mom doesn't, but that's because she's just so darn nice. Us kids go into the woods and get high, except of course for Jack, who's working on resurrecting Christ for the New Year.

"Eventually we try and eat mom's turkey. She does it a different way each year. She likes to add an odd cultural influence so it's Teriyaki Turkey or

Turkey mit sauerbraten. My mom's generally a pretty good cook, but she just can't do turkey. She's tried pretty much every Betty Crocker and Good Housekeeping recipe there is, stuffed it in a bag, cooked the hell out of it, barbecued it. You name it and she's tried it. Yet that poor bird always tastes like cardboard. And that's even when you have the munchies."

"We order in Chinese," Sam said. "Brooke invites whatever guy she's seeing at the time. If he shows up, they go to the movies afterwards."

"All of you?"

"Sometimes they bring me. Win never goes. That is, if he's even home for Thanksgiving. When I was nine, Brooke and some guy took me to *Last Tango in Paris*. Have you seen it?"

Lucy shook her head.

"Suffice it to say, it's wildly inappropriate for a nine year old. These two people have sex constantly. I have never been able to look at a stick of butter in quite the same way again. Still, it's better than being left alone with Win."

"Why is that?"

Sam made a face.

"Your brother's creepy?"

"He's unpredictable," Sam said. "And holidays don't improve his mood." She would have elaborated, but someone was literally breathing down her neck.

"You girls froshes?" the boy asked. His hair was cut painfully short. It exposed his pink scalp and a face that was devoid of acne, or personality. His blue and white team jacket read Columbia. Was it soccer, lacrosse, or tennis, anyone? Sam didn't care. She was not interested in preppies or their affiliates, jocks. Luckily those types of boys felt the same way about her. It was clearly prom queen Lucy whose siren call had prompted this.

He raised his hand to get the bartender's attention and was ignored. "Hey! I need some service here." The boy banged on the bar-top. "We want to buy these ladies a drink."

Lucy raised an eyebrow at Sam. "Did you hear something?" she asked Sam.

"Nope."

"Me neither," Lucy agreed.

"Don't be a bitch," the boy said. "It's just a drink, not the rest of your life."

Oh callow youth, Sam thought. On the jukebox, Donna Summer slyly promised some, "hot stuff, baby, this evening." Even more to the point there would be, "some hot stuff, baby, tonight!" Meanwhile the aura that surrounded Lucy's blond hair pulsed. Sam was reminded of the ending of *The Great Gatsby*. She loved the book and the way Fitzgerald described Daisy's essential power, her orgiastic light. The glow Lucy emitted was similar, but she wasn't Daisy. Lucy was neither insensitive nor selfish. Her looks were a genetic piece of good fortune. Lucy couldn't prevent the fantasies they spawned. Like any porch light lit on a hot summer evening, Lucy Westcott was attractive to all sorts of *Animalia Arthropoda Insecta Lepidoptera,* from a common witless cabbage moth to the sublime luna with its jade green wings. The ending was sadly the same for all and sundry, signaled by the thwack of those suicidal bodies as they hit the glass.

"You're drinking a tequila, right?" the boy said to Lucy. When she was silent in response, he insisted. "You could answer at least. You're being rude."

Lucy rolled her eyes.

"What's that about?" he demanded. "Hey, don't worry, our sperm's good. It's so good, it's blue."

They were blue bloods with blue sperm, hailing from Collegiate or Trinity and treading the well-worn path through the Ivy Leagues. They were a lot like Win's crowd, his supposedly bosom buddies. Win had attended Collegiate but transferred to Browning when he almost flunked out. For his time at Collegiate and her first two years at St. Ann's, their grandfather was alive and paying their way. Those were the halcyon days, although Sam had been too young to truly appreciate them. If only he'd lived, instead of dying of cancer. Surely then Brooke wouldn't be so sad, or desperate, or let's face it, fragile or maybe she would, Sam thought. Who knows? It was time to let go of Brooke. Sam tried, admiring the bottles of liquor stacked behind the bar. There were so many ways to say you were drunk. You could be *inebriated,* or *smashed,* or *wasted,* or *skunked.* When *skunked,* did your body turn black and white? Did you grow a tail and gain the ability to spray all those around you with an ungodly stench?

She felt free and then weightless. Sam floated up until she was hanging above the bar. Looking down, she spotted her own doppelganger next to golden haired Lucy, hemmed in by the group of prepster boys. Their clipped heads looked like perfectly plowed fields.

"Aho Kono kuso-ttare," Lucy said.

Sam plummeted back into her body.

"What the fuck does that mean?" the boy demanded.

"Aho Kono kuso-ttare," Lucy repeated.

"What's that, huh? Are you cursing me? Is that some sort of witch's curse? Jesus, I was only being friendly."

"You weren't being friendly," Lucy said. "You were being an asshole."

Lucy's tone was cuttingly neutral. She was dismissing this boy and his friends; but not just dismissing him, giving him clear directions on where and how to get lost. Lucy was sending him deep underground. If he followed her advice he'd end up wandering through the tunnels that branched off from Grand Central. It was where the homeless set up their encampments. That would certainly be novel for him. It might even be educational. Sam could have felt sorry about it, if he hadn't resorted to calling them "bitches." Then again, Sam's chosen attitude was defensive. She muttered, "Fuck you," or punched the guy on the subway who stuck his hand under her skirt. She was assertive, and aggressive, and told herself that there was no lasting effect from any of it, because at least she'd responded. She was showing them she wasn't their willing victim.

But Lucy was a real pro. She had upended these boys' ideas of who they were, turning their arrogance to dust and their bodies to salt. When the door opened, a stiff breeze would gather their molecules and blow them far, far away.

"What are you, lesbians?" the boy demanded, shrilly, his confidence shot.

"Hmm, not a bad idea," Lucy said. She put her hands on either side of Sam's face. I am so wasted, Sam thought just as Lucy pulled her close and kissed her full on the lips.

6

Muriel
October 1980

MURIEL SAT AT her desk, trying to write. It used to be comforting to be in this room that was all Amelia, all the time. Underfoot, a hooked rug sported her sister's profile. Even the desk lamp's metal pulls were modeled on her older sister's plane, the Electra. She used to think of it as a sanctuary. Now it felt like a prison.

The speech. She'd had a moment of impetuous enthusiasm; on its heels, regret. That song swam up from the depths, and she hummed along. "Regrets I've had a few, but then again, too few to mention." She had one. Why on earth was she giving a talk and traveling to New York to do it? Muriel shivered, thinking of where it would undoubtedly take place, one of those stuffy, oak paneled rooms half filled with academics and curiosity seekers. Some called them fans.

It had been the note from the Samantha Barry girl that had gotten her started off, down this wrong path. Now she had to write something. Unsurprising, that in the harsh light of day, words escaped her. Thought went up in a puff of steam. She would return the round trip ticket and overly generous stipend. She would give her regrets.

Muriel stuck her pen on the blank page and left it there, digging at the paper. Of course, what came to her was the gun. Albert's gun, upstairs, hidden where she'd found it, inside the drawer of his desk in that closet-sized home office. It was a shock coming on it that first time. But the second? The third? The twelfth? Albert was the one who told her they had to move on. Albert was the one who got up and went about his business. "It's important to stay busy," Albert had insisted. "It helps to take one's mind off things."

"Things?" Muriel had shot back.

He was so mild in response to the unimaginable. Just went through his day, and his daily routine. Then one morning, he was reading to her aloud from the newspaper while sitting at the breakfast table. He stood up with an expression of total astonishment and tumbled backward. Her heart had chipped off in little pieces. It turned out his broke all at once.

And to think, she'd thought him the braver one, better suited than she was for the job at hand.

It stunned her how wrong she'd been about him.

The gun.

Muriel stood up and went out into the hall, then climbed the stairs. She paused by the bedside table. There was the book Virgil had lent her. She'd read it straight through. *The Transit of Venus*. What did the title mean? It was, on the face of it, an astronomical oddity. Venus crossed the sun twice in eight years. If you lived to see it twice, you'd never see it again. More than a century would pass before one got another opportunity. The same could be said about true love. Or rather, the author thought as much. The writing was elaborate, so elaborate that Muriel wasn't sure of the ending and had to go back, flicking through the pages to see. Yes, it was just as she feared. They were star-crossed lovers. Muriel found herself crying. It was unfair but all too true; those you love are often on different trajectories, and it's lucky that you even brush against them in passing.

If Albert had come upon her like this, he'd have said, "What's wrong?" If she'd told him the truth, he'd have been surprised. A grown woman crying over something she read in a book?

I wouldn't have told him, Muriel thought. I would have said something got in my eye. And he wouldn't have pressed me about it.

It came to her again, how much they didn't want to know about each other.

Albert read thrillers; they were fast paced and exciting, there was always something coming up round the next corner. He read them so fast, like popping candy into his mouth. There was still a pile of them on his side of the bed.

His bed.

His room.

His house.

No, Muriel thought, that's not fair. Hadn't she been the one to put the pictures up on every wall and pick out the bedspreads, not to mention the material for the curtains? She'd sewed them all herself on the Singer in the workroom and put up the wallpaper, too. What made it his? Nothing. It was theirs, yet it wasn't. It didn't feel like it, even though she was the one left behind to live here.

Muriel walked into his small office directly off the bedroom. There was the desk, and the file cabinet with papers locked away that told everything about the house, the mortgage, the financing arrangements. She'd been going through them when she found it. He had records of every single incident for the last forty years. When the roof had needed repairs from that major leak, ice forming over it, dripping down into the bathroom. When the boiler had burst, when the oak tree in the backyard had fallen over, luckily missing the house by inches. Every piece of history that they'd shared together was in here too, the children's birth certificates, their wedding license, his work history, his social security card, his life insurance policy.

The key was in the desk drawer. She'd known that. He'd known that she knew, but why would she look inside? He hadn't expected her to. He hadn't expected to die like that. In the hospital, surrounded by beeping machines, he hadn't been able to utter a word. Perhaps if he had, he'd have offered her a warning.

Watch out for that right hand drawer. You might be surprised.

Muriel unlocked the second drawer down, lifted the files of papers and took out the box underneath. She opened it and looked at the black Colt and Wesson. The gun lay in its case, the smell of grease rising off of it. She lifted it out and held it with both hands, held it away. Not a big gun, and because it wasn't, heavier than it seemed like it should be.

Muriel knew how to shoot. She and Amelia had begged their father for a rifle. He'd given it to them one Christmas. Therein, a story.

Father had asked, "What should Santa bring?" Santa was a family joke. Amelia had debunked the Yuletide legend early. At five she'd peppered their parents with unanswerable questions.

"How does Santa get to every chimney in one night?"

"How does he fit down it? He's just too fat."

"Where exactly is this workshop? Show me on the map."

"How do reindeer fly? They don't have wings. And even if they did, their bodies are too heavy."

What was the expression children used these days? Poor Santa was "toast." Their parents gave up and gave in, their faces contorting. They'd found a joke and Muriel knew, even at four, the lie. Amelia did her best to comfort her after the fact. "It's not like there won't be Christmas," she'd said.

But back to the rifle. They'd wanted a Winchester like their cousin Tom had. Muriel remembered how they'd been sent to their grandparents to live while their parents established themselves. That December a brutal winter storm roared in. Would the train arrive? But it did, their father and mother emerging at the Atchison station, bearing three valises. In one was the longed-for rifle. The card was made out to both of them. It read, "For our remarkable offspring. Ready yourselves. Then take aim."

"What on earth? That's not theirs, I hope," Grandmother Otis exclaimed. "They can't have that, it's totally inappropriate. Not in my house."

MURIEL HAD SET the box on her lap. She removed the ammunition, then cocked the barrel of Albert's handgun and loaded it up. What had Virgil Washinawack said? That Albert had wanted it for protection? That was a good one.

When the going gets tough, the tough get going.

Marriage was certainly a mystery. The secrets one kept from each other. In retrospect, the rifle was the best present their father had ever given them.

Of course, the day after their parents left, it disappeared. Grandmother had swiped it. Amelia was the one who marched into their Grandmother's bedroom to demand it back.

"Young lady, are you accusing me of stealing from you?" she'd said, all up on her high horse.

And that was supposed to be that. She didn't know whom she was dealing with, Muriel thought. Amelia searched the entire house. She found an old trunk in the attic and picked the lock with a hairpin. There it was. They spent weeks practicing in the woods. One Sunday night at dinner, Grandmother said, "You have something that belongs to me. I expect it returned."

"I don't know what you're referring to," Amelia retorted.

That was when the war of wills began. Their grandmother's ironclad resolve pitted against Amelia's steely determination. Who would bend first?

When March blew in like a lion, the stories came with it. Mexico ravaged by plague. Photographs of the stacked victims, waiting for burial, featured on the front page of the Atchison Daily Globe. "Symptoms are chills, fever, severe headache. The patient experiences nausea and vomiting. As the disease progresses there is delirium and finally death," Amelia read with relish. "This pestilence is spread by migratory rodents." Looking up, she said, "Have you seen how many rats there are in the barn, Grandmother? Why, the entire town could get it. This plague seems to spread like wildfire."

"It won't come here," Grandmother insisted.

"Rats are migratory creatures," Amelia had continued. "They go north for the summer just like the birds."

"They do not. I don't believe a word of it."

"Poor Mrs. Michaels looked so healthy last week," Amelia mused. "And then just like that." She snapped her fingers. Mrs. Michaels had been a perfectly pleasant woman, and ancient. She'd been far from hale or hearty.

"You know, there's only one thing they can do to stop it. They have to exterminate the vermin. Now say we were to do it. Putting down poison is dangerous. Other animals might eat it. Daisy might get into it." Daisy. Grandmother's spaniel. The dog had consumed more than her share of pastries and other sweets and lived to tell the tale. Rat poison could possibly have as little effect as anything else had on that cast iron stomach, but did one really want to take that chance? My sister was always clever, Muriel thought. And it was funny, when an idea was implanted it was hard to rid yourself of it. Suddenly Grandmother Otis was fussing because her husband had a cough. "Just leave me be," he insisted. She put her hand to their heads, checking for fever whenever they came home flushed from running. "I'm sure there's nothing at all wrong with us," Amelia said, but her tone lacked conviction.

Then an acquaintance, Martin Roth, died in his sleep. Roth had been in a wheelchair for years. Usually their Grandmother would have noted his passing with a pithy remark like "Death comes to every man," or "We come into this world naked and we go out, similarly clothed," but when she heard the news, she went unnaturally quiet.

"He was a nice man, wasn't he, Grandmother?" Amelia said. In truth, he wasn't nice at all. He used to try and get them to sit on his lap and give them a ride. Girls would say other things happened. He tried it with Muriel who refused to climb on, then Amelia hopped up and there was this horrible scream from him. Everyone turned to look.

"It's nothing," Martin Roth said, much too quickly.

Later, Amelia showed her the hat pin she'd stuck him with. "If anyone tries something it fixes them."

Now Martin Roth was dead. He'd lived a long, full life. He'd had his fun, sometimes at the expense of unfortunate little girls. In death he was about to be put to better use. "You know what else I read today about the rats? They're drawn to warm weather. That's why we only see them in the spring and summer."

"We don't see them because they hibernate," Grandmother told her.

"Oh no. After they migrate, they nest."

"You have it wrong." But Grandmother didn't sound confident.

She had Nichols, the man who worked for them, check. He affirmed that the barn was the home of rats and other "unclean creatures." Poison would work, but it would also be a danger for anything else that sniffed round it. "And you have such a fine dog," he said. "I wouldn't want to be responsible for anything that might happen to it."

On his way out, he gave Amelia a conspiratorial wink.

The following morning Grandmother turned to Amelia at breakfast and said, "I give up."

"I'm sorry?"

"You can kill them. Go on. Go and do it. Do it now before I change my mind."

"Who would you like me to murder?" Amelia asked, innocently.

"There's no 'who' involved. Get that rifle you're hiding. Dispose of the rats. I don't care anymore. I don't care if you shoot yourselves in the process."

"What rifle?" Amelia asked. Muriel kicked her under the table.

"Amelia Earhart, there is no need to be impertinent!"

"I'm not being impertinent, I'm trying to understand. Father gave us a rifle for Christmas. Then it went missing and you said you didn't know anything about it. It can't be that rifle you're referring to."

"I removed it because it was unseemly to have you toting that thing around with you. People would talk. Girls who want boys to like them don't walk around with weapons under their arms."

"Who said I wanted a boy to like me?"

"You most certainly will."

"If I do, they'll take me as I am," Amelia said. "Now grandmother, saying we do what you want, then we can use the rifle without any obstruction from you afterwards, correct?"

Grandmother's face went red. She sputtered, "Just get on with it. One more word from you, and I'll end up doing something we'll all regret."

In the hayloft, Amelia had cracked open the rifle and inserted ammunition. Only then did it sink in and Muriel's heart shrank. "Couldn't we just tell her we did our best? She never goes out to the barn."

"Grandmother will want evidence."

Maybe the rifle wasn't worth it. Muriel had never actually killed anything before. Their cousins were the avid hunters. The boys brought down squirrels, raccoons, even a deer. But neither Muriel nor Amelia had ever taken a life; they'd slaughtered glass bottles and cans.

"I'll go first," Amelia said.

They baited the trap and hid in a corner, waiting. A half hour passed. Muriel's legs ached. Then she spied the whiskered nose, twitching. "Don't," she wanted to call out. Too late, the rat skittered across the floor to find the piece of cheese. Amelia aimed with precision and pulled the trigger. The beast fell, mortally wounded, its blind eye staring up. Amelia knelt down. "So sorry, old thing," she said. An elderly rat, the hair of its coat sprinkled with gray. Muriel forced herself to look and found it surprising. Whatever had animated the creature was gone.

"Is this what happens with us?" Muriel asked.

"It must be," Amelia said.

"But you have to still be alive somewhere?"

"In heaven, do you mean? It must be getting pretty crowded up there, what with all the spirits dancing around."

"It's only this? What's the point?" Muriel asked.

"Don't be silly. Whatever we do, whatever we make of what we have, that's the point."

"Is that enough?"

"I guess it has to be," Amelia said.

I GUESS IT has to be. Muriel heard Amelia saying it. She lowered the gun and walked back into their bedroom. She opened the closet, and found Albert's suits, the winter weight worsted wool and the summer weight striped cotton. She hadn't thrown any of his things away. She was wearing his cardigan sweater. She slept in his shirts.

Down to the end of the hall and up the stairs into the attic. It was nothing like the attic at her grandmother's. That was full of mystery. There had been a stuffed reindeer head mounted and left leaning against a wall, a wedding dress with a crinoline veil, old crockery, her grandfather's scimitar collection, a Chinese vase with a crack in it.

Here, her children's lives were boxed up. They had walked away and she'd said, "What do you want?" They'd replied, "Nothing."

The gun was shoved into the pocket of his trousers. They hung loosely on her, held up by a belt. It was loaded. Loaded for bear. Or smaller game. What did she weigh, anyhow? Not more than a hundred and thirty. Not even that.

The attic had been made into their son's room. He'd wanted to come up here once he hit Junior High. The walls were still painted dark blue. The curtains framed the one small window. His dresser still held his baseball and hockey trophies, Most Valuable Player 1949, 1950, and 1951, and a posed photo of the Medford high school baseball team, all smiles when they won the state championship.

Muriel opened the top of his dresser drawer. He'd left behind a change in case he slept over. She touched the plaid shirt. Then backed away and opened the closet. There were his old sports uniforms. An ancient Olympia typewriter sat on the desk. His bulletin board still had clippings of his favorite players; Ted Williams playing the last game he played before heading off to Korea.

Muriel set the gun on the desk. She sank into the chair, feeling her courage ebb. She forced herself to pull open the right hand drawer. Pencils worn down to the nub, old ball-point pens, an art gum eraser, letters opened but left inside their envelopes, gift cards, birthday cards, be my valentine, all mixed in together.

She swallowed, then lifted the gun and turned it on herself. Opened her mouth. Stuck the barrel inside. In movies they made it seem easy, natural. But the barrel tasted rancid and oily. She gagged. She wanted to spit it out. Muriel forced herself to hold the gun steady. When her breathing slowed, she reached round for the safety and took it off. A click. Her finger sank down to the trigger. She shut her eyes.

There were things to think about. How selfish this was . . . doing away with yourself. How there was no excuse for it. How there would be such a mess to clean up and someone would have to do it. How she was never inconsiderate, how she was kind and doting to a fault. Yet was it wrong? Every day all she wanted was for this misery to be over with. Why couldn't it be her turn?

Albert had wanted to do it.

He'd bought the gun.

Wasn't it as if he were giving her permission?

Her finger tucked round the metal trigger and pressed. She told herself, there'll be an end then and you won't have to think anymore, the thinking's what takes the most out of you. Waking up every day and trying to get through, waking up and for a moment thinking it was another day like all the other days that had gone before, then realizing that it wasn't, that it would never be that way again.

Amelia's answer to her question came back to her.

"Is that enough?" she'd asked.

"I guess it has to be."

The gun tasted horrid. She pulled it out of her mouth, retching. Then stood, needing to wash the taste out of her mouth. She had to get rid of the damn thing.

Years and years ago, she and Amelia had stood shoulder to shoulder inside that rundown barn, tucked behind a house on the main street in Atchison. It was a town set in the heartland of a great and powerful country. That country was only a part of the continent of North America, one of several continents dotting the planet. If you looked at life from that perspective, your own small part was inconsequential. Although it was all that you were given. It was all that you knew.

Muriel also knew what she'd done so long ago, taking a breath and steeling herself, then lifting the rifle onto her own shoulder. Narrowing her sight, she'd said, "My turn now."

7

Amelia
October 1980

FATHER HAD BROUGHT the rifle and hidden it with all the rest of the presents strewn under the tree. When Amelia opened it, Grandmother gasped and sprang to her feet. Trembling with anger, she pointed her finger at him. "Edwin Earhart, have you lost your mind?"

Amelia had written about this in her own book, *The Fun of It*. The book sat on the shelf, directly above Muriel's bent head. While Muriel read what she'd written, Amelia stewed. How was it possible to get everything wrong? In Muriel's version, Amelia was a wrecking crew of a sister, bent on destroying even the most benign fantasy. She used logic like a hat pin, sticking it into the colorful balloon and deflating Muriel's innocence. She'd murdered Santa Claus! All she'd said was that Christmas seemed a little, well, preposterous and besides, they weren't that young. Muriel had been at least nine, quite possibly ten. For that particular Christmas, Amelia was the one living with their grandparents in Atchison. Muriel had been in Des Moines. There were three travelers getting off the train to visit, Father, Mother, and Muriel disembarking in the middle of a blinding snowstorm. "It's in the book, just open it!" Muriel didn't hear a word. Amelia reached out impulsively, forgetting. Her fingers slid through the cover, the vellum, and out the other side. It was a nauseating visual. She pulled her hand back as if stung and curled it into a frustrated fist. Then panicked. She tried to breathe through her nerves. There was something she was missing, some clue that would lead to empowering her and give her back control. This was *her* dream. *Her* nightmare.

Amelia knew she was feverish. It was the only rational explanation. She was lying on the beach, delirious, and dying of exposure. This mental state was the beginning of the end. Soon she would stop breathing altogether, done in like that martyred rat. Her heart thrummed against her chest. Her breath came in snatches. *Stop!* Amelia couldn't. If she wasn't dying, then she was already dead and this was purgatory. She had been sent to live as a shade in Muriel's house in Medford. Hadn't she stood behind Muriel when her sister washed her hands in the bathroom and seen the evidence? Only one woman was reflected back in the mirror and that woman was Muriel. If she was a shade, if that was true, then God did exist and had a wicked sense of humor. Jehovah or Krishna or Mohammed or whatever it was, had sent her packing, sticking her here in the place she'd hated living in most of all, Medford. The more Amelia thought about it, the more this seemed the likely answer.

This morning had begun the same way all mornings seemed to, here in Muriel's house. At five a.m. on the dot, her younger sister awoke and went to the bathroom to perform her libations, wearing what had to be Albert's bathrobe. It was striped and way too large for her tiny frame. Albert was gone, but clearly not forgotten. There were photographs of him everywhere. It seemed to be a recent loss. Muriel's torpor was one clue. The pile of condolence cards, another.

Muriel moved slowly. It took her over an hour to get ready to descend to the first floor. When she did, she made a beeline for the kitchen. Water was put on for tea. Muriel sat at the breakfast table waiting, watching the sun come up. When the kettle whistled, she poured water into a teapot and let the tea seep. As she sipped on her first cup, she studied the view. At six twenty seven, the newspaper slapped the front door. Muriel retrieved the morning Globe. Then she cooked breakfast. One egg over easy and a slice of Wonder Bread, popped in to toast. It wasn't the same toaster Amelia had sent them; this model was thin, the burnished metal gleamed. Muriel set the dial to two and used the lightly toasted bread to scoop up the yolk of the egg.

Every day she ate the same dull meal. And every day, as Amelia watched her eat, her own stomach growled out a protest.

When Muriel was done, she set the dishes in the sink and went off to her study to work or really just stare at the walls.

So the morning passed. Muriel used the toilet several times and made another cup of tea. On an exciting day, the telephone rang. When she answered it, she sat in the comfortable chair set next to a small round table. The phone was also new. The one Amelia had paid for had been heavy and black. This was compact, a cheerful tomato red. The top fit neatly onto the bottom, nesting there. Sometimes Muriel made a call herself. When she did, she held the phone away from her and put her glasses on. The squares showing the numbers glowed.

"Hello," Muriel said brightly.

That was what passed for excitement for her sister. The workings of the house were far more interesting than its owner. Take the toilet, there was no chain pull to release the water. A handle in the back did the trick. What made it work? Amelia would have liked to take it apart and figure out the basic mechanics. But that would have meant more than the right sized wrench and a bag full of plumbing tools. She would have had to be able to grasp those same tools. Instead, she was forced to play the role of dispassionate observer, observing miracles as they appeared all around her. The burner on the stove lit without a match. Then there was that box at the end of Muriel's bed upstairs.

It flickered to life and on it all sorts of stories and news programs played as if on a movie screen. Two nights ago, it was something she knew, the wonderful *Mr. Deeds Goes to Town*. Gary Cooper was perfectly cast as a naïf. It was interrupted for commercial announcements. Muriel was bored; she'd use the time to get a snack. Amelia loved them. A cartoon tiger swore Frosted Flakes were *great*; a beaming mother presenting an orange box of Tide detergent claiming it made her whites *whiter*; and, best of all, planes flew the friendly skies heading east, west, north and south. *BOAC, TWA, Pan American.* Air travel was convenient. Do it and you, too, could see the changing of the guards at Buckingham Palace. A soothing voice said that the world was bigger than ever, with "More places to go, more things to see." The final shot was always a plane taking off and sailing away. How huge they were. And no propellers on the wings; instead, there were closed tubes that hid engines, hung below each wing. There were so many windows, surely room for more than a hundred passengers. *Pan American* boasted their fleet flew round the world every single day.

Impossible.

Amelia's reverie was interrupted. The phone rang. Muriel went to get it out in the hall.

Muriel ate lunch at noon. The meal consisted of whatever had been left in the fridge from dinner the night before. Muriel subsisted on a diet of chicken, chicken, and more chicken. To accompany it, she ingested fresh or leftover salad. The leftover version was kept in a glass mason jar overnight. The resulting mess was gray and desiccated. Once the meal was over, it was time to go. Muriel slipped into her coat and exited stage right, escaping through the front door. She returned approximately five hours later. In that time, Muriel might have gone for a constitutional or flown to the moon and back. Amelia could hardly know. She was not allowed to accompany her.

There were very strict rules. One of them was this. She wasn't allowed to leave the house. The first time Muriel pulled on her coat, Amelia walked with her to the door, intending on stepping out with her. She was rudely shoved back inside. Thinking Muriel had done it somehow, she turned and realized it wasn't possible. Her sister was busy, fumbling in her purse, extracting the house key. Muriel walked over the doorjamb and closed the door in Amelia's face. When Amelia tried to open it, no dice. Frustrated, she was left to wander. A kitchen window was open. Amelia put her hand out to feel the air, and her palm slapped against an invisible brick wall.

She was trapped here in Medford; worse, in the house she'd paid for, this place she'd fled from. It was deserved, this purgatory. It was payback for all those years of freedom.

When Amelia's legs began to ache, she slid down and sprawled on the floor. Through trial and error she had learned not to support herself by leaning against the furniture. It wouldn't hold her. More than once she'd toppled over, with painful results. At night, she slept on the Kashan rug she'd given to Muriel and Albert as a wedding present. It was a threadbare oriental, but better than the hardwood. The lack of comfort didn't bother her. She was used to roughing it. What did, was being trapped. Still, waking, she told herself things could change. It was a new day. Her optimism faded as the minutes ticked by. By the time night fell, she was spent and miserable.

There went Muriel, crunching the autumn leaves underfoot. Oh, to do that, to inhale the crisp air, to know the season full and close. Tuesdays and Fridays were shopping days. Muriel would return with two bags of groceries. She subsisted on skim milk, Cream of Wheat, eggs, Wonder Bread, the inedible chicken, a small roast, or chopped chuck.

Thinking of it made Amelia's mouth water. She was so hungry. She could literally eat a horse. Really, she could, carving it off the bone from fetlock to rump. She had to be starving to death. If she could only wake up, she might save herself. She was the one who had made the homemade fishing spear. It had worked well enough. She'd harpooned quite a few of those brightly colored fish. Then Fred sickened. She'd had to nurse him and it went on so long, there wasn't really enough food, even for one of them. By now, the signal fire would be out. She could try and start it again as she had the first time, rubbing sticks together until they sparked, then blowing cautiously until the spark became a flame and caught hold of the dry twigs she'd gathered.

"Weren't you ever a boy scout?" she'd asked Fred.

"Me?" he replied, laughing. "They knew better than to take me."

He was joking. That stopped soon enough. Poor Fred.

Poor her. He was gone, but she wasn't. Amelia salivated, thinking of how she'd grilled those iridescent bodies. All she wanted was that island back again. To feel the grains of sand under her fingers, to hold it, to hold onto something, to enjoy the sensation of a pebble rolling in the palm of her cupped hand. Yes, to start there and move on to save herself, but first the morsels of fish, charred to perfection, sucked right off the bone.

It's a puzzle, Amelia told herself. You've always been good at puzzles. You're the one with the logical mind. Father always said so. He'd sit us down and ask us both the question. "Mary is twice as old as her best friend Genevieve. Genevieve is five years older than Pauline. In five years Mary will be three times as old as Genevieve. Tell me my darlings, how old is Genevieve now?"

"Five." She'd known the answer immediately.

"How did you do that?" Muriel asked. She was still working it through on the paper.

THE FRONT DOOR shut with a bang. It was Muriel. Amelia found her in the kitchen, restocking the larder.

"There," Muriel sounded pleased. The bags were folded, put into the closet. Muriel opened a drawer and retrieved garden clippers. She headed out, leaving the screen door ajar. It offered a thin sliver of daylight. Amelia mentally measured the opening, and then edged closer. No brute force pushed back. Slowly. Surely. She lifted her right foot and put her toe into the opening.

The reproach was immediate. Her body was flung back. She landed hard on the checkerboard tile floor. The light fixture in the center of the ceiling buzzed and fizzed. A breeze blew in through the screen, taunting her.

"What did I ever do?" she demanded aloud, shaking a fist, "What do you want from me?"

No one answered. That was when she thought it.

When you're dead, you're dead.

As soon as she did, she fought back. *I'm not. This isn't death. It can't be.*

What was it then? Madness? Amelia thought of those boys she'd cared for up in Toronto. Back from the front, they'd changed forever. She'd seen firsthand what a fragile organ the brain was. How unprotected. Only a slim carapace sheltered it from the elements. When those shocked soldiers awoke, they'd lost so much. Some couldn't lift a fork to their mouths. Others had to relearn how to walk. There were doughboys whose memories were shattered. The doctors termed some of the cases *fascinating.* Amelia hated that word. She went home and cried for them. Blond, blue-eyed Tom Luddow, a farmer's son from Calgary, saw everything as fresh and new. She would have a conversation with him and then have it again two minutes later. For Tom, it was always now. His parents sat with him, looking wild-eyed at each other. Down the ward at the other end, Richard Jones could only communicate using an invented language. He thought everyone else was at fault, that he was speaking clearly and rationally, and that they were doing it to torture him. He grew so agitated he had to be put into restraints. It was horrid and humbling, bearing witness to what happened when human wiring shorted out.

Hers was clearly fizzing, the circuits gone awry. She was going mad, mad as the proverbial hatter. Amelia sat up on Muriel's kitchen floor, grabbing her knees and rocking rhythmically.

Muriel entered, bearing a clutch of roses. She snipped the thorny ends off, then used the shears to cut the stems in two. She took a plain white vase from a shelf above her head, filled it with cold water, and made an arrangement. The honeyed fragrance filled the room. "Oh," Muriel said, stepping back to admire her own handiwork. Hot pink. Orange. Vibrant Reds. The last breath of summer, the last hope.

Amelia got to her feet.

Muriel filled a kettle and set it on the stove. An orange ring of flame shot out, inside a cerulean blue heart. When the whistle shrilled, Muriel poured the boiling water into the waiting teacup. She dunked the bag several times then set it on the side to reuse. "Waste not, want not," Muriel said. It was one of Grandmother Otis' axioms. Funny to imagine that, in this version of her life, Muriel was frugal. The Muriel she knew better had been a bit more profligate. It was one of their ongoing disputes, how money Amelia lent to them never lasted long. She'd paid her ransom and gotten out. The down payment for this house, help with the mortgage, children's clothes and toys, appliances, she'd offered to do whatever they needed, even to take in Muriel when she wanted to leave Albert. Was it out of guilt or love? How did one separate the two?

Amelia felt a pang. Memories flooded in. Laughing with each other in the bedroom the two of them shared in Des Moines. X marks the spot written with their index fingers on each other's backs as they lay out on the beach at Lake Okabena. Finding the best places to hide in their cousin's farmhouse in Atchison. Scaring each other into and out of having the hiccups. Stuck inside on a rainy day and playing rummy, then poker, then canasta, card games that lasted for an eternity. Girls together. Best friends.

Muriel walked by, mug in hand. Her hair was pinned up and there was that beauty spot on the back of her neck. Amelia leaned over and blew on it, just the way she used to when they were girls. Muriel would shiver and cry out, "Stop it, Meely!" half irritated, half amused.

Muriel shivered and then stopped in her tracks. She turned and stared. Amelia's pulse raced, but then Muriel blinked and shrugged and off she went down the hall.

She'd felt something, hadn't she?

Hadn't she?

Amelia was afraid to hope.

In the living room, Muriel thumbed through the mail.

If a tree falls in the forest, what does it matter? A philosophical question, yet she wasn't a tree, she was a person.

"You haven't gotten it right," Amelia said, moving close to Muriel. "You knew Father was bringing the rifle with him. You knew because you were at home with him when he packed up the presents. You wrote me and told me exactly what we were getting for Christmas. It wasn't a surprise to either one of us. The box was there under the tree. You handed it to me to unwrap and winked at me. When Grandmother Otis saw what it was, she went crazy. Mother tried to calm her down. Father pretended not to be pleased, and Grandfather just went on talking about the law because it was beneath him to get involved."

Muriel wrinkled her forehead as if she was thinking too hard. Her mouth quivered and she muttered, "She took it away. I know she did."

Further proof. "You hear me!" Amelia insisted.

Muriel didn't look up.

"Admit it. You do. And speaking of guns, I know what you do. I've seen you up there. What are you thinking of doing?"

Muriel shrugged. Then she made a face as if to say, you guess. Go ahead. What world was this, Amelia wondered, where her sister kept a gun in the attic? What world was this that she had manufactured for herself? But Muriel said, "Grandmother hid it from us. She thought girls should be prim and proper. But you talked her into letting us use it in the end and you never got punished for taking it back. You were always her favorite. It must have been something, being able to talk anyone into doing anything. It must have been something, being you." Then Muriel looked right at her. Amelia knew she saw her.

"I could write about that. How willful you were. How deliberately you made your choices. How selfish you were. I'll read them an excerpt from the letter you sent me explaining to me why you couldn't tell me 'certain things.' Why you had to keep me in the dark. One flies away, the other doesn't. One is responsible and acts like an adult, the other gets to be a child forever. That would go over well, I bet."

Then Muriel swept all the mail off the table into the garbage can. She stood, grabbed the teacup, and exited stage right.

8

Sam
October 1980

LUCY SPRAWLED ON her never made bed. She wore a man's white t-shirt and bikini briefs. Sam would have titled a portrait of her *Lucy In Repose*. The work of art would have been worthy of the Modern. No Titian she, no Renaissance nymphet, Lucy was lanky, undeniably curvaceous, more a mix of Playboy magazine style and gritty realism. Two white paper boxes sat at her roommate's feet, the remnants of last night's take out delight from Hunan Balcony. Inside, congealed sesame noodles and rock-hard fried pork dumplings. Sam could have used them to conduct a science experiment, dropping them out the window and onto the heads of unsuspecting passersby. *Murder Most Foul: Barnard coeds arrested when Chinese food prank goes awry.* It was obviously not the best kind of research to undertake, nor would it replace Sam's fruit fly data. Sadly, last night when Sam had gone to the lab to give the captive insects sugar water, she'd been a little too lax with the locking mechanism and her control group had made good their escape.

Sam didn't know what to do. She had already bred the flies. There was no time to start from scratch. Radio Clash played in the background. Sam studied the final paragraph of her essay for English class and tried not to panic. Meanwhile, Lucy read *Plato's Republic*, busily highlighting every other passage with yellow indelible marker. It had been such a simple experiment, Sam thought. One that high school students did routinely. She told herself there was a solution, but the only one that meant keeping a decent grade was cribbing the results. Cheating. Sam had never cheated. She was the good daughter, the perfect student. Put on your thinking cap, she told herself.

She stared at the essay. It was an analysis of D.H. Lawrence, aka *The Virgin and the Gypsy*, *Women In Love*, *The Rainbow*, and his ridiculous concept of the godhead. Her English professor Maggie Swift was intimidating. She wore severely cut pants suits with oversized lapels and made withering asides. Swift was brilliant, passionate, and didn't suffer fools gladly. Next week they were starting on Thomas Hardy in her Lawrence and Hardy class. It might have been funny, but Maggie Swift betrayed no obvious sense of humor. Sam had already read *Tess of the D'Ubervilles* and was halfway through *The Mill on the Floss*. Hardy seemed to have a very nihilistic view of the world, which was pretty modern of him. He was right up her alley, the alley of the sophisticated and artfully morose, those who wore black as a fashion statement and if you asked, might tell you that color of any kind was an error, even though the sky at that moment was a robin's egg blue and the roses were startlingly scarlet. Bright sunshine poured in through the window, too nice out there to stay stuck inside.

Sam was losing her train of thought. Back to work, she chided herself. Back to the paper she was writing, arguing Lawrence was wrong about women, (oh Gudrun, Oh Ursula!). Sam thought that his idea of sex was baroque and homoerotic. She was deflating his purple prose and thus, his manhood. Sam needed to skillfully indict and convict, then throw away the key. By doing this she hoped to blow Professor Maggie Swift away in the process.

"Can I read you something?" she asked Lucy.

Lucy nodded.

"Lawrence's depiction of women is totally unrealistic. The men are all drawn as powerful beings, emotionally unstable yet resolutely sexual. The women are in their thrall, enraptured by their historically dark masculinity."

"What does 'historically dark masculinity' mean?"

"What do you mean, what does it mean?" Sam demanded, her anxiety ratcheting up another full notch. "What's wrong with it?"

"I don't understand. That's all."

"Well I do." Although, suddenly, Sam didn't. It seemed like total bullshit. Now she would have to worry about both classes. *Great, just fucking great.* She'd been in school less than a month and she was already courting failure.

"I had a teacher in AP English who told us that Lawrence was gay," Lucy said.

"He knew from personal experience?"

"It was a she, actually."

Sam felt odd discussing this with Lucy. Lucy acted as if the kiss at the West End Bar had never taken place. But Sam had never used her lips as a tool for strategic deployment. Having Lucy do so had put her at a disadvantage. Not that she was a lesbian, though she'd gone through a phase where she obsessively eyed other girls' legs and breasts. Only when her friend Nora confessed to watching every woman on the subway like a hawk, comparing and contrasting herself to them, did Sam realize that she was taking part in a rite of passage, gathering visual data to competitively place her own thin, somewhat angular body in its rightful place inside the pantheon of nubile females.

Her nightly sexual fantasies always starred boys, or boyish men. Sam's taste veered between demigods like Joe Strummer and Elvis Costello, and a teenage boy two grades ahead of her who boasted scraggly brown hair, an incipient beard and a steady girlfriend. Sam had started dating once she hit puberty. But her experience was so limited. She and her two boyfriends had groped along in the dark, with Sam having no desire to go any further than mutual masturbation. Now, here she was at Barnard, still a virgin. Unfortunately, she'd told Lucy this in a moment of truth and dare weakness.

She'd immediately felt exposed and vulnerable.

Once again, Sam reminded herself that Lucy was on her side.

Meanwhile, the tacked up sheet stolen from the supply closet that doubled as curtains fluttered, making an odd hissing noise. In Sam's dreams, the noise posed as either a reptile or a creepily insinuating stranger. Staring out the window, Sam tried to find a solution to her problems. All that came to her was the word "virgin." Then there was Lucy, the rodeo girl, Lucy, who was adventurous, self-assured, and sexually adept. Sam told herself that Lucy wasn't superior, just different. After all, what she described as her typical evening of sex with a boy was a round of "wham, bam, thank you, ma'am." Sam bravely told herself she knew better than to settle for that. Her own deflowering would be romantic and extra special. She would be in love. There would be no animal grunting or sweaty, tangled limbs. It would take place in soft focus with the camera pulling away and something romantic playing. Sam hoped for either Joni or Emmylou pining in the background.

"We've got to get you laid," Lucy said, breaking into her reverie. "It's exactly what you need to write that paper."

Sam flushed. "You think no virgin has ever written a paper on Lawrence?"

"Not a really excellent paper."

Lucy pulled on her clothing, added a jacket, and said, "Let's go to the Village."

"And do what?"

"We're going to find *him* for you," Lucy said.

"I can't. I'm busy."

"You don't look busy," Lucy noted. "Trust me. Just have faith."

Faith? Lucy was already at the door. Sam sighed. In truth, it was a relief. Outside there would be no fruit flies making a beeline for the open window and no imperious godhead banging at the door. Sam lifted her own jacket, a used and abused forties hounds-tooth number complete with lapels and a monogram on the inside pocket and followed Lucy out into the brave new world.

SAM HAD PLAYED tour guide for weeks, the two of them racing down the dizzying tilted floor of the Guggenheim, or sipping on a flask they'd snuck into the sculpture garden at the Museum of Modern Art. They'd toted up the movie stars at Bloomingdales, stopped by the Bethesda Fountain to admire the stoners, and traveled East to Avenue A during the smart daylight hours, venturing into galleries that were the size of their own small dorm room, then slurping borscht at Vaselka. Locking arms, they'd sauntered through Soho and slipped onto bar stools at Fanelli's. At a table nearby, Debbie Harry held court. Lucy didn't even know who Debbie Harry was, so Sam educated her in all things Blondie.

"I love it here," Lucy said over and over again. "I don't know why anyone would even want to live anywhere else."

Sam had reasons, but what was the point of enumerating them? And she did love New York, especially now, seeing it new through Lucy's eyes.

THEY EMERGED FROM the IRT at West 12th and strolled by the emergency room doors of St. Vincent's hospital. Two homeless men begged for spare change. Sam automatically put on her usual stone-faced mask of denial, eyes fixed on some obscure point in the distance. Lucy paused, digging deep into her pocket. This, even after Sam had already explained that it was a con, that they were alcoholics and junkies, homeless because of their addictions, and that some weren't even homeless at all. They were just making a living doing this, that it was always, always a scam.

"It doesn't matter," Lucy responded, "They wouldn't ask for help if they didn't need it."

Naïve. And oddly refreshing.

In fact, Sam found it changed her own opinion. She reached into her jacket pocket but it was empty; her wallet had been shoved deep down in the front of her jeans as a safety precaution to ward off pickpockets. Meanwhile Lucy turned left on Greenwich and disappeared from view. Sam raced to catch up.

It was a perfect fall day, the temperature hovering near seventy. Soon it would be Sam's favorite holiday, Halloween. She and Brooke had marched in the parade for years with a coterie of Brooke's friends. Rob, Mitch, and Duane transformed themselves into Tallulah, Harlow, and Joanie. Brooke went stag. Her hair was cut short or capped by a wig. She wore suits and once, a vintage tuxedo. There was always a provocatively sexual element; she never wore a shirt under the jacket, and went braless to boot.

Shit, Sam thought, it's Mother Dearest. That's whom I've been channeling when I'm wearing my hounds-tooth jacket. Brooke had worn her own version, waving her hair and dying it blond. She'd been Leslie Howard that year, point counterpoint to Rob's Scarlet O'Hara. Brooke even took Sam to a revival house showing of *Gone With the Wind* so she could understand the brilliance of her transformation.

Sam shivered. She was clearly doomed. There was a tiny version of her mother living inside of her. No matter where she went or who she became, she would never break free. Sam thought of the last Halloween they'd celebrated together. She'd been twelve and begged Brooke to dress as Glinda the good witch, to play a woman just this once. Sam had an ulterior motive: then she would get to be Dorothy. She'd found the perfect outfit at Secondhand Rose, a forties gingham dress with red shoes to match. Brooke agreed. The dress she designed gave her the ultimate hourglass figure, featuring puffed sleeves. It was cut out of billowing blue satin. But when Sam took out her own find to show it off, Brooke laughed. "Oh no, darling, you're Toto."

"What? No way."

"But darling, Larry has his heart set on Dorothy. We can't disappoint. Don't worry. I have a costume for you. You'll look so adorable."

"I'm not going to do it."

"Why on earth not? Those floppy ears. That sweet smile. Toto saves her, remember?"

"I'm not playing a pet."

"Oh please, pretty please. Larry will be so upset and I promised him."

"Why would you promise him?"

"Because, well, you know how he gets. It's so important for him."

For Larry, or for you? Sam could have said, but there were extenuating circumstances. She caved. She always caved. In the end, she'd let Brooke zip her into the brown fur outfit complete with fake nose and painted whiskers. Brooke invited Win to join them and he gave her a look.

"As what?" he asked.

"A Munchkin?"

"I'm six foot two," he said. "Some munchkin I'd make. No, Mom, you couldn't pay me enough. That is, if you even had the money."

Brooke made a spectacular Glinda. All along the parade route people applauded her. Larry threw out rose petals from his straw basket, Larry with his five o'clock shadow and his brown wig, Larry who she wanted to hate except that he was one of her favorite babysitters and the nicest person on earth. He always let her have ice cream before he put her to bed. Toto dutifully padded along behind, there for comfort and there to save the day, the dogged and dependable woman's best friend. Come to think of it, marching in that parade with Brooke was a little too much like walking around with Lucy. Except that when she was with her mother, she at least got hungry looks from younger men. There were those who preferred her punk affected style to Brooke's blowsy, take me and be done with it you manly man, come on. With Lucy, she was always doomed to play Toto.

Except, Sam thought, Lucy zeroed in on Sam with laser sharp precision. Lucy adored her. Lucy said that Sam was the coolest girl she'd ever had the privilege of knowing. Her admiration took the sting out of being ignored by certain significant others.

Almost.

"Earth to Sam, where are you?" Lucy asked just then, looping her arm familiarly through hers.

They sauntered past Elephant and Castle, a restaurant with a slim white brick façade. Three storefronts down, Sam paused, admiring her favorite seasonal display, an artfully arranged window featured Mexican Day of the Dead dioramas. Boxed miniature skeletons played music, cleaned house, hoed the fields, and shot stray soccer balls towards a goal.

"Creepy," Lucy said, pursing her lips in distaste. "What are they?"

"They're traditional. They're made for *Dia de Los Muertos*. It's a Mexican holiday, the Day of the Dead."

"What's that?"

"It's the day they set aside for mourning. You're supposed to remember the dead by doing things that they liked to do, eating their favorite food, playing their favorite song, telling stories about them. At the end of the day there's a big party."

"Too bad the guest of honor never shows," Lucy said coldly. She made a face at Sam, indicating her displeasure.

"Did I say something wrong?" Sam asked.

Lucy shrugged. Then walked past the Jefferson library. Inside the iron fence, a homeless encampment had taken over what had once been a garden. A man with a puppy sat on the ground. Next to him a handwritten sign read, "FEED US!" Lucy obediently dropped money into his lap. Sam dug out her wallet to add a dollar. Lucy forged ahead, crossing Sixth Avenue against the light, snaking through the traffic.

Something was wrong. Sam grabbed her friend's arm as they made it across. "What is it?"

Lucy was stone-faced.

"Come on . . . tell me."

"It's not important."

"Obviously it is. Did I say something?"

"No." Then Lucy braved an inauthentic smile. "It's just that one of my brothers killed himself."

"Oh god, Lucy, I'm so sorry."

"It's not your fault. No reason to be sorry." Lucy started off again, but Sam held fast.

"I'm here, Luce," Sam said softly.

Lucy nodded. "You really are. I don't know how you can do that."

"Do what?" Sam asked.

"Be so present. Never get rattled. Most people you tell that to, they don't know what to say or do."

"I'm not sure I'm so great at it either," Sam said.

"But you wouldn't start acting odd just because of it. You're not like that."

"No," Sam conceded.

"How come it doesn't scare you?" Lucy asked.

"Scare me? Why should it?"

"It freaks other people out."

Sam shrugged.

"You're so different from anyone else I've ever met," Lucy said.

"I doubt it," Sam told her.

"Yes, you are." Lucy took her arm. They walked together. "It was last year. Donnie and this bunch of guys he was friends with went to a party on a Saturday night. Donnie was driving. He crossed the divider on the interstate and smashed into a tree. All three of them died, so I guess technically that makes it a murder-suicide."

Sam had a stark image of Lucy's brother's car surfing across the divider and slamming into a giant oak. Impulsively, she turned and hugged Lucy tight.

Lucy let go first. She smiled shyly. They walked on toward Washington Square Park. "Donnie was always getting high," Lucy said. "It's not the way we do it. I mean, Donnie, he didn't know how to be moderate. That was part of what was so great about him. When he got high, he wanted to get wasted. My mom knew and she begged him to stop. Each time she did, he promised he would. But that was just to make her leave him alone. He lied and she always believed him. I guess she just wanted to believe he could change, because he was so obviously out of it whenever he came home. He'd be starving because he was stoned, and his eyes were always bloodshot. Then, when we moved north, he started drinking. My dad was so relieved. He thought alcohol was better. He thought it was like what he'd done, I guess, because my dad was this big jock in high school and, of course, being in the service all the guys went to bars. My dad saw drinking as what a man did. He wanted Donnie to act like a man. That was his big disappointment, that Donnie was such a *girl*."

"Your parents must be miserable."

"They must," Lucy agreed. "Not that you could tell."

"What do you mean?"

"It's like I said before, everyone in my family pretends everything's fine. Even this. If you pretend hard enough then you can make it true, right?" Lucy was angry. Her voice shook. She blinked the way a nocturnal creature would as it emerged into daylight. "You know what? We should go to Mexico. We should go there for the Day of the Dead. When is it?"

"November."

"You'll go with me, won't you?"

"Yes," Sam said, even though she knew what they both knew, that it was pure fantasy.

Lucy slipped her hand into Sam's and squeezed hard. Letting go, she added, "Sometimes I miss Donnie, but sometimes I resent him for doing what he did. And you know what's even worse? Most of the time I don't think about him. I'm just like the rest of them. I can't even remember what Donnie looked like, unless I'm dreaming. It's terrible. You wouldn't do that, Sam. You'd never forget him."

"Who knows what I'd do? Who knows how I'd act?" Sam said.

"You'd be different," Lucy insisted. "You'd always have a place for your brother. You'd do it no matter how much it hurt, just because. You'd keep him alive in your heart."

"You give me a lot of credit," Sam said. She didn't want to be that good. She didn't want to be the person who was obligated to remember; remembering meant you were forced into doing certain things you didn't want to do, being places you didn't want to be, making choices you really didn't want to make. Remembering made it impossible to be selfish. Being selfish didn't always have to be a sin, did it?

Although she had to admit, she liked being seen as perfect. It was nice to have Lucy compliment her and hold her in such high esteem. There was no way Sam was going to disappoint her by telling her how much she ached to be bad.

Lucy took a right down Waverly. Sam admired her military posture. Sam was good at guessing what people's careers were from the way they looked. Years of living in the city had offered her plenty of research opportunities: a female dance student's feet turned out in perfect plies and her hair was bound into a modest bun; strikingly tall, painfully thin models owned chiseled features; actresses were often unremarkable looking, yet hauntingly familiar. There was more to Sam's gift than that. You had to make yourself available. Look interested, and people believed you were. Strangers told Sam their most intimate secrets. It happened to her repeatedly, in stores, on subway platforms, even in front of the sink in a public bathroom. People confessed and she listened, taking in everything they said and tucking it away for later consumption. Lucy was impossible to quantify though. She wasn't just a prom queen, or a rodeo star, or an Army brat, or the sum of her looks. She wasn't just a brainy philosophy major. She was all of that and more, a constant surprise.

The playground in Washington Square Park was packed with children. Once Sam had found interesting things under the jungle gym, crack vials, a hypodermic needle, and an ever-changing assortment of used condoms. Undoubtedly this next generation was unearthing similar buried treasure. A mom wiped the runny nose of her screaming child. The woman appeared to be much older than Brooke, but looking closer, Sam saw it was an illusion. This woman was au natural, wearing distressed jeans, a distressed t-shirt, a distressed mien, and not a smidgen of makeup. If Brooke had been sitting next to Sam, she would have smirked, saying, "God, has she let herself go."

"I'm never having kids," Sam declared to Lucy.

"Me neither. They ruin your life."

Lucy pulled out a pack of Camels and lit one, the smoke trailing off.

"How about him?" Lucy said, jerking her head.

"Him?" Sam had no idea what she was referring to. Then she remembered their bogus mission. They'd come south to deflower her. Lucy had to be making a joke, right? She'd assumed as much, but it had been an excuse to get out of there and away from her troubles. The man Lucy pointed out leaned against the Washington Square arch, the breeze caressing his hair. He was terrifyingly blond, with agate blue eyes.

"Just to let you know, he's gay," Sam said.

"He is not."

"He is so. Plus, he's not my type."

"He's totally perfect. You'd make beautiful babies."

"I just said I didn't want babies. Lucy, even if he was straight, which he isn't, I wouldn't know what to say to a guy that pretty."

"How do you know he's not a Nietzsche scholar?"

"That would appeal to you," Sam pointed out. "You're the philosophy major."

"He could be an artist or a musician. You'd like that."

"He's a male model," Sam said with certitude.

"Or he isn't, let's go ask him," Lucy suggested, trashing her cigarette and grinding it underfoot. Sam was saved by the appearance of another stunningly attractive male who sauntered up to Mr. Aryan Nation, grabbed him in his hot hands and gave him an ardent tongue kiss.

"How did you know?" Lucy asked, astonished.

Sam shrugged.

Lucy shook her head. "I need a cup of coffee," she said, and then made for Café Figaro.

The Café was Sam's favorite West Village haunt. She'd spent weekends in High School sitting there nursing a cup of cappuccino. Sam liked to imagine that when she stepped out she would find herself in North Beach or Venice. It was that kind of place.

Lucy and Sam wended their way to their favorite table at the very back of the small room. It was round and too small to sit at comfortably, but discomfort was part of the tithe collected to gain entrance to this pseudo-bohemian world. The cafe doubled as a library. Patrons bent over their writing journals or the latest novel. A man with a black beret sunk into *Being and Nothingness,* and a lanky blond immersed herself in *The World According to Garp.* Sam had read both. She much preferred Garp. That John Irving was a handsome man. Maybe she could tap him for her deflowering.

Their waitress was the one who always wore a black dance skirt and leotard top. Sam had dubbed her "Miss Capezio." She moved at a crablike crawl. Eventually, she deigned to note their existence and decided to make her way over, staring past them without even asking what they wanted.

"An espresso, please," Lucy said.

"A cappuccino," Sam added.

Off Miss Capezio went, but not toward the espresso machine. She paused at a nearby table to flirt with its male occupant.

"So he was gay," Lucy said. "That doesn't mean he's not a candidate."

"Yes, it does."

"I slept with a boy who was gay."

"You didn't."

"Rodney Smith. He was from Appleton. I did it as a favor, took him for a test drive. Showed him what to do. I'll tell you what, he was a lot better at making me feel good than most of the rest of them were. Rodney had sensitive fingers."

"Look, Luce, that's you. I want to be in love with the first guy I sleep with."

"In love? How are you going to manage that?"

"By waiting," Sam said firmly. She was done with this as a topic, done with the hunt, and done with the absurdity of it. "I should never have told you," she said, under her breath.

"I'm trying to help," Lucy insisted.

"I don't need help. I'm not a project."

"Oh come on, this is fun," Lucy said. She was smiling, knowingly. Sam flushed.

"I'm fine the way I am," Sam said.

"It's not about being fine, it's about—" Lucy began.

Sam cut in, needing her to stop. "So how is having an accident the same as killing yourself?"

As soon as the words were out of her mouth, Sam regretted them. Lucy turned a ghastly, ghostly white. "I didn't mean that Luce, I'm so sorry." Sam reached for Lucy's hand, but her friend pulled it away. An uneasy silence reigned.

Why did I have to do that? Sam wondered. She ached to roll the film back to when she was the one being picked apart. It was so much easier than this. Lucy looked stricken. Sam couldn't blame her. My fault, she thought, wincing internally. A minute ticked by. Then two. Then five.

"You were making me feel stupid," Sam said.

Lucy nodded. "I see." Relenting, she asked, "Where in Mexico would be good?"

She was willing to forgive her. "Pretty much anywhere," Sam said enthusiastically.

"It has to be really exotic," Lucy said, mischievously.

"Isla Mujeres, then."

"What's that?"

"The Island of Women." Sam had picked it on purpose, a subtle reference to that kiss. She watched Lucy closely.

"That's a thought," Lucy said. "Although I couldn't live there forever. Not just with women. I mean, could you?"

"Nope," Sam said.

"The problem is how do you find a guy who you can talk to seriously? You know, the way we talk with each other."

"There must be one," Sam said.

"There must be one or two," Lucy agreed, as her smile expanded. The wattage increased exponentially, warming both of them.

And right at that moment, a boy sauntered through the door. He walked past their ever-unhelpful waitress. "Hey Mikey, how's tricks?" Miss Capezio inquired.

"Good as good can be, Evie."

Evie. So that was her name. Lucy nudged Sam and pointed out this Mikey. He wore threadbare blue jeans and a yellow t-shirt advertising Elvis Costello's aim as always on target and true. In the silkscreen, Elvis looked extremely gawky and pissed off, yet he still managed to exude a sterling confidence. That man knew exactly who he was and what he deserved. He flaunted his punk roots, but most of all he wanted to be famous. And Elvis was getting there. He had his moments, but he'd done nothing irreparable, not like Sid Vicious or Lucy's brother, turning that car wheel on purpose. Suicide was the biggest "Fuck you" there was. You left everyone else behind to deal with the misery you inflicted. You left them having to bargain with your ghost. Or run from it.

"The usual?" Evie asked.

Mikey was obviously a nickname for Michael. This Michael smiled. His smile was as inviting as Lucy's, but more shopworn and relaxed. It was an open invitation to who so ever might be proximate. He was handsome in a funky way. His auburn hair curled to his shoulders. He had blue eyes and a Cary Grant dimple stamped into the middle of his chin. This Michael was half boy-half man. His shoulders were wide as a competitive swimmer's. Sam saw his feet were shod in black Converse hi-tops. These marked him as both unaffectedly hip and pretty nearly perfect, if one were, say, thinking of a specific type.

Her type.

Evie, a.k.a. "the waitress from hell," hadn't done a thing about getting their order. But she sure got busy making his. Michael smiled a sleepy smile as she returned posthaste with his coffee.

"How's the witch?" Evie inquired.

"Watch out, she'll ride in on her broomstick and carry you off."

"I'm not afraid."

"Thanks," he said, reaching for the pitcher of milk and dismissing her. Evie pouted, but not in the bored way she exhibited with them. This pout was pathetic, peevish, and desperate. She wanted his attention. He steadfastly refused to give it and cracked open the book he'd brought with him. Evie sighed loudly. Michael didn't look up. She wandered away heartbroken.

Any month now we'll get our order, Sam thought.

But Lucy was up, off to protest. Wait. She was making a beeline for Michael's table with an unlit cigarette.

"Do you have a match?" Lucy inquired.

"Don't smoke, sorry. They have matches up at the front."

Lucy waited just as Evie had, assuming that when he realized she was standing there, he'd do a double take. He read on, literature trumping beauty. Giving up, Lucy strode cowboy style to the counter, palmed a book of matches, crossed back to their table, and lit one with a flourish. Drawing in the smoke and exhaling, she narrowed her eyes. "He's definitely gay."

Sam watched Michael's smile deepen, dimpling his cheeks. "Nope," Sam said with conviction.

Just then, Evie dumped their order on the table and waltzed away.

Michael drank the dregs of his coffee. He dropped a bill on the table and shoved his book into his back pocket.

"See you," Evie said to him hopefully.

"Absolutely," he told her. He was out the door.

The man who got away, Sam thought. Handsome without being sculpted, masculine without being arrogant, perfect without wanting Lucy, the very same Lucy who was up and pulling her to her feet. Sam threw down some money.

"What now?" Sam demanded, as Lucy dragged her outside.

There went Michael, bopping down Bleecker Street listening to some internal, infernal music. He turned the corner. Lucy pursued.

"We didn't pay," Sam yelled after her.

Inside Dauber and Pine Used and Antique Booksellers there were stray piles of books on every flat surface, overloaded shelves, and the musty smell of mildewing paper. Michael lounged behind the cash register, chatting with an older woman whose abundant white hair perched atop her head in a lopsided bun. Her face wore that familiar, pissed off New York expression. Glasses hung from a librarian's chain round her neck. She wore a man's button-down vest over a black turtleneck. Sam estimated she was about the same age as the collector's editions the store advertised. This had to be the aforementioned *witch*.

"You're always finding things funny," the woman said to him. "What about when they come for you, what then?"

"Who's coming for me this time?" Michael asked, raising an eyebrow.

"Everything's a joke to you, Michael. Some things one shouldn't joke about." Just then a cat jumped up on the counter and rubbed against the cash register. The old woman batted it away. "Out of here, you," she hissed.

"You're unfair to him," Michael said. "It's not right, Lydia. He kills the mice. He does what he's supposed to do."

"Which is more than I can say for you." She whirled round and confronted Sam. "What do you want?"

"I'll help her," Mike said.

"You mean you'd actually consider working? A first." Snorting, she lurched at Sam, who recoiled instinctually. The woman shot her the evil eye, then veered away, and grabbed onto the handrail of a spiral staircase. She ascended, grunting and groaning her way to the top. Above them floorboards creaked. Then, a door slammed.

"Don't mind her," Michael told them. "She's been in a bad mood since Stalin turned out to be . . . well . . . Stalin. Are you looking for a book? I see you found some matches, do you intend to burn it?"

He was speaking to Lucy, who was pretending an interest in British Architecture. Her magnetic tractor beam had sucked him in after all. But Sam wasn't going to cede her rights so easily this time.

"Your boss has been pissed off since the forties?" Sam asked.

He laughed, turning her way. "Actually, I think it's a fairly recent development. Right up until 1960 she was convinced Stalin wasn't a mass murderer at all and that it was a myth made up by the right wing American press."

"People believe what they need to believe," Sam agreed.

"Just like being religious." They exchanged a knowing smile. "Are you two stalking me?"

"You don't think we're bibliophiles?" Sam countered.

"You look exactly like our typical customer."

As if to prove his point, the bell rang and an elderly man wearing a stained cardigan and threadbare corduroy pants entered.

"Did you get the Benjamin?" he demanded.

Michael shook his head. The old man spit out an "ach" of disappointment then turned on his heel and slammed the door in his wake.

"Point taken," Sam said.

"Do you go to NYU?"

"Barnard."

"So you've come down to the village to see how the other half lives?"

"You're busting our chops because?" Sam countered.

"Because I can?"

Lucy was combing through the pile of art books. "These are gorgeous," she exclaimed.

"*The Garden of Love*," Michael said.

"It's at the *Met*," Sam said to Lucy. "We should go see it.'"

"I take it you're from the city and she's not."

Sam nodded.

"Where did you go to school?" Michael asked.

"St. Ann's."

"One of those certified geniuses? I must bow down and scrape the floor for you."

Sam burst out laughing. It was the crazy principal's selling point to the parents. According to him, only children who scored in the genius range on the Stanford Binet were admitted. It had certainly made the clientele happy to shell out the dough. Who didn't want to believe how special their precious little darling was? The good thing about that same principal was his generosity. She'd gotten a full ride when Brooke was disinherited. "Don't think about it," was what he told Brooke. And she never had to.

"How about you?" Sam asked.

"Dalton."

"And you're making fun of St. Ann's? Please. I assume you graduated from college?"

"I'm on sabbatical. This is the first day of the rest of my life."

"Where did you go?"

He seemed embarrassed to admit, "Harvard."

"You left Harvard to work in a bookstore?"

"Actually, to work in the basement of a bookstore. That's what happens when you shirk your undergraduate responsibilities; your loving parents decide it's high time you supported yourself."

"Mikhail!" a voice thundered from above.

"You don't have to buy anything, but you do have to leave," Michael said. "I'm off at five."

When they were outside, Lucy beamed. "He's perfect for you."

She'd pursued him to make him into a gift? If so, Sam wasn't about to argue.

TWO HOURS LATER they waited for Michael to lock the metal gates. "Chinese?"

"Sure."

The three headed southeast.

"You're an Elvis fan," Sam said, eyeing the t-shirt.

"He's amazing, though I have to admit I'm getting sick of the bad boy routine. You can't go after Ray Charles and James Brown. That's unacceptable behavior."

"Elvis Presley?" Lucy asked.

"Have I taught you nothing?" Sam said.

Lucy shrugged.

"Costello. He got drunk and went into this rant, acted like a total asshole."

"What did he say?"

Sam couldn't bring herself to explain that part. What he'd said had been heinous. He'd used the N word. It was easier to skirt the truth. If I were black, Sam thought, I'd never forgive him.

"If I were black, I'd never forgive him for going on like that. In fact, I'd probably want to kill him," Michael said, echoing her thoughts. "The trouble is, there's the music, and then the artist's personality. Elvis is just too damn good, especially live."

"He's amazing," Sam agreed. "Who else do you like?"

"The Clash, of course, and X. I got to see everyone. My brother worked at Max's. He'd always sneak me inside."

"That's too cool."

It turned out Michael had seen Blondie eleven times, and Springsteen playing "Rosalita," plus Lou Reed, Nico, and the B-52's. His taste was eclectic. He loved Aretha, but also Sonny Rollins and Brahms. He even admitted to liking opera.

"Were you a music major?" Sam asked.

"No. I guess I don't want to ruin it for myself."

Sam laughed. It was true. Too much analysis could suck the life out of something.

"What about you?" he asked. "What are your hopes and dreams?"

"To be a medical professional," Sam said.

"You're pre-med? That's too funny. My girlfriend Dani is, too."

"Oh." As in, *oh shit*. Sam's heart sank. She valiantly tried to repair her crestfallen expression, forcing the corners of her lips back up. It felt painful, more of a grimace than a smile.

"Sam plays me all sorts of music," Lucy said, into the sudden silence. "You wouldn't believe how uneducated I was when I got here. Such a hick."

"Sam is turning you into a snob just like the rest of us native New Yorkers?"

"You guys aren't snobs."

"Oh yes, we are," Michael said. "Everyone everywhere else in this country hates the city, so we believe it's our duty to prove them right by acting superior."

"I don't know about anyone else, but I love it here," Lucy avowed.

They went to the Phoenix Garden, a Chinese restaurant in an underground shopping mall. The noise was overwhelming; dishes clattered, metal pots slammed, and all around diners conversed in high-pitched Mandarin. Mike beckoned to the waiter then said, "我 们 能 得 到 三 瓶 啤 酒?"

The reply came and off he went.

"I asked him for some beers, I hope that's okay. I come here a lot."

"You speak Chinese?" Sam asked.

"I took it at Harvard. They give you a different menu this way. Better food."

Sam decided it was best to get the bad news over with. "How long have you been with Dani?"

Lucy kicked her under the table. Sam didn't flinch.

"We started dating in our senior year of high school. So are there any particular things you like? Maybe I should put it another way, what don't the two of you eat?" Michael asked, changing the subject on his own.

"I draw the line at entrails," Sam said.

He laughed. "Me, too."

"Why don't you order for us," Lucy said coyly.

"Really?"'

Under better circumstances Sam would have protested. She liked to pick and choose for herself. But in this case, she was dealing with how attractive this guy was to her and the unfortunate existence of a Boston based competitor.

"I'll do my best," Michael agreed.

Thankfully, the alcohol arrived. Lifting her beer, Sam wished upon whatever star was twinkling over New York City, the home of totally ambient light. Her wish was for Dani to vanish. She really liked this boy. Who would have thought it possible? She and *Miss Capezio* evidently had this in common, if nothing else.

The food came posthaste. The waiter served salt and pepper shrimp, pea pod shoots in garlic sauce, and a whole sea bass with its deadeye staring up at them. Sam winked at it. The poor fish couldn't exactly wink back.

"How come you left school?" Lucy asked.

"I told my parents I didn't want to go into the law, and they told me that, in that case, I'd have to pay my useless liberal arts education on my own. I'm saving up to go back."

"How's it working out?" Sam asked.

"It might take a little longer than I anticipated."

"They'll change their mind," Sam said.

"Aren't you the cockeyed optimist?"

"Not usually," she admitted.

AFTER DINNER HE invited them over. You had to walk up Bowery to get there as it was the only well-lit street. They made the left onto Delancey and something skittered past their feet.

"What was that?" Lucy asked, recoiling.

"A rat," Sam said, nonchalantly. It had paused as if to prove her right, staring up at them quizzically.

"That's not a rat," Lucy said, flinching. "It's huge."

"They grow them as big as cats up here," Michael said, as a passing car sprayed water. The rodent shivered and slid down the nearest gutter drain.

"Then there are our gators," Sam said.

"Giants. Sometimes they come up out of the toilet," Michael chimed in.

"Come on, you guys," Lucy said.

"Kids get them as presents," Sam insisted. "They're cute when they're little, but then when they grow, they have to be flushed. They live down there, roaming the sewers."

"You two are pulling my leg!" Lucy exclaimed.

"No, we aren't," Sam said. "This is New York, the greatest city in the world."

They took Eldridge. Half the streetlights on the block were broken. It was too dark. Sam felt that uncomfortable prickling in the back of her neck. She kept twisting round to make sure no thugs were following them.

"How far away is your building?" she asked him.

"Another block and a half."

Michael and Sam exchanged that knowing, slightly paranoid look all native New Yorkers wore as armor. He picked up the pace. Reaching the corner, Sam exhaled her relief. Just a half a block to go and they would be safe and warm. As she stepped into the street, a man slid in front of her. There was a gun in his right hand pointed at her chest. He twitched as if someone were pulling his limbs with marionette strings.

"Empty your pockets!" he ordered.

Sam did as commanded, throwing the contents into the street. Michael added his own bills and coins.

"Your turn," he told Lucy.

She glared and didn't make a move to comply. Sam's heart was pounding. She wanted to say something, but was afraid that it would set him off. She nudged Lucy's arm. Then the mugger reached for Lucy himself, using the gun. He was going to shoot her!

"No, don't," Sam begged. He gave an odd smile and used the barrel as an extension of his own hand to brush Lucy's hair out of her eyes. Lucy smacked at him and at the gun. It dropped into the street and slid away.

There was a second when the four of them stood there, frozen. A horrified tableau.

"Run!" Lucy commanded.

They did. They ran because their lives depended on it. They ran as if the hounds of hell were nipping at their heels in the shape of one pissed off junkie scrambling after his weapon, screaming, "You fucking shitheads, when I get you I'm gonna tear you apart!"

Michael stuck his key in the lock. It jammed. "Shit!" he hissed. Then the key turned and the metal security door flew open. They were through the portal, through the second security door and inside. Both clanged shut. Michael led the way up to the fourth floor and down the hall to E. He unlocked the police lock. In they tumbled, panting.

"Is he still out there?" Lucy asked, running to the window. "We should call the police."

Sam stared down at the now empty street.

"And say what?" Michael asked.

"That someone just tried to rob us. To kill us."

"Relax, I'll take care of it," Michael said. "Just be cool."

"Relax? How?"

"Let him make the call," Sam told her.

He lifted the phone and punched in 911. "There's a man who just tried to mug us. No. No! Look he's armed and in his late twenties. He has pockmarks on his face, dark hair. Yes, I'd say dark brown or black. He's wearing a blue jacket and tan pants. He's got a scar right above his left eyebrow. He's just been on Eldridge Street between Grand and Hester. No. No!" Then he hung up.

"You didn't give them your name," Lucy said.

"You never give your name," Sam explained.

"But they need to interview us."

"That's the last thing we want them to do," Michael said.

"What do you mean?" Lucy asked, clearly shocked.

"Because if we give them the option, they'll come here instead of looking for him. They'll take us down to the precinct, have us look through some mug shots, and that's on a good day. Or they'll just write down the notes, asking us a ton of questions. They prefer to do that. It's safer than combing the streets and possibly happening upon someone with a gun who might shoot before they do. It's not like in the movies. This is real life. They want to live to go home to their kids. They want to do what's easier. Coming here first is easier. And safer."

"That's can't be true."

"It is," Sam insisted. She still saw the junkie's pockmarked face, his glittering brown eyes, and his shock of dark hair. She felt the desperation that had oozed from his every pore. Sam shuddered.

Michael got up and went into the bedroom. He returned with a zip-lock bag. After crumbling pieces of hash into a pipe, he lit it, sucked in the balm, and passed the pipe to Sam. They smoked in silence. It was ironic that they'd almost been killed for a fix and now they were up here getting high. Outside there was a crash of thunder, then a bolt of lightning.

"My mother had these friends," Sam said. "They used to live on Avenue B. One day a man with a gun shoved his way into their apartment. He tied up Tod and then raped his wife, Emma, in front of him. He tied her up too, ransacked the place, and left. When they managed to get free, they called 911. Emma went to the hospital. There were rape kits. Statements. Mug shots. An endless hit parade of felons. Was he black? Was he Hispanic? Was he tall? Did he have any facial hair? They spent all this time trying to figure out who he was, but there was no mug shot of him, so Tod and Emma went home. The next day there was a note was in their mailbox. It was a death threat. They called the police who said they were sorry and would do everything in their power. The day after that, they came home to find their cat lying gutted on the kitchen floor. He could get in and out of their apartment. The police couldn't help them with that either, other than to suggest changing the locks. That weekend, Tod and Emma packed up and moved to upstate New York. They got an unlisted number. True story."

"Jesus," Lucy said.

"That's life in the big city," Sam told her.

The best thing was to take another toke. Then swig from the jug of wine Michael had opened. Outside it was raining cats, dogs, and kitchen implements.

Michael put on Coltrane's *Giant Steps*. It was frenetic and upbeat, a perfect counter to a near death experience.

"If you became a lawyer would you be defending that guy or prosecuting him?" Sam asked Michael.

He smiled. "It's hard to say. There's the sympathy route. Poor guy never had a chance, an unhappy childhood, messed up by the system, fell into addiction. My mother works as a public defender, so I've heard all the stories. Or there's the flip side. My dad says 'you make your own bed, then lie in it.' He's a corporate lawyer and feels no guilt. My brother is black sheep number one in that his MBA is going to help him work in the music business. He went to Princeton, now he's at Columbia. As for me, I think that some people don't have as much choice as others, that some of us are lucky, and that my parents are probably right. I should put away childish things. Instead I choose working at a shitty job, and I can choose to not do it, too. I can have a better life. That guy out there likely wasn't born with my same options. But I still despise him. He just stuck a gun in our faces and scared the shit out of us. And we all know it could have been a hell of a lot worse."

"That's why you have to do what you care about doing most," Sam said.

"So you can die happy?" Michael asked.

"Don't say that." She shuddered.

"But it's what you mean, isn't it?"

"She's right," Lucy agreed. "You can't sell yourself short."

"You know, what you did was crazy," Michael told her.

"I guess," Lucy said. "I didn't know I was going to do it, believe me."

"But the beauty of it is, it worked."

Exactly, Sam thought. They had done the smart thing, she and Michael. She was of two minds, angry that Lucy had put them in mortal danger, but aware that she might also have saved their lives. If that junkie had decided to shoot them, what chance would they have really had? He could have taken them out cleanly and coldly, then sauntered off? Who was to say that wasn't the story he'd worked out in advance, his perfect ending to a perfect crime?

"There's no way to be safe," Lucy said. "No fucking way in the world."

She knew whereof she spoke, Sam thought, setting her hand Lucy's knee. They sat together on the couch, bonded by this knowledge, united by just how close they'd come.

The record ended. Michael put on Keith Jarrett. He specialized in lyrical piano riffs. Lovely. This cramped apartment was their ivory tower. Michael sucked in on the pipe and exhaled the residue. Crop circles of hash smoke floated to the ceiling.

Outside, thunder crashed and lightning seared the sky, burning away all things wicked.

"Strange weather," Michael said. "Who'd we piss off, you think?"

"God," Lucy said.

"God knows," Sam added.

"I wish she'd let us in on the secret then." Michael giggled. They dissolved into laughter, and from that lapsed into hysterics. The tears were a relief. What a gift to be up here warm and dry, tucked away like Winnie the Pooh in that bedtime story!

Michael retrieved a pint of chocolate Haagen Daz from his freezer. He brought three spoons. Sam dug through the permafrost crust to get to the gooey heart of the matter. Outside the rain beat down.

"When I was thirteen, I was mugged four times," Michael said. "It was always the same stupid deal. A bunch of boys would come up to me. One had the knife. They would threaten to beat me up if I didn't give them my money. I told my parents I wanted to learn judo, so they sent me to a dojo. I never ended up having to use it. After that, every time I got mugged the asshole had a gun. You can't go all Bruce Lee when the other guy has a gun, unless you're in a Bruce Lee movie."

"It always feels like you can prevent it from happening, like somehow it's your fault when it does," Sam said.

"This wasn't our fault," Lucy said.

"My parents would disagree," Michael said. "They'd note that if I lived in a safer neighborhood, things like this wouldn't happen."

"That's bullshit," Sam said.

"Maybe. But it's also true. There's a whole lot less crime on the Upper East Side."

"How was it your fault when you were thirteen?" Lucy asked.

"Then I acted like I was an easy target. You know young, privileged, scrawny."

"There were three of us tonight. None of us are scrawny," Lucy pointed out.

"He had a gun. The great equalizer."

"When I was eleven, I was walking home from my friend's house," Sam said. "This creepy old guy came up to me. He grabbed me and said he wanted to buy me. I pulled away and ran, but he kept following me. I went into store after store to ask them to help. They told me to get lost. By the time I got home, I was completely hysterical. When I told my mother what happened, she said that was why she carried mace and gave me a can. She said, 'Just point and spray.' That was it. Problem solved. Unfortunately, when someone's grabbing your ass on a packed subway car, you can't go spraying mace around."

"Life in the big city," Michael agreed.

They whiled away the time playing poker, rummy, and spit. Then they got into his double bed. Conceptually, Sam knew this was every man's wet dream. In reality, it was intensely awkward. Lucy lay near the window, Michael was sandwiched between them, and Sam perched on the sliver of bed closest to the door. Lucy seemed to have no trouble falling asleep. Michael faded away. Only Sam was unable to enter the land of nod.

She returned to the scene of the almost crime. She saw them dropping one at a time, then the police arriving to sketch their chalk-marked outlines onto the slick pavement.

Yet, they were alive. The proof was that she was lying here, in bed next to Michael. Her extremities tingled. Across the room, a photograph of brown-haired, blue-eyed Dani beamed at her from the makeshift desk. Sam shut her eyes, trying to force sleep to come. Soon it would be morning. Soon, very soon, they could go. Then all of this would fade away. Meeting him, being with him, and facing danger, then lying in bed together, would turn into a story. She and Lucy could share it with each other to further cement their bond.

Still, it was impossible to fall asleep. Sam got up and went into the front of the apartment. The toilet was inside of a tiny closet. Sam closed the door quietly, then put the seat down and perched on it.

"Hey, are you okay?" a voice inquired.

"Sorry, did I wake you?" Sam said, emerging.

"I wasn't asleep, I was being polite," Michael told her. "Want some tea?"

"Sure."

He popped off the top of the kettle, filled it with water, and set it on the stove. When he opened the cupboard to retrieve two mugs, streams of cockroaches shot out.

"Shit!" The roaches descended. Michael swatted at them ineffectually and they both cracked up.

"In grade school our science teacher told us cockroaches would be the only survivors after the nuclear winter," Sam told him.

"I think your teacher might be wrong. You spray them with Raid and they shrivel up and die."

"I take it you've tried the Raid thing? How's that working out for you?"

"Actually, Dani won't let me use pesticides. She says they're carcinogenic. She made me put down some boric acid, but then told me she couldn't walk barefoot. I think I'm going to have to buy a gecko. Apparently, they feast on cockroaches. Or else I could give up and accept that to the victor belongs the spoils."

"It's kind of amazing how roaches act," Sam said. "Have you ever taken a picture down off the wall and think, wow, a shadow? Then you realize it's moving, that it's not a shadow at all. It's a roach army."

"And then you start screaming."

"You're a guy, you're not supposed to scream," Sam said.

"It's instinctual."

Sam laughed. She imagined cockroach metropolises complete with groceries and nurseries. It was an oddly comforting thought, worlds within worlds within worlds. They sat there quietly, their bodies touching.

"How come you came back here when your girlfriend lives in Boston? There are bookstores to work in there, right?"

"Plenty."

"And it's not because you wanted to live in this great apartment."

"This little slice of heaven, what do you mean?" Michael laughed. "I guess I ran away because I didn't want to face Dani every morning. She's so practical. She always has been. Dani thinks that dropping out is childish, that this 'trying to find myself' is ridiculous. When I'm with her, I see her point. Dani has this way of looking at you and not saying anything for a few seconds too long. It's as if she sees into the pit of your soul and boy, is it disappointing in there. She's always known what she wants to be and how to get there. She thought I was like her. Now it turns out that she might be wrong about that. One day she'll decide it's not worth waiting around for me to come to my senses."

"You love her," Sam said.

"I did. I guess I must still. But does she love me? Or does she love who she thought I was? I keep trying to break up with her and she keeps telling me I'm crazy and I don't know what I want. I suppose we've been together for so long, we're each other's best friends. I moved so we could get some distance, but we see each other every third weekend and fight. I think that it's over, but then one of us relents. Usually it's me. Does that answer your question?"

"Yes."

"That's enough about me. It's your turn. Boyfriend?"

"None."

"Why not?"

"Because." And then Sam kissed him, surprising them both. Michael tasted of hash, smoky and sweet.

"Are you sure?" he asked, holding her a little away.

"Positive." Saying it made it so. Kissing him made her forget that she was the reliable one, the predictable one, the one who stayed put because someone had to stay put. He slid closer and put his arm around her shoulder. They descended together onto the couch. Michael's hand roamed under her shirt. There was no bra to undo. Being a pert almost B cup came with certain fringe benefits. His hand moved back down, unzipping her jeans. Slim fingers explored the edges of her underwear, curling the elastic rim back to work their way inside. Sam moaned. Michael tugged off his own pants. He set his mouth over her right nipple and sucked. An electric charge shot through her body. It was too late to tell him that this was her first time.

He pushed his penis inside of her.

Shit! It hurt! It burned! All her desire was immediately squelched. Sam bit her lip to stop herself from crying out. Tears started in the corners of her eyes. Dani smirked at her from the side table as Michael moaned. The broken springs on the couch scraped the undersides of Sam's legs. To think that she'd imagined this as magical, that she'd thought of herself as being transported. Sam lay there, frozen.

"Are you okay?" Michael asked, hoisted up on his forearms. When she didn't say anything, he added, "You weren't ready, were you?"

He pulled out of her gently. His head descended. Sam knew where he was going. Blushing, she said, "No, no please. You don't have to."

It was too late. He'd bent to his work.

"Stop," she insisted, grabbing his hair and pulling him up. "Look, don't. I don't want that. I'm a virgin. What I mean is, I was a virgin."

"Oh shit!" Michael shook his head. He emitted a rueful laugh. "This was your first time? I'm sorry. I'm so sorry. How could I be that dense?"

"How could you have known?"

"Of course I could have known. I was just being selfish." He stared down at his hands as if they were the culprits. Sam picked up her underwear and jeans, then rushed into the bathroom thinking, *Why did I tell him? Why did I have to be so fucking honest? What on earth is wrong with me? I could have pretended. What would have been wrong with that?*

Sam turned on the light and the armed forces of the roach kingdom scattered. Wiping herself she discovered there was only a little blood. She thought of all the descriptions she'd read in soft porn and of D.H. Lawrence with his fucking godhead. She'd been so silly, waiting for the special one. Obviously, the first time wasn't great. She should have known from all she'd read, those clinical descriptions of tearing and piercing. How could that really feel good? But she'd been a romantic, imagining it would be different for her. If I'd just gone ahead and gotten this over with earlier, she thought, then he wouldn't have been my first and maybe this could have been the beginning of something. Instead it was clearly an embarrassing ending.

When she stepped out, Michael was still sitting on the couch. "I feel so bad."

"Don't," she said sternly. "I wanted to do it. I wanted to get it over with. Now I have."

"That's not all this is." He didn't sound entirely certain, though.

"You have Dani." She waited for him to challenge her, to tell her she was wrong.

Instead he said, "The thing with Dani is complicated."

Sam swallowed her disappointment. Why couldn't he tell her that knowing her for this one short evening had changed his life? That she was the one for him? Because if he did, Sam thought, I wouldn't believe him. He reached for her arm, but she slipped away.

Lying in bed next to Lucy, Sam shut her eyes. She lied to herself, telling herself it was good that she'd done this.

Jimi used to wail that question from Win's stereo.

Ohhh, but are you experienced?

Have you ever been experienced?

She had.

She was.

For all the good it did her.

9

Muriel
November 1980

LOUISE DE SCHWEINITZ Darrow was in town. Could Muriel drive into Boston to meet her? Louise knew it was two days before Thanksgiving, and likely an inconvenience. Still, she thought she would just give a call to see if Muriel might be free for lunch.

"Were your ears burning?" Muriel said.

"I was on your mind?"

Not on it so much as in it. Imbedded right inside.

There was fresh snow on the ground. All the tree limbs of the old oaks lining Newbury Street wore a silky white coating. The bell tinkled when Muriel pulled open the door of The English Tea Room. She saw Louise sitting in the far corner.

"It's so wonderful to see you," Muriel said, folding her diminutive friend in her arms. Releasing her, she added, "Tell me about the conference."

"It's nothing." Louise waved a hand dismissively. "Harvard Medical School is hosting a seminar on the role of women in medicine. They wanted an elder stateswoman. My more prominent colleagues were indisposed."

"When are you scheduled to speak?"

"I've already given the talk."

"But I wanted to come," Muriel protested.

"Trust me, you didn't."

"What would you girls like?" the waitress asked.

"Girls?" Louise mouthed slyly, her eyes twinkling.

Louise ordered the onion soup, Muriel, a grilled ham and cheese. Water arrived, courtesy of the busboy. With it, side salads adorned with a sweet milky dressing. She speared a piece of iceberg lettuce and let it settle on her tongue. At home she'd tried to replicate the dressing, but found her attempt to be a dismal failure.

"Were you just being polite when you said you were thinking of me?" Louise asked.

"Absolutely not. I was writing about you."

"I hope you were gentle."

"How could I be anything but?" Muriel returned the mischievous smile. "I was asked to give a talk myself. Columbia invited me down. There's a scholarship endowed in Amelia's name."

"Columbia? Of all places." Louise clucked her tongue. She would have said more, but the rolls arrived.

Muriel split hers and tried to butter it. The tab was so frozen, the stubborn pat ended up as stray clumps of desperate yellow. She was going to take a bite, then thought better of it. Her sandwich was coming. No need to ruin one's appetite.

Muriel thought that Louise was really the one who deserved the honor of having a scholarship at Columbia named after her. Louise had attended the school and gone on to become a doctor, while Amelia had never even applied to medical school. Of course, that wasn't Muriel's real concern. The speech was the trouble. In one impulsive moment she'd said *yes*. Apparently she had nothing further to add. Every attempt to write a speech had ended up in the trash. This morning, Muriel was staring dully into space for more than an hour. She'd finally come up with the idea of that spring break trip. And just then, the phone rang. Louise. Was it fated?

"You never answered my question," Louise said. "Why was I on your mind?"

"I was thinking of the time I came down and met you. When you and Meely were at Columbia."

"Ancient history," Louise said, glibly.

"True."

Louise studied her. "Plus, you've covered it before."

"Not exactly."

"Oh." Louise looked taken aback. Oh indeed. Muriel had never really told the truth about her visit.

Mercifully, her sandwich had arrived.

On that day so long ago, the sky had been a crystalline blue. Amelia met her at Grand Central station. They took the subway uptown and dropped her bag in the rooming house on Amsterdam Avenue. Then trotted off to meet Amelia's new great friend, Louise de Schweinitz at the science lab. The three of them headed to Low Library. On the way, Amelia bragged about how she'd gotten the janitor to show her where the key to the stairway up to the roof was hidden. "The poor man asked me if I intended to kill myself. I told him if I decided to do it, he'd be the first to know. I gave him a kiss for his trouble."

On the door, a sign warned *No Entry*. They ignored it, climbing the twisting metal stairs and shoving the hatch aside. After emerging, Muriel gasped. What a view! North, the farmland was sprinkled with mansions; to the west, the white stone cliffs of the Palisades loomed fortress high; due east, the river sparkled in the sun; south of them, workers on scaffolding raised the stone face of a gothic cathedral.

Muriel chewed on her sandwich. Going down, it stuck in her windpipe. She lifted her water glass and took a draught. The liquid sat atop of the obstruction. Muriel tried to cough it up. And failed. Louise was oblivious, spooning onion soup into her mouth.

Muriel tried to ask for help and discovered she couldn't talk. What to do? She reached round and hit herself on the back of the neck. Futile. She pushed back her chair, meaning to stand and gesture. Louise was a doctor. She'd be able to figure it out.

She was half in, half out of her seat when it came to her.

No house to return to. No clothing to pack up and give away. No ache to live with, day in and day out.

The clock above her head ticked away. Yet time seemed to expand. She flew back, back to Worthington, back to Amelia nudging her awake before the sun rose, the two of them sneaking out to the barn. It was the last day of vacation and they were going for one more ride together. Amelia slid the bridle on and gave her a leg up. Then they were off, winding their way through the pasture, the cattails whispering.

Don't do this, Pidge. Good things can still happen.

What good things? What was left to go right when all this had gone wrong? Yes, there were obligations, bills to be paid, gutters to be replaced, the car engine checked and retooled, but how could any of those things hold her? They were the dreary every day fabric of life, to be done and done and done again without reward. Things to take care of to make the hours pass. And then she saw the book, sitting by the side of the bed. She was supposed to return it, Virgil would want it back, but why worry about that, about him? Virgil would stop by the house to pay his respects, climb the stairs, and find it, and then he'd sit there, fingering it, understanding so much better than so many others would. He would know why she'd given in and let it all go. He would see why this was easier and better, yes, she was done with putting on a brave face.

Easier? Think again. You're not doing this, not on my watch.

Who was saying that?

It felt as though someone had taken hold of her shoulders. As if they were pulling her up, out of her seat. Louise looked at her, startled. And Muriel mimed choking. Louise was behind her in a flash, folding her arms round Muriel's ribs. Masticated bread rocketed out of her mouth, making a forced landing atop her half-finished salad.

Muriel stared down at it and then sank into her chair.

"Amazing," Louise said brightly. "It really does work."

The waitress ran over. "Is everything all right? Can I help?"

"Some tea, please," Muriel said. Her throat was burning. Tears had started in the corners of her eyes. She wiped them dry with the napkin. "What was that?"

"I read about it in the Journal of Emergency Medicine. The author seemed like a bit of a crackpot, still I did have occasion to try it out a few years later.

It worked like a charm. It's called The Heimlich Maneuver, named after its inventor."

"What happened to clapping a person on the back?"

"Oh, that wouldn't have helped. You were blue. We all hate to listen, but our parents told us to masticate thoroughly for a reason. The food was obstructing your esophagus. Next, I would have had to perform a tracheotomy."

"How would you have managed that?"

"With this." Louise lifted the knife. "One makes do in a pinch."

The hot tea arrived. As Muriel sipped on it, the rawness in her throat eased. They should be carting me away, she thought. The whole thing seemed like a dream. The disembodied voice she'd imagined hearing and that odd sensation, as if someone was tugging her out of the chair. *I know what it means to be of two minds. Literally.* She shuddered, rubbing her neck. It was far too easy to picture Louise taking a butter knife to it, jamming it in, in order to save her life.

"Amelia never forgave me," Louise said, interrupting her reverie. "That fight we had up on the roof when I announced my engagement."

"Forgave you? Shouldn't it have been the other way round?"

The three of them had perched atop the library dome, eating the sandwiches Amelia had lovingly prepared. From up there they lorded it over the other students making their way to and from class, those foolish souls all terminally earthbound.

"I have news," Louise had announced. "I'm engaged."

Muriel beamed. "Congratulations, how wonderful."

But Amelia's expression had darkened. "I thought you were going to say no."

"I changed my mind," Louise insisted.

"Did you? Because that man is a Neanderthal."

"What a horrible thing to say," Muriel interjected.

"Stay out of this," Amelia warned, turning her back pointedly. "He'll make you give up your career," she told Louise. "He'll want you at home raising his children. Does that sound rewarding?"

"Bert hasn't said to give up my studies. He wants me to take a little time off," Louise said, butting her chin out.

"Why bother coming to school at all? Why work so hard? Why bother doing any of it, when you're just going to throw it away?"

"But I love him," Louise insisted.

Amelia made a disgusted noise in the back of her throat. Then she stood and walked to the very edge of the roof.

"Come back," Muriel begged.

Muriel stood, meaning to go to her. Louise pulled out a camera. "We'll lose the light," she said softly.

Amelia didn't budge.

"Darling, I am sorry," Louise said, and then she got up, walked over to her friend, and embraced her. They made a fine tableau, framed by the setting sun. Amelia made a brave attempt at a smile. And Muriel knew what this was about. She felt sorry for her sister, even though she'd been jealous of Louise, of their apparent closeness. You always took a risk when you opened your heart.

"Go ahead," Amelia said. She meant go ahead with all of it. Then pulled away, crouched on the roof, and offered her profile to the lens.

Radcliffe owned the photograph. In it, Amelia stared off into the distance. She had on a smart hat and that long navy blue jacket, with the black skirt. People thought her so serene and regal, a figurehead, stuck onto a prow of a boat, always cutting first through the waves.

Let them. Let them make Amelia theirs. They have no idea who she really was. Amelia knew better than to reveal too much. She didn't even tell me certain things. But I could see what was going on with her that day, up on the roof. I knew how much she loved Louise. And how that fueled the critique. Amelia didn't want to lose her friend to this man. Is that a crime? If so, most of us would be guilty of it, Muriel thought. I was jealous of Louise. Amelia was jealous of Louise's lover. So it goes. The heart is such a fragile thing. And needs so much protection. That girl, Samantha Barry, was right. Amelia hid herself from public view. A slip of a girl saw my sister's hand in her own creation. And I suppose I continue the tradition. The question is, who am I protecting here? Not poor mother, she's long gone. Not Amelia either. She is hardly in a position to know or care. So I must do it for myself, I'm still trying to prove that I'm the better sister. Some things never change, no matter how old you get.

Muriel smiled, thinking of that. But lunch was over. She pulled on her coat and headed out into the warming day.

"Were we really ever that young?" Louise asked. Then she gave Muriel a hug. The taxi pulled up. Louise got inside and was spirited away.

What a funny thing love is, Muriel thought, how curious an emotion. Why do we imagine that it's borne by the heart when all the heart is, is muscle. It beats sparrow fast from a burst of adrenaline, then slows down to a dispassionate crawl when you drift off to sleep. It's the mind that tricks us into loving someone.

Muriel shut her eyes and found the three of them again as they'd been at the end of that day, sitting on the curved roof. The sun had set, a yellow fireball plummeting, tinting the sky orange, then scarlet. Night came and they lay back, using the metal for a pillow. Amelia had taken Muriel's hand and their fingers entwined. Above them, the quarter moon sliced the sky. Everywhere else the stars made pinpricks of light.

NOW, PARKED FURTHER down the street where she'd left it, she saw Albert's Caddy with its imperious headlights. She'd kept his car, giving away her decrepit Volvo sedan. The Cadillac was unwieldy, an ocean going cruiser that moved slowly and serenely with the current. I almost died today, Muriel thought. Whether it was true or not, it was true that she'd wanted to. But now that it was over, she felt differently about it. She had never liked the car. And she ached for something sleek, a vehicle that would slice through the water, throwing off a foaming wake.

Snow was thick on the tree branch. Muriel dug her gloved hand in and grabbed some, then shaped it. Then she threw it. The missile smacked the window of a passing bus, making a pleasurable thud. A passenger leaning against the glass started, and then stared out, trying to spot the culprit. He looked past Muriel, thinking her too staid and sedate, not up to making mischief. That was where he was wrong.

10

Amelia
November 1980

THAT DEEP-THROATED LAUGH marked her. It really was Louise. Amelia would never have known her. Her hair was no longer dark and waist length, but china white and cut into an unflattering bob. Her nose, set against sunken cheeks, was even more prominent. Muriel had just been writing about the three of them and that visit to Columbia when the phone rang. Had the fear that gripped Amelia when she realized she might miss this chance of getting to see Louise too, done it? There'd been an extra edge of desperation in her attempt; she'd thrown her arms round Muriel's neck at the last moment, actually begging, "Don't leave me here!" Then she was mounted on her sister, riding out the front door and into the snow-dappled day.

AS THE FOOD arrived, Amelia's stomach responded with a roar of distress. She watched Louise work on her soup. Stray voices of the other diners teased the air; a man pronounced himself "amazed" while his female companion was "distressed." Was she really here? Amelia touched her own arm. It seemed substantial. Still, she'd done this test countless times before. And Muriel had stepped through her, slicing her body in two. She'd been reconstituted. She'd tried and tried and tried. Now, miraculously, she was here. But was she really here?

They'd hung a mirror directly across from where Amelia stood. It was meant to create an illusion of depth, extending the room outwards, again and again. The diners were reflected in it. No sign of Amelia. Where she stood, an unbroken line of flocked wallpaper. Yet, today had obviously been different. She'd been allowed out of her Mudford cage. Her sister, Muriel had borne her here. It was really magnificent. Look at how energetic everyone was, waitresses and busboys rushing to and fro, bearing trays weighed down with goodies.

The car ride had been incredible enough. Muriel had unlocked the driver's side door and Amelia flung herself forward. She went headfirst, smacking against the other side of the car but staying put. Why hadn't she gone straight out again? There was no logic to it. But she didn't care. At least, she was out. Out of that house and there with Muriel as her younger sister clicked a belt round her middle and revved the engine. Backing out the driveway, Muriel swerved to avoid a trash can set by the curb. Twisting the wheel, she headed down the street, muttering, "I'll be late." Her right hand reached out blindly and spun a dial. A man sang, "New York, New York, it's a hell of a town."

Boston was, too, at least this incarnation. Tall buildings sprouted like a sea of giant sequoias. These were man-made, cut out of glass and stabilized with poured concrete. The cars on the road were sleek. Some had elegant fish-shaped fins at either end. Others were boxy. The biggest surprise was the way Muriel drove, commanding the wheel with quiet confidence. The speedometer worked its way from fifty-five to sixty m.p.h. Was this the same Muriel who had clutched the handle of the car door whenever Amelia took a curve too fast? In this imagined world, the rules were there to be broken. Maybe that was the point.

A perfect parking job, there, down the street, Muriel grabbed her purse and opened her door, Amelia slid out right after her, keeping so close she could see the hairs on the back of her sister's long, ropy neck. "Late, as usual," Muriel said aloud. They climbed the stairs in tandem. Muriel opened the door of the restaurant, and Amelia clung to her side like a leech.

Muriel waved and headed to the back, Amelia with her. She finally released her hold when Muriel got to the table. Partly, out of shock. Was that really Louise?

I never thought I'd see you again.

Amelia choked up. She averted her eyes, hoping to regain some semblance of control. There. Turning back, she saw Muriel reach for her water glass. And take a sip. Muriel set it back down and then swatted the back of her own neck. What an odd thing to do. Had a fly been hovering? Amelia bent closer, observing her sister's expression. Odd, she looked calm, like a statue, so still. Wait, she wasn't breathing! Was that possible? Instinctually, Amelia put her hand on Muriel's shoulder. It stayed. And she saw everything. Her nephew growing up and growing older, becoming a teenager, sprouting hair on his face, gaining wide shoulders and thinner hips, turning from that into a man. That same man marrying, Muriel proud of him at the wedding, prouder still as a grandmother, terrified when he went off to war and relieved when he returned relatively unscathed. His life lived. And then, unraveling. That man lying in a hospital room in a white gown laced at the back, shrinking away, shrinking down to nothing, suffering and then finally gone. "Oh," Amelia exclaimed, she tried to pull her hand away but it was stuck to Muriel's shoulder. They were twinned.

There was more. Albert going from youth to middle age to old age, his girth widening. Albert, standing behind Muriel in that same hospital room grieving for their son and Muriel's fury, turned on the one closest to her. Muriel was brutal in her judgment of her husband, his grief not as evident as her own. Muriel demanded what was wrong with him? Her life was wrecked, how could he go on? The days when she stayed in bed and refused to talk to him because her pain was deeper, it had to be. After all, she was the mother. Albert fighting with her and for her, persistent but gentle, forcing Muriel back into the world, trying to be courageous for the two of them, stifling his own feelings to save her from herself. But then there was Albert's desertion. She saw Albert, clutching his chest and falling to the floor. She heard her sister's voice. *No house to return to. No clothing to pack up and give away. No ache to live with, day in and day out.*

So that's it, Amelia thought.

"You're not getting away so easy!" She pinched Muriel right where she always did when she wanted her attention, hard, on her forearm. No response at all.

What now?

Her thoughts flew back, far back, to Worthington, that last good summer of their parents' marriage. It was the morning she'd nudged Muriel awake and escaped the still house to the barn. Atop the pony, they'd raced off together into the woods. Pine needles snapped under Indian's hooves, one kick and he was cantering; the next, he broke into a gallop. Trees fell away. They blew through a meadow strewn with wildflowers. And the sun rose red, a coin stuck onto the clean blue sky. Amelia saw herself lifting her own arms and letting go of the reins like a circus rider. Pidge refused to do it. She kept her hands clasped round Amelia's middle. If I go, she does too. Doesn't she know that? But Pidge wouldn't budge so it was up to her to pry her sister's fingers loose. To force her to balance.

Don't do this. Good things can still happen!

What good things? Muriel's ironic voice sounded back. Amelia knew what she meant. She knew how Muriel had tested out letting it all slip away. How she'd climbed the stairs and tried the gun, shoving it into her mouth. But she'd thought better of it.

Easier? Think again. You're not doing this, not on my watch.

Amelia tried again. She grabbed both of her sister's shoulders and urged her up, out of her chair.

This time it worked. Muriel rose like a marionette, tortured by strings.

AFTERWARDS, IT WAS hard to concentrate. The diners stared at Muriel and at her savior, Louise. Muriel pretended nothing had happened. Amelia had done the same more than once, walking away from a smoldering wreck. Louise was talking about Muriel's spring break visit to Amelia at Columbia. It hadn't been at all like that; perhaps she'd been a little less than generous about that boy, Bert, but honestly, she'd thought Louise was joking. She knew exactly what she'd said to her. "You'd murder him sooner than marry him." It was only afterward, when she saw Louise's expression, that she realized it was serious. Still, she had to say her piece. You couldn't let someone you loved make that kind of mistake. You had to try and stop them.

In the end, Louise had broken off the engagement and married someone else. Amelia had known she would. She'd known her better than Louise knew herself. But Muriel and Louise were shrugging on their coats. Amelia pursued them out the door and down the icy stairs, onto the winter street. Here. Here they all were. She stayed close to Muriel as Louise flagged a taxi.

They hugged.

Muriel waved.

Louise got in. It was now or never.

"Louise!" Amelia yelled and then, rushed past Muriel to pursue Louise who was stepping off the sidewalk and into the street. She got to the taxi almost in time. The door shut in her face and she reached out to bang on the window. Her hand touched the glass. Louise turned round, blinking, but the taxi was pulling into the street and rushing away. It turned the corner.

Amelia stared after it, dully.

She must have imagined the expression of surprise on Louise's face.

As she was imagining the chill, moving up from her the soles of her feet to her ankles. Up through the ankles to mid-calf. Looking down, Amelia saw she was ankle deep in slush. Backing up, she made the curb. Her whole body tingled. The air was crisp, her nose hairs singed. A man strode toward her and, looking up, saw her then swerved round.

Did that happen? Was it possible?

She turned to stare after him.

Then realized she'd forgotten Muriel. Her sister was opening the driver's side door of her car. Amelia ran to catch up and slid on the icy pavement. She went down hard, her legs splaying out.

The Cadillac was off, leaving her behind.

A boy stared down at her.

"Do you need help?" he asked, offering his gloved hand.

She hesitated, then took hold, the leather smooth under her fingers, his hand inside of it, inside of hers, amazing . . .

She was on her feet.

"Did you hit your head? Should I call 911?"

911? Was it code for something?

"You do see me."

He gave her a searching look. "I'm going to call. You might have a concussion."

She didn't. She knew the signs of that. "I'm fine," she said.

"Are you sure?"

"Yes, thank you so very much."

"No need to thank me." He looked relieved. He was likely late. *Late for an important date.* He rushed away.

She was here. Here on Newbury Street, according to the sign. Not the same Newbury Street she'd walked down countless times. There were shops where there had been private homes. Right in front of her, a dress store. The dresses were cut indecently short, thighs exposed almost completely. And there was her reflection winking back at her. I know that woman, she thought. She was wild eyed, her hair tousled, her cheeks flushed. Yet undeniably herself, she was her own Amelia.

Whose stomach rumbled discourteously. She'd thought she was hungry before; now, she was famished. The wind blew. Amelia opened her mouth, swallowing stray flakes. They melted on her tongue.

The door of the next store, Al's Deli, opened. The aroma of home cooking wafted out. The window display was enticing, a mix of savory and sweet; a whole roasted turkey, a ham on the bone, furrows of dried apricots and prunes, peaches and trays packed with baked goods, apple strudel, tricornered hamentashen, chocolate tipped cookies. Amelia's mouth watered.

Stepping inside, she discovered a cafeteria. Trays were stacked at one end of a glassed-in counter. Behind it, two men wearing white smocks filled orders. The menu featured Boston themed specials; there was either the overstuffed Harvard Square, a roast beef sandwich topped with lettuce, tomato, mustard, and mayonnaise on your choice of bread or the Red Sox platter, a hot dog with all the fixings and a choice of two sides. And there was traditional Hebrew fare. She and Louise once split an overstuffed Reuben at Katz's deli down on Houston. Amelia had been surprised by that sandwich, the base of peppery pastrami covered with melted tangy cheese over a layer of sauerkraut, all of it drenched in a sweet dressing. It had been a fine adventure, walking through the Lower East Side that day, remarking on all they saw. And since it was Louise who had ignited this change, she would order it now.

"Can I help you?" the man asked.

She ordered a Reuben, a side of potato salad, a spinach knish, and a slice of apple strudel. Drinks were kept inside the wall. She pulled the handle of the glass-faced door and discovered it was a cunning icebox. Amelia chose the one drink with a familiar name, a metal can of Coca Cola.

At the cash register, the woman said, "That will be six twenty four."

She gasped. It was outrageous. Only then did she stick her hands into her pockets and discover a more urgent problem. They were empty; even the cigarettes and lighter were gone. The food sat there, taunting her. She was faint from hunger. Would they let her wash dishes for a meal? Because, apparently, she was stone cold broke.

"Do you need to put something back?" the woman asked. The line was growing restive. At a restaurant she could have ordered and eaten the meal before the bill came. That English Tea Room was right down the block. In desperation she searched every pocket, went through her jacket, even the hidden one in the lining she used for her emergency cash. And discovered it was there, the entire stash. She had a thousand dollars in fifties. Peeling one off, she gave it to the cashier. The price was three times what a steak dinner at Delmonico's cost. It was highway robbery but what did she care?

The cashier held the bill up to the light. "Joe, take a look at this."

One of the countermen came over and Amelia held her breath. What holdup now? Was she going to be charged with forgery? Was she going to be taken to jail, was that what this had been, a tease? First freedom, then sustenance snatched away?

"You sure you want to pay with this?" he asked Amelia.

"Why? What's wrong with it?"

"Look at the date."

"It's good," she insisted, though really she had no way of knowing that.

"It just might be worth more money, that's all."

"Take it," she said. She would have begged if it came to that.

He shrugged. The cashier made change. Amelia shoved it into her pants pocket and found a seat at the nearest table. She grabbed the knish and took a savage bite. Then another. The spinach and dough melded with the spiciness of the mustard. She moaned her gratitude. The top of the can of Coca Cola had an odd seam in it, a metal piece that pulled up to create an opening. Tilting the can back, she misjudged the angle. Soda fizzed up her nose. Coughing, she covered her face with the napkin. Glancing round instinctually, Amelia was relieved to find no one looking at her. She was anonymous. When was the last time that had happened? She couldn't even recall. She might be in Timbuktu. Someone would still accost her. "Miss Earhart, you are my idol." *I would be your starving idol, actually. Thank god no one cares to know me. Thank God or whatever is responsible for this, whatever this is, because you've left me in peace. If someone tried to interrupt me, they'd be taking their own lives in their hands,* she thought. *I might eat them. That's how hungry I am. I might gnaw an arm off.*

Smiling at the absurdity of it, she lifted the first half of the sandwich. How lovely, the disparate elements, tart versus tangy. Pink liquid seeped out and ran over the webbing in the palm of her hand. Amelia hummed blissfully. She was the happiest of barbarians. The pickle was sliced into quarters. Brine sang in her mouth. Even the celery in the potato salad was crisp. And for dessert, the strudel's crust proved light and flaky. There, she'd eaten every last bite.

Revived, Amelia turned her attention to the room. A young woman seated just to her right was staring. *So it begins,* she thought. Initially, after the Friendship flight, she'd been charmed by the devotion. Strangers wanted to touch her, reaching for her arm, even stroking her head like she was a good luck talisman. It was all so new, so exhilarating. They explained how they'd been at the parade in Boston or New York. "You changed my life," they told her. Over time, the pleasure faded. Her smile atrophied. She never complained. She knew she was lucky, so much luckier than most, it would sound like petulance if she did, it would be unseemly and unattractive and ungrateful of her. Yes, it was trying. No, fame wasn't something she'd courted but once it came, she wasn't about to give it up. Here was another stranger, about to intrude on her privacy. Amelia would submit. It was the bargain she'd made to get free.

What would it be this time, she wondered? "Would you write your name on this napkin? I'll treasure it always. Could you sign my arm? I won't ever wash." Amelia nodded to the young woman who took that as an invitation, stood, and came right over.

"I'm sorry about staring. I know it's rude," she said.

"That's quite all right."

"It's just that your jacket is so fucking amazing. It's got to be vintage, right? Can I ask where you bought it?"

"My jacket?" Amelia reflexively felt the worn out leather. "I purchased it in New York."

"I should have known. They don't sell anything that cool here in Boston. Was it expensive?"

Not if you consider what this meal cost. "Fifty dollars," Amelia said. She'd been embarrassed by the extravagance at the time.

"No way. That's incredible. Was it at Secondhand Rose? They have great stuff."

Amelia shook her head. It had been custom made for her at De Palma Tailoring. The workshop was on the third floor of a building in midtown Manhattan. She went on Saturdays when the streets were deserted. Every pair of trousers, every button down shirt, every jacket she wore had been lovingly stitched by hand. "Worth every penny," G.P. insisted. Vincente De Palma made all of his suits and after the Friendship landed and the accolades poured in, he brought her there. Now that they called her Lady Lindy, she had to look the part.

"Come on, Sally," the man at the other table said to her interrogator. Off she went.

Amelia set her tray on the rack and found the ladies room. She stared at herself in the mirror. Yes, that was definitely her slightly shopworn face, looking back. After wetting her hair, she tamed it, and then pressed her thumb against the glass. It left behind a whorled print. Amelia used the paper towels, tugged from a metal canister that screwed into the wall, to wash up. She tore each one along the striated edge. She dried her hands and discarded the debris in the trash receptacle. Taking another look in the mirror, she realized she was quite tanned. Her skin was creased, crow's feet tucked into the corners of her eyes. One did get older, didn't one? Smiling broadly, she saw the gap in her top two teeth. It was her mouth, all right. G.P. had advised her to narrow her smile and hide this glaring imperfection.

Your public wants.

Your public expects.

Your public requires.

What if in this dream world, her public no longer existed? Was that so bad?

But of course they did. After all, there was Muriel. Her speech. That odd shrine she'd constructed. Muriel would know her.

Her heart sank, seeing the truth. She would have to go back to Mudford.

THE CASHIER TOLD her the T station was in Copley Square. Amelia was positive she knew the way. Hadn't she strolled through these streets a hundred times? A block in, her confidence waned. Where there had surely been an empty lot, a private home now sprouted. A once great mansion was now a ten-story apartment house. And there was no corner grocery or livery. The styles the women wore distracted her. The skirts were cut incredibly short. A passerby let her coat flare open to expose her legs. Couples held hands or hooked arms. Some wore matching jackets with fur-fringed hoods. Women favored trousers over dresses or skirts. She was pleased with that trend.

At a red light, a city bus made a turn. It was huge, twice the size of the ones she used to ride to work at Denison House. There was no extra tire attached on the back in case of a blowout. Everything was incredibly different from what she recalled. Was it possible that her imagination was this fertile? She'd had trouble writing a decent poem.

The mind is a remarkably supple thing, she told herself. Still, there was the thrum of anxiety.

Amelia changed at North Station for the train to Medford. Once there, her memory served her better. She found her way. Here was her old house at 76 Brooks. In front, a plaque bore her name. The inscription read, "The famed flier lived here from 1925 until she left to make the first transatlantic flight by a woman on July 17,1928. Here she wrote the poem *Courage*."

She was almost to Muriel's. What would happen there? Would she be sucked inside by a tornado style vortex? The image of it happening stopped her in her tracks. And up in the sky, she watched a plane ascend. Its metal hull shimmered. "Courage is the price," she'd written. It was with the hubris of youth. Still, she wasn't about to turn tail and run. She'd come this far.

She'd see Muriel. Muriel would know her.

And then what?

But Amelia urged herself forward. Here was the block. Here, the brick faced walk. She rang the doorbell and heard the familiar, sonorous chimes. She imagined Muriel's progress, blinking like an owl, as she made her way down that dimly lit hall.

"Who's there?" the familiar voice inquired. Before she could find her tongue, the door extended to the length of the guard chain. Muriel peered out, dressed in that wretched paisley dressing gown. "Can I help you?"

"It's me," Amelia said.

Muriel frowned, looking her over. Then understanding dawned. "Why Nora Morris. Look at you, all grown up."

"Not Nora." I should have said my name, she thought. Muriel imagined me dead.

"You girls do change so much."

"I'm not actually a former student," Amelia tried because, now faced with an explanation, she found she didn't have one. Dead? Alive. Muriel eighty, she looking much like she did in those photographs of her plastered all over the study.

"No? Who then?" Muriel's lips pursed, a sign she was thinking it over. Then comprehension came. "You're one of those. Please, not today." As she tried to shut the door, Amelia reflexively stuck her foot inside, jamming it open.

"You people never give up," Muriel complained. "Why on earth do you think you need my blessing?"

"I don't need your blessing," she tried.

"But you want an opinion. Fine, here it is then." Muriel gave her a long look. "You bear some slight resemblance to her. But your nose is too long, your chin far too weak. Your hair is completely wrong. And the way you're dressed? Amelia was dapper. She knew how to present herself. You, on the other hand. . ."

"It might be hard to keep everything pressed," Amelia interrupted, "and cleaned if you've been flying halfway round the world."

"Is the play set in the cockpit, or rather, the monologue? You must be a monologist just like the rest. You all seem to imagine you've embodied her. There you go. I've done my part."

"You clearly know everything about her," Amelia said, piqued. It was hard not to be, considering Muriel's tone.

"Why else come here?"

"Why indeed." But she had to prove herself, especially now. "Resistless. It feels a little forced."

Muriel stiffened. "What did you just say?"

"Resistless, it feels a little forced," Amelia said, louder, stronger. "Wasn't that your critique to me when I asked you to listen to a certain piece of poetry? I was so proud. I'd worked so hard on it. 'No mean achievement' is how you began, because you had a feeling that it was best to leave me totally defenseless. I assumed that meant the response was going to be positive. You paused just long enough for me to get comfortable and let down my guard. Then you went for the jugular. *What did it mean, 'courage is the price?' The price of what, exactly?* You said you were doing me a favor, showing me the error of my ways. You pointed out if I wanted this to be for public consumption, the editors would be similarly merciless. You were only trying to prepare me as best you could for my inevitable disappointment when I submitted it to the magazines. 'You might make a decent writer someday.' Isn't that exactly what you said?"

Muriel paled. I've done it, Amelia thought. She knows me. Then she had a stab of conscience. Muriel was mourning. What was she thinking, confronting her like this? This was her sister! Amelia put out her hand and Muriel slapped it away.

"Don't you dare, don't try to touch me! Get away from here now. Go on. Get." Amelia reeled back, and the door slammed in her face.

She stood there, stunned. She thought Pidge would open up to say she'd seen her mistake. She had to. How could she do anything else?

The door didn't open. She went round to the living room window and peered inside. The room was empty. Muriel wasn't coming back. Amelia knocked on the glass. There was no response. She went back to the door and buzzed. From inside, a voice yelled, "I'm calling the police."

And have them do what, arrest me?

She rang again and stood there, waiting. Then she heard the wail of a siren. Muriel had actually done it. She'd turned her in.

Amelia hurried off.

Passing the plaque, she remembered her own excitement on the day she finished that first opus.

> *Courage is the price that life exacts for granting peace,*
> *The soul that knows it not, knows no release*
> *From little things:*
>
> *Knows not the livid loneliness of fear*
> *Nor mountain heights, where bitter joy can hear*
> *The sound of wings.*
>
> *How can life grant us boon of living, compensate*
> *For dull gray ugliness and pregnant hate*
> *Unless we dare*
>
> *The soul's dominion? Each time we make a choice we pay*
> *With courage to behold the resistless day*
> *And count it fair.*

She'd read it to Muriel. Her sister nodded as if to say, "good effort." Then launched in. When she was done, Amelia had no words left. Which was, Amelia thought, the point. Muriel wanted to be a writer herself. Muriel tried her hand at poetry. Muriel had even written that book sitting directly above her desk titled *Courage is the Price*. "I'm trying to help," she'd insisted when she saw Amelia was upset. "You always claim it's most important to tell the truth."

There were all kinds of truths, but you had to grow old to realize that. Young, you resisted the notion. You thought that your truth was clean and quick and sure and easy. That it wasn't a piece of all that whirred inside of you, petty jealousies and slights and your own ambition. You couldn't recognize me, Amelia thought. And I know why. You only see your version of me. You're as bad as the rest of them.

AMELIA FELL ASLEEP on the T. The conductor roused her. "North Station. Last stop." Outside, she used the public phone booth, finding the number for the YWCA at 140 Clarendon. A phone call was outrageously expensive, fifteen cents for three minutes. She punched in the numbers on the bas-relief squares and asked for a room. "We don't have rooms here," the woman said and gave her the hostel address at 40 Berkeley. The Orange Line went to Back Bay. A short while later, she paid the admission and then climbed the stairs to the room. She fell across a single bed, so exhausted she didn't care if she slept forever.

Amelia woke, drenched in sweat. She'd been transported back to the tropics. Opening her eyes, she expected the listless palm fronds. And found a web of cracks radiating out from a hole in the plaster ceiling. Next to her, the radiator pumped steam. There was a bed, a broken down dresser, and a window that looked out to the street. She stood, pulled up the sash, and inhaled. The air was cool. The snow had melted. Only stray patches were left like remembrances on car roofs and tree limbs. Passersby hurried along. Cars swished by. Everyone had somewhere to get to.

Everyone but her, she wasn't expected. Or wanted. Or needed. If a tree falls in a forest, she thought. I am that proverbial tree. My own sister doesn't know me.

Yet I pretend to know myself.

I must be mad.

Amelia took a hot shower, luxuriating underneath the stream of water. She used her fingers to comb the knots from her hair. Now she was at least a little presentable. Her stomach growled. Mealtime.

At the Bravo Diner she ordered the Number 3 special; two eggs over easy, a side of bacon, rye toast, and all the refills you could handle. All this was a mere ninety-nine cents. Compared to yesterday's meal, it was a bargain. The newspaper lay on the counter. She unfolded the first section and read the date, November 20th, 1980. In the context of her time spent at Muriel's, this was undoubtedly correct. In the context of everything else, it seemed absurd. Yet here she was.

Amelia's fingers slid under the seat. She felt the metal studs that kept the cover on. She spun round lazily, the way she used to at the Soda Stop in Des Moines. She and Muriel would spin faster and faster, till one got too dizzy and cried "uncle."

Above her head a clock ticked away the minutes, nine seventeen, nine eighteen, nine nineteen.

It had been six forty two when she and Fred lifted off from Lae on July 2, 1937. Now it was forty-three years later and she was seated in a coffee shop, half a world away.

Amelia lifted her hand from the paper and saw the black smudge left by the newsprint. Behind the far counter, the red haired, short order cook flipped and fried and scrambled. He joked with the waitress. "Midge, you're too much. You slay me."

Her heart expanded. She loved him. She loved Midge. She loved everyone in this coffee shop. They were her best, her dearest friends. The carrot topped cook was freckled and sly. He was surely Irish. The Irish were the backbone of Boston. He winked at Midge, who made a scornful face. Still, Amelia could tell she liked him.

She turned back to the newspaper. A Republican presidential candidate named Ronald Reagan promised that if he was elected, he would force every last "welfare bum" to find gainful employment. In local news, an eighteen-year old boy from Plymouth swore God had made him hack his father to death with a bread knife. The Boston Bruins, a local team, were hosting the Rangers, who they would surely obliterate. This writer held out high hopes for a winning season.

"Anything else I can get you?" Midge inquired.

Nothing she could think of, yet she wanted to linger. It was so perfect in here and so perfectly mundane. Their days unfolded the same way always. If she stayed put, maybe hers would, too.

Know thyself. That was Socrates advice. Father's as well.

THE MAIN LIBRARY was exactly as Amelia remembered, the exterior an imposing white brick façade topped with a red slate roof. The research room had Windsor chairs and long wooden desks. Light poured in through huge, arched windows. She carried the books to a front table. Her life seemed to have spawned a veritable cottage industry. Muriel's bookshelves had held only a part of the oeuvre. So many words expended on her, including Muriel's own *Courage is the Price*. Among the books, *The Search for Amelia Earhart; Last Flight; Winged Legend: The story of Amelia Earhart; Women of Courage: Profiles of five remarkable Americans; Soaring Wings: A Biography of Amelia Earhart; Amelia Earhart, First Lady of the Air; Amelia Earhart Lives*. She heaved a sigh, cracking the top one. The biography began with their parent's turbulent marriage. She'd been over this ground herself. But she'd treaded lightly, no need to pain Mother or embarrass Father. Enough that the four of them had had to live through the acrimony and messiness of a divorce; it was surely no one else's business. Apparently it was. The writer glibly described Father as a drunk, a ne'er do well, a disappointment to both his wife and in-laws. This author drew conclusions from what he termed "historical fact." Wasn't that phrase redundant? "Amelia Earhart was shaped by her Father's failures," he opined. Who was he, Dr. Freud? Amelia seethed, slapping it shut and shoving it aside. "Idiot!" she hissed.

"Sssh!" The man across the table set his finger to his lips.

This was a library, a bastion of contemplative thought.

Amelia nodded. "Sorry," she whispered.

She took a deep breath and opened the next book. In this one, the author took her mother apart. No longer a strong-willed woman who had bucked convention, first by marrying a man her parents disapproved of, then sticking with him. Gone, the Amy who raised her daughters to always think carefully about their choices and know that they were capable of being anyone and doing anything. That mother had sewn them bloomers instead of skirts, encouraged them to play sports and read the classics. That mother had ridden in planes and trains and as a passenger in Amelia's own car, racing up unpaved mountain roads high in the Rockies, the two of them shrieking together as they rounded hairpin turns. This version of Amy Otis Earhart was unrecognizable, a needy, clinging wreck of a woman. After her eldest daughter disappeared, she made her disappointment and anger into a public spectacle, complaining about her son in law, G.P. , and how he was cheating her out of her daughter's fortune.

"Please!"

The man glared, then stood, and took his work to a quieter corner. Amelia opened the next book. It was about her, or rather the writer's vision of her. "Amelia was in the right place at the right time." According to this idiot, she was G.P.'s pawn. She'd been putty in his hands. First as her promoter, then as her husband. "Her resemblance to Lindbergh sealed the deal. Putnam saw her and knew he could use her." This so called biographer combed through the details of the last flight from Lae to Howland. There were copious radio transmissions sent from the Itasca. Odd, since she'd never heard a word from them. She'd assumed she'd flown off course and was out of range. Yet they'd heard her, transmitting. The writer believed, "Earhart was not up to this sort of flight. She was not a skillful pilot." Thank you very much. Amelia checked the sources and wasn't surprised to find Elinor Smith's name. Her nemesis was finally getting her say, now that Amelia wasn't around to contradict her. Elinor had always been jealous, believing herself a better pilot and more worthy of attention. She was the main source for the book. No wonder the writer believed "the around the world flight was an elaborate and ill-conceived publicity stunt."

"Trash!" she exclaimed.

G.P.'s book *Last Flight* was next. It was the book she was supposed to write. She'd sent cables back from each port of call. He'd cobbled it together, after the fact. And done it in his maddening style, revising her copy and adding his unfortunate flourishes. Her writing was always clear and to the point. His was verbose, the prose style florid and overwrought. "Fate willed otherwise," G.P. told his readers. He painted a pretty picture. In it, Amelia predicted her demise. It was like a movie, perfectly imagined. According to him, she'd said, "It's a very big ocean, so much water." They were words she'd never uttered. She fully intended on coming back in one piece and taking advantage of the promise she'd extracted from him. "It just seems that I must try this flight. I've weighed it all carefully. With it behind me life will be fuller and richer. I can be content. Afterward it will be fun to grow old." Not with him. They'd had a different conversation in their own living room. February in California brought a cold, clean rain. She'd said her piece. She'd told him she was done, after this. Once gone, he'd managed to twist it round, appropriating her.

"Ugh."

G.P. who she'd married in 1931, was dead. The other biographies said as much. If it was true, then there was no point in trying to set the record straight with him. Anyhow, there was nothing that man liked better than an argument. He was such a force of nature. It was hard to imagine that the world went on without him. They'd had their differences, but she had loved him. It wasn't passionate, but it was real love. A lump in her throat, next, she'd tear up. Amelia took a deep breath. This wasn't the time for sentiment. There. She was calmer. She reached for the next book. *The Search for Amelia Earhart* would present factual information. There would be maps. Charts. An analysis of where they'd looked. And how they'd missed finding her. According to the newspapers Franklin had sent the entire Navy out.

Wrong. The book had nothing to do with the physical search. The author believed the Navy had been sent on a wild goose chase. The President was the one who was at fault. He'd sent her on a secret mission. She'd flown off course on purpose, spying on the Japanese, and gone down near Mili Atoll. There, she and Fred were captured by the army and summarily executed. The writer had testimony from the natives to that effect.

Except, she'd never been sent to scout out the Japanese Army. Franklin had never asked her to do anything like that. She, as a pacifist, would never have agreed. The theory was laughable. The writer claimed her remains were dug up after a Second World War, this a war where the Japanese were part of something called the *Axis*, fighting America and its allies. Her bones had been shipped back to Washington and were hidden away in a vault, presumably beside Judge Crater's own.

Amelia sighed. Why had she come here? What did she hope to discover? *Amelia Earhart Lives* was next. With trepidation, she cracked it open. This writer believed she'd been captured by the Japanese, but survived to turn traitor. She was someone infamous, a *Tokyo Rose*. Apparently this was a radio personality who chided Americans and the world in English for taking up arms against Japan. The writer was, of course, male. He'd gone to great lengths to provide documentation, including photographs of her after the war. She was apparently a woman named Irene Bolam who lived in New Jersey and unfortunately enjoyed a limited reputation as a flier. The man insisted Irene was Amelia. When a man claimed something was true, how could a woman dare to disagree with him?

It was absurd.

Muriel's book came next. *Courage is the Price.* Amelia steeled herself.

The dedication read, "To all who knew and loved Amelia and to all who want to know her, this book is offered gratefully in her memory."

That was actually quite sweet.

Muriel began with family history, the oft-told story of great grandmother seeing George Washington. She described how Father and Mother met and fell in love, how they married, producing their small family. On to Muriel and Amelia. Yes, the details were off. That rollercoaster in the backyard had been something they'd both wanted to build. They'd been complicit, gathering the lumber in secret. And the dialogue was original. She'd never said those words. But Muriel had captured the essentials. Plus, she was circumspect; more than that, kind. Especially when she described Amelia's own mistakes, like the time she talked their mother into investing the last of her savings into that disastrous mining operation. Muriel painted a picture of an Amelia who was brave, selfless, a good friend, someone who did her best to balance fame and family duties. She was busy; still, she never forgot them. Not even after all the record shattering flights and business deals, the fame, the fortune, the adventures, her teaching job at Purdue, her married life in Los Angeles. Muriel wrote that they'd always kept in touch.

Amelia winced. The truth was a little more complicated. Wasn't it always? Even yesterday Muriel had been doing her best to defend her, albeit from herself. This world was truly Dickensian. She had to wake up. Wake up and get back and fix everything. This couldn't be the ending.

Amelia rushed out of the library. What to do now? First things first, she'd go back to Medford. She'd ring that doorbell and confront Muriel and get her to believe in her. In who she really was. She'd tell her the truth. Muriel deserved that much.

Pulled roughly backwards, by unseen hands, Amelia turned and blinked and realized she'd walked straight out into traffic. Horns blared at her. A car had been inches away from running her down.

"Lady, are you trying to kill yourself?" the man asked.

She was about to agree and thank him when she saw his crooked smile. Recognized that and the stray lock of blond hair that always threatened to fall into his eyes. There, those eyes, sparkling with humor and good will. Winston Manning. Young again. Shifting the backpack onto his right shoulder, saying, "You're one lucky woman."

He walked away from her.

She'd let him leave once before.

How cruel she'd been. How purposely cold when he'd asked her why. She'd told herself it was necessary, that she was being brave for both of them.

Courage is the price.

It was a young girl's folly, that poem, a young girl's vision that courage was the currency used. What she'd done to Winston Manning hadn't been courageous, it had been purely expedient. Amelia had known it then. She knew it now.

"Wait," Amelia called out, rushing to catch up to him.

11

Sam
November 1980

"THANKSGIVING'S ONE OF those crazy American naming things, right? I mean, who's the one giving the thanks? The turkey? The Indians?" Kim threw this out to Sam as Sam polished the last line of Kim's term paper.

Fixing her awkward syntax was Sam's penance. She hadn't told her Bio teacher about the fleeing fruit flies; instead, she'd gone and cribbed the results and gotten an A for her trouble. Kim was her biggest competition for the Amelia Earhart award. Even if she hadn't cheated, Sam felt Kim deserved to win more than she did. As a boat person, Kim had had her own run-in with American benevolence. Her father was a Colonel in the South Vietnamese Army. When it became clear the North Vietnamese would breach the city, the Americans abandoned Saigon, leaving most of those who'd supported them to their fate. Her father had paid handsomely for passage on a boat across the South China Sea. Then the engines failed and they ran out of food. The crew decided it was time to throw the weakest overboard. Kim's father staged a successful revolt. He was the sole reason many of Kim's friends and neighbors in Flushing were alive today.

Kim Nguyen was a puritan. She didn't drink or get high. She liked things to be stable and controlled. Sam understood. Kim had been twelve years old on that boat. What she'd witnessed had been brutal and terrifying.

"The committee will like her story better," Lucy warned Sam. "They'll feel guilty and decide that they can make up for American imperialism by doing right by her. And you'll have been part of the reason. You shouldn't be helping her write those papers. To win you have to be merciless."

"It's fairer this way," Sam said.

"You doing her work for her is fair?"

Sam shrugged. She couldn't bear to tell Lucy what she'd done. Lucy admired her. Besides, if she didn't tell anyone, she could pretend it hadn't happened.

"Let someone else write the papers for her," Lucy insisted. "She might get a B."

"I don't write them, I edit them," Sam said.

"Oh Sam, don't kid a kidder."

Oddly, revising papers for Kim had turned out to be a lucrative business. Kim sent friends to Sam who paid handsomely for her services. Right now,

Sam was working on a musicology paper for Sascha, a Russian émigré. He had told her how his Russian passport was stamped with the word "Jew." There, he had had no opportunity to get ahead. "Here, it is all greatness," he said. Sam liked him, but even more she enjoyed revising what he'd written for his Music elective, on John Coltrane's *Giant Steps*. The paper reminded her of Michael. She'd slipped out with Lucy the next morning, leaving him wrapped in a blanket on the couch. Her note read, "Thanks, it was fun."

It was so unbelievably lame. Fun?

Since that night, Sam had had a recurring nightmare. In it, the junkie with the gun mowed them down in order. First Michael, then Lucy, then Sam. She woke drenched in sweat.

"What do you give thanks for?" Kim asked, interrupting her reverie.

Sam had an answer. Being alive. All three of them had made it through that night. She was grateful for that. Of course, Kim was grateful because she'd gotten through worse than an encounter with a strung out junkie. But she was referring to the holiday.

"I give thanks to the Indians for giving us the food that enabled my predecessors to survive, live long, and prosper, and infect those same Indians with diseases that ravaged them, slaughtering them, taking their country away. That's American generosity at its finest."

"Yes, the names Americans use. You know what they called it when they sprayed herbicides in Vietnam? Trail Dust."

Trail dust. A little dust kicked up by the horses. America ruled the earth and ruined much of it, yet Kim and Sascha still came here. They still bought into the myth of America as the one place on earth where everything was possible. They weren't wrong. It was that sort of place. You still could become anyone here. Though it helped immensely if you were white and upper middle class or better than that, rich.

Look at Amelia Earhart, though. She'd reinvented herself. She'd been an ordinary girl from the Midwest, a failure until she was almost thirty, a social worker in Boston with a hobby, flying planes. Then overnight, she was the most famous woman in the world. It was more than either she or Kim expected. All we hope for, Sam thought, is a career; this scholarship would obviously help us in the most basic way. Not having to pay back those loans, for example. It's simply a means to an end.

Kim was spending Thanksgiving Day in the library studying for her Bio and Chem midterms. Sam wished she could do the same but Brooke would have had a cow so she was going to Brooklyn, sucked back into the primeval swamp. The only good part was Lucy would be with her, riding shotgun.

BROOKE'S APARTMENT WAS on the third floor of a building a few blocks away from the Jay Street/Boro Hall subway stop. She opened the door and called out, "Mom, it's me." There was no response. The apartment was dark, the proverbial cupboard bare. Brooke's bedroom door was flung open, the room an unalloyed mess. Thankfully, no corpses were in evidence.

Sam backed out to find Lucy admiring the photographs on the hallway walls. She and Win had dubbed this, "the palace of Brooke." Young Brooke framed by her parents' clapboard summer house in Bar Harbor; teenage Brooke, languid and lean, snapped on the couch of the five bedroom apartment on Museum Row on Upper Fifth; and thespian Brooke as Juliet, Maria of *West Side Story* fame, and Auntie Mame. Brooke with her father Winston Armstead Manning II, who had been devilishly handsome, he of the sharp chin, blue eyes, and streaks of salt and pepper gray in his hair. He'd exuded confidence, that man. Brooke gazed adoringly at him in all the photos. But on it went, Brooke touring as Hedda Gabler, as Maggie in *A Cat on a Hot Tin Roof*, Brooke out in La La Land with her pals Dennis, Warren, Roman, and Mick.

"Your mom knows everyone," Lucy said.

"She claims to."

"I'm impressed," Lucy said.

"That's the point."

Lucy laughed. "You're too much."

Sam shrugged. It depressed her, being here. A pile of dirty dishes was stacked up in the kitchen sink. On the counter there was a loaf of rock hard Italian bread, an open jar of jam, and a melted stick of butter. Home life was just as she remembered. Sam squished a roach without blinking.

"We could leave. I can pretend I forgot what day it was."

"You're not being serious," Lucy said.

"Half serious."

"We can't do that."

"I know." But if only they could. If only she knew how to run, how to run fast and far. Amelia Earhart had done it, Sam thought. She'd had a mother, a sister, even an old boyfriend who'd wanted to marry her and turn her into a hausfrau. She'd gotten up the nerve and gotten into a plane, and look at what she'd become.

One flies away, the other doesn't.

She was the other, staying close, staying put, just in case.

The living room held the evidence of her mother's long lost loves, Larry's Afghani rug, two leather couches from Jean Paul's old loft apartment, and pentagonal paintings, courtesy of Ricardo, whose palette favored day-glo orange and neon green. Brooke's men all left tokens behind. Sam thought of it as a barter system: let me go, and you can keep this. But it was also possible that they just decided to run and didn't have time to gather their belongings.

Only one had left nothing tangible behind, no paintings, no furnishings, no books, no clothing. Dear old dad. Oh wait, he'd left his kids. They were two animate trophies.

Lucy dropped onto the couch. The remains of a joint lay in the ashtray in front of her. "Look at that," Lucy said.

Sam was glad she'd omitted the obligatory "cool." Sam's other friends loved Brooke. This apartment had been the hangout spot in high school. Everyone said they wished her life was theirs because her mom was such a blast. Brooke preferred rock to Bach. Brooke knew famous musicians. Shit, she'd even slept with some of them and snorted coke off their chests. And Brooke was willing to listen to their problems, Ms. Tea and Sympathy offering them her sage wisdom. Their parents were so rigid! They wished their moms were more like hers.

No, you really don't.

Sam never told them why. She let them fall in love with Brooke. Not Lucy too. Please, not Lucy, Sam thought. Couldn't she keep one friend, just for herself? She had tempted fate by bringing her here. Lucy wouldn't be able to withstand Brooke's seductive need. "Let's go," she said, grabbing Lucy's arm.

But, just then the front door swung open.

"We're home!" Brooke announced.

Win walked in behind her, carrying a bag of groceries. "Hello sis."

"I'm going to cook after all," Brooke sang out, making her way into the kitchen.

"God help us," Sam muttered.

Win winked at her. "How's college treating you, little sister?"

"Fine," Sam said.

"Fine for you too, beautiful?" Win asked Lucy.

"Yes," she told him.

"What's fine?" Brooke called from the kitchen.

"College is fine. Or so says Sam's friend."

"The name is Lucy Westcott."

"Sam's friend Miss Lucy," Win amended. He swept into the living room, pulled out the bag of weed he kept with him at all times, and rolled a perfect joint. He took out the lighter he'd stolen from grandfather's study. When their grandmother discovered it was missing, she'd gone ballistic, but Brooke never gave Win away. Grandfather had used it to light his after dinner cigar. Their grandfather had liked his whiskey neat. He'd worn a white fedora. He'd taken his drink on the porch overlooking Bar Harbor on summer nights. Sam's scant memories included sitting in his lap out there as he told her a story. "Once long ago in a land far, far away there was this girl named Samantha."

If he'd lived, everything would have been different. But he hadn't, and all they had left was the lighter with the two roses engraved on it, reminding her of that folk song where the roses grew up in the old churchyard till they could grow no higher.

Win inhaled and passed the joint to Sam.

"No, thanks," Sam said.

"You've given up?" Win asked.

"I'm taking a hiatus."

"College usually has the opposite effect," Win said.

"I'm just not in the mood right now," Sam told him.

"That's surprising. Why?"

"Leave her alone," Lucy said.

"Look, a protector. What have you been telling your friend about me, Sammy?"

"The truth," Lucy said calmly as she took the joint.

"How would you recognize the truth?"

"Sam doesn't lie to me."

"Wow, really?" He was looking at Sam now. "You two are that close? Soul sisters? I'm impressed."

Lucy stood and tugged on Sam to join her. They went into the kitchen, leaving him there, out in the cold.

"You girls came to help me?" Brooke asked. "That's sweet."

Expedient. Brooke didn't know how to boil an egg. The raw turkey sat on the counter, its poor plucked carcass weighing in at twenty-five pounds and seven full ounces.

"That won't be ready for hours," Sam said.

"We'll play charades. It'll be fun," Brooke said.

Sam sighed. Charades was Brooke's favorite game. She got to act out everything.

"I'm not really up for that," Sam said.

"Of course you are, darling."

Brooke's lone cookbook, the ironically titled *Joy of Cooking,* lay open.

"Can you read it to me?" Brooke asked. Her eyes were bloodshot. Win's pot was fueling this agitprop attempt at culinary mothering.

"You need a pan," Sam said, "One big enough to hold a turkey in. You don't have any."

"You really think I'm an idiot, don't you?" Brooke pulled a disposable aluminum-roasting pan out of the last shopping bag. "Let's try it out," she said, lifting the turkey and dropping it in. Miraculously, it was a perfect fit.

"You have to take it out of the plastic bag," Sam noted.

This would surely put an end to the farce. Brooke never responded favorably to raw meat. She wasn't vegetarian as much as utilitarian. If someone else had shot, flayed, and cooked her meal, she ate it. If Brooke was asked to prepare dinner, paroxysms of anxiety, then despair ensued. *That poor slab of meat had been a pig or a cow!* Easy to be squeamish when you were raised with a full-time cook who made bone sucking good fried chicken. Little Brooke had never had to dirty her hands doing real life chores. Big, disinherited Brooke chose to keep up the pretense of being royalty. She foisted the duties of feeding the family onto her children. In response, Win refused to learn how to scramble an egg. Sam cooked for the three of them. She was great at breakfast. Her pancakes were to die for and she could make a mean waffle. Anything dripping in maple syrup worked out just fine. For lunch, there was tuna salad or a PB and J. Dinner was beyond her but they lived in New York, so they could order out cheaply. Chinese, Pizza, Mexican, or Indian. Yet Brooke had gone and purchased this white mottled bird with blood pooling underneath it. Sam watched her mother reach out as if she were actually going to remove the plastic bag, then recoil.

Turning to Sam, she begged, "Darling, could you?"

"Could I do what? You bought it, Mom. You must have a plan."

"You're so good at everything. I'm sure you'll do a much better job than I ever could. You just have to follow a recipe."

Sam's heart sank. Here was the Faustian bargain she'd struck by getting onto the 1 train and heading south. Peking Duck seemed more appetizing by the minute. Brooke was right, though, better Sam did the cooking. Brooke would turn them into the family who spent turkey day at LICH in the emergency room, waiting to get their stomachs pumped.

Sam read the directions. You had to baste, butter, and rub the fowl with a variety of basic spices. None of the condiments necessary were in the shopping bags, cupboards, or fridge.

"Just preheat the oven to 375," Sam said to Brooke. "We'll get everything else. You can manage that, right?"

"I wish you wouldn't treat me like a baby," Brooke said, pouting.

How else can I treat you? But Sam said gently, "I'm going to need money."

"Right. Of course." Brooke handed her a five.

"There are a lot of things to buy still." Sam made sure her voice was scrubbed clean of emotion.

Another five. Sam waited. Finally, grudgingly, an additional ten emerged.

It was a gas oven. Sam told herself Brooke was capable of lighting it yet, as they trudged down the three flights of stairs, she had this horrible, sinking feeling. What if her mother turned on the gas and Win's siren song of incredibly potent Hawaiian pot tempted her? What if Brooke chose to continue what had obviously begun hours ago, and in mid puff remembered, headed back into the kitchen, struck a match, and blew them both to kingdom come?

"I'll just be a sec," Sam said, racing back. Win and Brooke were in the kitchen. Win was digging into a pint of Haagen Daz coffee ice cream while Brooke puffed away on her Gitane.

"That was more than enough money," Brooke said to her. "For god's sake, economize."

THEY CORRALLED THE last cart at Met Foods. "I don't even remember what we need," Sam admitted. "I should have made a list. I guess the whole thing was kind of unnerving."

"Don't worry. I can handle this. I've helped my mom cook Thanksgiving dinner a billion times." Lucy filled the cart with stuffing mix, eggs, milk, potatoes, butter, even a bag of real cranberries. "Do you think she has sugar?"

"Some of those free Domino packets."

"You get a box of sugar, I'll get everything else."

The baking section was stocked with dusty boxes of food coloring, mismatched sprinkles, and bricks of unsweetened chocolate. There was one box of sugar. She took it, went to look for Lucy, and found her three aisles away. At the other end, a tall, angularly beautiful woman gave Lucy the evil eye, then made sure her boyfriend was securely fastened.

There was one cashier open. The line snaked back to the other end of the store.

"Your brother's back in town," Lucy said.

"He must have run out of money."

"Maybe he missed you guys?"

"A thin wallet makes the heart grow fonder," Sam said.

"I wasn't too mean?"

"Never feel sorry for him," Sam warned. "He senses weakness, then pounces." She wasn't being completely fair. Win wasn't soulless; he was just an opportunist. "I love him. But he's unreliable."

"I know the type," Lucy said.

"I wish he could figure out how to make it on his own. That sounds like I'm his mother, right? Then again, I shouldn't talk. I live twenty minutes away from home. I barely left. I should be all the way across the country, though even then Brooke would still be stuck inside my head. I wonder if you can ever escape?"

"Just so you know, you're nothing like her," Lucy said.

Sam smiled, wanting to believe her. She so did.

As for Win, the problem was he broke hearts. Littered New York with them. There was that disaster with Charlotte, her best friend in eleventh grade. Poor Charlotte had ignored Sam's warnings and snuck off to Win's bedroom during one of their sleepovers. The next morning, her brother and her friend were giggling over Cheerios. Sam watched warily, knowing how it would end. Sure enough, a month later he dumped her. Charlotte was bereft and of course, blamed Sam.

Sam told herself Lucy was different. She had experience and better yet, she was on Sam's side. I give thanks for this Thanksgiving, Sam thought. Those corny posters with the woman standing in front of the crashing waves are true. This is the first day of the rest of my life.

Back at the apartment, the oven was pre-heating. The turkey waited, shrouded in plastic. Brooke and Win were bent over the living room table, snorting cocaine. Brooke removed the rolled up ten-dollar bill from her nostril, Brooke rubbed the residue into her gums and said, "Sorry, Win just had enough coke for the two of us."

What a shame, oh my, what a terrible pity. In the kitchen, Lucy was rinsing the naked, plucked bird. "Ready?" she asked.

Sam took one wing, Lucy the other. They wrestled the obstinate fowl into the aluminum pan. Lucy rubbed butter on the carcass, and then sprinkled it with salt, two packets of ground pepper, and a dash of poultry seasoning. Giggles wafted from the living room. Lucy raised a significant eyebrow as she opened the egg carton. "Can you get me a bowl? Your mom must have a bowl, right?"

Sam found several in varying heights and widths. "This one?"

"Perfect."

Lucy cracked the eggs and whisked. She added Pepperidge Farm stuffing mix and used her fingers, molding it like clay, before shoving it into the turkey's gutted maw.

"Done," Lucy said. She pulled down the oven door and in went the turkey. After kicking the door shut, she reached into her breast pocket and withdrew a pack of Lucky Strikes. "I can't believe you don't smoke."

Sam refrained from describing the ravages of lung cancer.

Donna Summer was calling to them from the living room. She was singing about those "bad, bad girls." Brooke pranced.

Win winked, holding the phone. "Yeah, here, yeah, come on over," he said into the receiver.

Lucy in tow, Sam made a beeline for her bedroom. Posters of her heroes and heroines hung on the walls, Joe Strummer, Patti Smith, and of course, Mr. Elvis Costello.

But Lucy had discovered her high school yearbooks.

"Don't!" Sam protested.

"But I must, I must," Lucy said, paging through junior year. "You look amazing."

She pushed the open page toward Sam to show her. Sam was seated on a bench in Central Park. That year her hair was short and spiky and she wore her leather biker's jacket, black jeans, and the Beatle boots she'd scored at Secondhand Rose. The caption read, *Too Cool For School.*

"You absolutely are, Dr. Barry. Yet here you are with little old me."

"What do you mean?"

"I am so far from cool."

"You're absolutely mistaken."

"I was a prom queen. Since when are we cool?"

"Since you're the most popular people in high school."

"Being popular is boring and completely different from being cool."

"I'll let you in on a secret. Even the coolest kid wishes she could be prom queen, just once."

"And those very same prom queens wish they were the cool kids. When you're cool, you're defiant. That's how I always wished I was."

"You aren't exactly a pushover," Sam said.

"You'd be surprised," Lucy admitted. "At least back home. My room gives it away. It's just like those curtains my mom brought with me, all pretty in pink. I always kept my mouth shut tight, what's the point of bringing things up? I mean no one really wants to know my opinion. But you, you don't care what other people think of you. You say your piece, regardless. And you certainly don't smile and nod and act like some idiot guy is the boss of you because that will make him comfortable."

"You aren't like that," Sam said firmly, thinking of how Lucy had turned those freshmen into dust at the West End.

Lucy opened her mouth, apparently ready to disagree.

Just then the door opened. "Sam, Mom is freaking," Win said.

Smoke filled the hallway. Sam ran to the oven and opened it. Flames spat out. She slammed the door shut and spun the dial to off.

In the living room, Brooke waited, hapless and helpless.

"I don't know what happened," Brooke said mournfully.

"There was probably something in the oven. When was the last time you cleaned it, Mom?" Or even looked inside to see if anything lived there. Sam shuddered at the thought of some poor rodent burned alive.

"Where there's smoke," Win quipped.

Sam opened the windows, clearing the air. She felt relief, realizing that now they could simply order Chinese and leave. Win was obviously planning on a party and Sam wanted to as far away as possible when that went down.

"The poor turkey," Brooke exclaimed, standing in the doorway watching. Her face crumpled and then she was sobbing. "I can't do anything right."

"Oh god," Sam said, turning to Win. Those who do not study history, Sam thought, as Win knelt down in front of her.

"Mom, please stop," Win tried. "It's no big deal."

He looked up at Sam. She met his gaze. They both knew exactly where this could go. Sam shuddered.

"It wasn't your fault," Sam pleaded. "We can fix it. You'll see."

"Really?" Brooke sounded pathetically hopeful.

They weren't having that turkey, though. The fire was smothered, but the charred bird was inedible. "I just wanted to make a nice dinner," Brooke said, from the safety of the doorway. A sad little hiccup escaped.

Two from column A, three from column B; roasted Duck with Hoisin sauce, Moo Shu pork, a little Chow Fun, and Five Spice chicken.

"I FELL IN love with this place when I looked out this window," Brooke explained.

"It's pretty spectacular," Lucy agreed.

There was a view of downtown Manhattan right out the dining room window. The twin towers, Nelson and David, ruled the island, shimmering. From here it seemed like a magical kingdom, a place where everything was possible.

Lucy deftly used her chopsticks to lift the red paper wrapper they came in and tossed it at Sam.

"You're talented," Win said.

"It's what got me into Barnard. They like us to be adept."

Brooke tittered. "What's your opinion of my alma mater?"

"I love it," Lucy said.

"All I get out of Sam is that it's fine," Brooke said. She shot a look Sam's way and Sam avoided it, using the wrapper Lucy had thrown at her as a foil. She rolled it into a tube, then shredded it into little pieces.

"Barnard's exceptional," Brooke said.

Lucy nodded, smiling gamely.

"I spent the most marvelous four years there," Brooke continued. "What are you thinking of majoring in, Lucy?"

"Philosophy," Lucy said.

"Win considered philosophy."

"I did?" Win said. "Where was I when this happened?"

"Don't joke about it," Brooke said.

"I'm my mother's longest running disappointment," Win said.

"There's nothing wrong with you," Brooke insisted. "You're experimenting, everyone does. You'll find yourself. It just takes time."

"A lifetime," Win quipped.

Brooke winced. "Not everyone is as directed as Sam. She always knew she was going to become a doctor. Remember that pigeon she brought home?"

"I remember you freaking out about it," Win said.

"She thought she could nurse it back to health. She's always been so sentimental, so humane. Even with that nasty, rabid bird."

"It wasn't rabid," Sam said. "It was a baby pigeon."

"The babies are carriers too," Brooke said. "But of course you're such a Good Samaritan. Has Sam told you how she volunteered at the local hospital and worked for Planned Parenthood last summer? She's just as good with science as with math. All her teachers were in awe. She could be the next Marie Curie."

"I think not," Sam said, drily.

"Can't a mother boast?"

"Veering closer to the truth would help." Sam speared a dumpling.

"I'm proud of both of my children," Brooke told Lucy.

"God knows what you're proud of me for," Win threw out.

"Stop it!" Brooke hissed.

There was an awkward silence.

Lucy broke in, saying, "I was looking at the photographs. You know everyone. It's so incredible."

Win caught Sam's eye.

"Did you always want to be an actress?" Lucy continued.

"It was the only thing I ever wanted."

"How did you get the courage? I hate being on stage and having people look at me."

"You hate having people look at you? I find that hard to believe," Brooke said.

"It's true." Sam knocked knees with Lucy under the table, a silent thank you.

"Really?" Brooke smiled. "In my case there were objections. My mother believed that acting was beneath me. Luckily, my father was always supportive. He told me that I should follow my heart. He was a dear man. An angel."

Win smiled at Sam. They knew the rest of the speech by heart.

"My father was a Broadway angel. By that, I mean an investor. He loved the theatre. He would bring me along as his guest because my mother was, well, let's just say she didn't care for any of it. She thought theatrical productions beneath her. My father and I went to all the openings and after parties. We'd stay up late, waiting for the reviews to come in. I used to bring my autograph book. They were so kind, all of them, all the greats . . . Mary, Ethel, Rex. They were so, so welcoming.

"I knew I wanted to perform. Even in grade school I loved getting up on stage. But my mother resisted. She had other ideas, the cotillion and all the rest and then a good marriage and children. She never understood me at all." Brooke stared out, into her own past. Sam imagined she saw the disapproval her grandmother freely expressed. Brooke could be doing something as trivial as showing off a new dress and Katherine would give her that withering look. Brooke shrank away from it, from her. Win called their grandmother "the old battle-axe." Yet in person, she was surprisingly prim and diminutive.

Brooke said, "There was no stopping me once I got my feet wet."

Win raised an eyebrow, mouthing the rest. *I took to it like a duck to water.*

"I took to it like a duck to water," Brooke continued. "The surprise was that I was even rewarded at all. It's not easy. But then again, what is? And I've made such good friends. They're like a second family."

Actually, *we're* your second family, Sam thought, as she exchanged another knowing look with Win. Brooke had abandoned them willingly, eagerly. They'd submitted to the worst babysitting on earth. Blasted out teens, lecherous boyfriends, come one, come all. It might have been different if their own father had stayed put, instead of running north, the twenty-two-year-old au pair in tow. It would definitely have been different if Grandfather had gone to see the doctor when he first started feeling ill, then the cancer would have been curable. It wasn't by the time it was finally diagnosed. That funeral was huge, with everyone who was anyone in New York society paying his or her respects. Afterwards, Win snuck into his study to steal the lighter, to tuck it away and have something to keep. *Once there was a girl named Samantha who lived in a house at the edge of a great dark forest.*

"Are you performing in anything now?" Lucy inquired.

"As it happens, I do have a project. A one woman show."

"That's so cool. What about?"

"You'll have to come and see," Brooke said. "You and Sam."

"Really? That would be so great."

Lucy was enthusiastic, nary a wrong note struck. *Great.* Sam rolled the adjective round on her tongue. It seemed so long ago, yet she'd once idolized this same mother.

The doorbell rang. Win jumped up to get it. Sam recognized the voice. It was Dusty, nee Alexander Preston McQueen, asking, "How long are you back for?"

"A while."

"How was Vegas?"

"Interesting. Like I told you on the phone, different."

"What about Boston?" Dusty asked.

"Cold. Icy."

Sam got the subtext. Win was always looking for love in all the wrong places. Undoubtedly there had been yet another girl, another misstep, another painful breakup.

"Sorry to hear it."

"It wasn't all bad." Some other girl was, as usual, waiting in the wings.

Time to make good their escape. Sam lifted the white boxes of half-finished Chinese food off the table and dumped them in the plastic bags tagged with the ubiquitous "I Love New York" slogan. In the kitchen, she washed their plates and Lucy dried. The bell rang again and again. Win's crowd poured in in a steady stream, all preppy Upper East Side party boys and girls.

"Hey, Sammy Pammy." Dusty set a six-pack down on the kitchen counter. "Allow me to introduce myself," he said to Lucy, extending a hand. "Dusty."

"To his friends," Sam said.

"We're all friends here, I trust."

"Exactly."

Dusty smiled at her, cocking his head ever so slightly. Sam had a soft spot for him. He'd been Win's best friend since the beginning of time or really just starting in kindergarten. He was six foot one with dirty blond hair, a square chin, blue eyes, and a muscular torso, courtesy of hours spent rowing crew.

Lucy shook his hand and smiled her winning smile. "Lucy Westcott."

"How do you two know each other?"

"Roommates," Sam said. "How's grad school?"

"Not bad. College?"

"Fine," she said.

"That's it?"

"Actually, it's pretty great," Sam admitted.

"That's more like it, Sam I am. I keep meaning to check up on you, but they keep us L 1's busy." He gave her shoulder a brotherly squeeze. He lifted one of the beers, popped open the top, and went off to join the fray.

"He seems nice," Lucy said.

"He is. He goes to Columbia Law."

"Really?" Lucy was clearly impressed.

A girl could do worse than Dusty, Sam thought. She believed Dusty's trajectory was pre-ordained. No matter how high Dusty got tonight, he would make his way through the world without a hitch. In ten years, she was positive he'd be up for a partnership at Simpson, Thatcher. If things went on the way they'd been going, he and Win would drift apart. At some point, Win would call him for legal advice and Dusty would throw up his hands, then tell his faithful secretary to say he was out of town on business.

Win could still be Dusty. He was just as intelligent. But, instead, he was the perennial fuck up.

Yet, he was beloved. That was a gift, she supposed. Win worked the crowd. Sam wished she could help him. If only she had enough money to give him so that he would go away for good and figure out how to actually be grown up, not that she was sure what that actually meant considering their very real examples. Plus, Sam knew in her heart of hearts, it wasn't about the money. Whatever he made, Win spent or gave away, then gave his heart to the wrong person, then came back to this place where the very air was poisonous to him. It was worse for him than for her, or at least she told herself that. Sam kept assuring Win that he was covered. He kept pretending not to hear her or understand what she meant. Or that she was sacrificing a lot to stay close and watch over Brooke for the two of them so he could make his way. Sam, frankly, resented it, resented him turning up like a bad penny. Or how he blew her worries about him off, saying, "I'm fine, just fine, Sammy Pammy."

"I've got to go," Sam said to Lucy.

"All right."

Lucy turned to head out, but Dusty stood in the doorway.

"You guys are sticking around, right?"

"I don't think so," Sam said.

"Hey, come on. Where are you rushing off to?"

Lucy gave her a pleading look.

"I guess we could hang out for a little while more," Sam allowed.

Twenty-seven people shoehorned into the living room. Six packs of Miller and Bud, a jug of cheap white wine, and a baggie full of pot were on the coffee table. When in Rome, Sam thought, duly smoking a bowl. It didn't dent her somber mood. Her brain was clear as a bell jar. The rest of the group got sodden and wasted. It was lonely, perched high above the fray. Win bent in Lucy's direction; indeed, Lucy was the fulcrum. All available males spun round her.

"It was like the desert opened up and grabbed onto me," Win said. "It's such a mystical place. Shit, you should go."

Lucy nodded, but she turned away and found Sam. "Dance with me?"

It was the last thing on earth Sam wanted to do in front of these preppies with their half fried brains and noblesse oblige attitude. Still, Lucy had made a personal request. Her friend took her hand and led her into the center of the room. The O'Jays were getting on the love train in their striped bell bottoms, their hair combed into perfect Afros. Lucy was a tidy dancer, no weaving, no shimmying, and no shaking.

"You're good," Lucy yelled over the music.

"Not really." Sam had exactly two signature moves. The first involved rocking from side to side. The second was more full body, clapping and twirling. Lucy grabbed Sam's hands and pulled her close, spun her away, then back, square dance style. And then Lucy gave her an ebullient kiss on the cheek. "Thanks so much for staying."

"It's no big deal."

"I have so much fun with you."

Sam blushed, her extremities warming. She'd stayed because Lucy was clearly interested in Dusty. Yet, Lucy was also making it clear how important

Sam was to her. Sam thought of what Lucy had said to her when she'd worried about Brooke and Win back at the store, "You're nothing like her." It wasn't completely true. All children were a little like their parents. Still, having Lucy buoy her and believe in her mattered so much. Sam swore she would not disappoint her friend.

Another record dropped. Sly and his stoned family were taking them higher. Brooke danced free form, smacking into everyone as she went, a one-woman wrecking crew. Sam tugged Lucy off to a corner of the room for privacy and safety's sake. They weren't alone for long. While Brooke bumped and ground away, a small crowd gathered round them; Dusty, Win, and an old friend of Win's, Larry. They zeroed in on Lucy. Sam thought that she'd gotten it all wrong to even compare her to Fitzgerald's Daisy, Lucy wasn't at all shallow or careless. She was the opposite of that in every possible way. Meanwhile, Debbie Harry demanded that everyone call. Sam pumped the air with her fist. Lucy did the same.

The tempo slowed and Mr. Sledge crooned, "When a man loves a woman, he can't keep his mind on himself."

"May I have this dance?" Dusty asked.

Lucy looked to Sam, asking permission. Sam nodded, smiling, and retired to the couch. Brooke plopped down beside her. Thankfully, Brooke was focusing her attention on a girl who stared dolefully at Win. It turned out she'd met him in Boston and her name was Marnie. She was an undergraduate at Boston University. She had no idea what she was going to do with her life but Win was so incredible, wasn't he? She'd given him a ride to New York. She was coming home to visit her parents. She said how special and fragile Win was, how he needed care and watering.

It was a recipe for disaster. Win would dump her. Those who loved him, he disdained; those who treated him like shit, he adored. But Sam couldn't warn the poor girl. She would just have to experience it for herself.

The slow dance ended. Win played DJ.

"When are you getting some new records?" he yelled at their mother. To prove his point, he set the Bee Gees on the turntable. It was Saturday Night. They were feverish. Lucy tried to keep up with Dusty's Travolta imitation. Win cut in. He was a far better dancer than Dusty but he'd lost out already. When the night fever ended, the record changed. Brooke took over as instructor; everybody was being schooled in the *hustle*.

Sam shut her eyes and wished for sleep. If only someone would transport her back to her dorm room.

"Hey."

Lucy slid in beside her. Dusty wedged himself next to Lucy. The three of them took up the couch. Sam watched Dusty's fingers wrap possessively round the curve of Lucy's knee.

Win appeared. "How about another go?" he said to Lucy.

"I'm tired."

"Really?" But Win grinned, acknowledging his defeat. "Dusty, my man." He made a faux military salute and backed away.

Sam got up and went to the bathroom. She lay down on the black and white diamond shaped tiles, cooling her overheated body. She thought about Dusty and Lucy. He was decent. He was fair. He would make a good boyfriend. And then she thought of Michael. Suddenly that night came back, complete with its miserable ending and her furtive escape. Why couldn't it have been different? Why couldn't it have been the way she had always imagined?

Fantasy, meet reality.

Sam doused her face with cold water. The music was so loud it shook the bathroom walls. Outside the door, Van Morrison was begging her to listen to the lion. She was the lion or rather, lioness. In the living room, Sam found Dusty dancing with Lucy. Lucy had propped her head on his shoulder, and her eyes were shut. What did she wish for, Sam wondered? But she guessed that it was much like her own wish, that same absurd fantasy. She hoped that Dusty would be the one, her one and only love. It was silly, unrealistic, and yet it was what you were told to aspire to.

Real love wasn't like that at all. Real love meant loving a real person, flaws and all.

Win was making out with Marnie. Sam admired the girl's outfit, a velvet mini skirt over white tights, go go boots, a ruffled shirt, and vest. The buttons on her shirt were half undone. His hand was inside, prospecting for gold.

Then she realized Brooke was gone. Her body stiffened. She told herself not to panic, but rushed down the hall to her mother's room. And found her face down on her bed, snoring softly.

Sam exhaled. All was well tonight in this microcosm of the great wide world.

She found refuge in her own bedroom. A pile of books sat on the floor. Digging through, she found her favorite children's story, *The Superlative Horse.*

Long, long ago in China, Duke Mu was the ruler of the Five Provinces. The Duke was elegant, accomplished, and admired. But, most of all, he was a horseman and in charge of selecting the Emperor's private stock. One day the Duke proclaimed that whoever brought him the *superlative* horse would become the head of the imperial stable. All the best horsemen in the kingdom chose their version of perfection; sleek black, white and brown stallions with flaring nostrils, pawed at the ground. Only one lowly boy looked elsewhere. His horse was from a country stable, used for nothing much, a dull-coated stallion with little grace and no apparent virtues. Yet, in the race to see which of these horses was really the best, the lowly country horse beat all the others, leaving them in its dust. That boy had seen what was below the surface and discovered the warrior's heart, beating true, underneath the matted coat.

Good looks were only that, no more. And the lesson worked in reverse. Look at Lucy whose beauty was just as blinding as the superlative horse's dun colored, matted coat. People didn't think to dig beneath her glittering surface. They thought they knew the real Lucy, but all they knew was who they thought she was. Sam was the only one who dug down to find the real Lucy.

She smiled, then set the book down on the floor next to her bed and clicked off the light.

In her dream, she and Lucy rode through Central Park. Sam was astride a bay, Lucy, a black. Lucy's horse leapt over a downed tree. Then it was Sam's turn. The ground dropped away and they were airborne. It was incredible. Free of the earth. Free of restraints. The horse touched ground. Sam leaned in close, her face against its neck as its hooves pounded. They were racing flat out through the woods, and into a meadow, high grass brushing against the horse's legs, against Sam's own.

"Sam!" Lucy yelled, and Sam looked up to find her friend lifting her arms, letting go of the reins. Lucy stayed tight to the back of her horse, her legs gripping. She truly was fearless. *My turn now,* Sam thought as she followed her friend's lead and let out a war whoop.

12

Muriel
November 1980

MURIEL SHOVED THE newspaper aside. They'd elected that terrible actor as president! You tried to explain to people what was in their own best interests, yet they were so impatient. Every four years they herded into voting booths like cattle, pressing the buttons on their way down the chute to the slaughterhouse. Ronald Reagan. She hadn't cared for his acting, not one little bit. And worse than that, he'd been a red-baiter.

"Amazing what we do to ourselves," Virgil said. He had snuck up on her again. "How did you like that book?"

Muriel had brought it back, intending to leave it here in the reading area. *The Transit of Venus.* Lovers who were fated never to be together, like Romeo and his Juliet. "I had to read it twice," she said. "I wasn't sure I got it right the first time."

"The prose is pretty dense."

Dense like a fog. You had to push your way through, feeling the edge of things. She set it aside on the table.

"I guess you didn't care for it."

"But I did," she told him. "I was just so shocked when I realized what happened. The man you barely recognize gets onto a plane that crashes with the hero Ted, after he and Caro have waited so long, after they're finally ready to start a life together. Then it's over. It seems so unfair."

"Yes, it does," Virgil agreed.

He took the other leather easy chair beside her. Didn't he have business to attend to? But he was settling in. This was apparently going to be one of those conversations he struck up with strangers every day. She'd overheard him; he seemed to relish talking to students, town gossips, and tourists. No matter who they were, he had a kind word.

He was, Albert had said once, a born salesman. Albert had never cared for him. They'd frequented the same circles without ever really socializing. Then Virgil's wife had died. Muriel brought over a casserole. He'd answered the door, and she'd just walked in and taken over. Cleaned for him. Cooked the casserole in the oven. She'd sat with him and watched television with him. She hadn't asked one question. They'd seen that detective program, *Hawaii Five O*, with McGarrett solving the crime, then she'd said good night and gone home. The next day she'd gone to the funeral with Albert.

Muriel couldn't remember what Virgil's wife's face had looked like. She remembered the way she'd dressed, lots of hammered metal jewelry hanging from her ears and round her neck. Virgil had gone right back to work and now here he was, still working. Work was his balm, she thought. He loved the customers, knew many intimately enough to ask about their mom, their dad, their kids. He knew the professors at Tufts and what classes they taught.

As for knowing her, they'd spoken mainly about books. But Muriel thought that sometimes, what happened in books seemed more real than real life. Virgil was thumbing through the one he'd loaned her.

"I had to read it again because I wanted it to be different," Muriel said.

Virgil nodded. "I felt the same way." He smiled. It was a genuine smile, full of commiseration and affection. "You know, I've been thinking about that gun you mentioned."

She froze. Why did I tell him, she wondered. "Yes," she said quietly, "That."

"Did you turn it in?"

"Of course," she said too quickly.

"Ah." Don't kid a kidder, she thought. He knew the lie.

"I will," she said.

"No time like the present." And just like that he stood up.

"You mean now?"

"We can go by and get it."

"Oh no," she said. "I don't want to bother you about it."

Virgil said firmly, "No bother at all."

She looked around. The store was crowded. He only had the one assistant. Surely he wasn't going to do this. Surely he wasn't going to insist.

"Bob, watch the register," Virgil said.

Muriel floated along after him, out the back of the store, past the dumpster where they threw the empty cardboard boxes that had the names of the publishers stamped on them. Virgil opened the passenger door of his car and held it for her. Muriel slid inside and he went round.

"Don't forget to buckle up," he said, his eyes twinkling.

"Funny man."

"I do my best."

Muriel clicked the metal fastener shut and set her handbag on her lap.

Virgil drove down the alley and out onto the main street. He jiggled the radio till he found a jazz station.

"I can't," she said, thickly.

"What?" Virgil asked, lowering the volume on the radio. "What can't you do?"

"I can't get rid of any of it."

He nodded. He knew.

"When did you finally do it?"

"After the funeral," Virgil told her. "I had her friends come and take what they wanted, then I put all the rest of her things into bags and gave them away. I'll tell you what's odd. A girl came into the store a few weeks later wearing Laura Lee's favorite sheath dress. It had this print of palm trees on it. The girl was maybe seventeen but it fit her perfectly. I took one look and started crying. She must have thought I was crazy. But you know, it makes you crazy, losing someone."

"Yes," she agreed.

"They were all *her* friends you see," Virgil said. "Me, I'm great at talking to people. But getting close to them, that's a whole lot harder. I let her do all that, all the socializing, all the planning. She was good at that. I was good at pretending to be everyone's best friend. But I only had one best friend, as it turned out." He pulled over to the side of the street. There was her house, staring at them.

She didn't want him to come inside. She couldn't bear it.

"They were the ones who planned everything for her. They figured out the service, the wake. You saw how it was. All of them getting up and talking about my Laura Lee. All of them telling stories, all that love. They missed her. They didn't see how they'd manage without her. They came through the house and it was all about them, Laura Lee and them. They would tell me they knew just how I felt but they didn't know a thing about it. Then you showed up. You weren't friends with her. You knew me from the store, I guess, from the church. I thought you'd do what the rest of the acquaintances did. Set the dish down in the kitchen and go. I had so many of those dishes in there. I wasn't eating. How could I eat? But you heated it up and you talked to me like I was a human being. You didn't talk about her or how I must feel. You cleaned up just enough to make me feel human. We watched TV together. That was what you did for me. You treated me like it was just another day and there would be another one after it."

"I didn't want to presume," Muriel said.

"Which was what I needed." Virgil had kept the engine running. It was cold outside and the windshield was fogging up.

"I'm not ready," she said.

"It's okay." He rubbed his hand against the glass on the side window, clearing a hole. "It's peaceful in here, isn't it? A little world all its own."

A world between worlds, Muriel thought, here in the car with the radio humming.

"I think you're the kind of person who looks out for everyone else," he said. "It's a gift, being like that. But then when you don't have anyone left but yourself to look out for, you might find you don't know how to look out for you."

"Albert kept telling me I had to get on with things."

Virgil nodded.

"You and Laura Lee never had children," she said.

"We tried. Then when it came down to it, she decided she didn't want to adopt. I don't pretend to know how she felt. It would be insulting." He touched her arm lightly. Then dropped his hand. "I'll be looking for you tomorrow."

"Now you're my keeper," she tried.

"You don't need a keeper," he said firmly.

She had serious doubts about that. Still, she said goodbye and walked inside her own, still house. Then back to the office. There, on the desk, her latest effort. Amelia hung overhead, her lips wreathed in that infuriatingly cryptic smile.

"Why don't you write the damn talk for me?" Muriel demanded, "Clean out the house, too, while you're about it." As if.

The dead were useless for grunt work.

She sat down, then swiveled in the desk chair, once, twice, a third time round. Her kids would spin each other in it. Back when. Back then.

"It's like flying," her son used to say.

Don't. Don't think about him. Don't let yourself sink like that.

Think about flying instead.

Yes, going up and up and up and away.

She'd lied in those interviews, said she never cared for air travel. Why not? For obvious reasons, her own sister had crashed and burned. Why tempt fate twice? They never pressed but there was a different story, a truer story. Once they'd gone up in a plane. What flight could ever match that one?

AFTER GRADUATION FROM Smith, Muriel had gone home, riding west on the train. The darkened stations looked like stage sets, empty platforms with unclaimed luggage stacked on carts. Dozing, she'd woken to the desert, cacti saluting with pitchfork arms. Their parents had reconciled and moved in together in Los Angeles. Amelia met her at Union Station. They drove up to the canyon, to the new house. But some things hadn't changed at all. Inside, you could cut the tension with a knife. It was a miserable place, with those two, miserable people whose reconciliation had foundered. By the time Muriel arrived, they were no longer speaking to each other.

She'd purposely found a teaching job that took an hour to get to, just to escape. It was peaceful on the bus, Muriel grading papers and going over her lesson plans. After work, she spent time with friends or co-workers or with Amelia and her lover Samuel Chapman. Ironic, how Amelia had met him. Samuel rented an upstairs room from their parents. So they were unaware of what was going on, literally, above their heads. But then, Muriel thought, their parents had always worn blinders. It was the only way to account for their decision to make one last attempt to save their clearly extinct marriage.

"Are you ready? Let's go." Amelia was always ready first, impatient for Muriel, who spent way too much time perfecting how she looked. Muriel had no steady boyfriend. She felt it was important to make a good first impression at the parties, or picnics, or dances. Muriel liked to catch someone's eye and flirt with him. But she purposely dressed down for the political meetings. Politically minded men were dull. Samuel Chapman was an exception to that rule. Dark. Handsome. Intense and intensely interesting, a chemical engineer by profession, born and bred back east in Marblehead. He was a staunch progressive. It fit in neatly with Amelia's world-view. Muriel agreed in theory, but she could have done without those interminable, testosterone heavy meetings. All the men seemed to want to be the top progressive dog. The few times Muriel got a word in edgewise, they rolled on, ignoring her contribution. She only kept going because the two of them were such enthusiasts. Amelia. Samuel. They believed that there was a better world coming. It was being young, Muriel thought, you had the heady notion that you were part of the vanguard of real, lasting change.

The long winter passed. Then came spring and with it, a riot of red and purple flowers, the hillsides suddenly verdant. The International Workers of the World called for a strike in support of the dockworkers, meaning to make a stand for a living wage with benefits. To the surprise of everyone, including the IWW, the strike caught on. By May, ninety ships full of cargo were stranded in Los Angeles harbor. There were daily protests in support. The police went wild, clubbing protesters indiscriminately and sticking them in outdoor holding cells in Griffith Park. A huge rally was organized, yet whenever anyone tried to leaflet, they were arrested. How best to get the word out?

"We could drop them from the sky," Amelia suggested at a meeting.

A woman spoke, thus no one listened.

"I said, we could drop them from the sky!" Her voice rang out, impossible to ignore.

"From the sky? Like a miracle?" a man mocked.

"No miracle necessary. I have a plane." She certainly did. It was lodged in a hanger just outside the Los Angeles city limits. Muriel had gone in on the purchase with Amelia. Their father had tried to warn her away from taking flying lessons, but she'd ignored his entreaties. Once airborne, she fell in love with it. And once Amelia set her mind to something, there was no standing in her way.

"You have a plane?" He was incredulous.

"Why would I suggest it otherwise?" Amelia demanded.

"And you intend to fly it?"

"Of course I intend to fly it. I fly every weekend. Why would I own a plane otherwise?"

It was delicious to watch the man's expression mutate as he tried to find something clever and demeaning to say. Instead, his mouth gaped open.

"That could work," Samuel noted into the ever-expanding silence.

So the three of them painted the fuselage red, it was homage to the IWW leadership who'd fled to Russia, or been deported. It was a small plane with room enough for two, Amelia would pilot as Samuel dropped the leaflets.

They worked on through the night, and then Samuel went to get their cargo, hot off the press. Coffee bubbled, the pot set on a fire built from dry sage. It was bitter, triple strong. As day broke, the landscape emerged showing distant mountains with snow frosting the peaks; closer in, arroyos cutting hard lines. To the east, the light pushed aside the inky blue, and the sun rose up, serene, queen of a cloudless sky.

Amelia had lit a cigarette. "Want one?" she'd asked.

"All right." They'd smoked in companionable silence. Stubbing hers out, Amelia looked squarely at Muriel. "I'm taking you up with me."

"No, Meely. Samuel wants to go."

"And I want you with me. Are you afraid?" Amelia was daring her; nothing new in that. Yes, she was afraid, who wouldn't be?

"He'll be disappointed," she'd said, playing for time.

"He'll live with that. It's my plane, my choice," Amelia insisted.

She gave in, who could ever resist? She climbed the ladder and sat in the passenger seat. Amelia reached round her to slam the metal door shut. The engine coughed, then sputtered. Muriel wished it would fail but of course it roared to outsized life. Amelia waved to Samuel. He backed away, shading his eyes as the dust kicked up. Then the plane rolled out of the hangar and onto the firmly packed desert floor.

Inside that noisy cockpit, Muriel shut her eyes and tried to find an oasis of calm. She opened her eyes and saw Amelia pulling back hard on the throttle. The plane bucked, resisting, clinging to earth. Muriel gripped the leather cushion on the seat with both hands. The plane's nose tipped up, the wheels followed, the body lifted whole off the ground.

They dipped.

They rose.

They dipped again, her stomach dropping out of her.

She wanted to scream. And found she couldn't. Someone had absconded with her voice. Her stomach lay on the cockpit floor. But then the terror passed. She noticed that there were white threads of clouds directly in front of her, adorning a blue backdrop. The plane cut a swathe right through to the other side.

"Look." Amelia pointed out of Muriel's side window and there, right beneath them was a patchwork of stray roads and canyons. Beyond that was the Pacific, stretching forever, bold breakers riding the shoreline and white curls frosting a cerulean blue.

"Isn't it incredible?"

It was indeed, the plane cruising over the mountains just north of Los Angeles. Beneath them canyons were covered with green foliage, lush from the spring rains. The engine thrummed. The mother ship rode steady. They flew in above the San Pedro Docks. Beyond them, Liberty Hill and the courthouse.

"Are you ready?" Amelia asked.

Muriel tugged the top of the box open. She took a handful and shoved back the passenger side window. The wind whipped hard, blowing her hair into her mouth. She spit it out as the plane dipped. The ants below turned human, lines of strikers picketing. She dropped what she held in her hand and dug for more. When that box was empty, she reached for the next while paper rained down on the city of angels.

Afterward, their mission accomplished, they circled back. "There's the old homestead," Amelia said, pointing at their parent's house.

Muriel spotted it, so tiny from above, the yard thick with apricot trees.

"Who do you think is torturing who now?" Amelia asked.

She said it gaily. Muriel saw why. Up here, you were so far away. Up here, none of it mattered; none of it touched you. Up here, you could finally breathe and be yourself.

Down below them, their parents continued the war of words and worse than that, pregnant silences. Amelia headed dead north above the cloud cover, white puffs of cotton sewn together to make a luxurious aerial carpet.

"I'm glad I brought you," she said.

"Me, too," Muriel agreed, and this time she was the one reaching over to put her hand, reassuringly on her sister's, lacing the fingers through.

"Red Plane Buzzes City" was the newspaper headline the next day. They had alerted everyone to the rally; leaflets had even fallen into the open air holding pens at Griffith Park. No one ever knew who'd done it. No one ever learned the truth.

Muriel had kept that secret all these years, held it close to her heart.

"OH," MURIEL SAID aloud. Once they'd thought their luck would hold. But luck gave out, inevitably.

One flew away, the other didn't.

"Courage is the price," Amelia had written. It was an oddly enigmatic line. They all said Amelia was brave because she'd risked her life. It was true. She was brave. She'd flown off over the Atlantic, then over the Pacific and finally disappeared over the rainbow. It was horrible, imagining how she'd died. But in the end, Muriel decided that Amelia might have had it easier. She hadn't lived long enough to have to endure being abandoned, again and again. How many days had Muriel punished herself, wondering why she was the one who kept on breathing? To go on, to find some reason to get through the day, that took a whole different kind of courage.

13

Amelia
November 1980

GRABBING ONTO HIS shoulder, Amelia felt a mixture of relief and chagrin. So this was it. This was why she'd come.

"You can't mean it," Winston Manning had insisted.

"I don't love you anymore," she'd said coldly.

She hadn't meant it then. She could tell him that now. If she did, would everything change? Was that why no one knew her here, because to be here meant to be anonymous, having given it all up?

The boy turned and Amelia saw her mistake. He was a stranger.

"No good deed goes unpunished?" he asked.

He was in his early twenties and had a thicker nose than her Winston, a higher forehead. "Well?" he asked.

"I wanted to thank you."

"Thank me? For that?" He craned his neck past her, looking into the oncoming traffic.

"Are you waiting for someone?" she asked.

"My ride."

He dug into his pocket and extracted a crumpled pack of cigarettes. After sticking one in his mouth, he pulled out a lighter and clicked it open. Gold. Delicate engraving on the side, showing roses, intertwined. She peered at it and knew it. His, her Winston's own. There were the initials, carved into the intricate floral display.

"Where did you get that?" she demanded.

"Get what?"

She stuck her hand into her own pocket, meaning to extract its twin. It was gone. Only the money was there. What a mad, mad world this was.

Hers had had an AE; his, WM. She'd bought his for him in a shop off of Bleecker in the West Village and had it engraved. Next time they saw each other, he'd produced its twin, giving it to her.

Now the boy slid it away as if she might try to steal it from him. He had used it to light his cigarette. Amelia recognized the sickly sweet odor of maryjane. Musicians swore by the stuff. Was he a musician? He had no instrument with him. A passing car braked to a stop directly in front of him.

He reached for the passenger side door.

"Wait!" Amelia tried to think of what to say to detain him.

The boy looked askance, as though he thought her some kind of lunatic. She was indeed a desperate lunatic.

"I don't know your name," she blurted out. "For the reward."

"Are you shitting me?" He shook his head, one foot already in the car. "Is this being filmed? Am I on *Candid Camera*?" He swung round, searching for something, dropping the illicit cigarette instinctually.

"I'll need to get in touch," she insisted.

"I don't live in Boston," he said, still searching the street.

"How can I contact you?"

He was clearly nervous. "Wow, you can't show this, you know. Not without a release. You have to have my permission."

"Whatever you need," she insisted.

"Will they let me restage it? Maybe they can cut the second part out. You can do that, right?"

"I can do anything you want," Amelia said.

"My mom would die if she saw me on TV." He paused, considering, then leaned into the car and requested something to write with and on. "This is pretty cool, I guess. I mean, where are they? I don't even see them. You people are good."

"We are," she agreed. "We're incredibly gifted."

"Gifted. That's a funny one."

Then he got into the slope backed orange car and drove away.

She looked down at the paper. He was Winston, but a Winston Barry, who resided at 11 Willow Street, Brooklyn, New York. That street was literally around the corner from the Hotel St. Georges. The lighter, the same first name, the way his looks had tricked her, they all had to be clues. This was a bread crumb trail, she thought, and if so, she'd have to follow it.

It struck her, then, that this corner was all too familiar. It was where she'd said goodbye to Winston Manning, thinking it was for the last time. Of course, the room at the Hotel St. Georges was where they'd improperly said hello again.

Yet, she was years removed from both those events. That is, if she were to believe the newspapers.

At the edge of her peripheral vision, a plane sliced through the clouds; Amelia knew exactly what to do.

IT WAS NO longer Boston Airport, but Logan. No more metal hangars or mowed fields, either. Amelia emerged from a public bus, followed the lead of the man in front of her and stilled her surprise when the unmanned glass door swung open in front of them. Inside, she found a hive packed with worker bees, all dedicated to flight. A black board ticked off the names of the airlines, arrivals on one side and departures on the other. You could fly from Boston to Milwaukee, Los Angeles, even Juneau.

And of course, New York. The next flight left in forty minutes. Amelia walked down a long hallway to Gate 15 and the Eastern Air Line shuttle. Out the windows, planes were docked at other bays. They were sleek, massive, and most had no propellers. Their engines were soldered under the wing. If this was an act of imagination, it was truly remarkable. In her mind she'd apparently invented an airship where the engine's thrust had to be great enough to achieve maximum acceleration without the use of propellers.

Then how, precisely, did it work?

Amelia walked by Continental, Northeast, and United Airlines to find Eastern. An advertisement touted it as *the largest airline in the free world*. Was the other half of the world enslaved? Her fellow passengers filled out slips of paper at stand up desks, pens tethered to them with metal chains. Amelia did her best to answer the questions as honestly as she could. Name. Address. Destination. They accepted payment in cash, by check or via a credit card. Credit card? She could credit her intelligence or her luck in having fifty-nine dollars in hand.

The covered walkway to the plane swayed underfoot. At the open cockpit door, a woman in uniform greeted them. "Welcome aboard the Eastern shuttle."

Amelia tried to see into the cockpit but her view was obscured by the pilot and co-pilot, who stood in the doorway, chatting.

"Just take any seat," the woman urged.

Halfway down the aisle, Amelia chose one next to the window. It was upholstered and quite comfortable. The right armrest hid an ashtray. As she looked out the window, a voice boomed from the loudspeaker. "Ladies and gentlemen, in a few minutes we will be closing the cabin door."

An Esso truck sat directly under the wing. A member of the ground crew unhooked the hose. It drove away, leaving behind iridescent puddles on the tarmac.

If only she could be in that cockpit during takeoff! Still, just to be inside a plane again was a treat. And to think, Winston had gotten her here.

Amelia thought back to the first time she'd met Winston. It was December 1927, at a Christmas party in Cambridge. She'd been engaged to Samuel and trying to figure out how to get out of it. Either Samuel had changed, or he'd let down his guard and shown his true self. He'd started off as a staunch supporter of all things progressive, including the Wobblies. But it turned out that he had very conservative ideas about the role of women, or rather, one woman in particular. His wife. They'd live in Medford, right near Muriel, Mother, and quite possibly Albert. No need for her to pursue a career, she'd be staying happy at home. They'd raise two point three children in their modest house. She would tie on an apron to cook him dinner every night.

"I can barely boil water," Amelia had pointed out.

"Don't be silly. Anyone can learn how to cook."

"I have no interest."

"When you're married you will."

He was in love with some other Amelia, the figment of his own parochial imagination.

"I don't have a motherly bone in my body," she'd said.

"That's not true, you're wonderful with children."

"I'm a social worker," she told him patiently. "That's part of my job, not my life."

"You'll feel differently when they're your own kids."

"I won't. Really I won't. I don't want children," she tried.

"You don't know what you want," Samuel had insisted. "Look at how you change your mind. You were going to go to medical school a few years ago, remember?"

Her inconstancy should have been ample warning. Instead, Samuel thought that her progressive ideas had been a phase. That she, like he, was ready to put away such childish things. This, the same man who'd preached revolution . . . the new Samuel was stable, reliable, the sort of rock you could tie to your ankle before you leapt into the ocean and drowned.

At that party, she stepped out of the packed living room to find some air. An open window led to the fire escape. She slipped through it and was greeted by the winter constellations laid out above her head.

"There's Orion," a voice said. Its owner sat below her on the fire escape ladder. He was remarkably handsome, the sort of man who would routinely turn heads, with an aquiline nose, a strong chin, a thatch of blond hair and stalwart blue eyes. There was mischief in them.

"I see it," she said.

"Canis Major and Minor."

"I recognize those as well."

"You've studied the stars," he said.

"Enough to know the basics."

"And well enough not to be taken in by a flirtatious remark from a man such as myself."

"Exactly."

"Still, on such a beautiful night, wouldn't it be lovely to take a stroll?"

His smile was a dare. And she was in the mood to accept. She'd ditch him at the corner and head back to Medford. She would tell Samuel she'd had a headache and hadn't wanted to ruin his fun.

Amelia dug her coat out of the pile in the bedroom and snuck downstairs. They walked through Harvard Yard and over to the Charles. She told herself there was nothing wrong with admiring the river or talking to him. It was a way to pass what had, up until that moment, been a dull evening.

His name was Winston Manning. He was a Ph.D. candidate in Economics at Harvard. She introduced herself in turn. She was Miss Amelia Earhart, a social worker at Denison House. He told her about his own ambitions and how they countered the ones his father held for him. His father believed he would fall to earth. "Not quite like Icarus did," Winston said. "Though it feels that way to me. I so dislike business, he so believes I'll come round to his view and run the company so he can retire."

"You're the only child?"

"I have two sisters."

"He should pick one of them."

"If only he would. Imagine? A woman sitting on the Stock Exchange."

"Your father sits on the Stock Exchange?" She admired him from a knowing distance. He was rich. She was barely making ends meet.

"You think I'm made of money now."

She touched his arm. "No. Just the usual flesh and bone."

He took that as an invitation and tried to kiss her. She pulled away from him, but didn't slap his face.

"I'm engaged to be married," she said, primly.

"Yet here you are with me."

"Yes."

"Do you love him?"

"I thought I did," she said. God, she'd told a perfect stranger the truth.

"Ah, so I'm to be your way out."

This time when he tried to kiss her, she let him. What was unexpected was how pleasurable it was. What was even more surprising was how she let him continue the kiss, cupping her chin under his hand, tipping her face to his.

"I think I should go," she said eventually.

But she didn't mean it. There was no point in denying the animal attraction. It was impulsive, impractical, but that was how she lived. She flew into bad weather, knowing the forecast. She took all the precautions she could, then got into the cockpit and the engine turned over and she soared up. Amelia accepted the risks. That was what it was like that night, too.

THE LOUDSPEAKER CRACKLED again. A man's voice this time. "Good afternoon, ladies and gentleman. I'm Captain Laurence Miles. I want to welcome you to Eastern Flight 219. We are bound for our final destination, LaGuardia airport in New York City. Once aloft, our flying time should be approximately forty-seven minutes. Now, I'm going to turn you back over to our excellent cabin crew."

Forty-seven minutes. It had taken half a day to make the same flight with a tail wind. How was it possible? The woman in the tailored uniform stood at the front and asked that passengers remove the safety card from their seat pockets. Amelia watched the man across the aisle pull something from the netting by his knees. She did the same. This was a Boeing 727 jetliner. What was a jetliner, exactly?

The plane lurched. They were leaving the gate. Up at the front, another woman was assisting the first, demonstrating how to strap on the oxygen mask that would apparently fall from the ceiling unit above them if cabin pressure dropped. She wore a flat orange vest.

If the flight went badly, none of it would matter. But let them pretend, Amelia thought. Let them coddle the passengers into believing there would be a way to save themselves. She and Fred had been lucky and skilled. Even then they'd only had seconds to get out before the plane sank, taking everything that could have helped them survive with it. If only there had been wreckage spread across the water, it would have been something to pinpoint their location. Then everything might have been different. The ships would have known where to look. That is, if you believed the books she'd read, if you believed that any of it happened the way they said it did.

And if it had, what was she doing here?

They were third in line for takeoff. Ahead of them a plane raced down the runway, its nose lifted, its body followed, it melded seamlessly with the air.

"I HAVE ANOTHER hobby," Amelia had said to Winston Manning later that night.

"Not just astronomy?"

She'd been lying next to him in the double bed. They'd registered under assumed names at a less than upright establishment on the outskirts of Cambridge, Mass.

"Let me guess. You must be artistic. Do you paint? Or is it watercolors?"

"I do write poetry," she admitted. "But I'm not very good. And that's not what I meant. I'm a pilot."

"You're joking." But he saw that she wasn't. "I've fallen in love with an aviatrix."

"You're not in love with me. You barely know me."

"I'm making you nervous."

"It's a stupid thing to say, that's all," she told him. "Bandying about that word, love."

"Is this about your fiancé?" he asked. "Because he's nothing compared to me."

"Please. Don't."

"Don't what? I am in love with you. But don't panic. I don't expect a thing in return. Funny, isn't it? Usually it's the man who thinks of an escape clause. I promise you, you won't need one for me."

"Why's that?" she asked, playing along a little.

"I love you just as you are."

"Again, you don't even know me." She was up on one elbow, staring at him.

"I do, and not just in the carnal sense. I know you better than you know yourself."

There was something impressive in his insistence. And something insane. She didn't believe he could know her. Not who she was inside. Not any of that. Yet he was oddly beguiling. In truth, his smile was a wonderfully, crinkly, curious thing. Amelia suddenly ached to reach out and smooth down the rough edges. She was Mrs. Jones that night, the desk clerk giving them a knowing look. They had no bags. They arrived in the clothing they'd worn to the party. What if this man was not just one in a hundred, or one in a thousand, but *the* one, she thought? Oh, that was absurd, impossible. There was no such thing. That was a romantic fantasy out of the Austen novels Muriel preferred to read. Amelia told herself that, when morning came, she would write a note and give him nothing to go on. She would leave and never see him again. She would use him as an excuse to break things off with Samuel. That was all this was, that was all this could ever be.

She meant to do it. Meant to leave surreptitiously, and leave him in her dust. But it turned out that breaking it off with Samuel was the easy part.

Winston Manning woke the next morning when she did. He insisted on accompanying her almost all the way home. He kissed her repeatedly in public view. She didn't just let him. She wanted him to. In fact, she'd never felt so hungry for a man's touch, never known what it could make you feel-between night and morning an entire universe carved out, with him at its core.

Winston Manning made love to her with such confidence, such passion. During the day when she remembered, she'd gasp aloud. The way he encircled her breast with his fingers, and then slowly moved his hand down, caressing her stomach, laying the palm flat, his fingers splaying out across her hip and toying with her, resting on the jutting bone, the osa coxae, waiting her out so that she was the one to direct him, to push his hand to the v between her thighs, to moan.

Time stopped ticking away when they were together. Hours later, he'd turn to her and say, "Well?" It was a one-word question that called up a host of answers. It turned out Winston Manning had been right after all. He did know who she was.

"You should take me up in that plane."

"I should," she agreed.

Amelia hadn't been to the airfield in weeks. She'd lied to everyone, telling Muriel and Mother she was off on an overnight flight, telling the boys at the field she had too much work to do at Denison House. She was adept at making brilliant excuses; espionage would actually have suited her if her goal had been to protect this. It turned out if you told someone something with total conviction, they thought they were hearing the truth.

On weekends, the two of them drove away from Boston to smaller towns. She slid the gold ring on the ring finger of her left hand. They became newlyweds. Still, she insisted on paying her way with him, half the meal and half the spare accommodations.

"As you want."

"You're humoring me," she said.

"I'm saving money."

That made her laugh. "You?"

"Why not? Don't try to make this something where you've bested me."

Put like that, she saw her own trick. How had he known before she'd even guessed? Love with Samuel had seemed passionate, but it was a desert by comparison. That love was dependable, solid, a reaction to the endless acrimony that had been the meat of her parents' miserable marriage. When she'd ended their engagement, Samuel had been so surprised.

"Have you met someone else?" Samuel asked.

She told him, "No." Not the absolute truth. But then, she would have broken it off with him, either way. She knew that much.

Of course, she had met someone else. And with him, she could truly be herself. Gone was any attachment to convention, however meager. They painted the ceiling of whatever place they'd come to for the night with their dreams and aspirations. Winston wanted nothing more than to travel the world. Why couldn't they do it together? They would trek across Mongolia, home of the hordes. They would stand on the shore of Lake Victoria, watching the wildebeests throng.

His father thought his graduate degree impractical. His view was that the only thing that mattered at all in this world was making money. Winston would have to understand the nuts and bolts of their own business; his education was a frill, an intellectual pursuit, something you could do if you were born useless; an aristocratic notion. The Manning fortune was built on iron ore, and then steel, but it truly came of age during the First World War when Winston Manning Senior, his father, decided to retool and go into munitions. "The man believes it is the patriotic duty of every American to help this country kill with the greatest of ease," Winston explained. "Blood money," as he termed it, had made them richer than Croesus. It kept them rich right through the Great Depression. His father didn't believe in something as ephemeral as a stock market. He thought anyone who did a fool. He thought Winston a fool, too.

"You've given me nerve," Winston said to her. He would tell his father to go to hell. "Wait till he finds out I'm in love with a pacifist."

Wait. They could wait forever. Their love would never end. Although deep down, Amelia knew it had to. She was afraid of meeting this father, this wolf of a man in his drawing room in that mansion on Upper Fifth. She, who was never intimidated by much, was intimidated by this, worrying that it would go wrong. That Winston would be disappointed. That she would fail him in some way.

In February, Winston said, "We'll stay in Boston."

"Here?"

"Absolutely. Normally I'd say we should get married, but I know you'd be angry. We can do whatever you want. We can live together or marry. Your choice."

"This is how you propose to me?" She laughed carelessly, but inside everything was whirring round. It came to her that she wanted two things at once; both for him to get down on one knee and offer a ring, and for him to laugh, denying the seriousness of what he'd just said.

"I don't want to trap you," he said firmly. "I want a partner, not a slave."

"Then you think marriage equals slavery."

"I think you think that it can be. Though I don't think it would be with me."

"You give yourself a great deal of credit."

He smiled at her "I give you a choice."

Happy. She had never been happier in her entire life. "I choose you."

THE ENGINES ROARED. Her fellow passengers seemed decidedly unimpressed. Many had shut their eyes, feigning sleep. Their calmness was an affront. Her body coiled as it always did on takeoff. Up in the cockpit, the captain would be ticking off the list one last time with his hand resting on the throttle, and then he would pull it back. This plane was a thoroughbred. Urged forward it gathered momentum and here, here it came, the metal body lifting powerfully and that perfect moment when gravity was defied and the earth fell away.

They were aloft.

A remarkable ship; no lurching or stomach curdling drops as it rose to cruising altitude, only mild dips, then responding slight adjustments. No wonder it was possible to ignore all of it, to doze, read a newspaper, open a briefcase. The engines on this *jetliner* were evidently powerful. Amelia had an urge to climb back over the hull of the ship when it landed and examine one close up. Better yet, she would shadow a mechanic as they took it apart, then lift a wrench, slip on coveralls, and put it back together herself.

One of the uniformed women announced, "Ladies and gentlemen, we have reached our cruising altitude and the captain has turned off the seat belt sign. You are free to move about the cabin."

The result was immediate. Passengers unbuckled themselves. They rose and lined up for the toilets. The uniformed women came round with offers of pillows, blankets, and reading material. Amelia chose *Life* and *Time* and set them next to her on the empty seat. She made her way to the flight deck and found the cockpit door ajar. Inside the captain and co-pilot were working, surrounded by instrument panels.

"Can I help you?" It was the woman who had greeted her at the door, Amelia read her name on the tag, "Tammy."

"I was wondering if there was a way to get a tour of the cockpit?"

"I'll see if I can get you inside when we land." Tammy pulled the curtains shut against inquiring eyes. "Where are you sitting? Okay. Now don't y'all worry, I won't forget." She beamed a smile that said the conversation was officially over.

From her seat, Amelia spotted a clearing in the cumulus clouds. Below the plane, snow covered fields and houses. They flew at a much higher altitude than she was used to; everything down below looked model sized.

"Can you put your tray down, please?" Tammy requested. Amelia saw the man across the aisle flipping a small lever. She did the same and down it fell to her lap. "Here you go, darling." The food was packaged separately; a hard roll, a tin of cling peaches, and a main course. "It's Salisbury Steak," Tammy told Amelia. They'd had the same dish at the Horn and Hardart Automat; more expensive than chicken, it was a treat you could only afford once in a blue moon.

"Tea, coffee, soda?"

Amelia chose coffee. It was served in a cup shaped container made of some odd, water- tight material. The fork and knife were also unfamiliar, not metal, perhaps a type of polyethylene? She began with the steak, trying to cut it using the knife. But the meat resisted. Fine. She lifted the entire piece to her mouth, using her teeth inelegantly, and then tried the bread. Dollops of cold butter quivered atop the soft filling. It was doughy and tasteless, but she was hungry. *Down the gullet* was another of Grandmother Otis' favorite expressions. Amelia sipped on the coffee. It was watery, truly puerile. Still, she finished it and requested a refill. Then came dessert, the slices of fruit both sugary and cloying. But it was the same as eating a meal after a long hike up a mountain. The quality of the food was beside the point.

Across from her, Tammy was talking with the male passenger.

"How was it last night?" he asked.

"Not bad."

The man had loosened his tie. His cheeks were florid, his nose bulbous and veined. He nursed a whisky. "You find trouble, I know you girls."

"Oh, no we don't. We're good."

"What fun is being good? You should have come over to my place."

"Now, Frank, you know I couldn't. Why, I'm a married woman."

"I'm a married man."

This was the same. The men in the cockpit, the women caring for the passengers, la plus ca change. If this world was her own invention, why hadn't she put women in the driver's seat? Why hadn't she reversed the roles and made men refill the coffee cups and give out the blankets?

Even my imagination fails when it comes to imagining that, she decided. Because this must be a dream, if it's not, what is it?

Trying to figure that out made her head hurt. She looked out the window and saw below an endless triangulation of roads and bridges with cars rushing headlong across them. They were approaching the outskirts of the city. New York City, the place where things had begun for her, first at Columbia and then again years later, on May the tenth, in the year of our lord one thousand nine hundred and twenty eight.

There was a plan afoot, a group spearheaded by Amy Guest who had bought a plane, assuming she'd be the one to go in it. Her family had other ideas, so they were searching for another woman pilot to send across the Atlantic. When Amelia got the phone call, she assumed it was a bad joke. It was a phenomenal idea, proof that women could do exactly what men could. Then, it turned out they were dead serious. She was invited to New York. She would have to meet with the promoter G.P. Putnam. She knew who he was, knew that he was Lindbergh's publicist and publisher.

That man, Putnam, made her cool her heels for over an hour. By the time she was let inside, she was more than a little annoyed. Did he think he was the pope? "You're Miss Earhart?" Then he proceeded to lecture her about who he was and how he'd made Lindbergh, *Lindbergh*. Charlie this, and Charlie that, and how Charlie could write his own ticket, all because of G.P. Putnam. If you believed him, you'd have believed that the world famous pilot had done nothing but sit there, while Putnam worked the controls.

Finally, she couldn't bear it. "Do you ever stop talking about yourself?" she'd demanded.

"About myself? How do you mean?"

"Don't you want to know something about me?"

"You're an amateur flyer. Not that it matters. You won't be doing any flying. I'm sure the others have explained that you'll be sitting on a crate in the back of the plane."

"What did I come down to New York for then? You could have said all this over the phone."

"I wanted to look at you," Putnam said. "Now I have."

And that was all. She was being dismissed. Amelia got up, steaming, but he wasn't done with her. Not quite. "You're not entangled with anyone, are you? You're not engaged?"

"How on earth is that your business?"

"Because you have a better than even chance of dying on this flight. If I do decide on you, I don't want to hear that someone has talked you out of making the trip. There's a great deal of expense involved, and a lot of publicity. I don't want to waste my time. "

"Why would I have come all the way down here if I wasn't willing to go?" she demanded.

"Women are such changeable creatures."

"And men are such idiots."

He'd laughed. But Amelia didn't. She'd hated him. She strode out of the office, muttering under her breath. He caught up to her, took her in a cab to the station. The whole trip there, they barely spoke a word to each other. She was stewing. It had been a fool's errand. Why on earth had she come? It was just a publicity stunt. The man was impossible, cynical, overbearing, puffed up with self-importance. The nerve of him, saying that he'd made Lindbergh! As if! Telling her that he wanted to look her over. She wasn't a prize Guernsey. He probably expected her to knit a sweater in the back of the plane while they ferried her across the Atlantic. Then he'd sell it at auction.

On the way down from Boston, she'd been beside herself with excitement. The importance of all of it! It hardly seemed real, but still she fantasized. A woman making this flight would make history. Then, the meeting was delayed. And the man was impossible. But as the train wended its way north again, her bad temper dissipated. Can't see the forest for the trees? That was what came to mind. Putnam had irritated her, then enraged her, and that had made her forget what she wanted most. Oh. She so regretted losing her temper. Why couldn't Amelia have just let him talk? Men loved to talk, loved hearing the sound of their own voices. She'd blown her chance, why was she always so damn impulsive?

THE PLANE DIPPED. There was the emerald city.

"Ladies and gentlemen, the captain has put on the no smoking sign. We ask that you fasten your seat belts. Make sure your tray tables are put away and that your seat backs are in the upright position as we make our final approach to La Guardia."

The engines revved. The plane dropped over the water and the landing gear whined. Amelia heard the click and felt the familiar tug as the wheels locked into place. They flew low to the ground, sweeping close to the automobile traffic. Then they were over the runway and the plane landed with a bump. The brakes were applied, hard. Her body tilted forward. They slowed, taxiing into the terminal and coming to a stop.

"On behalf of Captain Miles and our entire flight crew we want to thank you for flying Eastern Air Lines."

People rose, eager to disembark. As she got to the front, Tammy caught her arm. "You thought I forgot, didn't you?" Tammy was as good as her word. Amelia was escorted inside the small cockpit. She tried to spot something familiar. There were the control yokes and the throttle quadrant, the landing gear selector, the airspeed and pitch trim indicators, and right between the captain and copilot's seats an array of engine monitoring gauges.

"It's incredibly complicated. Way too much for poor little me," Tammy said.

"I doubt that," Amelia told her.

Tammy laughed. "Aren't you nice."

Not really, Amelia thought. Nice isn't an adjective anyone has ever used to describe me. But Tammy was done, ushering her out.

La Guardia airport looked like Logan, with its newspaper kiosks, snack bars, and a line of yellow taxis waiting for fares.

"Where to?" the driver asked.

Across the river and through the woods . . . swept back, even as she was hurtling forward.

"The Hotel St. Georges."

The driver gave her a quizzical look. "Ten dollars extra to go to Brooklyn."

Amelia knew a lie when she heard one. She looked through the partition that separated them. Was it for his protection or her own? His license had a photograph and a number of who to contact if you had a complaint about service. "Mr. Abner Rice, is it? I can call and verify the charge."

"The charge for what?"

"That it's standard to pay ten dollars extra to go to Brooklyn."

"Go ahead, lady. Feel free."

"I'll just jot down your number."

"No one's taking you to Brooklyn without paying more," he said.

She saw a uniformed policeman directing traffic.

"Perhaps I'll just speak to him," she said, pointing. "I'll tell him you're committing highway robbery."

He grunted. "Jesus, lady, bust a guy's balls, why don't you? Everyone knows you can't get a fare back from Brooklyn. Why pick my cab? I have all the luck."

But the taxi pulled out.

Luck was not the right word for it. Some things just happened. Take this cab. It had been first in line. She'd gotten in. There. Done. Was it luck that she'd offered resistance to being overcharged? She couldn't have been the first. She would hardly be the last. Yes, he had to make a living but she also deserved fair treatment. Everything in life was a negotiation, Amelia thought. This was only a skirmish in what was the larger war. Each battle, won or lost, was a way to move forward towards your goal, that table where the treaties were signed and sealed and peace finally declared.

Yet that was the truest misconception. There was never an ending to it, never real peace found until you drew your final breath. Life was about the war, not about the peace. What the driver didn't know was that she would feel guilty and over-tip him to compensate for standing her ground. The scales tipped one way, then back again. The numbers on the meter flipped over. They merged with the steady stream of Manhattan bound traffic. There was the island, packed with majestic buildings, brimming with electric light. Her driver paid the toll. They rode across a Tri-borough bridge. She knew of no bridge connecting Queens to Manhattan, yet the evidence was under their wheels, the roadway clacking.

G.P. had chosen her after all. "I knew you were perfect," he said after her photograph was front page on every newspaper in the world.

"You couldn't have," she insisted.

"Of course I could have. I'm prescient."

G.P. Putnam was the sort of man who never imagined himself wrong about anything. He told her he had picked her because she looked so much like Lindbergh. He knew that if he styled her hair a certain way and dressed her accordingly, she would catch on. It was simple for him, a matter of genetics and timing and, of course, economics. What he didn't know was what she'd done before getting on that southbound train, cutting her hair purposely short and styling it just so. Choosing to wear pants instead of a skirt. She'd had the idea before he did. She'd seen what he'd done for Lindbergh. She'd helped him see what he'd wanted to see in her. She hadn't expected to lose her temper. That was the only surprise. Yet, in the end, even that helped her cause.

"I like a woman with spirit," he'd said.

Do you have a fiancé? She didn't. Not a fiancé. No lover. No man at all who would hold her back.

Liar.

Sitting on a milk crate in the *Friendship*, Amelia had known what could happen, she could plummet into the ocean like so many others had done before her. She, Slim, and Bill strained to see where they were. Below they spotted an ocean going liner. Then nothing. It had been over nineteen hours. Then it was twenty. The plane flew lower, trying to conserve fuel.

Finally they saw the fleet of fishing boats. They'd made it all the way across the Atlantic.

An ocean lay between the woman she'd been and the one she would become. Was it luck? Courage? Or the confluence of a thousand separate events beginning with her birth, and ending in Burry Port, Wales? Whatever it was, it had threaded together to make this penultimate moment. Stepping off the plane, Amelia had believed she finally knew what she was meant for.

14

Sam
November 26-December 8 1980

WHEN SAM WOKE up the morning after Thanksgiving, Lucy was gone. Breakfast with Brooke consisted of a bowl of dry Cheerios and an earful of Brooke's unbridled elation. The prodigal son had returned to the fold.

"Your brother is thinking of applying to school again," Brooke said. "Columbia. Up by you."

"Really? I don't see him going there." A kind way of saying Columbia would not take him. Win had flunked out of Williams his first year and then tried the University of Santa Cruz for half a semester. He hardly seemed Ivy League material at this point.

"There's no reason to sound so negative about it. They'd be lucky to have him."

"Bye, Mom," Sam said. And she flew out the door. Back to Barnard and her dorm room sanctuary.

But the weekend passed without any sign of Lucy. No calls. No letters. Not even a postcard. Sam was getting a little worried, although she knew Lucy had to be with Dusty. Still, Monday came, then Monday evening. By which time Sam was moving from acceptance, through anxiety, right to annoyance.

It was Tuesday, at five forty seven p.m. when Lucy waltzed in, looking only a little abashed. "I'm sorry, I should have left you a note. I should have called to see how you were."

"You should have," Sam agreed. And left it at that.

"I thought you'd figure out I was with Dusty."

She had after all. There was no real harm done.

Lucy blushed, dropping two full shopping bags on the floor. She flopped backward onto her own bed. The clothing she wore was new and elegantly hip, tight black jeans and a navy camel hair jacket boasting an oversized metal zipper and Nehru collar.

"You've been busy."

"Dusty wanted to go shopping. He insisted. I told him it was crazy."

And more than a little unnerving; it was as if Dusty were paying for her favors. But Sam wasn't going to mention what was obvious to both of them. She could read Lucy's embarrassment.

"I didn't want to buy anything. But he talked me into it. He's really pretty persuasive. I don't even need new clothes. I tried to explain why it felt wrong to me, and he said that I could return all of it and give the money to charity. It was so ridiculous when he put it like that. I felt like I was in one of those old movies, and he was David Niven," Lucy said.

"Not Cary Grant?"

"David Niven, for sure. He's so dapper and breezy and oddly sentimental. Every time I thought I was making myself clear to Dusty, he'd turn it around and put it on me. 'But don't you like that sweater? Didn't you say you wanted a shirt like the one that girl was wearing?' I tried explaining what I meant but he twisted it and by the end I was so exhausted, I just gave up."

"The lawyer in him is strong," Sam said.

Still, it was a tasteful assortment of jeans, shirts, and jackets. She'd done well for herself. Like Holly Golightly, Sam thought. Which made Dusty well, no, not George Peppard.

Life wasn't like a movie. It didn't have tidy beginnings, middles, and ends. "Dusty is basically a good guy," Sam said, leaving it at that.

Lucy nodded, gratefully.

"That's what I thought, too," she agreed. Then stripped off her clothes, grabbed a towel, and headed for the relative safety of the shower.

"WHAT'S COOKING, SAM I am?" Dusty inquired later that afternoon. He sat on a couch in the shabby waiting area of her dorm, one leg casually crossed over the other knee. He was decked out in a camelhair coat and a natty blue and red striped scarf. His feet were shod in Docksiders. Sam detested those shoes and the men who wore them. To her, they were a signifier of social status, indicating the wearer's affection for sailing and university clubs. In the interests of full disclosure, this meant that she hated a piece of herself. Grandmother Katherine owned a compound in Bar Harbor with its own private beach and two boathouses filled with a mini flotilla of *yar* sloops, ketches, and dinghies.

Dusty's leather briefcase perched on the worn-out couch next to him. He looked a completely solid citizen, staid, upstanding, and impeccable. One would never have guessed he liked snorting coke. What Win did for work, he did for fun. One day Dusty might boast about his youthful indiscretions. Will I remember, Sam wondered, or will I conveniently forget that I ever strayed from the straight and narrow? No self-respecting doctor could spend her nights getting high and blaring punk music. They were both going to have give up on being rebellious. Even in the mildest way. Sam saw herself in hospital whites, a stethoscope hanging from her neck, patrolling the halls of Brooklyn Methodist. The vision was real and really unnerving.

"What's wrong?" Dusty asked, reflexively wiping his mouth to dislodge what he assumed was a stray piece of food. She had been staring at him that fixedly.

"Nothing," she said, rushing up the stairs.

FOR A WHILE there was no more Sam and Lucy. Sam made friends with three other girls on her hall. They got stoned together when their class-work was done. Without Lucy, she had more time for her own work. She caught up on Jude in all his obscurity and aced her Bio and Chem midterms. When she asked Professor Hartley, her Chemistry professor, if he would nominate her for the Earhart award, he said, "Miss Barry, you didn't have to ask me. It's done."

Sam told herself that those fruit flies were ancient history. After all, no one was entirely honest or morally upright. And the answers were available to anyone who looked up Mendel's law. Sam knew she'd hidden her mistake so artfully it would never be caught. Yet, every day she saw Kim in the library. She knew the truth and it tortured her. Finally, she stopped Professor Grayson in the hall and said, "Can I see you in your office?" There, she blurted out, "I have something to confess."

After it was done with, she felt immeasurably lighter. Her heart had been pounding as she recounted the whole sorry, ridiculous incident. Then Sam realized Professor Grayson was trying not to smile. "You've come clean," her professor said, "Good for you."

"I know I don't deserve the grade I got."

"I agree. I'll mark you down. I trust you've learned your lesson."

"I so have."

"Well then, you'll be the first." That was it. She was dismissed.

Sam knew her chances to win the scholarship were blown. She felt relief, then despair. And there was no Lucy to tell. On the other hand, she wondered if Lucy wouldn't have tried to talk her out of confessing in the first place. Lucy saw the endgame much more clearly than she did. Sam felt a little idiotic for being so scrupulously honest after the fact. How did she expect to get ahead in life if she wasn't willing to cut some corners?

After their next class, Professor Grayson said she'd decided to mark Sam down two grades but if she did two further experiments outside of the coursework and followed the directions to the letter, making sure to write her results up clearly and completely, she would get extra credit.

"Yes, oh yes." And there it was, a second chance.

BY DECEMBER SHE was back on track.

Sam was running one of the extra credit experiments. Her test subjects were white lab rats. There were two groups; one was being fed protein rich food, the other no protein at all. It meant that one group of rats would live, while the other would waste away and die. The animals had been bred for this purpose. Sam didn't want to make a big deal out of it, but she did feel terrible watching the poor animals weaken. It was odd because more than half a century before, Amelia Earhart had done the same stupid experiment. Back then it had meant something, though. Now, they knew the results. Sam had read how Earhart had made the mistake of naming her rats after Santa's reindeers. Sam took her charges out of their cages and held them in her lap. They shivered, but submitted. She told herself there was no room for sentiment, that they weren't pets. If she couldn't stand lab rats dying, how was she going to manage the rest of it?

But it seemed so unnecessary.

Sam found Professor Grayson in her office.

"I want to thank you so much for giving me the chance to make things right," Sam began.

"No need. You're not the first student I've had who's cheated. But you're one of the few to confess." Professor Grayson was bent over the stack of papers. Sam waited until she looked up. "Is there something else?"

"I don't understand. Why let the rats die when we already know the result?"

Professor Grayson sighed. "Because, Ms. Barry, as a scientist you must learn to follow the protocol."

"I just . . . I don't see the point. It seems cruel."

"Life is cruel." Professor Grayson clucked her tongue. "Have I made a mistake with you? I gave you a second chance because you're exceptionally good at this. Or so I thought."

"I know, it's just that . . ."

"I see that you have philosophical questions about this. That's commendable. However, if you wish to become a doctor, which you claim you do, you'll certainly have to learn to cope with the death of a few lab animals."

Sam nodded.

"Good. One further word of advice for you. Accept that you will not be able to save everyone."

It was true. She understood as much. Sam found little comfort in her English class. After Jude came Tess. Fate ground poor Tess down. She was doomed, just as Jude had been. The novel was bleak and depressing. Sam searched for a suitably grim musical accompaniment. What befits a wounded heroine most? She set *Mother Earth*, a bargain basement find, on the turntable. Tracy Nelson belted out *Down So Low*. "When you went away, I cried for so long. I wanted you to stay, but that was all wrong. The pain you left behind has become part of me and it's burned out a hole where my love used to be." Sam wailed away with Tracy. Then she spun Marianne Faithful, who was tearing her cheating lover another one. Wondering why he did what he did to her.

The world was a cold, cruel place and apparently she was going to play her part in it. Where was Michael when you needed him. But she knew where he was, safe in the arms of his real girlfriend.

The door opened and in walked Lucy, who flopped onto Sam's bed.

"Busy?"

"Swamped."

"What with?" Lucy asked.

"Work."

"I can see that," Lucy said, raising an elegant eyebrow.

"What's going on with you?"

"Nothing."

There was evidently something. "Tell me," Sam said.

"Dusty insists I come to dinner and meet his parents tomorrow night."

"Out or in?" Sam asked.

"Out. The Tavern on the Green. Please come with me."

"I don't think so. I know them already and they make me really nervous."

"Think of how I feel," Lucy said.

"Just tell him you don't want to go."

"I tried that. He got really upset. He said to understand him I had to meet his parents. The thing is, I need him to slow down a little." Lucy's nostrils flared the way an animal's did, when it scented danger. "He's kind of freaking me out. You know him so much better than I do."

"As a friend, not as a boyfriend."

"I know he'll hate me if I refuse to go," Lucy said. "I can't bear thinking of that."

"Dusty won't hate you."

Where had the other Lucy disappeared to, the one who brimmed with confidence? Lucy had said she acted differently without Sam. Here was the proof. The window was open a crack to counteract the potent steam heat. A bowl of water sat on top of the radiator to keep the air moist and their skins daisy fresh. Their curtain sheets flapped in the breeze.

"He says he loves me," Lucy confessed. "But how can he love me? He doesn't know me."

"Maybe he doesn't mean it as seriously as you're taking it," Sam tried. "Dusty's had lots of girlfriends."

"I know. He's told me about them."

"And?"

"He said he was always careful. He never said he loved one of them. Not even the one in high school he was with for two years."

"You mean Natalie? Really?"

"He wants me to say it back to him," Lucy told her. "But I can't."

"Tell him you can't say it, then. Tell him the truth."

"It's not that easy for me, telling the truth," Lucy said. She looked absolutely miserable.

Above Lucy's bed were remnants of the super-sticky tape used to hang up posters. The posters themselves had slumped and fallen off. Only one remained, Klimt's *The Kiss.* It showed a man and woman's intertwined bodies built out of specks of gilt and dabs of color. It was a taunt, considering their mutual situations. Sam's nonexistent, a fantasy that had succumbed to the reality of an awkward one-night stand, and now Lucy's dance with Dusty. Sam realized that Lucy was clueless in her own way. In fact, they were both naïve when it came to dealing with what was expected of them, lost in the same, treacherous woods.

"You don't want to break up with him," Sam said. "On the other hand, you don't want to start pledging your troth."

"I guess that's pretty much it."

"How many guys have you broken up with?"

Lucy counted back on her fingers and reached the end of both hands, then kept on going.

"Eleven, I think, no actually, twelve. Does elementary school count?"

"If you want it to." Sam was impressed, and a little unnerved. "Why did you break up with them?"

"They did something to upset me, I guess. But look, I don't want to do that to Dusty. I mean, he's nice and besides, well, you're friends with him."

"This isn't about me."

"I know," Lucy admitted. "I guess I like him in a different way. It's just that I don't know how to get him to stop."

"Stop what?"

"Stop pushing," Lucy said. "How do you get him to listen to you. I mean, really listen."

Sam smiled. "It's not the easiest thing," she admitted.

"So what's the secret exactly?"

"What happened with the others?" Sam asked, avoiding the question for the moment.

"It's like a switch gets turned and everything after that is wrong," Lucy said. "Of course, once they sense I'm pulling away, the guys get frantic. The simplest thing would be to change my name and go into a witness protection program. Instead, I have to see them in the halls at school, or in town. I end up dosing out humiliation and then I hate myself for doing it. Yet, this is who I am. I try to act like a nice girl and in the end I always have to act like a bitch."

"Just say *no* to him," Sam said firmly. The last thing she wanted was the blowback from Lucy breaking up this way with Dusty. Why had she ever taken her to Thanksgiving? Why hadn't she forced her to leave when they had the chance? This is what comes of having friends date each other, Sam thought.

"I've tried that." Lucy had an odd look on her face.

"What?" Sam asked. It clearly wasn't just advice that she wanted.

"Dusty invited us to Puerto Rico."

"Us? Us, as in you and me? You said no on that one. Tell me you did. Luce, come on! I can't go on a trip with the two of you."

"I know." But she was giving Sam a pleading look. "It would be a vacation, though. I mean, it's nice down there, right?"

"What do you need me for?" Sam asked. But she knew. Lucy had basically said as much to her, Sam would support her, Sam would show her how to fix things with Dusty, Sam would help her be strong, thereby saving her from acting like her worst version of herself. And, by doing that, she would also be helping Dusty. "Shit," Sam muttered under her breath.

Just then, there was a pounding on the door. Kim yelled out, "Sam! Lucy! You have to get out."

"A fire!" Lucy said, grabbing Sam's hand.

But there was no fire. It was an unnatural disaster. Some lunatic with a gun had murdered John Lennon. He'd been shot dead in the street in front of his apartment.

"Why?" Sam asked aloud. As if there were ever a reason.

The TV in the common room played clips of the Beatle who was more famous than Jesus, then a video from his new album. In the video, John ambled through Central Park. They cut to the crowd of fans gathered outside the Dakota.

"My mom was so into Paul," one of the coeds exclaimed.

"Which one's Paul?"

"He's the one with the baby face. You know, the cute one."

Brooke swore she'd met the Beatles. Sam didn't believe her. There was no photographic evidence on the wall of shame. Brooke claimed a lot of things that weren't even close to true. Still, when Sam was little, Brooke played every Beatle album in order and interpreted the songs for her, "This one's about John's aunt," she'd say. "And this one is about tripping."

"Why would someone sing about tripping? That's just silly. It's an accident. All you do is fall down and get up again."

Brooke started laughing and couldn't stop. "You are so cute."

She was a kid. Kids are cute. They don't know about acid. Or grass. Or hash. Or coke. Or how disappointment can become habitual. How it can turn into a lifestyle choice.

Sam learned all that later.

As did Win. Oh God, Win! He'd be crushed. Win was a total Beatles fanatic. He bought two of every album. One was in the original sealed cellophane wrapping, the other was meant for personal use. When Win listened to their music, he was the sternest apostle. "Quiet," he'd order Sam if she snuck into his room. The records he spun were treated with consummate care. Win used a special soft cloth to clean them. He held the vinyl cautiously, thumb on the edge, middle finger supporting the disc. That way no fingerprints marred the pristine surface.

He was devoted, but so were millions upon millions of others. John had been the best sort of God. He'd wanted those who believed in him to be happy. Listening to that music, they were.

Sam had the urge to go find Win and try to comfort him. But she knew him too well. He'd shrug her off, shrug her sympathy away. She was his little sister, what could she do for him? The one thing Win had left was his pride.

Tears welled up. Sam tamped them down. She wasn't going to cry in front of these girls who were asking stupid questions and making ridiculous comments. Sam remembered her own John Lennon sighting. She was on her favorite Central Park bench when he walked by holding his young son's hand. She was with her friends. They all did that New York thing, feigning disinterest. It was how you were raised, to pretend famous people were the same as anyone else. It was considerate, but more to the point, no self respecting New Yorker would squeal or shriek or demand an autograph like a rube. That just wasn't cool.

In the common room, plenty of New York City girls crowded round the TV.

"It must hurt like hell to get shot."

"Who shoots a musician anyway? That's just weird."

"Who shoots a Beatle? I mean, if it was someone really famous. Like Clint Eastwood, or Charles Bronson."

"You can't shoot Clint Eastwood. He'd get you first. He's Dirty Harry."

Did that girl actually laugh? How was this, in any way, funny?

Sam wanted to smack her. These were supposedly the cream of the crop, top of the Seven Sisters pyramid. She backed out, Lucy at her heels, her own face ashen.

"We should go down there," Lucy said.

It was past one a.m. They crossed the deserted campus in the rain. The number 104 bus ran erratically after midnight. When it finally pulled up and the doors heaved open, the other passengers were dressed for work. Lucy and Sam took the worst seat, the one over the motor at the very back. The bus cruised past Salter's Bookstore and the Mill Luncheonette. It dipped down the hill at Ninety-Sixth Street, then climbed back up. Out the window, Sam watched as the Thalia, the New Yorker, and Blimpies rolled by. In Blimpies, once, Sam had ordered a sub. It arrived with stringy lettuce, watery tomatoes and slivers of processed meat. That thing was truly inedible.

Why would anyone bother with that when they could walk a block west to Barney Greengrass and eat an overstuffed corned beef on rye, or take a ride downtown to Manganaro's for a real hero with all the fixings? New York was amazing, the people who lived here eccentric and magnificent and gruff, but kind in totally surprising ways. It was the city that never slept, a place where ingenuity mattered, where being unique was seen as a positive. John Lennon had chosen to live here. He'd loved living here. Why was this his reward?

At Seventy-Second Street, Sam and Lucy merged with a steady stream of people heading for the Dakota. A light rain fell. The reflections from the streetlights gave the wet cement an opalescent sheen. No one spoke. They were numbed to the core.

It was horrible, ghoulish, yet Sam was glad they'd come. Staying in that dorm and watching it unfold, while listening to those stupid comments from those girls, that had been unbearable. At least here everyone was united in shock, pulled along by the tractor beam of fame and senseless death. Ahead of them, an older couple held onto each other. The woman turned, and Sam saw her eyes were puffy from crying. She blinked hard, like a bird after slamming headfirst into a pane of glass.

Stunned.

They all were.

At the Dakota the crowd sang "Give Peace A Chance."

Sam choked up. Last spring, they'd been smoking a joint. "We should see if John wants some," they'd joked, but too late. She had been close enough to touch his jacket. If she'd only reached out. But father and son were past by then, walking up the hill and disappearing from view.

Now he was gone forever.

Being happy should be easy and effortless. It should just come, Sam thought. But it didn't happen that way. It was hard to be happy, even if you were famous and rich and successful beyond anyone's wildest dreams. John had been so many different people in his life, the original mop-top, a husband and young father turned hippie and druggie, then a man so truly in love he would give up everything for it, for her, for his son.

Life was so desperately unfair.

The policemen standing vigil looked stricken themselves, solemn and grim. They were probably Beatle fans, too. Who wasn't? Being a fan, you felt touched by the person you admired in a special way. It was as if that famous person was your very best friend. They weren't. You were no one to them, but they were everything to you. It was odd how deluded fans became. How being near your idol was enough to lighten your mood. Their specialness rubbed off, or so you imagined. She'd found herself telling the story of John Lennon walking right by her. It had made her feel brighter and better, she'd felt important solely because of that proximity.

But all he'd wanted to do was to walk through the park like any other father holding onto his son's hand, his own lovely son. It was true, she hadn't hounded him or asked for his autograph, she'd left him alone because she was a New Yorker and that was what you were trained to do from birth and it was a good thing to be like that. To pretend as if it didn't matter, even though it did.

Sam was crying. She wiped the tears away. The rain fell steadily, chilling her. There were lights lit in the apartments above them. The yellow crime scene tape flapped wildly. Faces appeared at the windows.

"I'm Patricia Whitten from the BBC. Can I ask you a few questions?" The reporter had a clipped British accent. Arc lights flared, illuminating Sam and Lucy, trapping them.

"I guess," Sam said.

"Super! Can I have your names then?"

"Sam. Samantha Barry."

"And you?"

Lucy shrugged.

"Why are you girls down here?"

"We just wanted to come," Sam said. "We thought we should."

"Why come to the Dakota?"

"This is where John lived," Sam said.

"You don't think it an intrusion?"

Sam stared at the woman. Of course it was. Yet here they all were. It felt right to stand vigil but now that she'd said it, Sam saw how horribly wrong it was. She flushed, embarrassed. She thought of how Win had blasted the White Album the day it came out. How Win had taught her the words to every one of those songs. "So you say it's your birthday." Then she imagined John Lennon arriving home, thinking it a normal day, that he would have all the time in the world left to say and do whatever needed to be done for Yoko, for Sean. Sam was sobbing. She turned away, wiping at the tears.

"We're here because we don't know where else to go," Lucy said, taking over.

The woman swung towards her. "How old are you, if you don't mind me asking?"

"Why does that matter?"

"It's a point of interest. Fans of all ages you know."

"I'm eighteen," Lucy said.

"To you he was more the later Lennon than John the Beatle."

Lucy nodded bravely.

"It wasn't a question of him being your favorite?"

"My favorite?" Lucy's jaw dropped.

The woman persisted. "One did have favorites, you see. Some liked John, others preferred Paul."

"That's a terrible thing to say," Lucy told her.

"You shouldn't ask that question. Can't you hear yourself?" Sam agreed. "What sort of person are you?"

"Excuse me?" The reporter smiled brightly.

"I can't excuse you," Sam said firmly.

She grabbed Lucy and pulled her through the crowd, finding an exit on the far side.

"Favorites," Lucy said in disgust.

They crossed the street and clambered up on a park bench. Sam's jacket was soaked, her feet numb inside the canvas Converse sneakers. Above their heads, the limbs of a naked oak helped to thwart a little of the water.

"We shouldn't be here. We should leave Yoko alone," Lucy said. Just then, an entire floor in the Dakota went dark. Lucy grabbed Sam's hand. Her cold breath made smoke signals. "No one really knows what it's like until it happens to you. No one realizes." Lucy's gaze was fixed on some foreign, miserable spot. "Donnie was the first person I ever got stoned with. I was fourteen and straight as an arrow, junior barrel racing champion, queen of the pep club. I was my dad's daughter, did everything the way he wanted it done. My parents were out to a movie that night. Donnie and some friends were going to the drive-in to see *Star Wars.* They'd seen it like six times or something. It wasn't the kind of movie I liked. I didn't care about science fiction at all. But Donnie got me to come along. He could really get you to do anything. He was like that. It was the first time I ever smoked pot. They took out the joint and passed it. Donnie said, 'Go on, Lucy, it won't kill you to try it.' He was always daring you to step outside of yourself, outside of what you were comfortable doing. But not in a really dangerous way, it was like he was promising he'd be there for you if something happened." Lucy sighed. "I still think *Star Wars* is a comedy. He and his friends were making jokes through the whole thing."

"You must miss him so much."

"I do miss him," she said softly. "What's even worse is when I forget about him. What kind of person forgets?"

"Everyone forgets. It's normal."

"No, it's not. It's wrong. Because if I forget, then what happens to him? He'll be gone, and I don't want him to be gone." Lucy was desolate.

Sam's heart expanded. It included Lucy, of course, but also everyone who'd ever lost someone near and dear to themselves, who'd suffered and ached, finally understanding that once that person was gone they could never be replaced, that living with the absence was all you could do. To do that, you had to be brave in ways that tested you. It wasn't obvious bravery. It was something that you tucked inside, something that was rooted down deep, a very specific kind of courage. Everyone was forced to see how he or she would manage this if they were the ones who lived. Survival required adaptation, just as in nature. It was better to survive, but it wasn't easy to know how to live afterwards.

Lucy let go of Sam's hand and stuffed her own into her pocket. The crowd across the street had fallen silent.

"My mom never thought that Donnie could do anything wrong," Lucy said. "He was her favorite so to Mom, he was perfect in every way. Donnie fooled her. If she'd looked a little harder, maybe she would have seen who he really was. Then again, maybe you just can't see who your kids are. Maybe you love them too much for that."

"What about your dad?"

"My dad thought Donnie was soft. He was always ragging on him to be a man and toughen up. It was his special Donnie litany. I remember this one time Donnie and my mom were watching TV together. Donnie couldn't have been more than nine years old, just a little kid. My mom was stroking his hair and hugging him and they had this special smile they shared, this special secret way of looking at each other. Maybe my dad was jealous, I don't know. That day, my dad got this look on his own face. It was the one that meant you ought to go hide until he cooled down. I tried to warn them. I waved at them, but they didn't see. Then it was too late. He went ballistic. 'You're ruining him. You keep up like that and that boy will be a fag. It'll be your fault.' He went into a total rage, throwing things around, scaring the shit out of me. After that, Donnie wouldn't let my mom touch him."

"That's horrible," Sam said.

"I know. I do love my dad," Lucy said. "But he's a Neanderthal, he really is. I mean, he does his best, considering. But sometimes his best isn't even close to good enough."

"I know what you mean," Sam said. She would tell her now. She would tell her what she had never told anyone else. Lucy deserved to hear it. And imagine letting it out, finally. How would that even feel?

But Lucy was going on. "The fucking police, they were such cowards. When they phoned, my mom just kept saying, 'no.' Then she handed my dad the phone. I was sitting in the living room watching TV and half watching them. I knew something was wrong. I had this knot in my stomach. You want to know what it is, then again, you don't. You want it to go away. You want everything to stop, to just stop. At the funeral, none of the other boys' parents showed up. Everyone blamed Donnie because he was driving."

"You said he killed himself."

"He turned the car into oncoming traffic. I went out there to see where it happened. He rode right across the median to do it. I know he was drunk, but even so, you see what's coming at you. You know that much."

"Sometimes you don't," Sam insisted.

"Sometimes you just want it to be over," Lucy said. "Sometimes that's all that matters. You don't think about the rest. Sometimes I guess some people just are selfish. I hate him for being that way. Which is the worst part you know, because I loved him so much. I mean, how can it be that he didn't care how we were going to feel? How could he not think about that?"

Lucy jumped down off the bench.

How indeed, Sam thought. She knew what Lucy meant all too well.

They walked back to the uptown bus and sat in the back again, drying off their clammy clothing. Sam saw their reflection, cemented inside the double-paned glass of the bus window.

"Listen, I shouldn't be asking for advice with Dusty. I know I have to figure it out myself, I'm a big girl."

Dusty. There it was. Sam couldn't escape.

"But there's this other thing."

Sam held her breath, afraid of what that was.

"My mom invited you out for Christmas. Would you consider coming?"

"Oh." It was a relief. In fact, when Sam thought about the bare bones Christmas tree in Brooke's living room she wanted to escape. Brooke and Win waking past noon, all bleary eyed, to open the presents, then all of them trooping across the river and through the Central Park thickets to Grandmother Katherine's apartment for their ritualistic dressing down. Win usually got her CDs boosted from the local record store; once he even stole Lanvin perfume for her. She wore it faithfully, dabbing it on the sides of her neck for a month until Brooke told her she smelled like an old Parisian lady. The best present he ever gave her was won at the San Gennaro fair. It was a black and white stuffed dog. She named it Spot and slept with it for weeks. Then one day, it was gone.

"Tracy thought it was cute," Win said. When she started sobbing, he added, "I'll get you something better. Don't cry. Please, I can't bear it when you cry."

True to his word, the next day a teddy bear was on her bed. Win did his best but it wasn't enough because how could it be? Brooke's all his this year, Sam decided. He came back home just in time for Christmas. So why not let him have Brooke, have her and coddle her and get stoned with her and get fed up with her and disappear again maybe after New Years'? In the interim, she would escape. There was no earthly reason not to. It was her turn now, Sam told herself, burying the guilt as deep as she dared.

"I'd love to go to Wisconsin with you," she said, squeezing Lucy's hand.

As they walked from the bus stop, Sam looked over her shoulder, checking for predators. An icy wind blew up off the river.

"What have you girls been up to?" the guard at the campus gate asked, tossing a wink.

"Wouldn't you like to know," Lucy replied. Then she took off. In a footrace she had the advantage, outpacing Sam by a yard, her long hair flying.

15

Muriel
December 1980

CELIA SAID, "I do" at the nave of the church. Muriel beamed. Then she joined the guests in the reception hall just across the street. A band was setting up on the raised dais. Above them, a banner proclaimed "Celia and Gary. Partners Forever." Exquisite pink, red, and yellow flower centerpieces graced the tables. Muriel enjoyed her pig in a blanket as she contemplated what *forever* meant these days. Celia and Gary had been high school sweethearts, so they'd had more time than most of their contemporaries to ponder the innumerable imponderables. Still, Muriel had read the statistics; one out of two marriages ended in divorce.

But here came the new bride and her groom. "Look at you, all grown up," Muriel said, giving Celia a hug.

"Auntie Muriel." Celia beamed. It was a fond nickname; Muriel wasn't a real relation. Muriel shook Gary's hand. His sky blue jacket shimmered. It reminded Muriel of the ones that singer Presley favored. Gary had a strong chin, but he wasn't traditionally handsome. He was really more pleasant looking than anything else. Youth held its own attractions.

Five months pregnant, Celia's yellow dress clung to her stomach. Muriel's old friend Julie had been so upset when her granddaughter announced that she preferred to live in common law sin. "Monstrous," she'd declared. Muriel disagreed. "Why not test the waters?" Julie was positively scandalized by Muriel's *laissez faire* attitude. In the end, the temptation of gifts and money had proven too much. Celia and Gary were both art students and as broke as could be. They caved. Now here they were, married.

Muriel had always adored Celia. As a little girl Celia had been a wildcat, running her poor grandmother ragged. On an outing they'd all taken to the Harvard Museum of Natural History, Julie refused to buy three-year-old Celia some trinket. In protest, the child wailed, gnashing her teeth and pounding her tiny fists into the floor right next to the Kronosaurus. Julie begged her to stop, to no avail. She threw up her hands, walking away. That was when Muriel took over. Lifting the rag doll body from the floor, she said firmly, "Behave!" The tears dried right up. Children needed someone to set limits for them. That was how it was.

One friend then another came up to chat. Apparently the Medford Historical Society's campaign to refurbish the Royall House was causing trouble. Alliances were forming. Would she be at the next meeting? Muriel was such a calming influence, a voice of reason, someone said. She didn't commit. Then it was time for dinner. Muriel was at Julie's table. The waitress set shrimp cocktails in front of them. Four demure curls of pink and white shellfish were draped over a handsome glass goblet.

Julie was deep in conversation with her daughter Erica, mother of the bride. This was the very same Erica, who so many years ago, played hide and seek and capture the flag with Muriel's son. She'd met Julie back when her own children were in kindergarten. Just like that the knife went in, twisting in her gut.

Not here. Not now. Gritting her teeth, she turned to her right and discovered she knew the man slipping into the chair beside her. "Virgil, what on earth?"

"This is Mr. Washinawock." Julie's daughter, Erica, introduced him round the table. "He believed in our Celia from the very beginning." Muriel got it then. Celia had worked at the bookstore back when she was in high school and Virgil had her do the window displays. Muriel remembered a particularly eye catching Halloween one, complete with headless horseman and goblins.

"How are you?" he asked Muriel.

It was a simple question, but one that reverberated. After that drive home, she'd avoided going back to the store.

"Good," she said.

"Glad to hear it."

"Muriel's heading down to New York," Julie interjected. "She's giving a talk there. She'd going to be a keynote speaker at Columbia University."

"That sounds like fun," Virgil said.

"I'm not going to be a keynote speaker," Muriel corrected. "It's nothing that grand."

Mercifully, the waitress reappeared to remove the appetizers. The main course arrived seconds later, a feast of roast beef, mashed potatoes, and steamed carrots. Muriel dug in, grateful for the distraction. Her mouth was full when Virgil asked, "What are you doing then, if not being a keynote speaker? What's your talk about?"

She chewed, swallowed, took a sip of water, and said, "They're giving a student scholarship. I'm to introduce it somehow."

"When is this all happening?"

"In January."

"I'll be in New York myself in January. Our ABA chapter has a meeting," he said.

"ABA?"

"The booksellers association. I'm actually speaking to the group myself."

"About?" Muriel asked.

"About this new trend, book banning."

"Absurd, isn't it?"

"And yet . . ."

Muriel nodded. She knew what he meant. Bad ideas came right back, just the same as all the good ones. All you had to do was live for long enough to find that out.

"What will you speak about?" he asked.

"My sister."

Just then the best man stood, tapping on his glass.

The first speech was maudlin; the second, humorous; the third, verging on tasteless with its intimate knowledge of the bride and bridegroom's private foibles.

Celia's father got up and made a toast from their table. "I never thought I'd live to see the day," he said to general laughter. He went on to roast Celia amiably and broke down when he said how he was happy to be gaining a son; he only hoped the boy knew what he was doing.

After that, they cut the cake.

There was a pause as it was devoured. It was too sweet. Muriel set down her fork. She saw Virgil's piece was set aside as well, half eaten.

He saw her looking and leaned over. "Salt's my downfall, not sugar."

The microphone buzzed. The bandleader waited for the unpleasant noise to subside, then leaned in. "I want to welcome everyone to Celia and Gary's wedding. The first song, by request of the bride and groom."

The guitar player moved to the front and began to sing *Imagine*.

She glanced at Virgil and saw his eyes were filling with tears. It was a John Lennon song. She'd heard it on the radio. Her son had schooled her in the Beatles. She had enjoyed their music though she preferred jazz standards. It was horrible, how the poor man had been cut down in the prime of his life, leaving behind a wife and son. Celebrity brought all kinds of trouble with it. Amelia had had her share of demented fans.

"I still can't believe it," Virgil said. "There he was, not hurting a soul, and this maniac blows him to kingdom come."

"People think they own you when you become famous," Muriel agreed. "It's as if there's some sort of unwritten contract; we'll love you as long as you give us whatever we want."

When the song was over, Celia stood. "I want to thank all of you for coming and celebrating with us," she said, her face flushed with emotion. "And I want to thank John Lennon for giving us so much. We love you, John, wherever you are."

She sat down, and Gary embraced her. It was a mournful note to strike on such a lovely occasion, but then it was Celia's wedding. She was that kind of person, Muriel decided, always bursting with enthusiasms, with emotion.

There was something noble in being like that, being a young woman who felt with such intensity. It was unusual to be able to give in to your passion so easily.

Luckily, the bandleader knew how to change the mood. He struck up a waltz.

"Can I have this dance?" Virgil asked.

Muriel wasn't about to say no. She loved dancing. She and Albert had celebrated their anniversary every year at the Ritz Carlton rooftop restaurant where they spent the night on the dance floor. Albert had been amazingly adept. Virgil wasn't a match. He was graceful, though, without being flashy. Muriel eyed the other couples. All those on the dance floor were at least middle aged. The waltz ended and there was barely a pause. The band launched into, "It don't mean a thing, if it ain't got that swing."

"Game?" he inquired.

"If you are."

"You can't say 'no' to the Duke."

Muriel swiveled on her heels. Their hands meshed, up, down, up, down, and the room whirled by. Marvelous. Then the tempo changed, the band was playing rock and roll for the younger set.

"I'll sit this one out," she said.

Virgil escorted her back to the table. "Can I get you anything?" he asked.

"Ice water?"

"Your wish is my command." He poured her a glass.

Muriel sipped on it.

"I remember when the Beatles first came on the scene," Virgil said. "I was a big James Brown fan at the time. I was sure they were nothing. Going to fade away like all the rest of the pretenders. But they stuck. I thought to myself, look at those pretty boys. All the girls mooning over them, causing riots wherever they went. It seemed so silly. But then I gave half an ear to it, because you have to see what's out there. You have to keep things fresh. Besides, playing music myself, I don't like to get behind the times."

"I heard you were a musician. What do you play?"

"The tenor sax. It was how I met Laura Lee. I was in the house band at this club out west in Los Angeles, the Beachcomber. She was dating the manager, and he gave her a shot. She was a pro, worked her way up to starring. Poor Jimmy, the manager, got left in the dust. We toured all over the country. Had this beat-up old bus. One night, I figured I'd take my chance with her. I knew if it went wrong, I'd get fired. But it didn't. Turned out she'd liked me the whole time, too. She'd thought I was the one who was disinterested. To this day, I don't know why she settled for me when she could have had anyone. Love is really a mystery."

"What a story," Muriel said.

"Everyone has one." He meant she did, too. She didn't think hers anywhere near as glamorous.

The bride and groom were dancing close to their table. Celia's head rested on Gary's shoulder. They were so trusting with each other. It was lovely. Muriel's eyes misted over. She was really quite the pushover. But then, it was a wedding, one was supposed to be.

She willed herself back into their conversation.

"It was January," Virgil was saying. "We were playing the Hotel St. Georges. It was a palace, that place, with the biggest saltwater indoor pool in the city. The ballrooms were crammed with customers. We were second on the bill. That was where I saw her."

"Who?"

"Your sister."

Muriel stiffened. "Oh."

"I've never breathed a word about it to anyone. I never even told my wife."

"Well, bully for you." She stood.

Virgil got up, a look of surprise on his face.

"What's wrong?" Virgil asked. "What is it? Look, I never meant to presume."

BUT SHE WAS already saying goodbye. She had to get away. Muriel was in the coatroom, handing in her ticket, before she realized what had stung her so much.

He'd befriended her to get to this, to his special story, his moment with his own Amelia. He was hardly the first to try it with her. But he was the only one who'd gotten past her defenses. She'd believed he liked her, solely, for herself. Hearing her own internal voice she winced. It was Jealousy, plain and simple, she was jealous of a ghost.

He'd come after her. He took the coat from the checkroom girl and held it for her. It was the lamb's wool Albert had bought. Virgil got his own coat. She expunged all signs of hurt from her face and made for the door.

"Let me take you home," he insisted, pursuing her.

"It's only a few blocks. I can make my own way."

"Please."

They were outside by then. The cold air slapped some sense into her. Still, she couldn't help muttering under her breath, "You're like the rest of them."

He'd heard her. "The rest? What rest? I don't know what you're talking about."

She turned to confront him. "Vultures. That's what you all are."

"I was making conversation."

"Were you?" Muriel demanded.

"Of course. What else did you think?" Then he took her by the shoulders, suddenly leaned forward, and kissed her lightly on the mouth. He pulled back. "I shouldn't have done that."

She blushed, but she wasn't sorry. Not in the least. "You know what you are, Virgil Washinawack? You're the kissing bandit."

"Is that who I am?" He smiled, bashfully. Then Muriel tucked her arm into his, surprising them both.

THE DAY AMELIA'S plane disappeared photographers and reporters camped on her lawn. To afford everyone some measure of peace, Muriel finally invited them inside. Then they peppered Muriel with their inane questions.

Amelia would have known how to make the newshounds her friends. She would have answered their questions with tact and modesty. She could work a room. Muriel had no practice. But there was no one else to do it. Mother was a wreck. G.P. was impossible. There was no one else to protect her sister but her. Someone had to keep the pack of wolves at bay.

Muriel remembered exactly what she'd said to them.

I have every confidence she'll pull through. She's gotten into worse scrapes before and survived. No, I don't think she's dead at all. I know she's alive.

How could she be dead even now? Sometimes Muriel felt she was so close, brushing against her, whispering to her.

Had Virgil seen her at the St. Georges? Who was to say? Not me, Muriel thought. Once we told each other everything. But by the time she was lost, she was keeping secrets, keeping so much close. Had I judged her too sternly too many times, or did she decide it was safer to stop trusting me? Either way, it hurt.

But they were walking to Virgil's car. And, just like that, he was opening the door for her. Just like that, he was starting the engine and pulling out. She reached out then and put her hand on his knee thinking, I'll just give it a pat, but then she couldn't lift her hand away. It stayed there of its own volition. Virgil's own left the steering wheel to clasp hers tight. He squeezed it once, then left his on top, light enough for her to slide away from him.

She didn't. And he was wise enough not to say a word.

16

Amelia
December 14 1980

MAC WAS NO longer there to open the taxi door or call for the porter to take her luggage. Not that she had any. Two men stood on the corner, sharing a bottle hidden in a paper bag. One threw it down in disgust, the glass shattering. His companion said, "Man, you are such a goddamn fool!"

The dreary awning read Hotel St. Georges; otherwise, Amelia would have thought she was in the wrong place. Inside, Amelia saw shuttered shops and stairs leading down to a subway entrance. There was no oriental carpet leading you up the stairs to the lobby. No main desk. No waiting area with leather armchairs. And no Colorama ballroom, where it was standing room only when the big name bands played. To get inside the new version of the Hotel St. Georges, you had to go round to a side entrance on Hicks Street. A glass divider separated Amelia from the desk in a tawdry lobby. A man stared up at her when she pressed the buzzer.

"Whatcha want?" he demanded.

"I was wondering about renting a room?"

"We're full up."

Amelia was relieved. It was not an inviting establishment. Indeed, sleeping on a park bench seemed preferable. Still, back outside, a cold wind chased her down Clark to Willow. There, she ascertained that the number of the apartment building this Winston Barry had written on the paper existed. Inside there was a mailbox with the name Barry taped above it. What had he asked about, a "candid camera" of some sort? What was that, she wondered.

She'd have to do some research before she confronted him again. Tonight, what she wanted most was to go to sleep. But where could she stay? This wasn't the Brooklyn she'd expected. The air was frigid; her legs chilled inside her rayon trousers. No "Room for Rent" signs hung out. Above her head, a glimpse through a window showed a family sitting down to dinner. Inside the next, a mother held her little girl on her lap, reading a book. I had a mother once, Amelia thought, and her eyes clouded. Mother was gone. They were all gone, if you believed those biographies. With the exception of Muriel; Muriel, who didn't even know her.

She wandered past to the Promenade. The view of Manhattan Island was breathtaking; a cluster of monumental buildings at the tip searing the night sky. They'd been imagined and built out of ambition. She understood that, why you strained against what was predictable, why you attempted something new. Why else was one born? She leaned against the railing, and her eyes filled with tears, only partly from the cold wind whipping off the water. What if she climbed up and jumped down into the drink? Would she go back then? Would she end the day where she'd begun after burying Fred, lying on the beach, exhausted? Or would it be different, would she find herself in Lae, feverish, not even having climbed into the plane?

Amelia had no way of knowing. She could just drown and die and no one would ever be the wiser. Was that what this was? Was that all she was meant for? Underfoot the walkway, cars rushed to and fro. Everyone in this world had something pulling at them, some purpose that they knew of, someone's will they refused to bend to. She was the only one left completely rudderless.

Yet it had to have something to do with him. Why else had that boy brandished her gift?

Amelia had come here once, years ago to assure Winston Manning that the flight circumnavigating the globe would be her last, her greatest adventure. She had promised him then that on her return, they would finally be together for good. Had she even believed it? She had told him it was true, so she must have. Luckily, her resolve hadn't been tested.

Now here she was again. Death was death and life the absence thereof. So what was this?

This could only be a fantasy. She'd made up this world in order to keep her promise to him.

That is, if he actually existed in this world. If he does, Amelia thought, he'll be older than Muriel is.

Will he even know me when my own sister doesn't?

Will true love triumph in the end? She smiled ruefully. The odds weren't good on that score.

She had to sleep. In the morning, she'd figure out what to do next. Where to go? How to act? Who to pretend to be? Maybe then she'd discover what she was doing here in Brooklyn, New York, besides pursuing an ephemera.

She walked back to Montague and made a left. There was an open coffee shop. She found a telephone booth. The YWCA was on the corner of Third Avenue and Atlantic. They had rooms available at ten dollars a night.

Inside one of them, she lay on the bed and rested her head on folded arms. She recalled the weeks trapped inside Muriel's house in Medford. She relived her newfound freedom, the elation of flying, even as a passenger. And she reminded herself that her life was nothing if not a series of improvisations. First student, then nurse, then medical student, then social worker, then aviatrix, then clothing designer, then wife, and then, of course, lover. She'd been famous. She'd been poor, then rich, then stretched for money. She'd done everything she could, cramming it all in.

She woke refreshed. The girl at the desk advised her to try the Goodwill store and wrote down directions. Amelia bought two pairs of blue jeans, underwear, bras, button-down shirts, a navy blue wool coat, and, best of all, a pair of men's heavy soled Dunham Tyrolean work boots.

Showered and changed, she was ready to tackle the new day.

Amelia rang the buzzer for Barry.

A woman's voice asked, "Who is it?"

"I'm looking for Winston?"

The speaker crackled back at her. "For what, exactly?"

"I'm a friend," she said.

"If you're his friend, then you know where to find him." Click.

Amelia backed away. She could stand outside in the cold, watching and waiting like that Hammett novel she'd loved, featuring the Continental Op. She scoured the street and spied an orange car. It was much like the one he'd gotten into in Boston. She checked. Sure enough there were Massachusetts license plates. An odd collection of objects were displayed on the dashboard; a grinning tiger at rest, a strange troll like creature with blue hair extending in every direction, and a sticker that read, "Deadheads Welcome." A handwritten notice stuck in the side window said, "No Radio. No Nothing."

The voice had insisted a friend would know just where to find him. It was likely that same girl's voice. She was keeping him all to herself. Amelia would have to wait for him to emerge. But she was too cold to stand here all day long without a cup of coffee to warm her.

Inside the coffee shop, the booths were on one wall, the counter seats opposite. She ordered and looked in the bar-length mirror to discover Winston Barry. He sat in a horseshoe-shaped booth, at the center of a crowd of his contemporaries. Her breath quickened. She bent down, purposely hiding her face. She slid onto a stool and watched as a steady stream of young men and women came in to greet him, slipping in beside him, or standing and bending over to talk. The girl who'd been in the driver's seat was at to his side.

How to begin? "Isn't this a coincidence?" Or maybe, "Fancy meeting you here?"

Absurd. It was better to just try the truth. Oh yes, the truth. That would win him over. It had worked perfectly with Muriel.

"Are you stalking me?" The boy accosted her, slipping onto the stool right beside her, then adding in a snide tone, "Are you filming today?"

"I'm staying nearby," she said.

"Where?" He clearly distrusted her. Who wouldn't? She was like the stalkers who had pursued her mercilessly, showing up at events and talks, one of them even getting to her plane and trying to sabotage it. She seemed as mad as they had, doing this.

"I was on my way to the airport yesterday," she tried.

"Convenient." He smirked. "What name should I use for you?"

"Amelia."

"All right, Amelia. We're on a first name basis, then. Where are you staying that's so convenient?"

"At the Y."

"The Y?" He smiled. "That's the best they can afford? The government must really be in trouble."

"What do you mean?"

"We both know what I mean," he said.

Then the girl he was with was pulling on his arm. "Let's get out of here," she told him.

He got up.

"Wait," Amelia said.

"For what? Are you going to arrest me?"

"Why on earth would I arrest you?"

Winston Barry shook his head like she was playing him for a fool. Then he was out the door. She pursued him onto the sidewalk. "What do you want from me?" he demanded.

"That lighter," she said. "Did Winston Manning give it to you? Do you know him?"

"You know I know him. You're from the feds, not *Car 54, Where Are You*, right? Am I supposed to think you don't know who my grandfather was?"

Was.

"He's dead?"

"Of course he's dead. He died twelve years ago. Wait." His eyes narrowed, and a look of relief washed over his face. "Is this about getting it back? Did that bitch, Katherine, hire you?"

Amelia blanched. She knew exactly whom he meant. "How did your grandfather die?" she asked, trying for a neutral tone.

"Cancer." He peered at her. "What's it to you? What are you after here?"

"I'm curious, that's all." Conversationally, adding, "The lighter has his initials on it. Did you know? Take it out, I'll show you."

The girl was tugging on him, pouting a little. But he shrugged, and then complied. He slipped the elegant, metal object from his pocket and extended it, cupped in the palm of his hand. Carefully, she traced the letters, hidden inside the rosebush, WM. The corners of his mouth tugged up. "What about that? So it was Katherine who sent you. Well, mystery solved. I took it. So what. I'm not giving it back. Tell her whatever you want."

He slid it away and put his arm through the girl's. Then they were off, rounding the corner, leaving her behind eating their dust.

Dead. Dead twelve years. Gone. Gone without her. This was his grandchild. She saw the resemblance, of course; it was what had fooled her initially. The color of the eyes, the wide shoulders. Genetics were so powerful. There was the experiment all Biology students had to replicate, Mendel's principles proved by mating fruit flies to find the dominant genes. Vestigial wings or normal ones, brown eyes or white.

She had to wake up. She was done. Shutting her eyes, she wished for the miracle to occur. She needed her body to be sucked back. She wanted hot air to wash over her. She needed to hear the ocean tapping at her feet. Enter here those for whom all hope is lost, she begged.

Nothing changed. Someone bumped into her and said, "Sorry." She was on Montague Street. She gave in, letting the crowd take her with them to the subway entrance. She walked down the stairs and purchased a token.

This time she was all alone touring the city. No Louise. No G.P. No Winston Manning. Even her fame had abandoned her. There were wonders to behold, though. Twin towers gleamed from the tip of Manhattan Island. The banks of elevators shook as they rose. On the roof deck, she joined crowds of tourists clutching their cameras. You could see imperially far, north, south, east, and west. Along the Palisades, huge apartment towers tilted at the sun. The city had expanded everywhere at once.

CHINATOWN WAS OUTSIDE the Canal Street F train stop. In the more authentic restaurants she was one of the few white patrons. Amelia ordered fried chicken feet. All manner of dumplings were served in woven nests, proffered from rolling carts. She went north to Little Italy to get a cup of bitter espresso and a cannoli. Further north and west she found art galleries. On the walls, blotches of paint were smeared across huge canvases. She disliked much of it; what was wrong with representation? One artist appealed to her though, a man named Diebenkorn. His series of paintings was titled Ocean Park. It reminded her of the light, the depth, the wonder she'd seen watching the Pacific. Soothing. Remarkable.

Outside, music blasted from a store, the singer demanding, "Should I stay or should I go?"

She didn't seem to have a choice in the matter. She took the train to Thirty-Fourth and emerged to find a line of schoolchildren. Joining them, she admired the Macy's windows. Inside, the story of the Nutcracker unfolded, complete with sugarplum fairies. Altman's was no longer across the street, but the Empire State was down another block. The view from the observation deck was still striking, although eclipsed by the one visible from the uppermost floor of the trade center.

Her biggest disappointment was with the subways. They were filthy, the windows of the trains painted over. And people were camped out inside the subway stations. Many were mad, muttering to themselves. When beggars came through the cars, the other passengers usually ignored them. She always gave something.

It was a different New York, better in some ways, worse in others.

South to Coney on a warm day, she discovered that where there had been pleasure and elegance, there was now a broken boardwalk. The beach was dirty, bottles and litter all over the sand. Yet, there was still that magnificent view and, of course, the ocean. A world away, she'd crashed and watched her plane sink, then she and Fred had swum to shore. A world and several lifetimes away. Amelia sat on the garbage-strewn sand, watching as ships passed across the edge of the horizon.

A WEEK WENT by like this. Seven full days before she found the courage to go back. Inside the coffee shop, he was sitting in the same booth. She ordered at the counter. She watched the steady stream of people come and go and understood that whatever he was doing, it was illicit. It was obviously why he'd been suspicious of her, although wouldn't anyone have wondered what it was she wanted of them?

He came up to her finally.

"You told her what I said?" he asked.

She shook her head.

"What do you think you're going to get out of me?"

"Nothing," she said.

"Why come back?"

"I want to give you your reward."

"Reward?" He laughed. "That is so bogus. For what?"

"You saved my life."

"It was a set up."

"No. You did save me. I wish to thank you."

"You wish to thank me?" Winston Barry gave her a hooded look. "Fine. Buy me something. It's her money, right?"

She wasn't going to argue, if it pleased him to think that, so be it.

The girl was left to "mind the store."

They walked over to Square Circle. Inside, he was well known. Lots of chatter went on before he asked for what they'd been keeping for him. "She's paying for me," he said. The record was titled *The Beatles Yesterday and Today.* On the cover, four handsome young men with oddly long, bowl-shaped haircuts were holding pieces of raw meat and dismembered dolls.

"This is what you want?"

"Yes."

It was nineteen dollars. She could easily afford the money.

"You must like the Beatles," he said. "Or are you more of a Presley type? Wait, I have it, James Brown! You like to get down and dirty."

She had no idea what he was referring to, but it clearly amused him.

Outside the store, he shook her hand and said, "Mission accomplished. Now you can send in your report on me."

That was it, as far as he was concerned. But as for her?

THE NEXT MORNING the woman at the front desk was distraught. Some crazy acolyte had murdered John Lennon, the former Beatle. Wasn't it horrible? Who would do something like that?

Beatles? She read the coverage. It was tragic. She knew all about this sort of insane devotion and what it spawned. She thought immediately of the boy, Winston Barry, and how he would take it. She went to find him at the coffee shop but he wasn't there. Not that day or the next. Amelia stood outside the window of the apartment, waiting for him. He never emerged. She read on, fascinated by the fans' heartbroken laments, the outpouring of grief and affection.

On Saturday, Amelia went to Central Park. She thought of it as Olmsted's triumph, his vision of a wilderness artfully tucked inside a teeming metropolis. Amelia joined the steady stream of people heading for the band shell.

Love, love me do

Love was what this group sang about.

She'd heard the band's songs in every store this week. And blaring from street vendors radios. The park crowd was silent. Respectful. It was like Will Roger's funeral, she thought, when every movie theatre in the country went dark in mourning. Amelia had gone to see her dearest friend privately, slipping in ahead of the line of fans to view the casket, then going home to lock herself in her bedroom and cry.

The crowd began to sing *Imagine*.

There was no set age; bearded men, fresh faced boys, girls in jeans and short skirts, and children perching on their parent's shoulders made up the crowd. A voice over the loudspeaker announced it was time and the clock struck two.

Not one person spoke. No one broke the silence. Being so tall, she could see around her. She searched for Winston Barry as one minute ticked on into two. No one broke ranks. They stood transfixed, trapped in their own memory of this singular person.

He'd been a pacifist, this John Lennon, although Amelia thought it a little silly when she'd read about his bed-in for peace. Still, the impulse was genuine. That poor bereft widow beating at the policeman with her fists, screaming that it had to be wrong, it just wasn't possible. Those two had apparently had a passionate love affair; he'd left his wife and given up his famous band-mates for her, turning himself into a nonentity of sorts, wanting to just be a husband and father and upstanding citizen of this same city. His mistake had been to try and find the limelight again. Fame was its own reward. Now there was an odd saying.

By the time she ran into Winston Manning again, Amelia was the most famous woman in the world. It had been years since she'd broken it off with him on that corner near the library. Years and years since she'd come into her own, leaving him and all that they'd planned together, behind. Amelia kept tabs on her former beau. He'd gone and married a rich society coed from Barnard, a Katherine Benet. She pored over the grainy photos of the *perfect* society wedding. Sneered at it, almost. And eventually, she too had married, giving in to G.P.

When she attended that gathering on the Upper East Side, reading and discussing her best selling book, *Twenty Hours, Forty Minutes: Our Flight in Friendship*, it had been four full years. She'd sat at the back of the room, signing the flyleaves, writing inscriptions. And asking the same question over and over and over again, "Is there something special you'd like me to add?"

"Whatever you think might be appropriate."

Amelia knew his voice immediately. She swallowed hard, looking up at Winston.

"Go ahead," he said, and she opened the book.

There was a slip of paper there, inside the front cover. She quickly slid it inside her jacket pocket. She could have thrown it away. Instead, later she unfolded it to find an invitation.

And went. How could she not? She wore a black wig, a long dark dress, glasses with see-through lenses, and a hat that obscured her face. They sat above the ballroom floor, talking. When the main act came on, they went downstairs to dance. The woman singer had a sweet, silky voice. They danced cheek to cheek under the colored lights of the ballroom. No one seemed to recognize her. That was a relief. Winston leaned in and whispered, "Anything worth doing involves taking risks."

"It's unfair to use my own words against me," she told him.

"What's that?" Putting a hand to one ear, he pretended deafness.

It was, actually, more than fair. She knew that better than he did. She had become Amelia Earhart, brazen flier, the bravest woman in the world. She'd piloted the Atlantic solo, married her promoter, and started a clothing line. She'd been feted in Europe and had ticker tape parades given in her honor. Yet with him, she'd played the coward. She'd come to tell him the entire story. Why she'd done what she'd done to him. She was going to get it off her chest and let him judge her cleanly, clearly. Yet, she found that, when she was with him, she was afraid to do it. In this one thing, she lacked the courage of her convictions. She just couldn't bear for him to have a bad opinion of her. It would, quite literally, break her heart. He would never have to know, she told herself. What was the harm in keeping quiet now?

Back in Central Park, they were at seven minutes and counting. The cold pierced her bones. Striated sunlight dappled the crowd. People spilled out everywhere. There had to be enough gathered here to bring the city's humming heart to a stop.

Wrong. She heard the faint rush of traffic. Life went on, regardless.

Winston Manning's clearly had without her. She'd gone to the library right after she discovered he was dead and read his impressive obituary in the New York Times. He'd built his father's business into a hugely successful company. He'd gotten out of munitions and into making steel beams for construction projects. *Manning is survived by his loving wife Katherine, his daughter, Brooke, and two grandchildren, Samantha and Winston.*

This, the same Katherine his grandson had accused her of working for, irony of ironies. The same woman Winston had claimed was barren. Had he lied to her about it? Perhaps. What mattered was he'd had a child with his wife after all. He'd had a full life. The granddaughter's name couldn't help but strike her as familiar, and then she knew why. It was the name of the girl who was corresponding with Muriel about that talk at Columbia. She'd looked over her sister's shoulder enough times in that stifling office to be certain of that.

Oh, the perfect synchronicity of it all.

Nine minutes and counting. Winston Manning had told her that if she went away and never came back, it would kill him. Clearly it hadn't. She was glad to know that. In fact, he'd had many more years without her, than with her.

She turned, trying to find the grandson's face in the crowd. If she told him her truth, he'd think her truly mad. Still, she thought she might try. What did she have to lose?

Ten minutes.

There he was, just at the edge of the crowd. Time was up. A collective gasp and then everyone began to disperse. He stood alone, a miserable, lost, and lonely boy.

Just then, the sky changed from crystalline blue to gray, and from above, white flakes rained down like God's own tears.

17

Sam
December 25 1980

SAM SAT IN the Westcott's living room Christmas morning. She had a cup of homemade cocoa, warming, in her hands. The marshmallows on top floated like tiny rectangular islands of processed sugar. The Westcotts were so nice to each other. Sam wasn't used to it, or to the host of holiday rituals that were a part of their Christmas. The youngest child gave out the presents. That was Lucy, but she would lose her place soon. Jack's wife Doris was pregnant, her huge belly covered by a pink maternity smock.

Pink just like those curtains, Sam thought. That first day they'd met each other seemed a million years ago. Sam had expected to find pink everywhere in the house, but Alma's taste was much more sedate. The walls were taupe or off white; the décor staid, plaid sofas and faux Chippendale chairs. Every spare table held a dried flower arrangement. Photographs showed the entire brood at every possible developmental stage, from posed infant on a bearskin rug, to toddler bopping a clown or playing in the snow, to boys in sports uniforms, to Lucy astride a Pinto quarter horse. The boys looked alike, all towheads with military haircuts. It was impossible to distinguish them by birth order because each photograph was snapped individually, but one had to be Donnie.

Lucy most resembled her father. On the mantel, he sported his high school football jersey, holding the trophy above his head. The inscription read, *ALL STATE CHAMPIONS 1951.*

The den was stuffed with memorabilia, including Tom's own personal trophies for *Most Valuable Player* and *All State Defensive End*. Sam had no idea what that was, but then she was ignorant when it came to team sports. In this house, sports were a birthright. Every member of the family excelled at something; baseball, football, basketball, hockey, and in Lucy's case, barrel racing.

A glass case at the end of the room held Tom's medals. Sam counted eleven. There were also plaques. One was from a battleship; the other, a submarine. Each had his name engraved next to the dates of service.

It was the most all American family she had ever come in contact with, a living, breathing Norman Rockwell portrait.

"Now isn't that lovely," Alma said. She held a pale green silk scarf up for all and sundry to admire.

"It's so you, Mom," Lucy said.

"Do you like it?" Phyllis, the second oldest brother Mike's wife said, her voice shrill.

"Of course."

"I was worried, wasn't I, Mike?"

"She sure was," Mike agreed. "Driving me nuts about it. We went everywhere looking."

"Well, it's perfect, just perfect," Alma exclaimed. She got up to kiss her daughter in law on the cheek.

"Thank you, Mother," Phyllis said.

Mother. Father. It was so quaint, Sam thought.

Alma wrapped the scarf twice round her neck. She'd already put on the bracelet Jack's wife, Doris, had gotten her. Doris was a big boned blonde with extremely pale skin. She was almost as tall as her husband. Indeed, every member of the family towered over Sam who, at five six, had never before imagined herself as diminutive. Here she was surrounded by a grove of redwoods. Even straining, Sam couldn't see the topmost branches or make out what these people actually thought through the thicket of pleasantries. It drove Lucy nuts, but to Sam, civility was a blessed relief. Lucy had no idea what it was like to have Christmas in that other world where everyone said whatever they liked, regardless of how much pain it caused.

"Isn't that cunning," Doris exclaimed. Lucy had given her a gold pin shaped like a butterfly.

There had actually been a load of gift-wrapped packages in Lucy's luggage.

"When did you buy those?" Sam asked, panicking.

"Don't worry," Lucy said. Once in Appleton, she'd taken Sam to the general store where Sam bought boxes of chocolates for everyone. "You'll be the most popular person in the room. At least they'll like that present. We all pretend to be thrilled, then we stuff whatever we get in the back of the drawer and forget all about it."

"Here's one from Sam," Lucy said, handing it off to Tom, who gave Lucy a warm, genuine smile.

Sam had witnessed the first of these at the airport. It came right after the endless bear hug, his eyes welling up as he clung to his daughter. Sam couldn't help choking up herself. It was like when she watched certain crappy TV shows, not to mention *Love Story.* Sam was envious. Since the divorce, her father had never shown up for Christmas. But Tom loved his daughter, and wasn't ashamed to show it.

Tom shook the rectangular package. "Hmm," he said. "I'm betting it's a tie."

"Dad."

"You know how I love ties."

Lucy had gotten him a light blue one. When he opened the package, Tom immediately stripped off the one he had been wearing to exchange it for hers. His uniform was the same as his sons, a neatly pressed button-down shirt and a pair of khaki slacks with the seam standing up straight, saluting. They all were shod in brown leather shoes. The two older boys wore sports jackets. This family's idea of casual was a far cry from what Sam was used to. She was ashamed of her faded blue jeans and short sleeve t-shirt.

"A book!" Tom said, managing to sound authentically surprised.

He held it up. The general store had a small selection. Sam had chosen *Famous Naval Battles,* one of those coffee table tomes that were printed for just this sort of occasion. It would likely sit on the table gathering dust. But not today, today they would all leaf through it. "Boys, take a look, there are some incredible pictures in here."

All of them did a bang up job of feigning enthusiasm.

Sweaters.

Scarves.

More scarves, oh my.

A pair of gold stud earrings for Alma.

Then, a coffee break with homemade cake that had been drizzled with sugar frosting sweet enough to bring on a diabetic coma.

"How is it?" Alma asked. A chorus of approval answered her.

"Delicious."

"Incredible."

"The best!"

"No one bakes like my mom!"

Then it was back to the present presentations,

"Here's one for Sam," Lucy said, handing her a box.

She'd received other things. All were clearly from Alma. Perfume. Soap. An embroidered pillowcase. Sam was touched, even though Lucy had told her that whatever she got was from the gift drawer. Apparently Alma shopped and stashed these things away for just such an occasion. The idea of a mother who had a drawer like that, who was thoughtful enough to prepare in advance was, well, remarkable. Sam was sure that Alma had fed and housed every stray child her brood brought home. She clearly deserved the mug one of those two sons had given her with the inscription *World's Best Mom.*

The group leaned forward expectantly.

Sam read the card aloud. "To Sam. From her Secret Santa."

Lots of Secret Santas had come and gone, and each had a tell. In Alma's case, a whirring of anxiety. *Was it what they wanted? If not, whoever might have gotten it would certainly be ready to return it, why everyone knew that people kept the store receipts.* Tom's sheepish smile gave him away. The older boys made bad jokes. Jack's wife giggled nervously, an Alma in the making. Mike's wife, Phyllis, started talking about how much it had cost or where it might have been bought. "Oops," she'd say, "Where Santa might have found it." As for Bill and Rich's presents, all, except the mug, wore the University of Wisconsin Badger colors.

Now, Sam used her nail to break through the tape without ripping the paper. Alma collected it in a pile. "Waste not, want not," she'd said more than once.

"That's just beautiful," Alma exclaimed, admiring it before placing it aside.

It was heavier than any of the other wrapping paper. On it, bas-relief angels blew golden trumpets.

Sam dug down through the tissue, flashing on those joke presents Win had tortured her with, a big box revealing a slightly smaller one. On it went until it got down to zip, zero, done. This wasn't a trick. It was just carefully wrapped. Inside, Sam found four tiny boxes. She removed the first. All of them craned forward, eager to see. Sam opened it to find a full mariachi band complete with bass player, horn section, and a singer crooning a festive tune underneath the twinkling lights at the *Casa De Hombres.*

"Oh, Lucy, it's so cool," Sam said, lifting it to show it off to the rest of the room. She handed it to Phyllis, who peered at the skeletons in the diorama, keeping it at arm's length.

"My lord, what is it?" Phyllis asked.

"A Day of the Dead shadow box," Sam said.

"A shadow box?" Phyllis passed it off to Mike.

It was the proverbial hot potato. He fingered the box cautiously, then handed it to Doris. On it went, making the rounds of the rest of the brothers, first Jack, then Rich, then Bill, and off to Tom, who handled it gingerly, then handed it to Alma.

She held it up to admire. "Why would you look at that, such detail!"

Sam opened the next. It was a boxing rink and the two opponents were locked in a clinch as a crowd of sepulchral fans cheered them on. In the far corner, the cut man was busy, his white towel sprinkled with blood.

"I don't understand what these are supposed to be about," Phyllis said.

"The Day of the Dead is a Mexican holiday," Sam explained. "Like Mardi Gras except, well, it's not just a big party, it's the holiday where people remember their loved ones." She paused, feeling awkward. She knew the subtext here, the missing party.

"I don't get it," Phyllis said. "Who would even make something this creepy?"

Sam darted a glance at Lucy. "Halloween didn't start off as kids going around saying trick or treat," she tried.

"I don't know what Halloween's got to do this." Phyllis shivered. "I don't get the joke, which I guess is the point. I'm just not that bright about this kind of thing. Not like Lucy here, the resident genius."

"Now Phyllis," Alma began.

"I bought them for Sam," Lucy said in a completely neutral tone. "This isn't meant to insult your intelligence, Phyllis. Everything isn't about you."

"Or about you either," Phyllis retorted.

"But I really like them," Sam said, earnestly.

The room was rife with tension. It was a shame. They'd all been so happy. Or, well, they'd seemed happy. Why wasn't that enough? It had been enough for her.

"You don't understand," Sam tried. "There's this store in Greenwich Village. We walked past and I pointed them out to Lucy."

"Sam *was* the one who told me about the Day of the Dead," Lucy told them. "And you know what, Phyllis? I think it's a pretty good holiday to have, to take one day out of the year to talk about well, let's say, maybe Donnie?"

"Now darling," Tom said. "Don't start."

"Start what? Remembering how it used to be on Christmas? How Donnie was always the first one up? He'd beat us all downstairs. Isn't that right? He'd make that list of whatever we thought was in the presents and keep it, then whoever guessed the closest got a special prize. Donnie made sure they were always things we wanted, like having peanut butter and jelly snuck into your lunch box when Mom went on that tuna fish salad kick, or having your homework done for you for a week. Do you remember how he did that for you with your chemistry, Mike? He got this friend of his from high school who was good at Chem to do it. No one ever knew. It was cheating, yeah, but it was only for a week. It was fun. It was always fun with him here."

Tom shook his head.

"What, Dad? You don't want to think about it? Is it easier for you to pretend he never existed? It's not for me. You guys remember the first night we moved in here?" Lucy turned to her brothers, trying to get them to meet her eyes. None did. She let out a low laugh. "That's how it is then. I see. Well I remember. It snowed and he woke us up. He made us get dressed and sneak out. We found sleds in the garage and then we went over to the hill by the High School. We were the only ones out that night, just the six of us. Everything he touched was better because of it. Tell me I'm wrong."

Her brothers stared at the floor, at their hands, at some point far off in the distance. Tom chewed hard on his cheek. Phyllis examined her very fine manicure. Doris seemed to be praying. Only Alma turned Lucy's way.

"Isn't Christmas supposed to be about Jesus and how he died for our sins?" Lucy asked, her voice cracking. "Isn't it about us remembering *him*? That's what we say all the presents are for and why we spend so much money on each other, right? So we can remember his sacrifice. Well, what if Donnie was like Jesus? What if he died for our sins?"

"That's enough, young lady," Tom said firmly.

Lucy was shaking.

"You went to Mexico, didn't you, Dad?" Jack interjected, loudly.

"Sure did," Tom agreed. "Veracruz. It was pretty down there, but poor, dirt poor. These kids ran after you in the street, begging for money. It made you feel sorry for them, though how could you have helped all of them? I didn't see the point in picking out one. That just would have made more of a problem."

"Remember how I thought we should go there for our honeymoon?" Phyllis said.

"Then the Murrays came back and told us how sick they got," Mike agreed. "That was the end of that idea."

"Dad traveled everywhere," Jack said to Sam.

"That's the Navy for you," Tom allowed. "Broadens the horizons."

Lucy was seething. They were going to go on as if she'd said nothing.

Sam couldn't bear it. "I know it's not any of my business—"

"It's not your business," Mike said firmly.

"Fuck you," Lucy threw out.

"Lucy. We don't use that kind of language here," Tom said.

"Maybe we should," she told him.

Mike cleared his throat, meaningfully. There was an awkward, lengthy silence. Doris stroked her cross. Phyllis smoothed her skirt. The boys exchanged meaningful looks.

"There's not a day goes by I don't think about Donnie," Alma said quietly, into the breach. Her hands were busy, knitting an invisible shroud. "I know that we all have our own way of remembering him. I'm sure your brothers do. I know your father does. But I also know you're right; we're scared to talk about it. Maybe you're also right that that's not a good thing. We talk about the weather with each other and what movie we saw. I guess we do tiptoe around the point more than a little."

"Now that's just not true," Tom said, raising his hands awkwardly, stretching them out in front of him, using them to plead his case.

"Yes it is." Alma stood, walked to the window, and turned to look out. Sam followed her gaze and realized it was snowing, hard. "We act like it never happened. The honest truth is, I don't know how I get through each and every day. I want to break down, but I tell myself I can't. No one prepares you for how you feel, losing your own child. There are no rules to follow on how to act, or what to do. And there's no end to it. No turning back or changing things round. Still, you do it in your mind, you do it awake and asleep.

Sometimes I think he's alive and think I've been dreaming all the rest. Then I see how wrong I am and how much I failed him."

"Now, Alma," Tom said soothingly. "There's just no point in getting all worked up. It's Christmas. We're all here together."

Lucy shot up. She went to her mother and put her arm around her. Alma turned toward her and sank a little into her daughter. Then she looked back at the room, at her family. Her eyes were damp. "We're not all here together. That's what your daughter here has been trying to say to you."

Six. Six children. It was what Alma had said when they first met. Tom had tried to quiet her then.

"You boys were so young," Alma said. "We were living in Okinawa and I'd made this one great friend. Mildred was black, that's what they call it now. Even so, she turned the white boy's heads more than once, even your dad's, as I remember. She was what we used to call, a live wire. She and I just hit it off.

"The thing is, black stayed with black, white with white on that base. We were the exception. None of the other women knew how to talk to us, but we didn't give two bits for what they thought. There are times in your life when you meet someone, and the two of you just click." Alma smiled, clearly remembering her friend.

Lucy's eyes met Sam's.

"It's about that trip we all took," Alma said. "Millie and her four kids and me and my five, you were even there too Lucy, in my belly. We took a boat over to the mainland and then caught the train. It was my first real adventure without Tom. You boys were so excited. You had real bunk beds, not that any of you slept much. Every two minutes you'd pop up the shades and look out.

"Buildings were different over there; most of them squat to the ground. Off in the distance, snowcapped mountains. When we pulled into Hiroshima station, there were signs in four different languages. We dropped off our bags and walked up to the castle. They've rebuilt it now, but at the time they were just starting. The castle had stood there for centuries until we dropped the bomb on them." Alma searched her sons' faces. "Do you remember Millie at all? Do any of you remember playing with her kids?"

They shook their heads.

She nodded, knowingly. "The point is Donnie did. He asked me where that castle was a few years ago. That was how that boy was. He remembered every little detail. And I think they haunted him." Alma smiled, weakly.

Odd how quiet it was, the sort of quiet that came when the snow fell, Sam thought, the world blanketed and softened because of it.

"No one deserves what we did to those people over in Japan; dropping those bombs out of the clear blue sky, experimenting on them like that. They were mothers and children, old people, all of them getting up to greet another day. Millie told me the Japanese thought they were leaflets. Everyone was looking up and then came the blast. I told Donnie where we'd gone and then that I was sorry if it upset him and he said, 'Don't ever be sorry. I'm glad you took me there. Glad I saw it.' But was he really glad or just saying that to make me feel better? I think it worried him. I think maybe taking him there was part of what went wrong. He was so sensitive, he cared so much about everyone and everything. I know I should have done more to protect him. I go over that night all the time, thinking if only I'd said something to him or made him stay put. Why didn't I keep him here? Why couldn't I keep him safe?" She moaned, and Lucy was there.

Lucy was right there, saying, "Oh, Mom." Lucy took her mother into her arms.

"ARE YOU OKAY?" Lucy asked Sam, an hour later.

They were up in her bedroom, taking a breather. After a trip to the same hill Donnie had snuck his brothers and sister out to, once, in the middle of the night. This time the parents had tagged along. They'd all come back to the house pink cheeked and half frozen, had more hot chocolate, warmed up, and greeted aunts, uncles, and cousins. Then came an early dinner of perfectly rare roast beef. Glasses were raised. Toasts rang out. Lucy and Sam helped to serve, clear, and dry. More than once, Alma and Lucy stood together, passing the plates without a word to each other, their bodies bending towards each other, a mother and daughter reunion.

"I'm fine," Sam said. And meant it.

Lucy gripped her hand for a second. "If you hadn't been here, I wouldn't have been able to say anything to them about Donnie."

Lucy's smile was so whole hearted and sincere, it made Sam choke up.

"That's silly, Lucy. You would have talked about it."

Lucy shook her head. "I know myself. I seem self-confident, but when it comes to this kind of thing, I'm not. Not at all."

"As opposed to say, kissing me in front of that boy in the bar?"

"That was funny, right? I wanted to freak him out."

"You definitely did." Sam paused, then added, "It sort of freaked me out too."

"Really? You?"

"Yes, me," Sam admitted. "I didn't know what it meant."

"Everything doesn't mean something," Lucy said.

"No?"

"I mean, some things just happen."

Lucy was sitting next to her on the bed, cross-legged, and it came to Sam that they were both thinking about the same moment, when Lucy had brazenly pushed the gun away from her face, and they'd all taken off.

"I could have gotten us killed," Lucy said, softly.

"But you saved us," Sam told her. Then she took Lucy's hand for a second, squeezed it hard, let it go.

"And you saved me." Lucy beamed a smile at her. "What about that story Mom told. Think of her having a black friend. Think of her taking us all to Hiroshima to educate us. I never would have guessed she had it in her."

"People surprise you."

Just then, voices rang out from below. "Lucy? Samantha? Girls, we need you."

Sighing, Lucy unwound herself and stood. They trooped down to form a circle round the piano with the rest. Christmas carols spun through the blessed holy night.

SHE WAS DOING it for Lucy. That was what Sam told herself, when she decided to say, "Yes," two days later. She got into a plane with Lucy and flew south to San Juan. That night she lubricated her misgivings with sangria and woke up at three a.m. to hear groaning and squeaking through the paper-thin walls. Sam put the pillow over her head and cursed at herself.

The next morning, early, she snuck down to the pool. The ocean was hidden from view behind a slatted metal fence, keeping the tenants safe from the riffraff.

"Does the senorita want anything?" The waiter who inquired wore a black vest and black pants over a long-sleeved white shirt topped off with a smart looking bowtie. It was eighty degrees and climbing outside. The sun was dull in the sky. Yes, she wanted something, a cup of strong coffee; sadly, she'd left her wallet upstairs.

"It's okay," Sam said, flashing a smile.

He turned to chat up another guest, an older woman with a mane of blow-dried blond hair whose bikini had a chain linking the top and bottom together. What kind of odd tan would that give you, Sam wondered?

Sam got out of the chair and dove into the water. The cold shocked her body into consciousness. From below, the ripples crested over her head. A child's plastic dolphin was under the rusted ladder, lost among old gum wrappers and palm fronds. Surfacing, Sam blinked and spun round slowly, then reared back. Floating, she shut her eyes, the image of a yellow disc seared into her pupils. She was probably doing irreparable damage to her corneas. It was a crystal clear summer day here. But back in New York, it was freezing and miserable. Sam knew it was a shallow excuse, but it was a good one, too. Or at least better in the daylight, as opposed to last night, listening to what went on through the wall. She swam to the ladder and then climbed up the rungs, walked over to her chair, and collapsed into it. The sun beat down, eradicating memory and purging further regretful thought.

"Hey." A finger jabbed her midsection. Sam's eyes snapped open. Lucy's tiny bikini was sculpted out of three triangular patches of jade green material. She sank into the chaise next to Sam's. Sam had bought her Hawaiian print two-piece at a store in Appleton. The bottom covered enough of her ass for comfort and the top had under-wire that miraculously gave her cleavage. Next to Lucy, though, the effect paled.

The eager waiter appeared. "Senorita, how can I help you?"

"Coffee," Lucy said. "Iced."

"Spot me?"

"Of course."

"I'll have one, too," Sam said.

"Si, senorita." He floated an insincere smile.

Sam squirmed. She didn't want to be perceived as what she so evidently was, the rich tourist gringa.

"I can't believe how warm it is here," Lucy said. "As soon as you get off the plane it smells like summer."

True. Heat, water, and tropical foliage combined, exuding the same pungent odor Sam inhaled when she lay down on the grass on a hot July day on the great lawn in front of her grandmother's house in Maine. Right now, though, she was inhaling coconut oil. The woman to their right slathered it on, even though her skin was already an otherworldly bronze.

"Where's Dusty?" Sam asked.

"Taking a shower. He'll be down."

The iced coffee arrived with a side pitcher of milk and packets of sugar.

"Gracias," Sam said.

"Gracias," Lucy repeated.

The waiter gave Lucy a lecherous wink. "Da nada, senorita," he said.

Lucy rolled her eyes at his back. Overhead a bi-plane pulled an advertisement for Ron Rico Rum.

"Dusty wants to go to this place where there's surfing," Lucy said.

"What will you and I do?"

"I thought we could all go."

"You couldn't pay me enough to get on a surf board. I'm a land based mammal."

"You can lie on the beach there," Lucy said. "Dusty goes to Rincon every time he comes down here."

"I think I'll stay put."

"It's supposed to be really beautiful. Plus, you'll get your own cabin. Please come, Sam."

Sam nodded, giving in.

An hour later, Dusty was expertly strapping two surfboards atop his parent's Jeep. Only then did Sam realize Lucy intended to surf. She'd be left alone on the beach as well as in her cabin. A nap was definitely in the cards. She could recuperate from her bad night's sleep, and maybe even think. Or better yet, not think.

"I didn't know you surfed," Sam said to Dusty.

"I'm a man of mystery," he told her.

"And the raddest dude ever?"

Dusty gave her a sisterly punch on the upper arm. "Do I detect a note of sarcasm, Sam I am?"

"You just might."

Sam lay down in the back of the Jeep but her stomach couldn't tolerate that position for long. When she sat up, her hair blew wildly. They sped past stands selling *Bebidas* and *Carnitas*. Dusty veered around slow moving trucks with panache. Salsa boomed out of the radio, and Lucy kissed Dusty on the cheek. Sam tipped sideways, leaning against the hard metal shell of the car, then shut her eyes. She dozed, only coming fully awake when they made a sudden hard left and bounced down a narrow road.

The landscape had changed. Scrubby bushes clung to rocky cliffs. They passed a faded sign for a roadside restaurant, then the restaurant itself shut tight, then a gas station littered with broken-down vehicles, then a row of houses painted in turquoise, pink, and lemon yellow. Chickens, goats, and dogs wandered along the side of the road. A truck rushed past, heading in the opposite direction, with only inches to spare. Suddenly they were braking to a stop. It seemed as if they'd come to the edge of the world. In front of them was the vast ocean. Ripples of white surf shredded across a deep blue sea. Dusty pulled over onto a narrow siding, and they stepped out to admire the view. Pelicans dive bombed while gulls wheeled, shrieking. Out past the breakwater a line of surfers waited for the perfect wave. Their reed-thin voices carried on the wind.

"You're still going out with me, right?" Dusty asked Lucy.

"Just try and stop me." Lucy stood closest to the edge, her blond hair blown back, her profile magnificent. She looked just like a ship's figurehead, cutting first through the wind and the wake.

THE HOTEL, A series of huts dubbed *La Villa Hermosa,* was shabby. The shacks were in no way hermosa. Cut from roughly hewn wood and unpainted, they fronted a rocky beach. Dusty went into the *oficina* to register.

Sam's cabin was number nine. It was basically a shack with a single bed, a rickety side table and a non-working floor lamp. Home sweet home. She changed into her bathing suit and emerged to find the jeep gone. Lucy sat on the sand, smoking.

"He went to get an extra wet suit from his surfing buddies," Lucy said.

"Do you even know how to surf?" Sam asked.

"I learned when my dad was posted in Hawaii. I can teach you."

"No way. Not ever."

"You'd like it."

"No, I'd never like it," Sam said. "Believe you me. Danger in the water is not my business."

Lucy laughed as the jeep roared up, spitting gravel. Dusty emerged, a wet suit in one hand, their lunch in the other.

THE SURFING BEACH was minutes away. The only sign it existed was a motley array of old, rusted American cars parked at odd angles on the nonexistent shoulder. Dusty unloaded the boards. He hoisted the first. Lucy grabbed the second. Sam retrieved her book and towel. They walked onto a slim quarter moon of sand that fronted the pounding surf. Near the breakwater, a line of surfers bobbed and weaved.

Lucy and Dusty pulled on their wet suits and grabbed their boards.

"Sure you don't want to come with us?" Dusty asked Sam.

She shook her head. "You know me better than that."

"You're so funny, Sam I am. You don't know what you're missing."

"Sage advice from my future legal counsel."

Off the two of them went, boards under their arms. Sam watched them drop down and paddle, making for the horizon. She cracked open the novel she'd brought along. But it was far too pleasant to read. She shut her eyes and gratefully sank into a stupor.

She was roused by a masculine voice. "Hey, you."

She opened her eyes and saw its owner standing above her toting a deep purple surfboard with a yellow lightning strike Z slashed across it. He was tall and blond; his chiseled features matched his wide-shouldered physique.

"What's up?" he asked.

"Nothing."

"Really? What have you got there?"

"A book."

"What are you doing with it?" he inquired.

"Reading."

"Cool. How did you get here?"

"I drove," Sam said.

"Really?"

"Dusty drove me," she amended. Was this guy for real? Was anyone this dense? Or were the questions he posed a put on?

"You're with Dusty?" He swiveled to face the water. "That's Dusty out there? Shit. Aren't you going out?"

"No."

He gave her a searching look. "Why not? Who's out there with him?"

"Lucy."

"Lucy." Mr. Surf and Sun pondered the name for what seemed like forever. He finally said, "And you're?"

"Sam."

"I'm Luke."

"Hi, Luke." Sam nodded a greeting. She'd assumed the stereotypes of surfers in movies were false but he was on his way to proving the opposite.

"You're not into surfing?" he asked.

"Nope."

"You should be. I mean, look at those bitchin' waves."

"Bitchin' all right." She assumed that meant obscenely huge and absolutely terrifying.

"I was out all morning. Just ran an errand. Now I'm back."

"I see." Another pregnant pause. Sam was getting a crick in her neck from looking up at him.

"I guess I'd better get out then," Luke allowed.

"I guess so," she agreed.

"See you later."

"Uh huh."

"It's Luke," he said again.

"I know."

He beamed a toothy smile and hoisted his board over his head, effortlessly. Luke wore no wet suit. Sam thought it entirely possible that the surf had beaten whatever sense he was born with out of him.

She leaned back and lifted the novel above her eyes to shield them from the sun. *The Transit of Venus* was Professor Swift's suggestion. On the cover, bearded gods hoisted a globe of the world. Inside, the characters twisted and turned away from each other with maddening efficiency. The book was a study in delayed gratification. Would the lovers ever live happily ever after? Professor Swift claimed the author was a genius. When Sam turned to the photograph at the back, she did a double take. Shirley Hazzard looked so much like Professor Swift she could have been her twin sister.

Sam rolled onto her stomach and concentrated. The writing was dense and lyrical. Sam was pretty sure that things would end badly. How could it go well for star-crossed lovers like the scientist Ted Tice and the love of his life, Caro? Still, Sam wanted them to get lucky, to be the exception, to enjoy a fairy tale ending.

She was so immersed in the novel that when she looked up, she was surprised to find herself back on the beach. Far out, six surfers waited for the perfect ride. It looked like such a pedestrian activity. But then a huge wave bore down on them, and all six crouched to catch it. One surfer fell, then the next, until only two were left. Sam was certain they were Luke and Lucy. She yelled out, "Go, Luce." Luke bobbled, then slipped from his board. Lucy rode the rest of the way in, alone.

Sam's heart swelled. She waved to Lucy, and Lucy waved back.

Sam picked up the book again. Poor Ted Tice was lost in the wilderness, but he never gave up searching for love. It was elusive, but maybe in the end true love would triumph and they would be together, always. Sam wished it were the case. One could hope, anyhow. Then she heard screams and looked up.

"Where is he?"

"He was right over there!"

"Where?"

"There, right there!"

Sam stood, straining to see. Two rider-less surfboards bobbed in the wake. The other surfers were converging on a spot close to treacherous looking rocks.

"Did you see where he went?"

"Come on, man, find him!"

Sam ran into the water. The undertow was powerful, knocking her over. She got to her feet and dug her toes in. She knew better than to try and swim out. She could do a decent breaststroke, but her skills eroded after that.

"Have you got him?"

"I can't see a fucking thing."

"What the fuck? What's going on?"

"Mother-fucking riptide!"

One huge wave, then another, crashed against the shoreline. One surfer, then the next, dove down and reemerged.

"Over here!"

It was Lucy, emerging with her arms round someone, shoving him onto a surfboard. Others helped her push the board in. Sam waded toward them as far as she dared and saw who it was. Dusty. Unconscious. With a bloody gash in his forehead. She rushed forward, grabbed hold, and tugged him to shore.

"Take him off, put him down here!" Sam bent over Dusty and swept his mouth for debris, then swept the airway. She tilted his head back and pinched his nose. She breathed into his mouth once, then again, counting down.

She pumped on his chest.

Don't leave.

Don't go.

Fuck you.

I won't let you go.

Not now.

Not here.

Not on my watch.

Sam forced her breath into Dusty's lungs, compressed his chest, and waited for the response. Waited for him to hear her and come back. Something moved. Out of the corner of her eye, she spotted a sleek white bird skimming across the surface of the water. Sam told herself it wasn't a sign. It meant nothing. It wasn't his soul taking leave.

Come back.

Please come back!

Don't leave me. Please. Not you!

She tried again. Pounded on him again.

And Dusty choked. Then coughed. His eyelids fluttered.

"Turn him on his side," Sam ordered.

Luke did, and Dusty heaved up half the ocean.

The surfers were all talking at once, their voices tinny, exposing the strain.

"That's the way, man."

"Back from the dead."

"Fuck."

"Didn't want to lose another one after Roger."

Dusty wheezed. His nose was running. His skin had taken on a greenish pallor. Luke helped him to his feet and wrapped his head with a towel to staunch the blood.

"You girls follow us," Luke said.

The keys were in the ignition. Lucy drove, the last car of a small parade.

"You were amazing," Lucy said. "How did you know what to do?"

"I have no idea. I mean, I guess it was because I took a class." Sam couldn't stop shaking.

"God, that was incredible," Lucy said. "Are you okay? Of course you're not." She put her hand on Sam's and held onto it tight.

"You found him. I saw you," Sam said.

"You saved his life."

Sam shook her head, not because she wanted to argue over credit, but because she wanted to shove all of it away. She wanted to go back. To go back to their dorm room, say on the afternoon of December eleventh and then go downtown to the Dakota, gothic home to the stars, and point out a nervous man standing by the entrance. She'd tell the police officer, "He's got a gun. He's crazy. He wants to kill John Lennon." She wanted to watch him being taken away, she wanted him to be locked up forever, and then she wanted to go back even further to a cold spring morning in Appleton, Wisconsin. She wanted to knock on the door of a house and say to Alma, "You don't know me, but trust me. Don't let your son go to that party tonight. Lock him in his room. Make him stay there. Talk to him. Tell him about your own mistakes and how it gets better. Explain that if he waits long enough, it will change. Then one day, he'll have his own kid to tell the same story to."

Sam said, "My mother keeps trying to kill herself."

"What?" Lucy asked.

"The first time, she slit her wrists."

"No!" But Lucy saw immediately that it was true. She reached out and took Sam's hand.

"I was twelve that time. Dusty's dad had gotten the three of us passes for the opening of *Jaws*. It was an extremely big deal. We saw Roy Scheider, and Robert Shaw, and Richard Dreyfuss. We walked in on the red carpet. We sat in these plush seats like we were important. It wasn't even a movie for kids my age. After the first scene, I had to hide my eyes. I guess that's really why I don't like to go swimming in the ocean. My stomach was in knots, but I was with the two of them, and they were acting like it was nothing, watching people get pulled under and eaten. I wanted to impress them, so I pretended that none of it scared the shit out of me. I think Dusty knew I was bluffing, because he kept telling me it was a mechanical shark. Then it was over and thank god, because all I had to do after that was boast about going to a premiere to my friends. We went back to our apartment. Brooke had said she was going to go out because she'd just broken up with Mr. Paris and she was hot to find a replacement."

Lucy gave her hand a hard squeeze. Sam hated the next part. Telling it meant seeing it. Seeing it meant feeling it. "We all thought we were home alone. Win and Dusty lit up a joint. They started calling people to see who might come by. I went to the bathroom, and it was locked. There was a puddle of water coming from under the door. I told myself it was a leak, but that didn't explain why the door was locked. Then I knew. I knew because Brooke had this record album from this play she loved, *Marat/Sade*. On the cover there's a reproduction of a painting of Marat in his bathtub, and his wrists are slashed. I knew that was what she'd done, and I didn't want to be the one to find her. For a second, I thought I'd hide in my room and let them find her."

"But you didn't," Lucy said. "You're too brave for that."

"Brave? Is that what it is?"

"Yes," Lucy said firmly. "Brave and noble and true."

"Sure, I'm one of the three musketeers. That's me, all right."

But Lucy was right. Sam had run back to get Win and Dusty, and they'd broken down the door. Brooke was lying in the tub. It didn't look anything like that drawing on the cast album. The tub wasn't pretty. Blood was everywhere; the water was pink with it. The police came and took her mother away. She was hospitalized, and Win refused to go to their grandmother's house, Sam did too, staying at home with her brother. Waiting for Brooke to come back to them. When she did, they made her a pancake breakfast and after that they treated her as if she were going to break.

"Her shrink said it was a cry for help," Sam said. "Win, Dusty, and I promised we would never tell. It was what she wanted. She begged us to keep it a secret. That time, then the next, then the time after that. I don't know. It's awkward to talk about it. Win and I, we promised each other that we would keep her safe. But sometimes you don't know how to keep that kind of promise, do you? I mean, sometimes it's not only up to you, right?"

Lucy nodded sagely. She knew. She knew exactly what Sam meant. Sam thought of what Alma had said, what Alma blamed herself for not being able to do and how she would likely blame herself for that for the rest of her life, how unfair it all was but how natural it was too. And then Sam thought that the people who had assigned Lucy to her room were actually geniuses, because she and Lucy seemed as if they had nothing in common, when they had this, this trumped everything else.

They had pulled into the lot at La Clinica. Lucy shut off the car engine.

"I used to imagine the worst," Sam said. "Just to try and prepare myself. It was kind of a relief. At least it would be over with, you know. Then, I'd hate myself for thinking about it like that."

Lucy pressed her forehead against Sam's for a long, significant second. She pulled away. "I understand. There's nothing wrong with that. It's natural. All of it is."

There was a sweet, merciful silence. Then Sam took a deep breath and opened her door. As she stepped out, she remembered Win turning off the water and Dusty helping him pull Brooke out of the tub. Her mother's body had flopped onto the floor. She had tried to cover her with the Indian print bedspread from the couch, because she shouldn't be naked like that, all the while saying to Brooke that she'd be a good girl, she'd be so good, she'd do anything she wanted if only Brooke would live.

In this waiting room, a mother comforted her wailing child. A man sat patiently, his arm in a sling. Dusty was wrapped in a blanket. His color had returned, pinches of red on each cheek. Luke got up and let Sam and Lucy sit on either side of him.

"Sam I am," he said to her. "You brought me back from the brink. Wait till I tell Win."

Poor Win. He'd been the one to find Brooke after she took the bottle of sleeping pills. He'd stuck his finger down her throat and made her throw up, then called 911 again. Win and Sam came home to find her with a gun after another miserable breakup. "What the fuck is wrong with you?" Win demanded, but he told Sam to go into her bedroom. He got the gun away, hid it, and made Brooke promise him *never again.*

Her promises were worthless. He knew it. Sam knew it. It was why Sam had chosen Barnard. Why she stayed close. It was why she was going to be a doctor, so she could be ready. Of course, she also liked the idea of helping people and she was good at it. It wasn't just because her mother might need her *in extremis.* Poor Win. How could he really leave when Brooke said things like, "I'm thinking Russian Roulette, for fun." Win tried Las Vegas. He tried the desert. He tried Mexico. He tried college. He tried everywhere he could think of, but he could have gone to China, for all the good it would do him. He would have ended up back there in that apartment, vigilant, angry, and evidently, terrified.

That was the sort of love they felt for their mother.

They were both suckers. But it wasn't that simple. Nothing was ever that simple. There was another Brooke. There was another mother. That Brooke had announced, "Today's your special day." Sam was told to choose anything she wanted so she decided on a ride in a hansom cab round the park, then ice cream at Rumpelmayer's, wolfing down every bite of the massive banana split. That Brooke said, "You are the best girl in the entire world, how did I ever get so lucky?" That mother said, "Straight A's. Marvelous. Where on earth did you come from?" That doting parent said, "So dashing," as she dressed up Sam as the pirate king for their rainy day theatrical in the living room.

That Brooke was the fun mother, the cool mother. That Brooke had taken her to the Fillmore East when she was seven to see the Allman Brothers. They had backstage passes because she was always a VIP.

"Isn't she sweet," the man with the ponytail said when they visited in the dressing room. "Woman, you surprise me. I didn't know you had kids. Wow."

"Wow, indeed," Brooke agreed.

She and Sam exchanged a knowing look. Sam wasn't a kid; she was a pal. She was Brooke's best pal and knew everything there was to know about making her way in the world. Brooke told her that and that she was "stupendous."

In the cab on their way home, Brooke asked her what part was best.

"When that man looked at you and played you the song," Sam said.

"That wasn't me he was looking at," Brooke said. "It was you." Then Brooke ruffled her hair. That was the other mother, the magical mother, the one with the radiant, heart-shattering smile.

18

Muriel
January 5 1981

MURIEL DUNKED THE toast into the soft-boiled egg and listened to the shower run. She'd woken up to the sound of footsteps. "Who is that?" Then she'd seen him. Virgil was bringing her breakfast in bed. Of all things! What a romantic.

Muriel swallowed the toast and sipped on the coffee. The curtains were open. Outside it was brilliantly sunny, the kind of sunny day that came in winter and fooled her into thinking she was back in Los Angeles again, back at the beginning, twinned to her sister. It was a nice image to hold onto. She felt so oddly peaceful.

"Hey," Virgil growled as the door to the bathroom opened. He stepped out, wrapped from the waist down in one of the hotel's towels. He was hairless, not even a little sprinkling on his chest.

Virgil sat down next to her on the bed and tucked his arm round her, then gave her a gentle squeeze.

"I've got to get over to the meeting," he said. "They're taking us out to lunch, so I won't be back till around five." He kissed her, and she tasted Crest toothpaste, minty fresh as advertised; underneath it, the bitter aftertaste from the last sip of coffee he'd drunk.

He turned away to dress. It was funny, his trying to be modest at his age. He put on his jockey shorts, pulled on a pair of blue serge suit pants, added a crisp, pin-striped oxford button-down shirt, and topped it off with the jacket, then over that a tan cashmere coat. The last touch was the shoes and they were serious, black cordovans.

"You look swell," she said.

"Do I?" It was an old time word, but they were old timers. Virgil took a look at himself in the hotel mirror. He didn't bother with a tie. A tie didn't fit with him, Muriel thought, and she liked that she knew that about him.

Virgil picked up his briefcase. They made quite the picture, she thought, a man heading out the door for his office, his loving wife seeing him off. Except Muriel wasn't Virgil's wife. He wasn't her husband. It wasn't illicit what they were doing, but it also wasn't anyone's business. A relief to discover that she was past putting names on things, or worrying about what people thought.

"Good luck," she said.

"You too." He kissed her. And then he was gone.

Muriel turned to check the clock. It was just after eight.

She got into the shower and let it run hot, so hot that it almost scalded her, but nothing could burn his touch off. She shut her eyes and remembered everything that had happened between them. She recalled the conversation they'd had, afterward. Virgil had talked about how angry he was and what he was going to do to fight against the idea that novels could influence young people to act in certain ways, this notion that fiction was the devil's workshop and somehow encouraged young people to be promiscuous. As if they had to be encouraged when their hormones were raging? Didn't they have sex wherever they could, in movie theatres, in the back seats of cars, in their parent's homes, in public parks? To which she'd added, mischievously, "Don't leave out hotel rooms." He'd laughed. He understood the reference, how could he not? Don't leave us out. Others would ask, "This, at your age?" If not now, when, exactly?

She got out of the shower, dressed, and then opened the curtains. Yellow cabs, cars, and trucks rushed past below. It was exhilarating, this city. Funny, Amelia was the reason she was here. Not just to give the talk, though that was one piece of it. It was the moment of pure jealousy she'd experienced at that wedding, when Virgil brought up Amelia. It had forced her to see herself so clearly. To understand that she really liked this man. And of course, he'd acted on impulse himself. To think, she might have missed out on all of this.

Instead, here she was.

But Muriel glanced at the clock. Time for her to get a move on, she was expected.

Downstairs, the doorman called her a taxicab.

She had envisioned an auburn-haired pixie with an impish smile and she could not have been more wrong. Samantha Barry's long black hair fell to just below her shoulders. She was quite attractive, with an angular face and a serious expression that made her look older than her seventeen years.

"I can't believe you're actually here," the girl said. "I'm so excited to hear your talk."

"Don't set the bar too high."

"You're being modest."

"I prefer to think of myself as a realist. But I hear you have your own news. Congratulations."

"Oh, yes. Thank you." She blushed as she led Muriel through the wrought iron gates and onto campus.

"You must be exceedingly talented," Muriel said.

"I don't think it has much to do with talent," Samantha Barry said. "It's more about being in the right place at the right time."

"Don't undersell yourself. My sister never did," Muriel said, amiably.

They walked along the red brick path onto campus. Columbia. Amelia had joked it was "the gem of the ocean." Hardly a gem from an architectural standpoint, the campus was a hodgepodge of old and new, brick facades stuck next to severe looking granite monoliths.

Still, Low Library stood guard atop the quad.

They climbed the marble stairs.

"This way," Samantha Barry said, and Muriel realized they were making for the library.

Inside, the ground floor was gutted of books. It was now a lecture hall. Folding chairs were set out to face the lectern and the only thing familiar to her was the cobalt blue arched ceiling.

A man bore down on them, extending his hand. "Mrs. Morrissey? I'm so glad you could make it. It's such a thrill for all of us."

This had to be her pen pal, Professor Price. He was exactly as she'd imagined him right down to the tufts of hair that sprung wildly off either side of his head, making him look a little too much like a crested penguin.

"My pleasure," she said, taking his hand.

"Can Miss Barry get you something? You must be famished. Tea? Coffee? A snack?"

"Tea would be heavenly."

"How do you like it?" Samantha Barry asked.

"A little milk."

The Barry girl returned with a Styrofoam cup and a slice of pound cake. Meanwhile, Fabian, as he insisted on being called, was telling her all about his undergraduate years at Tufts. "Imagine, you living right nearby all that time!"

"Yes, imagine," she agreed, although she had no idea what it was they were imagining. The man beamed at her as if they were long lost friends, reunited. He was professorial down to the faded cardigan and the sagging corduroy trousers.

"That Miss Barry is a gem," he said as the girl went off to greet the people streaming in through the open doors.

"And an award winner, too," Muriel noted.

"I wasn't on the committee. I didn't even know until two days ago myself."

Miss Barry reappeared, and Professor Price excused himself.

"This is Lucy Westcott," she said, introducing a statuesque blond.

Muriel shook hands, noting the contrast. Physically, they were polar opposites.

This Lucy Westcott said how interested she was to hear the talk, and that she'd known very little about Amelia Earhart until Sam had filled her in. Behind her, the room was getting crowded.

Muriel felt a horrible whirring sensation in her stomach, as though genies were spinning round inside her. She had imagined an intimate group but there were at least a hundred in attendance and more coming through the doors.

"I wonder if I could look over my notes," she said.

"Of course." It was Miss Barry who took her behind the lectern and then guarded the way so no one could interrupt her.

Muriel pretended to read over the pages, although really what she was trying to do was to calm herself down. The panic always came whenever she had to speak to a crowd. She tried to remind herself that it would subside once she began. The waiting was always the hardest part.

The Barry girl was at her elbow. "Can I introduce my family?"

"Of course."

"This is my mother, Brooke Barry, my brother, Win, and my grandmother, Katherine Manning."

The mother wore a purple dress with a sweeping neckline. It did her hourglass figure justice. The brother was handsome with a shock of blond hair that kept threatening to fall into his eyes. He swept it back with one hand, unconsciously. The grandmother had to be close to her own age. She was one of those women who sported a perpetual tan. She'd undergone some sort of cosmetic surgery as well. She had a wide-eyed, deer in the headlights, look. Miss Barry turned from one to the next, her own anxiety touchingly evident.

But Professor Price was tapping the microphone. It emitted a horrid shriek, and Miss Barry ran forward to adjust it.

19

Amelia
January 5 1980

WHEN THE SUBWAY doors opened, Amelia saw a man crouched by a wall. He was drawing with chalk. There were strange looking animals and a crude airship with flame spurting from its tail. It was the beginning of the story, but she wasn't going to get to see the end. The doors shut, and they lurched off.

At one hundred and sixteenth street, she exited the train and walked upstairs to find the campus gates. They were much as she remembered them but other things had changed. New buildings dotted the quad. Still, Alma Mater ruled, gripping her staff. And there was Winston Barry, standing in front of the library. The woman with him wore quite a coat. Was it made of horsehide? Possibly. It was piebald, brown spots on a white background, and cut short to reveal her legs. Her bright red hair completed whatever this look was.

They went inside. Amelia followed at a distance. Luckily she was cautious, pulling back at the entrance when she saw them huddling together. She overheard an older woman chiding the pair. "Can't you ever get anywhere on time?" The woman's hair was dyed an unearthly orange, and her skin was the same hue. Still, Amelia recognized her. This was his Katherine. *Industrialist's heir weds society beauty* the headline had read. A beauty no more, there was that.

"Let's go," Katherine Manning said sternly.

"And so it begins," the woman with Winston, clearly her daughter, said, *sotto voce.*

Families. As always, they were a mystery.

The former almost child bride, Katherine, wore an elegant black dress and high heels. She was dressed for a soiree.

Amelia had devoured the stories; the new Mrs. Manning's sublime figure, her mane of red hair, her peaches and cream complexion. Winston Manning's choice had been purposeful. The girl was the opposite of Amelia in every possible way.

At the front of the room Winston hugged a young girl. She had to be his sister, Samantha. There was Muriel, shaking Katherine Manning's hand. *The plot thickens,* Amelia thought, and then, *the game's afoot.* She smiled.

AT THAT READING long ago when he'd handed her, her own book to sign, Winston Manning requested Amelia write something personal. She'd complied.

For Winston, may your life always be a grand adventure, AE.

Later that night, in their room at the Hotel St. Georges, he'd claimed he'd never stopping loving her.

"You're married," she'd said. "What's that about then?"

"I made a mistake," he said. "At least I can admit it."

She didn't respond. He couldn't expect her to give up everything now. She was Miss Earhart. She'd gotten more attention than she'd ever dreamed of. But it wasn't the attention that counted, it was what came with it, she could finally be who she wanted to be.

Within reason.

Sadly, there was always a catch.

Winston Manning had run his hands down her body and pushed her lightly backward onto the bed. Then he lay down and set his mouth against the tip of her nose. His hand caressed her cheek. "It is you," he kept saying as his fingers unbuttoned the top button of her dress, then the next and the next. He smelled of aftershave and under that, the musky scent that was only his. Her dress was removed. His clothing. They were fully exposed. Years had passed but it seemed like nothing. He'd barely aged; a few more laugh lines in the corners of his eyes, but physically not much else had changed. Yet everything else was different. They were married to other people. Still, he was able to do what he'd been able to do before, stop her thinking, bringing her here, right here, into the urgency of now. And that was when she accepted that she was starving for him. They fell onto and into each other.

You're lucky if you have one great passion in life, Amelia thought. But I got greedy. I wanted to have two.

THE MAN AT the front of the room leaned into the microphone. In response there was an ear splitting shriek.

Samantha Barry ran up to adjust it. She bore little resemblance to her brother. Her eyes were brown, his blue; her complexion tawny, almost Semitic, his pale, lily white.

The speaker thanked her a little too profusely. He wore corduroy trousers, a cardigan sweater, and an ardent moustache. "Good afternoon, ladies and gentlemen. My name is Dr. Fabian Price. As chairman of Barnard's Biology Department it is my great pleasure and privilege to be your host on this banner day. Today we give out our very first Amelia Earhart Award. This wonderful and prestigious scholarship is being given to one outstanding female undergraduate who has chosen to complete her pre-medical training here at Barnard. I know some of you may be as ignorant as I was about that part of Miss Earhart's life. Most of us know of her exploits as a pilot. But before she conquered the air, she was a student right here at Columbia. She wished to go on to medical school and become a doctor. Miss Rachel Morrow, our generous benefactress, is a keen scholar of all that is Earhart, as well as a Barnard alumnae. It is her generosity that has made this award possible. Miss Morrow, would you stand?"

A woman with gray hair and a no-nonsense demeanor acceded to his demand. Amelia didn't know her. There was a round of applause.

As it died down, he continued. "We are extremely lucky to launch this scholarship with a lecture. Amelia Earhart's own sister has graciously agreed to come all the way from her home in Medford, Massachusetts, to be with us today. So without any further ado, our speaker, Mrs. Muriel Earhart Morrissey."

Muriel took over at the podium. Amelia leaned back against the far wall, wondering what subject she'd finally settled on. Was it the story of the rat and the rifle, subtitled Murder Most Foul? Or the one that exposed her supposed bad behavior here at Barnard, or rather, above their heads on the roof? I'm likely in for it now, Amelia thought.

Muriel's eyes swept the room without settling on any one person. Amelia recognized her own trick to calm the nerves. "Let me begin by congratulating the recipient of this award, Miss Samantha Barry." There was a round of applause and a war whoop from the front. Amelia was positive Winston was the culprit. "I also wish to thank Professor Price for extending this most unexpected invitation. I'm most grateful to be here today. Finally, I want to give thanks to Miss Morrow, for her most generous support." More applause.

Muriel paused to sip water. This was another way to still the panic. It was a sizable crowd, the room well past capacity, listeners spilling out into the hallway.

Muriel cleared her throat and finally launched in. "My sister Amelia would be pleased to have her name linked to this particular scholarship. Although she chose not to pursue a medical career, she had a keenly inquisitive mind. A scientific mind, really. Some of you may know about her project in our backyard. Amelia wanted to construct a working roller coaster. Unfortunately, she got only one good fast ride of it before our mother shut the project down. My older sister was also an amateur paleontologist. During an extended summer vacation, she found pieces of a cow's skeleton bleaching in the sun and set herself the task of finding all the rest. By summer's end, the entire animal was complete. Plus she'd discovered the cause of death, a broken neck. Amelia theorized wolves had chased it down. It made for a colorful story, but she was clear in her rationale. She always wanted to get to the truth of the matter. That was always Amelia's goal. To figure out the why, and of course, the how."

Amelia remembered that cow. Or what remained of it. She'd found stray bones in the field miles from their rented rooms on Lake Okabena. But she hadn't flown solo during the reconstruction. Pidge was right beside her, working just as hard. It was Pidge who'd found the femurs and a tibia. But now she was talking about Toronto.

"I attended St. Margaret's College in Toronto, Canada, for a year," Muriel was saying. "Amelia arrived to spend Christmas vacation. It was at the end of the First World War. Wounded veterans filled the city. There was so much desperation, so much need. When there was someone in need, my sister's first response was to try and help. Amelia enrolled in a Red Cross course and volunteered at a local hospital. This set her on the track that led to her year spent here, fulfilling pre-med requirements at Columbia.

"Unfortunately, there were financial considerations that made it impossible for her to complete her training and become a doctor. Amelia eventually settled on social work, a career she could work at without an expensive course of graduate study. She might have done that her whole life, but of course she would have deprived you of something marvelous. Luckily for you Amelia was never afraid of taking a risk. When she was offered an opportunity to become the first woman to fly across the Atlantic Ocean, she was well aware of the danger. She had better than even odds of crashing at sea. But Amelia knew it was a chance worth taking to make history. To lead, by example."

Muriel was making it sound quite heroic. It had been in one way, and of course, wholly selfish in another. She'd left Muriel and Mother behind, telling herself they would learn how to cope if she plummeted to her death. She'd left Winston Manning, too, lying, to extricate herself, lying to get free.

Four years later in that hotel room, he'd demanded an answer. "Why did you marry that man? I hear from everyone he's impossible. You can't love him."

"It's complicated. And you're one to talk. You with your child bride."

"For one thing, she was twenty. That's not a child. For another, you broke it off with me, not the other way round. I was well within my rights. Why didn't you tell me? I would never have tried to stop you from going. I would have been thrilled for you. It was the kind of adventure we always talked of having. How could you underestimate me so badly?"

"I might have died," she tried.

"We'll all die," Winston told her. "It's how we live that matters, isn't that what we both said?"

He was certain he was right, that he would have urged her to get into that plane and go. He had loved her passion, he argued, loved her for herself, never wanting some outdated notion of what a woman should be. Now they would start again, he insisted. He'd get a divorce. His wife wasn't able to conceive. There were be no children. Katherine would let him go. She was unhappy, too.

"I doubt your wife would divorce you. She's a strict Catholic."

"I can't go on like this," he said. "Can you?"

She said the publicity would ruin him. He said, "I don't care. But apparently you do."

But she was never really afraid of that. It was what she couldn't tell him, what she didn't tell him. Amelia promised she would think about it and so they went on illicitly, meeting when they could and torturing each other when they couldn't. He pushed her and pushed her and finally she promised that when she got back from the round the world flight they would get the divorces and be together.

Come live with me and be my love.

She'd lied. Or maybe she would have done it. Maybe she would have left G.P. and married him, after all. If he would have had her, once she told him the truth. Lucky I never got back, Amelia thought. As kind a man as he was, it was hard to predict whether he would have forgiven her. The devil was always in the details. She'd been carrying his child when she got into that plane. And she'd known as much.

They say you only live once. That life is a gift. One was true while the other? It was grand, strolling down a city street, reading the faces of the passersby. Just being able to imagine their anonymous lives unfolding, the rooms they lived in, the dreams they clung to. Gazing into a shop window and seeing a mannequin dressed to the nines. There was so much pleasure to be gotten from something so simple. To listen. To touch. To be in awe of the mystery at the heart of this magnificent thing called life.

Courage is the price. Muriel had been right to ask her what it meant. To be honest, she wasn't sure herself. She'd thought it sounded swell. That was the kind of word she'd used back then, swell. She'd been so young. The public saw her as courageous, risking her life whenever she flew. But it seemed such a small thing when she compared it to what Muriel had lived through, losing a father, a mother, a sister, a husband, a son, and finding a reason to go on. That took real courage.

Winston had lived on without her, too. Amelia winced, thinking of how the news might have come over the radio when her plane vanished. Then came the futile search and ultimately, acceptance that she was gone for good. He'd let her go. He'd let that part of himself go. But of course, there was a child. He'd held a baby in his arms and loved her and raised her. How could he have done anything else? He'd been a lovely man. A decent man. The sun rose every day in Medford, and in New York, and on an island in the Pacific, unnamed and unknown, where red tendrils of heat touched everything and made the air glow red, then orange, then a clean crystalline blue.

"There are a host of theories about Amelia's last flight," Muriel said. "I have no patience with most of them. My sister was neither a spy, nor a traitor. And she certainly didn't use her round the world excursion as an excuse to escape her marriage, to disguise herself and live in sin in some other country. Nor is she living under an assumed name up in my attic."

Amelia smiled. You'd be surprised.

"As a sister she was always with me whenever I needed her to be," Muriel said. "My closest ally, my dearest friend."

That was a stretch. She hadn't been a good sister. She'd kept the most important thing from Muriel. And that horrible conversation they had. At Christmas, Amelia swept in, bearing gifts. Mother pulled her aside, whispering the less than happy news. Muriel was pregnant; how could they have a child? They had no money to spare to raise it with. Besides, their young marriage was already rocky. "Talk to your sister. She'll listen to you."

Don't ask me to do this, Amelia begged, but silently. She did as she was told and went into the kitchen.

Muriel turned. "Meely! How wonderful to see you. I didn't think you could make it. Look at you." She took a step back from the hug to give her a once over, "So stylish."

"You look pretty great yourself."

Muriel shrugged. They both knew she didn't. She was worn down, worn out. She and Albert fought over everything. He didn't want her to work. He didn't want a career woman. He wanted the opposite of what he'd married, someone demure and predictable.

"I've heard your news," Amelia said, rolling up her own sleeves to help. "That was fast."

"That's how it is sometimes," Muriel said softly.

Amelia had no idea how to broach the subject politely. But it was her job. She'd been pressed into service. Or so she told herself.

"I thought you and Albert weren't speaking to each other."

"Do you have to be speaking?" Muriel let a rueful laugh slip out.

"You wrote you wanted to leave him. That you were going to come out and stay with me in California."

Muriel shrugged. "I never liked California. I couldn't wait to get out of there the first time."

"But Mother says you haven't told Albert you're pregnant."

Muriel shook her head. Amelia still could have held back. Could have let it go. But no, she plowed right ahead.

"It's not for him you're keeping the secret," Amelia said. "It's for you."

"That's not it." Muriel lowered her voice. "I just thought it would be better to talk about the baby after we got through the holidays."

Their heads were close. Passing secrets. "You don't have to go through with this," Amelia advised her.

Muriel pulled away and put her hands over her stomach, instinctually.

"I can arrange for it, if you want."

The expression on Muriel's face stung. She shook her head, hard.

Yet Amelia continued to press her. "I'm just trying to be practical," she said.

"I couldn't do that, Meely. I've thought it over. It's fine in theory, but it's not for me. Please, don't bring it up again." And Muriel swept out of the room.

It was awkward between them all the rest of the day. Only when Amelia was back in her car, driving to the plane, did she let herself break down. And cry. She wiped away the tears, angrily. Yes, she was a little jealous, which was absurd. What had it been anyway, just a mass of cells at that point, nothing more.

On the train to New York, on her way to that pivotal interview with G.P. Amelia felt nauseated. She put it down to nerves. Then, once they'd chosen her, there was so much to prepare for. She could hardly draw breath. It took her ten full days to realize how late she was and note the changes in her body. That was when she used an assumed name and had a test. Yes, she was pregnant. How could it be? She'd been so careful. What bad luck it was. What horrendous timing.

Amelia thought of Winston Manning, and of what he might say. She came up with a thousand different ways of framing it, running through it again and again in her head. And then took the coward's way out by breaking it off with him and not telling him she was pregnant. It was easier than arguing about it. And she told herself she would quite likely die at sea. He would never be the wiser. If she survived, she'd make up with him. She'd explain everything to him then. If she told him, she was afraid that he'd convince her. That he'd somehow prevent her from going.

When no one really could have done that.

Still, it was the story she told herself. And then she got into that plane. Flew across the ocean. Became "their" Amelia.

You have to make choices. You have to be savage about them sometimes. She'd gambled, and look at all she'd won. Once famous, she couldn't find her way back. Maybe she didn't really want to. She couldn't have a baby and do all the things she suddenly was able to do. She couldn't get into a plane and fly off when everything that having a child would be, would pull her back to earth. Maybe later on she would see her way clear to doing that, but not yet. She couldn't do it yet. Not now when she was suddenly *their* Amelia.

She had to confide in someone. So she told G.P. He knew a doctor. Amelia would come up to his estate in Rye afterwards to recuperate. They'd say she was working on the book about her flight. Sharing that secret was likely part of why she gave in to him and married him. In one way, he did know her better than anyone. He knew what she was willing to do. What she'd given up to do it.

The Park Avenue doctor explained the procedure. How he would use dilation and curettage. She knew what that meant. He said there would be bleeding afterward. She should keep an eye on things. "I'll be fine," she said to him. And she was. What was done was done.

But then there was that horrible conversation with Muriel. Muriel was only defending herself. Muriel who could never understand why it had hurt so much, hearing her own sister say those words.

20

Sam
January 5 1981

"I'M SO PROUD of you," Katherine said, giving Sam one of her patented air kisses.

Brooke grabbed her next, stifling her in a bear hug. "Look at you! Just look at you!"

Win offered a high five.

Lucy beamed.

"That speaker wasn't half bad," Katherine opined, turning to Brooke. "You should have brought the book to show her. She would have found it amusing."

"Mother, please," Brooke said, flushing.

"What have I done to you now?"

"You really were wonderful," Brooke told Sam, pointedly ignoring her mother. "And to think, you never wanted to perform at all."

"It was just a little speech," Sam said. The truth was, she'd been shaking like a leaf. Standing in front of the audience, she couldn't make out one face. She'd gone snow-blind from anxiety.

"We ought to go over to the bar and commandeer some tables," Win said. "You'll love this place, Grandmother, you can boast to all your friends how you've been slumming."

"But this isn't going to take the place of me giving you a little party," Katherine insisted. "I must show you off, darling. Don't say no."

Sam pictured herself standing in the huge living room of that overheated apartment with the museum worthy paintings and antiques, every single thing breakable and dear. Her grandmother's friends were all society people who barely knew she existed. She blanched.

"No, Grandmother," Win said firmly. "Sam's not going to let you give her a party and please, don't ask Sam again. Now come along and behave."

Katherine bristled. But Win smiled a charming smile and shook his head as if she were a bad tempered child. He set his finger on his lips. There was something funny in how he did it, and something else, a confidence that Sam didn't expect. It stopped their grandmother in her tracks. Win lifted Katherine's coat off the chair and held it for her to slide her arms into. It was a long black mink, the kind that became a legend most. Grandmother Katherine was a legend, at least in her own mind. Even though she wore heels,

Sam towered over her grandmother. Katherine was older and gaunter than she had remembered. It made her feel oddly powerful and thus magnanimous.

"I guess I'll have to make do," Katherine said, grudgingly. She gave Sam a pleading look but Win winked, took Katherine's arm, and moved her away.

They were going to the West End Bar. Sam couldn't quite imagine what Katherine would make of it. How had Win managed that? But it wasn't only Win who'd come to her rescue, Lucy was now escorting Katherine, chatting away gaily to her.

"Did that just happen?" Brooke asked. "Did she just give up without a fight?"

Sam nodded.

"Your brother is amazing."

"Yes," Sam agreed, "What book was Grandmother talking about?"

"It's not important." Brooke was buttoning her coat.

Sam gave her a searching look. "Mom, come on."

"All right. I sold it. So sue me." Brooke shrugged.

"Sold what?"

"Dad gave me a copy of Amelia Earhart's autobiography with a personal inscription in it."

"Why did you sell it?"

"I was broke. Your father had dumped me. We were stuck in court, fighting over child support, which he refused to pay. My dad was dead and the trust fund he'd promised me dried up because your grandmother decided that I needed to stand on my own two feet and learn a lesson. So I took everything that had any value, and I sold it. Rings, earrings, necklaces went first, but then I got desperate. I looked for other things to sell and there was that book. I got a hundred dollars for it, enough for a couple of meals."

"Oh, Mom," Sam said and hugged Brooke. "I'm sorry."

"You have nothing to be sorry for," Brooke told her. "I'm the one who should apologize. I haven't been much of a mother."

"That's not true," Sam said.

"It is. I should have listened when my father told me not to rush into getting married, but I was in love and pregnant with Win. He said he'd help me raise the child on my own. He said that your father wasn't capable of that sort of devotion." Brooke sighed. "Your grandfather told me your father wasn't a serious man. Those were his exact words to me. When your grandmother heard about it, she went ballistic." Brooke gave her a wry look, and Sam nodded. She knew exactly how Katherine could get, especially with her only daughter.

"How could he tell me such a thing?" Brooke said, mimicking Katherine's intonation. "How could he imply that it was acceptable to raise a child out of wedlock? In other words, *what would people think?*" Brooke shrugged apologetically. "In the end I did what she wanted. But I suppose it wasn't her fault. I wouldn't have listened to my dad anyway. I needed to get married. I needed to think that this was real love. I was always so romantic. Luckily, Win was an easy baby. He did everything right on schedule. I think your dad liked the image of himself having a son, raising a son. But that was when he was doing well and getting work."

"So it was having me that ruined everything?" Sam demanded.

"God no." Brooke reached out, as if to physically reassure her. Sam shook her head, refusing. "Look darling, this was all before you even came along. Win was three when he decided to leave me the first time."

Sam stuck out her chin. She looked past her mother to the room, to the clusters of people still having pleasant, mindless conversations. There was Muriel, chatting amiably with Professor Price.

"Samantha." Brooke's hand was the weight that pulled her back.

"What?"

"I'm not good with men. You know that. I always believe they're better than they are. I have this ridiculous optimism about them. It was never about you. Not you, or your brother. Neither of you are responsible for me being a naïve idiot. Don't ever think that." Brooke hugged her and wrapped her arms tightly around her.

And Sam felt odd. It was as if she were on the dock and they were calling "all aboard," it was that kind of embrace, that kind of goodbye. Sam saw the rest, saw herself on the deck as the boat pulled free of its moorings, looking east to the world that lay ahead of her.

"My wonderful daughter," Brooke said, releasing her, then reaching up to smooth Sam's brow. "You're amazing. Always believe that."

Then she was off.

SAM STAYED TO clear away the mess, helping Kim who was already hard at work. Kim had been magnanimous when she heard about Sam winning the award, inviting her over for a toast, and raising a glass of sparkling apple cider.

"I wish we both could have won," Sam said.

"No, you don't."

"Why not?"

"Because it's not possible."

True. But baldly put.

Professor Price waved her over. He was with Professor Hartley and Professor Grayson.

"Congratulations," Professor Hartley said.

"Well deserved," Professor Grayson added.

Sam thanked them and they smiled beneficently. Then she and Kim gathered up all the plastic knives and forks and paper plates and dumped them into the garbage bins. They covered the remaining food with plastic wrap and folded the chairs and stacked them.

Was it well deserved? Sam wondered. Being the best was a matter of opinion. She was lucky that when she'd owned up to making a mistake, it wasn't held against her. She was fortunate that they all liked her. They could just as easily not have. She was talented at math and science; balancing equations offered a satisfaction that was sadly lacking in much of life. There was a clear right answer. In the messy real world, logic evaporated in the face of all the vagaries and inconsistencies that made up the workings of the human heart.

"Done!" Kim exclaimed, pulling on her own jacket. "Coming?"

"I just have to find Mrs. Morrissey," Sam said. She'd lost track of the guest of honor. She'd meant to invite her along, not that Mrs. Morrissey would necessarily want to go out to a bar with them. She was staying at the Hilton. It had been so nice of her to come down there and speak, though in truth Sam had been so nervous she only half listened.

Sam went out into the hall. It was empty. She'd left Mrs. Morrissey's coat and bag upstairs in the office. Had someone gotten them for her? The door was locked and her things were still safely inside. Sam walked down the hall, carrying the coat with her, calling, "Mrs. Morrissey, are you here?"

21

Amelia
January 5 1981

THE STAIRS WERE quite different. No longer a curl of metal, they went straight up to the roof. The hatch was easy to push back. Amelia stepped out, shading her eyes in the bright winter sun. There were familiar landmarks, Riverside Church with its fine steeples arching into the sky and beyond it the Hudson, clots of ice choking the river traffic. Turning, she found the Empire State and Chrysler buildings. In between, the swathe of Central Park. These things remained while so much else had changed, the world spinning happily on without her. She squatted, studying her old campus. Students rushed on, oblivious, busy with their lives, imagining their futures. They were young enough to think that they could do anything they wanted, that there were no sacrifices to be made to get there.

"What a view!" The voice shocked her back. Muriel's upper half had emerged.

"It is indeed," Amelia agreed, reaching out a hand to help her sister.

"I tried the door. When I discovered it was open, the temptation was too much." Muriel shivered. She had no coat. "I was escaping," she admitted.

"From what?"

"From this pest with his charts, he'd gone back to get them to show me." Extending her hand, she said, "I'm Muriel Morrissey."

"I know. I enjoyed your lecture." Amelia took Muriel's hand in her own again. She wanted to clasp it in both of hers, to pull her close. And resisted the impulse.

Muriel turned away, taking in the view. They stood shoulder to shoulder.

"You must get a lot of that," Amelia said.

"You mean that man with his pet theory? Oh yes. It's always the men who have them. I used to wonder about that. I've come to the belief that they think, if they can prove where she died, they'll finally bring her to ground and to heel."

"A funny notion, proving themselves superior."

"Men think they were meant to rule the earth," Muriel said. "They still cling to that fantasy."

"So to avoid him, you lit out for the territories?" Amelia offered slyly.

"Just like Huck." Squinting in the sunlight. "It still is breathtaking up here."

"Different from the way it used to look, but yes, wonderful. Still an incredible city."

"You've snuck up before?"

"When I was at school here."

"And to think, I imagined it was my own little secret." Muriel turned to examine her.

Would she discover that inadequate impersonator who'd had the temerity to come to her door and confront her? Amelia waited, expecting that would be the result as Muriel tilted her head to the side, trying to nudge the memory to the fore. It was this very habit of cocking her head that had made Amelia nickname her Pidge. She'd always found it endearing.

Better to strike first, Amelia thought, this could be your last chance. "It was your sister who brought you up here originally, wasn't it?"

"No." But of course the answer was yes, and they both knew it.

"Back then you could see to Brooklyn, couldn't you?" Muriel didn't disagree. "No one had thought it necessary to build towers along the Palisades, they were pristine, like the White Cliffs of Dover." This is it, Amelia told herself, and plunged ahead. "It was the first day of your visit on spring break. You'd taken the 3:14 to Grand Central from Northampton. She met you. She stood at the entrance to track 44 on the lower level. She took the portmanteau from you, though you protested, the gift Mother gave you for college. It was a marvel of workmanship, that thing, with all those odd secret pockets hidden inside. You could pack up your secrets in that old kit bag. That was the joke."

Muriel stared. "What are you getting at?"

"I took the bag and we got into the subway. What a treat that was for you. You were amazed by the way the people dressed. You commented how New Yorkers were so different from the parochial Bostonites. How many races and ethnicities were packed together. You were so enthusiastic, so exuberant. You spoke with me about Smith and how one class stood out for you. Professor James. You idolized that woman. She was the reason you had decided to teach. Though you weren't going to teach on the college level, you thought that too hard to manage. Besides, what was better than shaping a child? There, you had a chance to really change someone; in that small way, you could reshape the world."

Muriel's mouth opened, but no words emerged. Instead, she reached across and touched Amelia on the cheek. Then her hand pulled back, as if stung.

"It isn't you," she said, shaken. "It can't be you."

"Who else could know the details?"

"You're making it up."

"But I'm not," Amelia insisted. "I'm telling the truth." She had so little time to prove herself. *Had we but world enough, and time.* She didn't, this was a gift. "You were thrilled to be invited to visit. The months we'd been separated. We'd been apart before, I'd gone to school for a while, but we were together for vacations and in Toronto. We'd always stayed faithful to each other, we'd always written, but this year I'd fallen off. You sent me letters. I left them unanswered for a week or two. And mine were all about what I'd done. You resented it, felt left out. So when I invited you, it was to make up for that, I promised you concerts, poetry readings, the museum, and, best of all, just being together, the two of us together again.

"We dropped off your bag at the rooming house on Amsterdam Avenue. The woman at the desk said, 'Is this your famous sister?' You were so pleased that I'd been talking about you. It took so little to make you happy. I felt sorry I'd forgotten that. I knew I should have been a better sister. So I packed the hamper, got my camera, and we went to find Louise."

"We?" Muriel backed away. "Wait, you're the woman who accosted me at my house. Did you follow me all the way here? You must be out of your mind."

Amelia stepped forward, grabbed Muriel's shoulder, and held fast.

"Let me go!"

"Not yet.'"

"I'm going to scream if you don't."

"I know. You'll call for the police. Do what you have to do. But isn't it true that you and I went into that science building over there? In the basement, Louise was writing up her findings on mitosis. We waited for her to finish up, and I showed you my rats. I was doing an experiment on them, but unfortunately I made the mistake of naming each and every one of them. Ironic that they were named after Santa's reindeer, Donner, Blitzen, and all the rest of his antlered steeds when I'd ruined Christmas for you."

Muriel tried to jerk her body away but Amelia held fast.

"I had to ask those stupid questions about Father Christmas because I always needed to prove a point. It just seemed so absurd; how could anyone believe there was some white bearded roly-poly man who was making stop after stop after stop? I told myself that it was more important to know the truth than to cling to a ridiculous myth."

"Help!" Muriel called out.

"I'll strike a bargain with you. I'll let you go if you just listen for a few more minutes. Remember the Reynolds? The Christmas party they gave in Cambridge. That night when I slipped out and left you behind with Mother and Albert and Samuel."

Muriel blinked, hard. "How on earth. . . ?"

"On *heaven* and earth," Amelia corrected. "There are more things, believe you me. I met someone at that party. I fell in love with him. I never told you about him, I never said a word to you or Mother. But every weekend when I said I was away, I was really with him. All that spring I saw him."

Muriel shook her head. "Now I understand. It's that kind of story. What if Amelia Earhart had a secret lover? Someone no one else ever knew about? Believe me, that's been done to death."

"And yet it happened. His name was Winston Manning. He was a graduate student at Harvard. Handsome. Amusing. Exceptionally charming. He was a man who knew how to chart the stars, a dreamer who went into business and made a second fortune. He was, in short, a walking, talking contradiction. He was the way most of us are. Imperfect. And lovely. Unexpected. Remarkable. Always, always surprising."

"Just stop," Muriel insisted, trying to break loose.

"You think it's that sort of story, don't you, about lost love? It's not. Remember when I visited on Christmas and you were pregnant? Remember that horrible piece of sisterly advice I offered? Put to you in your own kitchen. Said as if your older sister knew better how easy it would be to scrape away an almost child. You were right to be offended by it. Mother sent me on that fool's errand, but that's no excuse. I was jealous of what you had. You see, I'd made a different choice."

Muriel stopped trying to pry herself away. That had gotten her attention. "No one knows that."

"But me. I'd had an abortion," Amelia said. "I never told Winston about it. I had to make a choice and I did. How could I know that everything would change? How could I understand what it would mean to me? But you can't have everything. I knew that then, I know it now. I don't regret what I did. It was worth it. What I regret is that I didn't trust you and that I didn't tell you. We were sisters. Best friends. I should have known better and trusted you more. You've been a far better sister to me than I ever deserved."

She kissed Muriel on the cheek. Then, she released her.

"Is it really you?" Muriel asked, reaching out, but not quite touching her face, her hand hanging there, in midair. "It's not possible." Saying it to herself, reassuring herself.

"Yet, here I am," Amelia told her.

Muriel stared hard at her, and her expression softened. "What an odd thing," she said. "What a world."

"What a world, indeed," Amelia agreed.

They took each other in. Slowly. Completely. Seconds became a minute. Then two.

"Too funny." This, from Muriel, her lips turning up at the corners, twitching into an almost smile.

Amelia smiled back, more fully. "Yes. Life has its moments."

From down below, a voice broke in.

"Mrs. Morrissey? Are you up there?"

Muriel shook her head, then put a finger to her lips.

The voice insisted, coming closer, "Mrs. Morrissey?"

Not now. Not yet.

But what could one do?

Muriel shrugged. "You stay put, Miss Barry," she called out. "I'll be down directly." Muriel moved close to Amelia then. So close their frosted breath mingled in the air. She put out her hand. Amelia took it. And they made their way slowly to the ladder.

"Since you're here, I do have one thing I'd like to say," Muriel said.

"Yes. Anything."

"I've been meaning to tell you for a while." That smile blown fuller, as she said, "You never fooled me. I knew you weren't perfect. That was what I loved about you most of all." Muriel leaned forward then and kissed her on the cheek. Then wiped at the lipstick stain. "There. Cleaned you right up."

"Miss Morrissey, I have your coat," the girl called out.

"What to do, what to do?" Muriel asked.

But they both knew. She had to go.

Courage. Courage is the price. The world was tugging at them, pulling them apart. Muriel stood on the top rung of the ladder.

Amelia smiled so hard it hurt.

She watched her younger sister descend and disappear from view.

It was done. Finally, done.

Amelia walked back to the edge of the roof, waiting and watching. Off they went, Muriel and the Barry girl. At the top of the marble steps, Muriel turned back and looked up, waving.

Hello.

Goodbye.

Looking east, Amelia saw the Triboro Bridge. When she flew in to meet Winston in Brooklyn that very last time, she landed at Floyd Bennett and drove a hired car inland past the barren Coney Island beaches and the shuttered boardwalk vendors, past silent houses and Olmsted's other jewel, Prospect Park. In the hotel, she went up to their usual room, and he came to her. It was January then too, the depths of winter.

How lovely he'd been, how fervent his pleas. She'd agreed that when this last flight was over, she'd do just as he wanted. In that hotel room, it was easy to believe it was possible. Yet, long ago she'd made a different choice.

Two roads diverge in a yellow wood, and I took the one less traveled on.

THAT ROAD LED her to the cabin of the Electra. Outside, the tropical storm had raged, rain pelting on every side. The noise of the engine overwhelmed the senses. But finally, morning arrived. The rain let up, and

Amelia peered through the cockpit glass, trying to find some marking point. The gas gauge was running low. They'd had to fly at a higher altitude than they'd planned to cut through the worst of the storm. Still, Howland should be just below them. She lifting the radio and tried again. "Calling Itasca, we must be on you but cannot see you. Gas is running low."

Amelia strained to find a signpost in the frothing, gray green water. Where was the damn boat? The ocean was visible now as a wilderness of peaks and valleys. Glancing at the gauge, Amelia saw it was heading into the red. Just then the sun came up, piercing the horizon line, soaking everything, and making it a stunning gold. It took her breath away.

She dropped down to a thousand feet. Below her the waves bristled with whitecaps. There was no landing strip, no boat, nothing but the Pacific stretching forever.

Banking left, she reached for the radio. "We are circling but cannot hear you, go ahead on 7500 now or on the schedule time on half hour." Holding her breath, she waited. Then, out of nowhere, the radio came to life blurting out a rapid-fire dot and dash. She had no way to reply in Morse, but the response meant they had heard her. Surely they must be close.

They would make it. Amelia let out a breath, relief flooding her.

NOW IT WAS the year of our lord, nineteen eighty-one, the end of a crisp January day. Amelia sat on the edge of the library roof, watching as the sun set over the Hudson. She knew that Muriel was nearby, seated at a long table. At the other end of it, Miss Barry, her brother Winston, their good friends, Miss Barry's closest friend, that tall, striking blond, Lucy Westcott; all were there to celebrate her achievement. For young Samantha Barry, it was only the beginning.

In the back of the barroom, a band set up. The bass player twirled his oversized instrument with panache. The saxophonist wet his reed and blew on it, sending out a trill. Back at the table, Winston Barry lifted a glass. "To the best sister in the world." Samantha Barry blushed at what was clearly heartfelt. Lucy sat next to her. At the far end, Muriel leaned over to speak with Katherine. Amelia wondered what common ground they'd found? It was amusing to think of the two of them together and the tricks life played on one. The hapless Professor Fabian Price and Brooke Barry were also deep in conversation, though his gaze had drifted south to her cleavage. On the bandstand, a guitarist tuned his instrument. In a second, the music would start. Perhaps she'd know the song.

A young man had come up to Samantha Barry. He tapped her on the shoulder. She turned, registering surprise, then pleasure. He'd brought her a present, and she was being urged to unwrap it. Inside was a first edition of

Amelia's own first book. On the title page was an inscription, "For Winston, may your life always be a grand adventure, AE."

AMELIA SHUT HER eyes. It was odd, she could see further and further. She saw their future. Love, marriage, success, children, sadness; there was always that, too. Always sadness. Always loss to balance out the pleasure. The girl, Lucy, had arranged for the boy to show up. His name was Michael, and he was the one Sam would marry eventually. They'd have stops and starts, date other people, argue, break apart, but in the end they'd end up together. As for Lucy, she would thrive as well, becoming a professor of philosophy out in California. She would find love and lose it enough times to decide that there was only one way to mother, and adopt a child. A boy. Samantha would become a doctor just as she'd planned, she'd have her own children, two, no, three. Winston would write about music, he'd make a name for himself and leave home for good. Brooke Barry would find a good man but it would be too late, the cancer already consuming her. She'd die, and Winston would take her gallery of photographs home with him to San Francisco. Katherine would be gone long before all that. She wouldn't have to suffer the loss of her only child. But she and Brooke would be friends again, that friendship beginning here, on this very night. Katherine would loosen the purse strings a little, but more importantly, she'd resist blaming her daughter. She'd learn to be temperate and kind to Brooke. She'd grow old gracefully. Dead, she'd lie next to her late husband whose own wishes had been ignored. Winston Manning had wanted his ashes dumped at sea, but Katherine had stuck him in a graveyard in Maine. As for Muriel, her future was unclear. She was too close, Amelia thought. Or perhaps she had her own secrets, which was as it should be. They were sisters, after all.

For the rest, she hoped the future held something that passed for happiness, however fleeting. It was what one got if one was lucky. *I was lucky.* Still, she wanted more. She wanted to stay. *Just a little longer. Please, only a little.* It was all so fleeting. Above her head the North Star shone, bright and constant, a reminder of what she might find yet, if only she tried. There were worlds upon worlds out there. She told herself she'd always been a gambler, she'd always believed that anything was possible. Then, lifting her arms high above her head, Amelia let the wind take her.

Naomi Rand is the author of three mysteries featuring divorced criminal investigator, Emma Price, they are *The One That Got Away, Stealing For A Living,* and *It's Raining Men* (all from Harpercollins). She has stories in two great collections, *Crime and Music* (Three Rooms Press) and *Hard Boiled Brooklyn* (Bleak House Books). Her fiction and literary criticism has appeared in *The Flexible Persona, Other Voices, Melus, Cutbank, The Florida Review,* and *The North Dakota Quarterly.* Her non-fiction has appeared in many national publications including *Redbook, Parents, Ladies Home Journal,* and The *New York Times.* For longer than she cares to remember she was a non-fiction book reviewer for *The Boston Globe.* She is the recipient of a grant from the New Jersey State Council on the Arts for her fiction.

Visit Naomi's website: http://www.naomirand.com